REALWARE

Other Books by
Rudy Rucker

REALWARE

RUDY RUCKER

An Imprint of HarperCollins*Publishers*

This is a work of fiction. Names, characters, places, and incidents are products of the author's imagination or are used fictitiously and are not to be construed as real. Any resemblance to actual events, locales, organizations, or persons, living or dead, is entirely coincidental.

EOS
An Imprint of HarperCollins*Publishers*
10 East 53rd Street
New York, New York 10022-5299

Copyright © 2000 by Rudy Rucker
Front cover design by Raquel Jaramillo
Inside back cover author photo by Sylvia Rucker
Interior design by Kellan Peck
ISBN: 0-380-80877-3
www.avonbooks.com/eos

Library of Congress Cataloging in Publication Data:
Rucker, Rudy v. B. (Rudy von Bitter), 1946–
    Realware/Rudy Rucker
        p.   cm.
PS3568.U298 R4   2000   00-20152
813'.54 dc—21   CIP

First Eos Printing: June 2000

Eos Trademark Reg. U.S. Pat. Off. and in Other Countries, Marca Registrada, Hecho en U.S.A.

HarperCollins® is a trademark of HarperCollins Publishers Inc.

Printed in the U.S.A.

RRD   10 9 8 7 6 5 4 3 2 1

For Isabel, Rudy Jr., Georgia, and Pop

CONTENTS

Chapter One
PHIL
February 12 / 1
February 14 / 10
February 19 / 24
February 20 / 38

Chapter Two
YOKE
February 20 / 46
February 21 / 73

Chapter Three
PHIL
February 21 / 98
February 22 / 104
February 23 / 128

Chapter Four
YOKE
February 23 / 155

February 24 / 181

February 26 / 195

Chapter Five
RANDY, PHIL, BABS, PHIL
Randy / February 26 / 203

Phil / February 23–25 / 219

Babs / February 26 / 232

Phil / February 26 / 244

Chapter Six
YOKE, BABS, RANDY, YOKE
Yoke / February 26 / 255

Babs / April 1 / 268

Randy / May 1 / 282

Yoke / June 1 / 296

Genealogy of Characters
in the Ware Tetralogy

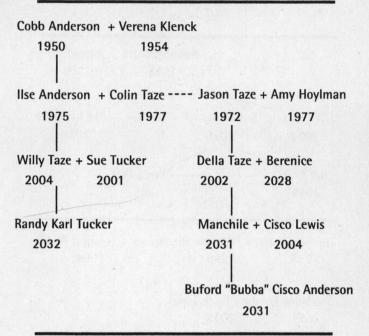

Cobb Anderson + Verena Klenck
   1950   1954

Ilse Anderson + Colin Taze ---- Jason Taze + Amy Hoylman
   1975   1977   1972   1977

Willy Taze + Sue Tucker   Della Taze + Berenice
  2004   2001   2002   2028

Randy Karl Tucker   Manchile + Cisco Lewis
   2032   2031   2004

                        Buford "Bubba" Cisco Anderson
                                    2031

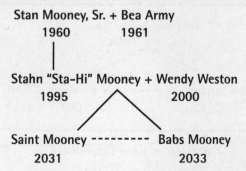

Stan Mooney, Sr. + Bea Army
     1960   1961

Stahn "Sta-Hi" Mooney + Wendy Weston
     1995   2000

Saint Mooney --------- Babs Mooney
     2031   2033

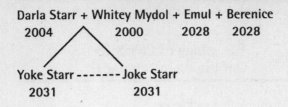

Darla Starr + Whitey Mydol + Emul + Berenice
2004   2000   2028   2028

Yoke Starr ------- Joke Starr
2031   2031

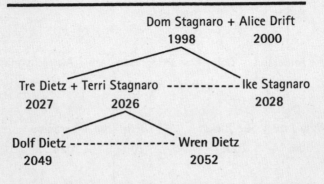

Dom Stagnaro + Alice Drift
1998   2000

Tre Dietz + Terri Stagnaro ----------- Ike Stagnaro
2027   2026   2028

Dolf Dietz ----------------- Wren Dietz
2049   2052

Berdoo Scragg + Rainbow Plenty ----- Tempest Plenty
1994   1999   1994

Starshine Plenty + Duck Tapin
2021   2016

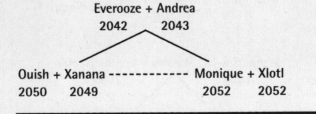

Everooze + Andrea
2042   2043

Ouish + Xanana ------------ Monique + Xlotl
2050   2049   2052   2052

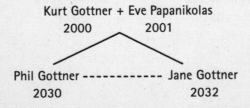

Kurt Gottner + Eve Papanikolas
2000   2001

Phil Gottner ------------ Jane Gottner
2030   2032

REALWARE

CHAPTER ONE

PHIL

February 12

"Wake up, Phil. It's your sister on the uvvy. Something's happened." Kevvie's breath was alkaloidal and bitter in the dawn.

Phil woke slowly. He liked to take the time to think about his dreams before they evanesced. Just now he'd been dreaming about hiking again. For some reason, he always dreamed about the same three or four places, and one of the places was an imaginary range of mountains, an arc of icy little peaks that were somehow very—domesticated. Easy to climb.

"Wake up!" repeated Kevvie. Her voice was, as usual, flat and practical, though now a bit louder than before. As Phil's eyes fluttered open an interesting thought occurred to him: maybe the mountains were his teeth. Sleepily he started to tell Kevvie his idea.

"My teeth are the mountains that—"

But she wasn't listening. Her blue eyes were intent, her fox-face was pinched with urgency. "You talk to Jane right now," she said, plopping the little uvvy onto the pillow next to Phil. The uvvy was displaying a tiny holographic image of Phil's sister.

Calm, practical Jane. But today Jane wasn't calm. Her eyes were red and wet with tears.

"Da's dead," quavered Jane. "It's horrible. A wowo got him? Willow says they were in bed and all of a sudden their wowo got really big, all bright and swirly, and it jumped inside of Da and the light was shining out of his eyes like searchlights and he was yelling and then his body collapsed and the wowo sucked him inside and crushed him. Da's gone! Willow's covered with his blood. It's so gnarly?" Jane's voice twisted up an octave on the last word and she began sobbing. "I can't believe it. Wowos are just a toy. Da and Tre made them up."

Phil felt a savage torrent of emotions, too fast to nail down. Relief, terror, joy, wonder, sorrow, confusion. His father was dead and he was free. No old man to judge him for not doing anything with his life. His father was dead and he was alone. No stand-up old guy between him and the Reaper.

"Dead? What—When did Willow call you?" Phil's eyes began throbbing.

"Just now. From the car. She's scared the wowo might get her next. She left the house to go to the gimmie. She told me to tell you and for you to call her. I'm flying out. You pick me up."

"Wait, wait, this is all too—" Phil broke off in confusion. Kevvie, who'd been avidly eavesdropping, smiled and offered him a piece of her chewing gum. Phil shook his head no. Kevvie tended never to have the correct emotional response. In company, she had to look at other people so she'd know when to laugh.

"What are you going to do?" demanded Jane's little face. Her pointy chin was trembling.

"I'll call Willow, then I'll drive Kevvie's car down to Palo Alto, and then I'll call you back. And yeah, I can pick you up. But—are you sure Da's really dead? From a wowo? It's just a fancy hollow graphic that Da made up a story about! Wowos are math and bullshit!"

"Willow said the wowo pulled Da in like it was—*a garbage*

disposal. She said that. She's hysterical. She shouldn't be driving."

"I'll call her. I love you, Jane."

"I love you too, Phil. Be strong. I'll see you tonight. I'm going to the airport right now."

Phil clicked off the uvvy and the room was quiet. His eyes felt so strange—bulging and puffy and aching. They wanted to cry, but for now they were dry. He imagined a wowo in his father's head. Light streaming out of his father's eye-sockets.

"Oh, poor Phil," said Kevvie. "It's terrible to lose your father. I want you to know that I'm here for you. But what was that about a wowo? That hologram thingie? Willow says that's what killed your father? A ball of colored light? The gimmie aren't going to buy it. She should get a top attorney right away."

"That's too—" Phil began, but broke off with a vague gesture. In his mind the full sentence was, "That's too stupid and autistic of you to deserve an answer," but he didn't have the heart to start a fight. Kevvie's inability to visualize other people's feelings was so extreme that Phil had come to think of it as a clinical psychiatric condition. Indeed, Kevvie habitually chewed a popular empathy-enhancement gum in a perhaps unconscious effort to try and correct her deficit. "E-gum makes you part-of," as the chanted commercials had it. But it seemed like the only person that e-gum made Kevvie more sensitive to was Kevvie. All these angry thoughts went racing through Phil's head as he made the little gesture. He reminded himself that he liked Kevvie. His father's death was filling him with irrational rage.

Da dead. Phil groaned and got out of bed, sliding the groan down into a keening moan. This hurt so much that he needed to keep making noise.

He wore only a plain white T-shirt. His butt was small, his legs were short and nimble. Phil's mother Eve was Greek, while his father Kurt had been German. Phil's body hair and chin-stubble were dark, but the hair on his head was a floppy shock of blond. His sly, hooded eyes and sardonic lips made him look dissipated, which was misleading: Phil had been clean and sober his whole life. When the mandatory grade-school screening had revealed that Phil carried the genes for alcoholism and drug addiction, Phil had taken it to heart and decided to spend his life Straight Edge. A singularly mature decision for one so young—with the bonus of providing a way to be superior to Da, who'd been quite fond of booze and pot.

Phil's room was bright and messy, an odd-shaped room with a peaked ceiling and walls that slanted out on two sides. There was a lot of empty space near the ceiling, and Phil had some home-built robot blimps cruising around up there like sluggish tropical fish. Flying machines of all kinds were Phil's hobby. The blimps were like pets, and Phil had names for them: one was Led Zep of course, the others were the Graf Z, the Macon, the Penile Implant, and the largest and most colorful was the Uffin' Wowo. The last name was a riff on Da's brilliant uvvy graphic that had somehow ended in disaster less than an hour ago. Da dead. Life ends in tears.

Distractedly humming, Phil put on some thick red tights he'd gotten from the thrift store. There was gray morning light from the room's skylight. Kevvie sat on a rolling desk chair, chewing e-gum and watching him.

Phil swung open his room's arched mouse-hole door to reveal the interior of what looked like a factory. His room was located inside a bigger room, that is, Phil's room was a wooden box on stilts inside a subdivided warehouse down near the bay-side Port of San Francisco. Some developer had sliced the giant warehouse up into five or six strips, and Phil rented one of the strips along with two other people: a guy called Derek and a woman named Calla. Derek was a chaos artist and Calla a genetic counselor, while Phil was a cook in an expensive restaurant. Each of the three lived in their own cobbled-together wooden box.

Phil's and Calla's boxes were on stilts, and Derek's hung by cables from the ceiling. The huge open warehouse floor was left free and clear for other purposes. The three boxes were a bit like birdhouses in an aviary—quite literally so in the case of

Phil's, as he'd designed his dwelling from the specs for a traditional pentagonal wren-house like a kid might bring home from shop class. He'd tried giving his room a round door, but after tripping over the curved threshold a few times, he'd compromised and made the door's bottom square and flush with his box's floor.

Phil started down his thin little chicken-walk of a staircase. He could see out the windows that lined the tops of the warehouse's walls: a view of the San Francisco Bay, of a floating gray ship and a docked red ship, of great four-legged cranes like giraffes or elephants, of concrete dockside elevators, of more warehouses beneath low clouds. Everything chilled and dismal. A Thursday in February.

High overhead hung a giant twisting model of DNA; this was Calla's. It was made of linked spheres that were hollow cocoons spun by a fabricant, a little DIM ant that could turn sunlight and wet leaves into filaments of rayon. The DNA model was a useful thing for Calla to show to her clients, who came here in person when the genetic information that Calla gave them was so harsh or so strange that uvvy contact wasn't enough. Phil well remembered when his genetic counselor had laid out his options: abstinence or addiction.

Down on the factory floor, two of Derek's "attractors" were active. One looked like a big wobbly green doughnut, the other like a purple cow-udder with twisting teats. They were patterns of air currents, flowing volumes of air made visible by color-lit fogs of vapor, fractally rich with eddies and schlieren. A dozen other attractor-devices sat idle: cryptic, mute technoclutter. Only when the attractors were powered up did they clothe themselves in beautiful, orderly chaos. Da's wowo had been a similar kind of thing.

Phil took a shortcut through the doughnut volume, careful not to bang into the machinery at its core. But he stepped on something anyway, something that yipped. Derek's mutt Umberto. The dog sometimes liked to sleep hidden inside the doughnut, warmed by the central generator.

"Hush, Umberto," said Phil. "It's okay." If only that were true.

In the bathroom, Phil drank some water. The water on his teeth like a mountain stream. Da dead? It was way too soon. There was still too much to say to the old man, too much to learn. Now the tears were beginning to come. A rough sob. He buried his face in a towel.

After a bit, Phil washed off his face with cold water, then cried some more and washed some more. The beautiful complexity of water, of its sounds and motions. Da wouldn't see water anymore. Phil's dream just before waking—he'd been climbing the teeth-mountains and—hadn't there been a ball of light in the dream? Phil leaned on the sink, resting his forehead against the mirror with his eyes closed, trying to look back into his dream. Wouldn't it make sense to have had a special dream just as his father died? Especially when Da had died so strangely.

"Here's some coffee," said Kevvie, who'd followed him as far as the kitchen—the little area of the factory floor that passed for a kitchen, a sink and a stove and a table with chairs on the concrete floor beneath the seventy-foot-high truss-supported corrugated steel ceiling. She'd brought the uvvy as well. "Get away, Umberto," she said, and aimed a sharp kick at the dog, who'd come over to see if he might get some breakfast. Kevvie couldn't stand Umberto.

"Don't hurt him, Kevvie." Phil took the coffee. "Thanks. I can't believe this. I feel so—it's like my head's exploding. Life's not a rehearsal. It's real." He took the coffee Kevvie handed him, but set it down without drinking.

"You better call Willow," said Kevvie. She glared at Umberto so hard that the dog went slinking away.

"I know." Phil told the uvvy to dial his stepmother Willow. Phil's father Kurt had left Phil and Jane's mother Eve for Willow when Phil was thirteen and Jane was eleven. Eve had successfully remarried, and the families had stayed reasonably close over the years, with Phil and Jane freely moving between the households of their two biological parents.

Willow answered on the second ring. "Willow Chen Gottner," her voice was loud and harsh, just short of a scream. Willow's image floated above the uvvy—she was a thoroughly Californian Chinese woman with a symmetric face, full lips, and blonde hair so shiny and processed that it looked like metal. She moved with abrupt, birdlike gestures. There were smears of blood on her hands and on her cheeks. Her normally tidy features were blurred and twisted with anguish.

"Hi, Willow, it's Phil. I just talked to Jane."

"Kurt's really dead, yes, this is his blood all over me. I'm so scared, Phil. The wowo ate him *like garbage*."

"I'm coming right down. Where are you?"

"I'm at the gimmie station. They don't know what the fuck I'm talking about. They think I murdered Kurt or some shit." Willow was notoriously foul-mouthed. This was something that Phil and Jane's mother always tut-tutted over, but it made Phil and Jane like Willow more than they might have otherwise.

"You see!" interjected Kevvie. "Tell her to get a top criminal attorney!"

Phil glared at Kevvie, but felt he had to pass the idea on. "Do you have a lawyer?"

"Right! As if I need a lawyer to deal with some stupid gimmie pigs who I'm paying in the first place. As if a lawyer's going to protect me from a fucking hole to the fourth dimension that ground up my brilliant handsome husband like garbage!" She glared angrily at someone out of view. "Stay away from me, you sow!" The uvvy-view jerked wildly. "Stop it!" Then the uvvy went dead. Phil immediately called again; a gimmie answered.

"Officer Grady, Wackerhut Police Services, Palo Alto Station."

"I was just talking to Willow Gottner?" Phil said. "We were cut off?" He could hear Willow screaming curses in the background.

"She's out of control, sir," said the gimmie officer. "We're concerned she could injure herself. I'm afraid we're going to have to restrain her and administer a sedative."

"Take it easy! I'll be right there. I'm Kurt Gottner's son Phil. Where's your station located? I'm driving down from the city."

The gimmie gave Kurt directions and added, "I'm very sorry about this, Mr. Gottner."

"My father's really dead?" Kurt asked.

"We've got a response team up there. We're still not entirely sure what the situation is. The material evidence indicates a fatality, but there's no body. And, yes, your father's missing." There was a shriek from Willow. "She wants to tell you one more thing. I'll hold the uvvy out to her."

The little image showed Willow, sitting on a plastic couch squeezed between two Wackerhut policewomen. They had their arms twined with hers in some special cop way and one of them was in the process of pulsing a drug-mist squeezie in front of Willow's tiny triangular nose.

"Phil, be sure to call Tre Dietz," said Willow, her features already slackening. "I forgot to tell Jane."

"Don't worry, Willow. I'll be right there."

"Call him!" insisted Willow. "Tell Tre the wowos are real! The bastard." The uvvy clicked off.

"Who's Tre?" Kevvie wanted to know.

"Oh, you've heard of him. He's the uvvy graphics hacker in Santa Cruz who runs that new company Philosophical Toys? He got interested in Da's work on this weird shape called a Klein bottle—and they did the wowo together. Just for a goof. Tre's only about thirty. He and Da used to hang together and tweak the wowos." The unreality of it all came crashing over Phil then and he was crying. "I don't understand, Kevvie. Da can't be dead."

"But who actually owns the rights to the wowo?" asked Kevvie.

"Kevvie, that's too—" Phil broke off and slumped in his chair. This had really taken the wind out of his sails. "Can you drive, Kevvie? I don't think I can drive. I'm all torn up."

"I'll go dress."

When Kevvie left, Umberto came skulking back out of the

doughnut. Phil petted him absently as he uvvied Tre. Tre was still in bed with his wife Terri, and none too talkative.

"Yaar?"

"Tre, this is Phil Gottner. One of the wowos just killed my dad. You better turn the rest of them off."

"Myoor! That's so xoxxed! I should have thought of this. Your poor dad. I'll kill the wowos right now. Later."

Phil left a message at the restaurant where he cooked, and then he put on his silver boots and black leather jacket and went outside with Kevvie. There was a stink like sewage and cheese from the big moldie nest in the abandoned red ship that sat in a silted-in slip across the street from Phil's warehouse—the Snooks family. A group of skungy sporeheads and slug-skaters were standing on the pavement by the ship talking to a couple of the Snooks moldies and buying camote, the sporeheads' drug of choice. Obviously they'd been up all night. Phil gave them the finger, pro forma. They jeered back; one of them halfheart-edly threw a rock. Phil and Kevvie headed out.

It started raining as they got on the road. The traffic was light; the former Silicon Valley of the Peninsula had become something of a Rust Belt, and there wasn't much reason for anyone to go down there from San Francisco. There were only a handful of cars on the road, all tiny electric jobbies with hy-drogen fuel-cells. Overhead you could see a few of the richer travelers riding on great flapping moldies.

Kevvie wanted to listen to an old-fashioned morning audio show she liked, a smugly cynical guy and a woman with a dead flat that's-the-way-it-is-and-nothing-more voice just like Kevvie's. The theme of the show was that flying saucer aliens had been invading Earth for over a century and that the government was keeping it a secret. As if there were a government that mattered. As if the actual aliens who'd briefly appeared on the Moon this winter weren't more exciting than hundred-year-old lies. But Kevvie loved this shit. Phil threw a fit and made her turn it off.

"You're in a nasty mood today."

"My father's been murdered!"

"It's not like you two got along all that well. You had a big fight the last time you saw him."

Phil sighed as if his heart would break. "Poor Da. I wish I could see him just one more time." Up above the rainy freeway was a big sign temporarily wrapped in black plastic, the wind picking at the plastic and making it flap and billow in a way that spooked Phil. It was like a shroud. The brutal synchronicity of the universe displaying this just for him. Phil shuddered; the hair on the back of his neck stood on end.

February 14

On Saturday they held the memorial service on the grounds of the Bass School, the private school where Kurt had worked. A quartet of students played sweet music on violin, viola, flute, and harp. A big redwood towered overhead, fog in its branches. It had rained all night, but now the sky was clearing. The mourners sat in folding chairs on the flat ground in front of the school's main building, an enormous old two-story house, all glass and redwood, the home of a deceased software tycoon, the Bass of Bass school.

People took turns getting up and saying things about Kurt Gottner. Phil didn't feel able to speak. If he opened his mouth he'd be likely to start howling. Why expose himself like that, especially with all the Bass mucky-mucks here? Though he'd gone to Bass School for four years, Phil had no great love for the place. Da had met Willow Chen through Bass—she was a professional fund-raiser who did contract work—and Phil tended irrationally to blame Bass for his parents' breakup.

Phil's mother Eve had pulled Phil and Jane out of Bass after the breakup, and from then on they'd gone to public school—which had been, on the whole, more fun. The larger classes of the public school made it likelier that you could find a kindred spirit. And public school had moldies working as teachers' aides. You could learn a lot really fast from an uvvy link with a moldie. Bass, on the other hand, prided itself on being moldie-free.

Eve hated Bass. According to her, the students and faculty at Bass were a pack of freaks and losers, and the parents of the Bass kids were snobby self-indulgent artsy-fartsy crypto-Heritagist poseurs trying to buy themselves the illusion that their neurotic drug-addicted promiscuous bulimic dyslexic brats had one single grain of brains or talent. This, Eve's opinion. Phil, however, had found many of the Bass teachers quaint and nice. Especially his father.

At the funeral, Eve sat at left end of the front row, next to Phil, Jane, Kevvie, Willow, Willow's mother Jia, Da's brother Rex, Rex's wife Zsuzsi, Rex and Zsuzsi's daughters Gina and Mary, Kurt and Rex's mother Isolde, and Isolde's kind old sister Hildegarde, whose face could stop a clock.

Rex got up and spoke a little, about how Kurt had always been accident-prone as a child. "One time when Kurt was little he fell off his bicycle and I carried him home. A few years later he broke his ankle in a soccer game and a friend and I carried him home. Today's the last time we'll do it. We're carrying Kurt home."

Not that there was going to be much of Kurt to carry. The gimmie had scraped together maybe an ounce of blood and tissue-fragments. After freezing a sample of the DNA, the gimmie had incinerated the remains for Willow, who'd placed the ashes in a tiny octagonal madrone-wood box. The box sat before the mourners on a small Oriental rug on the ground.

Isolde got up and talked about Kurt as a child. She was a little woman with white hair and a strong voice. "Kurt was a wise soul," said Isolde. "He knew more than other people. He was shy and he didn't like to talk about it, but I could always see it in his bright brown eyes—he *knew*. He knew more than anyone could teach him, and he spent his life exploring the world of ideas. Nothing else mattered to him. I used to say, 'Kurt, why don't you get a Ph.D, and work at a university?' 'I don't have time, Mom,' he'd say. 'I'm too busy.' And all he'd be doing would be sitting in his armchair looking at a sunbeam. Too busy. Maybe Kurt knew he wouldn't have as much time as the rest of us." She gave a mild, rueful laugh and wiped her eyes. "Kurt was so excited about his last discoveries, about his dimensions and his wowos. I only hope that some good can still come of them. We're all trying to understand this death. What happened? I'd like to think that Kurt knew—and that somewhere he's still knowing. My son was an explorer."

Willow spoke next. The gimmie had cleared Willow of any wrongdoing; the cause of death had been written off as a freak electrical phenomenon, perhaps ball lightning, perhaps a corona discharge from Kurt and Tre's holographic wowo projection equipment. Willow looked stunning, slim and chic in a black wool suit, her face composed and perfect below her shiny bright hair.

"He was the best man I've ever known," Willow was saying. "He shouldn't be forgotten. And I've been working to set up a fitting memorial. The trustees of the Bass School have agreed to start a Kurt Gottner Scholarship Fund. An anonymous donor has agreed to match dollar-for-dollar any pledges made to this fund today. So please give generously."

"*Sell* it, Willow," Phil murmured to Jane.

Pretty soon one of the Bass administrators was speaking, a Doctor Peck, stringing together a line of fund-raising platitudes. "Bass School one big family . . . Kurt Gottner the quintessential . . . quick mind and open inquiry . . . such a special place . . . your unique opportunity . . . Kurt Gottner Scholarship Fund . . ."

Phil couldn't listen anymore. There were as many people standing as sitting, so he felt free to sidle out of his seat and wander over toward the deck of the school building where some little kids were already nosing around a big table full of canapés catered by the Bass School parents. Funeral meats. Phil cast a professional eye over the spread. He could have done a much better job, but oh well. He ate a salty deviled egg and a crustless triangle of bread with tank-grown salmon. Now a town councilman was butt-kissing the mourners, marveling at how "eukaryotic" was the nucleus of the Bass School community for Palo Alto at large.

Phil pushed open the big glass-paned front door and went inside the school, flashing back to his years here as a student. Fourth through eighth grades, with Da a genial distant figure teaching math and uvvy graphics to the seniors. Eve happy at home, taking care of them all, doing uvvy work for her family's olive-import business by running a dragonfly camera that talked to farmers in Greek. Those had been cozy years. The little family, the parade of days.

Phil walked down the creaky wood-floored hall, looking at the rows of pictures by primary-school students on display. Lots of hearts; odd as it seemed, today was Valentine's Day. Monday the hearts would come down, and spring flowers would be next. Or perhaps dead presidents. George Birthington's Washday, his English teacher had liked to call it—a bit of wordplay that Phil had found the very apex of worldly wit. The old school smelled the same as ever. Yes, it had been peaceful here until Willow appeared. She'd flown in like some bright magpie, snatching up Phil's woolly father for her nest.

"Are you a teacher?"

Phil's reverie popped. A slender dark-haired girl his age was looking at him. Her jawline was strikingly angled, her eyes clear, her mouth intelligent and kind. Her one nonidealized feature was her nose, which was a bit larger than normal, though it sat quite harmoniously in the calm oval of her face.

"Me? My father was the teacher."

"Oh God, I'm sorry, you're Kurt Gottner's son, aren't you? You must be so weighted that you don't know what to do."

"Yes, exactly. Thank you. My name is Phil." He held out his hand.

"I'm Yoke."

"That's a nice easy name. What was your connection with my dad?"

"Oh, I'm visiting Terri and Tre Dietz, so I came along with them to pay my respects. Tre's been so excited about your father's work, he talks about him all the time. Your father must have been a great man. How horrible that the wowo killed him."

"It's a nightmare. Everyone's scared to sleep in his house anymore. I've been down here in a motel since Thursday—today's Saturday, right?"

"Yes. Time's strange for you now, isn't it? My mother died at Christmas—which is another reason I'm here—and for the few days afterward it was like there was this glowing light everywhere and time wasn't moving at all. I even started smoking for a week, something about the cigarettes made it easier to chop up the time. And where I come from, smoking is practically impossible."

"Cigarettes, what a concept," said Phil. "If I let myself, I'd be drunk and stoned through all this for sure. I'm glad I don't have to do that. I'm sorry to hear about your mother. She died on Christmas Day?"

"Christmas Eve. She was alone. I feel terrible." Yoke's eyes moistened.

"Poor Yoke," said Phil, and went on talking lest the two of them break down.

"You're right about the kind of glow everywhere. Luminous. Realer than real. My father's ashes are in that little box on the rug on the lawn and the rest of him is who knows where, he's really dead and someday I'm going to die too. This—" Phil gestured at the old building around them, at the misty trees and the people outside. "This is what there is. We're like ants under lichen. Actual organisms crawling around in this shallow layer of fuzz on the Earth."

"Lichen?" smiled Yoke, wiping off her eyes. "I just saw natural lichen for the first time this week—forest lichen instead of the stuff inside moldies. Terri took me on a tour of the Big Basin redwoods. The ranger said, 'Alice Alga took a *lichen* to Freddie Fungi, and ever since, their marriage has been on the rocks.'" When Yoke hit the "lichen" pun, she giggled and raised her eyebrows.

"Or maybe we're like beetles under bark," said Phil, trying to stay poetic and serious. "Or rabbits in a briar patch. I keep having this funny vision of how glued to the Earth's surface we are. And how shallow the atmosphere is. Gaia's skin."

"I totally know," said Yoke in a heavy Val accent. Phil couldn't tell if she was mocking him or if that was a way she really talked.

Outside, the last speaker had finished and people were standing up and starting to mill around.

"Everyone's going to hit the canapés now," said Yoke. "Big-time. Before the crowd gets here I need to go to the bathroom."

"So that's why you asked if I'm a teacher," said Phil. "It's up those stairs, Yoke."

"Thanks, Phil. It's nice to meet you. Let's talk some more in a minute."

Phil watched Yoke go up the stairs. She had a high, perfectly rounded butt. But she moved up the stairs very slowly, taking one step at a time. It was so painful to watch that Phil looked away for a minute. When he looked back, Yoke was at the top. She smiled and waved as if she'd just mounted some great peak.

"Oh there you are." It was Kevvie, chewing a stick of celery. "Why'd you run off in the middle of the service?"

"It was getting to be too much for me." Phil glanced up the stairs. No more Yoke. He sort of didn't want her to see him with Kevvie. "Let's go out on the porch."

"Aren't you supposed to be doing something about your father's ashes?"

"Oh God, I forgot."

Phil hurried back down the steps to where his family stood around the rug on the ground. The reddish madrone wood of the eight-sided box made Phil think of a stop sign. Da's ashes.

Angular little sister Jane hugged Phil. Willow gave him a brittle smile. Eve, Isolde, and great-aunt Hildegarde each gave him a kiss. Rex shook his hand and clapped his shoulder, Aunt Zsuzsi patted his cheek, cousins Gina and Mary smiled sadly.

Kurt had often said he wanted them to dig his ashes into the soil under a certain big oak tree in a park near Palo Alto;

he and the kids had strolled there together many times. The tree was split near its base into a pair of great twin trunks. Phil had been placed in charge of informally sneaking the ashes into the public land, so now he put the flat little box in his coat pocket. Eve had forced him to buy a suit for the funeral; it was the first time in his life Phil had ever worn one.

They stood around for a bit, sadly reminiscing. Jane recalled how Kurt had always rhapsodized about the oak tree, how he'd gone on about fractals and gnarliness and self-organized criticality.

"I remember another thing Da used to say about that tree," said Phil. "He talked about how the week before the psychologist C. G. Jung died, Jung had a dream about an oak tree blown over in a storm with great nuggets of gold found twined in its roots. 'I want to be remembered like that,' Da always said. 'That my life sent down deep roots that pulled up gold.' " Phil sighed heavily. "I don't know if he really made it."

"Of course he did," said Isolde. "Think of his students."

"And who knows what the wowo will lead to," said Rex. "Don't underestimate your old dad, Phil. He was a pisser, but he was deep."

"Your father loved you very much, Phil," said Willow reproachfully.

"When he wasn't too drunk," muttered Phil.

"*What?*"

"Never mind."

"Speaking of wowos, look at this," said Jane, hurriedly getting something out of her purse. "Willow gave this to me."

There was knotted little bit of metal in the palm of Jane's thin little hand—a gold ring tied in an overhand knot with no sign of a break or a weld. Like a tiny sculpture.

"It's his wedding-ring," said Willow. "The gimmie found it on our bedroom floor. If you look closely, you can still make out the inscription, 'To Kurt from Willow.' It's creepy the way it's knotted. I don't want it."

"I think it's been knotted in the fourth dimension," said

Jane. She'd always been a better student of their father's ideas than Phil. "In the fourth dimension you can knot a closed loop by lifting part of it ana out of our space, moving it across, and then pushing it back kata into our space." *Ana* and *kata* had been Kurt Gottner's special words for the four-dimensional analogs of up and down. Jane looked at Phil with intent eyes. "This means the thing that ate Da comes from a higher dimension."

"Oh sick, there's a moldie here," interrupted Kevvie, sniffing the air. She looked around. "Over there with Tre and Terri Dietz. Who invited a moldie?"

There was indeed a soft-looking figure standing with Tre and Terri Dietz, a plastic moldie shaped like a barrel-chested sixty-year-old man, white-bearded and white-haired, a man with a big head and high cheekbones, his skin somewhat papery in appearance. Even without the smell, you could tell he was a moldie from how flexibly he moved. Yoke was standing next to him, chatting and laughing with a bottle of soda in her hand. She looked like a fashion model.

"I think that's—you know—Cobb Anderson!" exclaimed Phil, glad for the distraction. Growing up as Kurt Gottner's son, he'd heard enough about higher dimensions to last him a lifetime. "We'll talk about it later, Jane." He hurried over to the other group, glad for another chance to be with Yoke.

"Hi, Phil," said Yoke. "Cobb, this is Phil Gottner. Phil, this is Cobb Anderson. Cobb flew me down here from the Moon. He's here to pick up one of his relatives from Santa Cruz. His great-grandson."

Phil was surprised. "You're from the Moon, Yoke?"

"Duh! Why do you think it took me so long to walk up those stairs? I could see you feeling sorry for me. Well, I'm getting stronger every day."

"Hello, Phil," said Cobb, insisting on shaking Phil's hand. His imipolex moldie flesh was cool and slightly slippery. "Tre says your father was a great man. I hope you don't mind my coming to the ceremony. I'm just so happy to be out with people doing regular things. I haven't done anything normal in I don't know how many years." He had a hearty, booming voice with a crackle in the lower registers. His speech membranes couldn't quite reproduce a true human bass.

"I don't mind if you're here, Mr. Anderson, it's an honor. My father would be happy. But—there are a lot of the people at the Bass School who really hate moldies. Not that you're a moldie exactly. I mean, at least you started out as human."

"I'm like a Wal-Mart greeter now," rumbled Cobb. "If that means anything to you. Pure plastic." He turned his massive head, slowly looking around. "Now that you mention it, Phil, I do notice a few frosty stares. I'll just take a little stroll around the neighborhood. This is Palo Alto, eh? Pretty snooty. I can see why my great-grandson didn't want to come." Cobb smiled, bowed, and undulated off down the school's gravel driveway.

"I don't get how he could fly you down here from the Moon," Phil said to Yoke.

"I was inside him. Like the wendy meat in a California corndog!"

"Yoke's been walking around the Santa Cruz Boardwalk absorbing Earth culture," said Terri. "She and I made friends when I was up on the Moon, so I invited her to stay with us when she came down." Terri was a trim, deeply tanned woman with straight dark hair and pink lipstick. Bright golden DIM beads crawled slowly about in her hair.

"Terri's teaching me about diving," said Yoke. "I love being underwater. Everything alive all around you. I want to go to the South Pacific pretty soon. Earth is wonderful. And not just the water. The sky!" She gestured upward. A low gauzy cloud was drifting against a background of distant high clouds that rose up like mountain ranges to a tender patch of blue. "How can you mudders ever get anything done? Whenever I look at the sky I forget all about whatever I've been doing. Such stuzzy soft fractals." But now her attention returned to Phil. "What kind of job do you have?"

"Non tech. I'm a cook at a three-star San Francisco restaurant named LoLo. My father was disappointed in me. But I'm good at what I do."

"We hardly have any restaurants on the Moon. Most people just eat food-paste from the tap. And raw fruits and veggies from week trees."

"Well then, Yoke, our food's another mudder thing you can enjoy learning about. I'd love to cook some special dishes for—"

"Hi, I'm Kevvie Inch," interrupted Kevvie, suddenly appearing between Phil and Yoke. "Phil and I live together. Who are you?"

"I'm Yoke Starr-Mydol. I'm from the Moon."

"What are you doing down here?"

"Oh, tourism, self-improvement. I'm interested in the ocean."

"You don't work?"

"Well, nobody's paying me," said Yoke. "I'm kind of a software artist. I like to think of algorithms for simulating natural processes. I plan to try and model some Earth things while I'm here."

"I'm a geezer-visitor," said Kevvie. "I go see old people all over San Francisco. They have little DIM machines to take care of them, but they don't have anyone to talk to them. It's sort of like being a sex-worker, except there's no sex. I have a girlfriend who's a sex-worker. Klara Blo. She and I had bacteria-style sex a few weeks back. Have you ever tried bacteria-style sex, Yoke?"

Phil groaned inwardly. This was a new obsession of Kevvie's and she was always talking about it. "Bacteria-style sex" was the current expression for getting in a tub with someone and taking the drug merge to make your bodies temporarily melt together. Phil refused to do it, because he figured that just one pleasure rush could blow him off the Straight Edge and down into the addict's 24–7–365 regimen, wasted twenty-four hours a day, seven days a week, 365 days a year. Kevvie had started out Straight Edge like Phil, but she'd started dipping and dabbing six months ago, and now she was getting worse all the time.

"I wouldn't want to," Yoke was saying matter-of-factly. "I

think it's skanky. My parents have been merge addicts since before I was born. Or were. My mother Darla died two months ago. That's something I wanted to talk to you about some more, Phil. The thing that killed Darla could have been the same thing that killed your dad. And maybe Tempest Plenty too."

"I've got it!" interrupted Kevvie. "Flying saucers took them! Have you ever seen a flying saucer, Yoke?"

"I saw the real aliens who were on the Moon in November," said Yoke. "But they didn't come in any flying machine. They travel in a form like radio waves."

"I don't buy that," said Kevvie, with irrational vehemence. Phil realized that she was lifted. "If those things you saw were really aliens, there has to have been a saucer that they came in. They use a special metal. I bet ISDN or the gimmie is covering it up."

"There goes a saucer now, Kevvie," said Tre, pointing up at the sky. "Yaaar." He had long, tangled, sun-bleached hair and he wore weird little brown sunglasses over his no doubt blood-shot eyes. Once he'd gotten Kevvie to start staring upward, Tre looked back down. "What Yoke was talking about, Phil, is that Darla and Whitey had a wowo in their cubby. Only nobody saw Darla dying, so it didn't occur to anyone that the wowo might have been involved. I should have thought of it when Tempest Plenty disappeared last month. She was the aunt of our neighbor Starshine Plenty; we were putting Tempest up in one of our spare rooms."

Phil could tell Kevvie wanted to butt in and say something else dumb, but Terri spoke first. "Tempest was this colorful red-neck pheezer," said Terri. "A dynamo. Mean as a snake. A lifter. She liked to work on Starshine's garden, always talking a mile a minute, whether or not anyone was listening. And then one morning she was gone, along with Starshine's wowo and Star-shine's dog Planet. Starshine figured Tempest had taken the dog and the wowo back to Florida. She says most of the people in her family are like that. Rip something off and head for home."

"The wowo Tempest took was in Starshine's garden," continued Tre. "It was the best and biggest wowo I ever made, but the base only weighed a couple of pounds. Tempest loved to look at it, especially when she was lifted. And she was crazy about that dog. So what Starshine thought seemed reasonable. We were like, 'So what, at least Tempest's gone.' But then — mur! — Willow saw the wowo swallow Kurt and I put it all together. I switched off all the wowos that I've distributed."

"How did you manage that?" demanded Kevvie.

"All of my Philosophical Toys maintain an uvvy link to me. That way I can send out upgrades and — in the case of a catastrophe like this — I can shut them down." Although Tre looked like a Santa Cruz lifter, his Philosophical Toys had made him reasonably wealthy, and he ran his business in an orderly and efficient way. "I've been wanting to ask Willow for a really detailed description of how it went down. But I don't want to tweak her out."

"You should see what Jane has," said Phil. "Hey, Jane!"

Jane was still in conversation with old Isolde and Hildegarde, and she gave Phil a sisterly "How rude!" kind of look, a big jokey frown. Isolde and Hildegarde used the interruption to begin creeping toward the buffet.

"What?" said Jane, giving Phil a gratuitous poke in the ribs as she joined them.

"Show Tre the ring."

"Way eldritch," said Tre as soon as he saw it. "Knotted in the fourth dimension. Like a calling card. Like it wants us to know."

"It?" said Phil.

"The thing that came through the wowo. It couldn't have been the wowo itself that ate poor Kurt — a wowo's just a hollow of a self-everting Klein bottle geometrized in this tasty gnarly way that Kurt dreamed up. The wowo must have attracted something." Tre gave a kind of shudder and hugged himself, looking around. "It could be inches away from us right now. Watching." He handed the ring back to Jane. "I wouldn't keep this near me if I were you."

"You take it, Phil," said Jane, handing it off like a hot potato. "Bury it with Da's ashes. If we need it again we can always dig it up."

"Like the goldfish," said Phil, referring to a dead goldfish that he and Jane had buried one winter, only to dig it up every few days to look at the progress of its decay.

"It doesn't feel right not to have all of Da to bury," said Jane. "Willow said the ashes are just part of his hand. Maybe the rest of him is in the fourth dimension."

Phil put the knotted ring in his pocket next to the box. Some of his father's stories about the fourth dimension were coming back to him. A four-dimensional monster would be able to touch the ring in his pocket without coming through the fabric. Even if he were to put the ring *inside* the box, a four-dimensional creature could still reach it, just like you can touch the middle of a sheet of paper without coming through the paper's edge. If the four-dimensional creature could see everything, what good would it do to bury the ring?

"There was a weird dimensional thing about Darla too," Yoke was telling Jane. "She disappeared on Christmas Eve. My dick of a father had left her alone, he was out with a girlfriend or something. Poor Darla. All Whitey could find of her was this little gory patch of blood. And then Whitey starts saying he's going to grow her back. He has a fairly recent S-cube of her personality, and he's gonna use her DNA to fast-grow a new body, a young sexy one of course. But when he gives some of Darla's blood to a pink-tank worker, about half of the DNA in the blood turns out to be *backward*. Clockwise twisties instead of counterclockwise." Yoke made mirror-twin helix motions in the air with her hands. "When I told Tre about it, he said that maybe some of the DNA had been flipped over in the fourth dimension."

"Your father is growing a new copy of your mother?" asked Kevvie.

"Clear," said Yoke. "The new Darla's gonna have a bitchin' real meat body, not an imipolex fake like Cobb's. Whitey's had a lot of fights with boppers and moldies. He wouldn't be able to stand it if Darla came back pure moldie. This way she'll have a meat body, although her personality will have to be off in a kind of moldie scarf that she wears all the time. A Happy Cloak."

"I've never heard of anyone doing that before," said Kevvie.

"Oh yeah they have," said Yoke. "You've heard of Stahn Mooney. Used to be a Senator? His wife Wendy is made of a meat body with a moldie Happy Cloak that drives the body. Wendy's 'Cloak is really just a moldie that doesn't have any of the original Wendy's personality at all. But we'll have Darla's personality in her 'Cloak to start with." Suddenly the confidence drained out of Yoke's voice. "I hope it works. I miss her."

"What are you guys talking about?" asked Willow, wandering up to the group. She had a glass of white wine in her hand and her voice was shrill. "Help yourself to the refreshments before they're all gone. The Bass parents made a very nice buffet. And this wine is from Doctor Peck's own vineyard. It was Kurt's favorite. Eat, drink, and be merry." She looked far from merry.

"It was a nice ceremony, Willow," said Tre carefully.

"You have a lot of nerve showing up here," said Willow. "Considering that your shitty wowo killed him."

"Tre thinks it wasn't really the wowo itself," put in Phil. "He thinks it was a creature from the fourth dimension that the wowo attracted."

"Big difference," said Willow.

"Maybe you could grow a new husband," suggested Kevvie. "Like Yoke's father is doing."

"I assume Yoke is this little chippie here? How many people did you bring along, Tre? I mean besides the moldie. Do you think this a fucking hairfarmer beach party?"

"I'm sorry, Willow," said Tre. "We'll go now."

"Good!" Willow burst into tears and Jane held her, letting Willow's metallic blonde head rest on her shoulder.

Cobb appeared in the driveway just then. Tre and Terri murmured a quick good-bye and went to meet him. And then, before Phil could really say a proper good-bye to her, Yoke was gone too.

"Ooops," said Kevvie, rolling her eyes and grinning. She never knew what to make of big dramatic situations. At a time like this, Kevvie's cheery emptiness was kind of a relief. Phil linked arms with her and walked back to the buffet.

February 19

Phil thought about Yoke all the time for the next few days—whenever he wasn't worrying about the wowos or thinking about his father. He'd hoped that with the old man dead, there'd be nobody nagging him to make something of himself. But the memory tapes were playing on. Thinking about Yoke was much better. Phil thought about Yoke so much that when she turned up at the LoLo restaurant on Thursday, sitting at a table right near the kitchen, he almost wasn't surprised. Just, "Whew, here it is."

"Is this the guy?" Naranjo was saying, Naranjo the waiter who'd called Phil out of the kitchen. "Is this the hombre you lookin' for?"

Yoke was all smiles, sitting at a table with two guys and a woman. Phil recognized two of them: Saint and Babs Mooney, regulars in the San Francisco art scene. "Hi, Phil!" called Yoke. "I was hoping I'd find you here. Can you come out with us later?"

"He gotta stay and scrub a lotta potatoes," said Naranjo. "He's just an assistant chef. He gonna be here till about three maybe four A.M."

"Don't listen to him," said Phil. "It's great to see you, Yoke. Hi, Saint. Hi, Babs. I'll be through at eleven-thirty. It's ten now, so take your time eating and I can leave with you. With any luck, you'll be tonight's last customers. Things are really slow." A big storm had come in off the Pacific this afternoon and it was raining like people were up on the roofs with hoses. You could hear the splashing of the water through the glass of the windows. "You haven't ordered yet, have you?"

"How's the squid?" asked the fourth member of the dining party, a tenor-voiced fellow with shoulder-length red-blond hair that was very straight and fine. "Do you serve it with tentacles?"

"Sure," said Phil, taking an immediate dislike to the man, probably because he was sitting next to Yoke. "We've even got ink. But I'd recommend our deep-sea oarfish today. Brought in by a moldie this afternoon, he caught it himself. You can't catch an oarfish with ordinary techniques; it swims too deep. It has a nice firm flesh from living at such a high pressure. If you like, Yoke, I'll make it in a special sauce with sherry, cream, and chanterelles. Some saffron basmati rice and asparagus on the side. A few black cherries in the sauce for the sweetness and the color. And a Belgian endive salad with fresh-roasted red bell peppers and a mustard vinaigrette."

"Ooh," said Yoke. "That sounds delish. I've read those fancy food words, but I've never eaten them."

"Should we all have the same thing?" said Saint. "Babs? Onar?" Babs nodded, but the handsome, long-haired Onar insisted that he be served squid. "Stir-fry it in canola oil," he instructed. "All tentacles. And don't let them get rubbery."

"Gnarly, sir," said Phil.

Naranjo jotted down the order and went off to serve another customer. Phil lingered, gazing at Yoke, admiring her.

"Did you bury your father's ashes?" asked Yoke. "And the knotted ring? How did it go?"

"Having my dad die hurts more than I ever imagined it would," said Phil. "Today it's been a week. Yeah, I buried the ashes and the ring. I dumped the ashes out of the box; there weren't many of them. Now I wish I'd kept the ring. I need to think about it some more. Maybe I should have paid more attention when Da tried to teach me about the fourth dimension."

"I was so sorry to hear about your father, Phil," put in Babs Mooney.

"Yaaar," chimed in her brother Saint. "Poor Kurt. It would

xoxx to get chopped up by a hyperspace blender." Babs and Saint had DIM lice in their hair, colorful little bugs that moved around on their scalps like tiny cars in traffic, arranging their hair in filigrees that could variously resemble shingles, paisley, crop circles, or herringbone tweed. Programming the lice was one of Saint's art projects.

"I have a theory about the wowo," proposed Onar, holding up a bony finger. "The wowos were a representation of the Klein bottle, were they not? Two Möbius strips sewn together?"

"I guess," said Phil. "But it was just a goof. An illusion."

"Perhaps the models set up a morphic resonance. Reality is, after all, a consensual hallucination. If enough people see something as a Klein bottle, then—*voilà*—it's a Klein bottle. It's not impossible to be killed by a dream."

"Don't make it a New Age fantasy, Onar," reproved Saint. "This thing was real."

"Reality is a hobgoblin for small minds," said Onar mildly. Yoke giggled. She seemed to find Onar entertaining.

Phil got the head chef to let him prepare most of the food for Yoke's table. He cooked with fervor, and the meal was a big success. Around midnight he and the four guests stepped out of LoLo together. It was still pouring rain. Yoke did something with her uvvy as they stepped outside, and a moldie suddenly came bouncing up the street, sending out great splashes of water with each jump. It was Cobb Anderson.

"Thanks for waiting, Cobb," said Yoke. "What did you do?"

"Oh, I was going around town with Randy Karl," said Cobb. "And then we split up and I was hanging out with some homeless people in an alley off Columbus Street. Talking with them. One of them was a very intelligent fellow. It's not so much that the homeless are crazy and addicted, it's that they don't have money for rent. Just that one simple lack. We need to find a way to make cheap housing for the poor. But hey, just for right now, let me be your umbrella." Cobb stuck up his arms, and his tissues flowed upward, spreading out and thinning to make a giant umbrella that they could all stand under, the five young people in a circle around the moldie. "Better hold up the edges," said Cobb. He'd used so much of his body flesh in the umbrella that his head had sunk down to chest-level.

"Where's Randy now?" asked Yoke.

"By now I imagine he's found a moldie hooker like he was looking for. I really should get that boy up to the Moon to be with his father. Eventually."

"Cobb's talking about his great-grandson," Yoke explained to the others. "Randy Karl Tucker. He's a cheeseball from Kentucky. He lives in Santa Cruz. Tre and Terri Dietz hate him. Randy kidnapped one of their moldies by putting a leech-DIM on her. But now Randy says he realizes it was wrong. Cobb's supposed to take him to the Moon to meet his father."

"What is this 'DIM' that everyone's always talking about?" asked Cobb.

"It stands for 'Designer Imipolex', Cobb," said Yoke. "It's what everyone uses instead of the old-time silicon computer chips anymore. A DIM is made of imipolex with some mold and algae in it. Just like your new body. You were out of it for a looong time, weren't you?"

"I'm still out of it," said Cobb. "That's another reason I want to have a good look around dear old Earth before I go back to the Moon. And Randy's in no hurry either. He's been busy spending the money his father keeps sending him. Sad to say, Willy's a little reluctant to meet his only son. At this rate, poor Randy could wind up being a remittance man—someone whose father pays him to stay away. I've told Willy he should be more excited about Randy, but so far Willy doesn't want to listen to his Grandpa. I think he's been on the Moon too long."

"Why didn't Randy come along for dinner?" asked Phil.

"Hell, he was in too big a rush to get to that scurvy place in North Beach," said Babs, laughing. "Real Compared To What. Can you even imagine? Randy's certainly a man who knows what he wants. Admirable, in a way."

They walked down the sidewalk as a single group dome. The plan was to go back to Babs's space in a warehouse not far from Phil's. Yoke, Cobb, and Randy were spending a few days with Babs. The rain made a nice reverberating sound against Cobb's taut moldie flesh, which smelled like a dank basement. Phil managed to be next to Yoke, though Onar was on her other side.

"So you're into helping people now, Cobb?" asked Onar. "Is this a result of some experiences you had while you were dead? And what was that like?"

"My original human personality was stored on an S-cube for over twenty years," said Cobb. "And, yes, that was more or less the same as being dead. That me is dead forever, and it's the same as the me right now. Memories of it? A big white light. The SUN. Endlessly falling into it, but never reaching the core. A cloud of other souls around me. The end of time, forever and ever."

"You mean 'Sun' like our home star?" asked Phil.

"No," said Cobb, "I mean capital S-U-N. At least that's the name I use. The Divine Light, the universal rain that moistens all creatures. The SUN is a little like the eye on the top of the pyramid on the old dollar bills. Except SUN isn't about money, the SUN is about love and peace."

"Oh look," said Babs, changing the subject by noticing a shop window, and the group stopped to gaze in. Colorful felt hats, each a single pastel shade, were suspended in the window, funny and bright, with an intricate patterning in their fabric. "I'm getting so into fashion," added Babs. "I've been designing lace. It's too bad nobody ever wears lace. They should." Babs herself wore a silky shawl of thick, intricate nonrepeating lace. A mantilla.

"How did that work, your getting an imipolex body?" Phil asked Cobb.

"It was interesting," said Cobb. "These two loonie moldies each started running a simulation of me. They pulled me back from the SUN. They were running two simulations of me so they could compare and contrast and get the parameters tweaked. And meanwhile they had a new imipolex body ready for me. So there were two simulations of me waiting for the one body. I and I got into a telepathic uvvy link so that we could merge and share — instead of doing sudden-death musical chairs. From that merging experience, and from being with the SUN, I got the conviction that each of us is the same person. And that's why we should be really kind. Which answers Onar's question of why I want to do good."

"How do you make the lace?" Yoke was asking Babs.

"I use fabricants," said Babs. "I don't think you have those on the Moon yet? They're crawly little DIMs like the lice in my hair, plastic ants that can spin fabric like spiders. People are using them for everything in the fashion business. I bet those hats were made by fabricants. Fabricants eat just any old thing — weeds, scrap wood, cardboard — and they spin it into fiber. I'll show them to you when we go back to my place."

"If we're going to Babs's," said Onar, "let's get some kind of transport. I don't want to walk the whole way under a vile-smelling live toadstool."

"Randy would love it," said Babs. "But we can get the street-car at the corner up there. You can ride too, Cobb, it's run by a moldie."

The streetcar with its moldie conductor came clanking up then. Cobb and the five young people got aboard. Phil ended up between Yoke and Cobb.

"Do you think I smell bad?" Cobb asked Phil.

"Of course," said Phil. "That's the way moldies are."

"Well then, that's another problem I want to work on," said Cobb. "Besides more housing. I want to make moldies smell good. I bet a little biotech research could do it. The moldies just haven't bothered to fix their smell before because they don't care. What if the moldies made themselves smell good and built a whole lot of free housing!"

"Maybe Cobb should run for mayor of San Francisco," said Yoke. "He's friends with ex-Senator Mooney, you know. Babs and Saint's dad."

"I've got a new life and I want to help people," said Cobb.

"A moldie run for an election?" exclaimed Phil. "You'd get all the moldie votes, but that's ten percent of the city at best. What human would vote for a moldie? Even if you did used to be a person. And you've only been in San Francisco for, what, two days? Talk about a carpetbagger!"

"Well, it would be very popular to help people find housing," said Babs. "That's like the biggest problem. Cobb could win a lot of votes by fixing up abandoned warehouses."

"Are you rich, Cobb?" asked Onar.

"I don't actually own much of anything," said Cobb. "My estate was divvied up a long time ago. My grandson Willy is wealthy, though I doubt he'd be much interested in this issue. But even without money, I have a very high recognition factor. As a politician I could act as a 'facilitator.'" Cobb smirked a little at the bogus word. "How about this?" he added, and started up a series of impressions, changing his voice and features to resemble half-remembered images of dead Presidents. "The last four letters of 'American' are 'I can.' Mo' folks, mo' better. Ask not—"

"Stow it, Cobb," said Yoke, cutting him off. "Presidents suck."

They got off the streetcar a block from Babs's warehouse, and the five humans ran there, with Cobb bouncing along next to them, hitting every puddle on the way. The inner walls of Babs's warehouse space were decorated with great webs of shiny woven fiber, bright-colored and iridescent. There was a polyglass keg of beer that Saint had brewed, and he and Onar got into drinking it.

Babs's fabricants lived in a little glass box like a terrarium, with strong lights and with a dish of wet paper for food. There were dozens of them, shiny little hourglass shapes with six legs. Babs showed Yoke how to use an uvvy to program them, and Yoke picked up on it right away. Within half an hour she'd gotten the fabricants to spin her a mantilla filled with spidery copies of her name.

Cobb sat quietly on the couch, taking everything in. He'd

tightened up his body so that he was dense and practically odorless.

Onar found a great sheet of piezoplastic in Babs's supplies and flopped it out onto an open space on the floor. With a deft move of his long fingers, Onar pinched off a bit of his own uvvy to make a receiver-DIM which he affixed to the big sheet of plastic. Now the imipolex came alive with colors and shapes: some abstract, some like cartoon images and blurred photographs, all coming directly from Onar's brain. Saint put on his uvvy and got in on the act too, moving around playing air guitar and sending thought-sounds to the blanket of piezoplastic. The great sheet began to buzz and vibrate like a giant speaker, its rapid undulations sending out Saint's brain-made music. It sounded like spacey horns with cymbals and heavy-metal guitars. Everyone watched and listened in fascination, everyone except Phil, who kept worrying about how to get Yoke's attention.

Finally, Phil distracted Yoke by getting Babs to show off her old worm-farm, which was a big layer of humus between two transparent plastic walls. If you shone lights against a wall, the lavender, red-banded worms would appear, writhing up against the plastic.

"I have some smart imipolex worms mixed in," said Babs. "There goes one." A gold flicker went writhing past. "You can actually uvvy into them to get a worm's eye view if you like."

Now Babs went to get a beer, and Phil took the opportunity to get Yoke to step outside alone with him. It had stopped raining and there was some dramatic moonlight in the clouds. "If you're interested, Yoke," said Phil, "we could take a little walk and I could show you where I live. It's not far from here. My housemate Calla has a big fabricant DNA sculpture, and Derek makes machines that do things with colored air. I have some toy blimps I made in my room. Would you like to come look at them?"

"What will Kevvie say?" asked Yoke.

"I don't think she's home," said Phil. "She was going to do something with Klara Blo tonight."

"Her friend the sex worker!" said Yoke. "I remember."

"Kevvie and I aren't totally linked or anything," said Phil, feeling himself blush. "We just happen to—"

"Live with each other," said Yoke. "Like an old married couple. Babs said you've been together for over a year. I was asking her about you."

"I'd leave Kevvie for you in a minute, Yoke," blurted Phil. "I can't stop thinking about you." There was something about Yoke—her smell, her voice, the way she moved, the things she said—she fit into Phil's heart like a key in a lock.

Yoke widened her eyes and arched her eyebrows. She slipped her hand into Phil's. "So show me where you live."

It was a beautiful night. The moon floated out from behind the drifting clouds; it was nearly full. "Where exactly on the Moon are you from?" asked Phil.

"I was talking to Terri about that yesterday," said Yoke. "She was showing me how you mudders think there's a face in the Moon. And for everyone it's different. To me it looks like a girl. And if you see it that way, then Einstein would be just at the bottom of her left eye. Which is the Sea of Tranquility."

"I've always thought the Moon looked like a smiling pig," said Phil. "With a snaggle snout."

They walked a block and turned a corner. It was dark and quiet, with calm puddles staring up at the night sky. "I feel like my father's up there," said Phil. "Hanging in the sky like an ornament. His face looking down."

"I can feel Ma like that too," said Yoke. "Dear, loud Darla. I feel kind of weird about my pop's plan to bring her back. That's not really, truly going to be Darla. I mean, don't you think there's such a thing as a soul?" Yoke sighed and looked at the sky. "The dead are kind. They want us to live. You have to believe that."

"I want to. The last time I saw my father, I fought with him. He always wanted me to be a scientist instead of a cook. He was needling me. I lost it. I told him I hated him for leaving my mother, and that his work was stupid. And then, bam, he started crying. I couldn't deal. I left. And that was the last time I ever saw him. I need to feel like he forgives me."

"Then you have to forgive *him*. Forgive him so you can forgive yourself."

Silently, Phil tried the notion on. He let forgiveness fill him; and it felt like unwrapping a rusty wire from around his heart. "This is good, Yoke, this helps." It was wonderful to be with this girl. Nobody had ever understood him so well before.

Yoke stood quietly next to him, her face turned up toward the sky—or toward him. Phil decided to try and kiss her. But just then a high ecstatic yodeling caught Yoke's attention and made her draw away.

"What is that?" she asked. "It's coming from those colored lights way down at the end of the block. Is that a ship?"

"It's an abandoned ship that's stuck in the mud at a slip right across from my warehouse," said Phil. "The Snooks family lives there. A big nest of moldies. They're betty-lifters, cheeseball whores, camote dealers, way xoxxy. If old Cobb wonders why most people don't like moldies, he should get to know the Snookses."

"What's the ship's name?"

"*Anubis*. It's decorated all ancient Egyptian. It used to be a party boat, and before that it was a freighter."

They walked the rest of the block hand in hand, the crazy urgent yelling of the Snooks moldies and their customers getting louder.

"On the Moon we hardly mingle with moldies at all," said Yoke. "They stay in their underground Nest and we stay in the Einstein dome."

A shiny gold moldie came humping across the street like a big inchworm and reared up in front of them. He had a stylized chin-beard and a striped scarf on his head just like a pharaoh. "Come aboard the ship *Anubis*, spiritual seekers. We feature the stuzziest camote in town. Key a timewave to ancient Egypt."

"It's just me, Thutmosis," said Phil.

"Neighbor Phil?" said the moldie, peering closer. "The eternal return. Metempsychosis. Yet never the same river twice. Who's the woman?"

"I'm Yoke Starr-Mydol," said Yoke. "I've just come here from the Moon."

"How about those crazy loonie moldies?" asked Thutmosis. "Are they still kidnapping Earth moldies?"

"Maybe they are," said Yoke, cocking her thumbs and pointing her forefingers at Thutmosis like guns. "Maybe I'm about to put a leech-DIM on you. Better run!" Thutmosis Snooks grunted and went undulating back toward his ship.

Phil undid the heavy locks on his warehouse door and ushered Yoke inside. The lights were on; Derek was in his workshop in the far corner, doing something with one of his air-sculpture machines. Umberto the dog peered watchfully out from under Derek's workbench. Derek caught Phil's eye right away and pointed meaningfully toward the bathroom. Phil's heart sank as he went to look. Yoke followed along behind.

There was a throw of skin in the bathtub, bumpily billowing like a sheet with lovers under it. Now the mass surged and Phil could see four eyes in two faces; it was Kevvie and Klara Blo, merged together into one ungainly bod; the skin was theirs.

"Hi there, Phil and Yoke," said Kevvie, except it seemed like she said it out of Klara Blo's mouth, a somewhat hard-looking mouth in a rough-skinned face the color of a lemon. Ungainly lumps moved beneath the fused skin: the bones of beckoning arms. "You two wanna lift and join us in some bacteria-style sex, Phil?" came Klara's voice. "You and your new little cookie? You're missing everything with your stupid Straight Edge, Phil. Merge is the best. It's like the air is an orgasm."

"Naranjo told me you went off with Yoke," said Kevvie, talking out of her own mouth now. "So I brought Klara over here to help me wait for you." Slowly, she sat up in the tub. Her neck and shoulders pulled free of Klara. Her still-fused breasts stretched and jiggled.

"Phil, I'm going back to Babs's," said Yoke, and in an instant she was across the floor and out the door into the shadows.

"You're trying to sneak around," said Kevvie. She looked wildly unpretty. "You like that little moon-maid more than me. Her and her bullshit about aliens with no flying saucers."

With a sudden great wallowing motion, Klara tore completely loose and got up out of the tub. "You're a zerk, Phil," she said, pulling on her clothes and pushing past him. "You have no idea how much Kevvie loves you."

Kevvie went on a crying jag then, and Phil held her. She felt unsettlingly fluid—as if she might pop. After a while Phil helped her to go up to their room and get into bed. As soon as she lay down, she nodded out. He went back downstairs.

"This isn't good, Phil," said Derek. "Calla wants to evict you two."

"Is she in her room?"

"No, man, she walked in on them in the bathroom with *her* date, and he's this very clean wetware engineer, so you can imagine. They went back to his place in Cole Valley."

"And you?"

"You know me, Phil, I'm an anarchist. I think it's wavy to have two skanks merged in our tub. Local color. But I'm worried about Umberto here." Derek leaned down to pet his dog, who'd perked up at the sound of his name. "I'm afraid Kevvie might really hurt him one of these times. She doesn't like him, fine, I can accept that. But when Kevvie's lifted she gets so harsh and rigid, you wave? Like a killer robot. And I don't like cleaning up after her either." Derek's attention turned back to the machine he was working on. "Hey, I've got this new effect, man. Channel this." Derek turned on his machine and a big tongue of flame went whipping up into the air. "Looks like a dragon-fart, hey? And it's not really fire. It's a plasma. Cool to the touch." Derek ran his arm through the forking pillar of flame.

"I have to go back out, Derek."

"Oh no you don't."

"Kevvie's asleep for the night, Derek. When she gets like this it means she took quaak or gabba behind the merge."

"I don't want to be sitting here with her crying and melting on my shoulder when she gets up to puke, man."

"I promise I'll be right back, Derek. I just want to run over to Babs's."

"To try and square it with that other girl. What's up with her?" Derek did something to make his fire tongue reach way across the room toward Phil. "Confess to the fire-god, my son."

"I think I love her," said Phil as the cool flames licked all about him.

"Go in peace."

Phil's simple declaration to Derek crystallized his feelings. He had to find Yoke and tell her. He hurried back outside.

Across the street some wasted sporeheads were capering along the ship's railing, doing the flat-footed newt dance that sporeheads always did, their diagonally opposite legs and arms rising and falling together. A purple Snooks moldie named Ramses was playing them some trance music from a long horn he'd grown out of his nose. Gold Thutmosis came bustling over once again.

"Was that moon-girl really packing a leech-DIM?" Thutmosis wanted to know. Moldies were terrified of leech-DIMs, which were control patches that could turn them into slaves. For the sake of human-moldie relations, the leech-DIMs were illegal, just as were the thinking-cap devices that moldies could use to enslave humans. But there was a lively commerce in both products just the same.

"Where did she go?" Phil countered.

"Back the way she came."

Phil took off running down the block and around the corner to Babs's. But when he got inside, Saint and Babs were alone with a pale gangly guy who was lounging back in a beanbag chair, fondling a handful of Babs's imipolex worms. Cobb, Yoke, and Onar were gone.

"Where's Yoke?" demanded Phil.

"Out flying," said Babs. "Onar bought Cobb that sheet of piezoplastic from me. And then Cobb grew wings and took Yoke and Onar out to see the Golden Gate Bridge. Yoke knew you'd come back, Phil. She said she didn't want to see you again tonight. Maybe you should try again in the morning."

"Let me introduce you, Phil," said Saint, kindly changing the subject. "Randy Karl Tucker. He's Cobb's great-grandson."

"Hi guy," said the lanky yokel, only it sounded more like "Haaah gaaah." He had pale hair and a narrow head. He was dressed in very generic clothes: white shirt and black pants. "This is a stuzzy art scene y'all got goin' here," he opined. "If I could get my dad to give me the money, I wouldn't mind buyin' me one o' these warehouses. Reckon a fella can do pretty much whatever he wants here." He smiled at Babs.

"Put the worms back now, Randy," said Babs. "You're going to hurt them. Randy just got back here from Real Compared To What, Phil. That moldie sex-club in North Beach?"

"Oh yeah," said Phil noncommittally.

"I laaahked what I saw," said Randy. "But I didn't have the dough for a real date with a San Francisco moldie. I'm still all fired up."

"Gnarly!" whooped Saint. "A true cheeseball."

"It's a lift," said Randy mildly. "Don't knock it if you ain't tried it."

"You'd probably like the *Anubis*," said Phil. "It's just down the block from here. Though if you go aboard you better know how to take care of yourself."

"Oh, I've been around all kinds of moldies," said Randy. "Thanks for the tip. Hey, Babs, I'm gonna feed one of your worms to Willa Jean. This oughta be a hoot. *Chick-chick-chee!*"

At Randy's call, a little imipolex chicken appeared from the depths of the warehouse. It walked with a jerky strut, abruptly turning its little head this way and that. It was yellow, with a dark patch on its back.

"My pet chicken," said Randy Karl. "See that purple spot on her back? That's a special leech-DIM that's controlled by my uvvy. Willa Jean's practically like an extra hand for me. Want a worm, chick-chick?" The grinning Randy dangled a twisting green imipolex worm a few feet above the floor.

Willa Jean beat her stubby wings and hopped, trying to get at the worm. The worm was writhing and Willa Jean was cheeping frantically. Finally Randy dropped the worm and the little chicken caught it in midair. Now the chicken squatted on the floor, stretching out her neck so as to swallow her prey the faster.

"Gobble gobble," said Randy. "Want 'nother one, Willa Jean?"

"One more, but that's the last one, Randy," said Babs. She didn't seem as annoyed with Randy as Phil might have expected. It was almost as if Babs thought Randy were cute and interesting. No accounting for tastes.

Phil looked out Babs's warehouse door, scanning the dark sky for a sign of Yoke, Onar, and Cobb.

"Poor Phil," said Babs. "You'd be much better for her than Onar."

"Yaaar," agreed Saint. "Onar's a windbag. A sneak. I know him from work. Normally I don't hang with him, but somehow he heard we were going out with Yoke tonight and he begged me to come along."

"Oh well," sighed Phil. " 'Night, guys."

February 20

By the time Phil got back to his place, Kevvie had started throwing up. Derek was nowhere to be seen, but of course Umberto was right there sniffing at the vomit, and Kevvie was cursing at the dog and trying to kick him, which made her lose her footing and fall down really hard. Seeing the toll drugs took on Kevvie made Phil grateful that he didn't have to be doing the same thing. But as always, there was a part of him that wished he could. Being a druggie would be so easy.

"Are you mad at me?" Kevvie asked him.

Over the years, Phil had picked up some tools for coping

with addicts. "I can't afford to be mad. It's not your fault, and I can't fix it." He tried hard to believe the words, to put his own serenity first.

It was three A.M. when they were finally settled in, Kevvie all cleaned up and the two of them in bed together. Phil couldn't immediately fall asleep. He kept thinking about his father, wishing for the zillionth time he hadn't called the emotional old man stupid, hadn't reduced him to tears.

The image of the buried wedding ring formed in Phil's mind, and he worked at trying to visualize how the ring could have knotted, trying to think about ana and kata, doing this mental homework as a kind of offering to his dad. Maybe he should dig the ring back up.

He drifted into sleep with the ring still in his mind, and in his dream he began climbing up a mountain, the ring floating in front of him, except now it was a glowing ball, a wowo that was his father's face, a face with a seam on it like a baseball, the seam continually shifting along itself, warping his father's features in a way that was painful to behold. The baseball split in half and started talking to him, Phil climbing the steep hill all the while.

"Can you forgive me for leaving your mother?" his father's voice was saying. "I can't forgive myself, Phil. Forgive me." The voice seemed to touch Phil all over his face, touch him with sticky little baby hands.

"Oh, Da," Phil answered. "Don't. We're the same flesh. I remember crawling on you when I was little. You smelled like freckles."

"Forgive me."

And then Kevvie was waking Phil up again. She was bright and perky in a brittle kind of way. Chewing gum and drinking a cup of coffee, smiling, modulating her voice.

"I'm sorry to wake you, but it's Willow on the uvvy again," she said. "There's something new about your father. It sounds like the flying saucers came back."

Phil put the uvvy on his neck and let the image of Willow

form inside his head. "The fucking tree fell over," said Willow. "The tree where you buried him."

"What?"

"Half an hour ago I rode my bike there for my morning exercise, and the tree was flat on its side. Its roots are all pulled out of the ground."

"Did you find any gold in the roots?" asked Phil. Anything seemed possible now.

"Fat chance," said Willow. "I took one look and got out of there. This scares the shit out of me, Phil."

"Yeah," agreed Phil. "I wonder if it uncovered his ashes and the ring."

"That's exactly why I'm calling. I'm worried some busybody might find the ring and I get hassled for burying that little bit of Kurt on public property. I want you to come down here and find the ring before someone else does." As well as showing a model of her face, Willow's uvvy signal showed a real-time view of what she was seeing, which was the kitchen of Phil's father's house. She'd moved back in after the funeral.

"All right, Willow," said Phil. He was pleased and surprised at the readiness of his response. "I'd be glad to." Do the right thing.

"It's the least you can do," said Willow, who'd been expecting a refusal. "After the way you treated Kurt. I called Jane and she thinks it's a good idea too."

"I already said I'm coming, didn't I? I'll get the train this morning. But I have to be back up here by four for work."

"Thank you very much," said Willow, and hung up.

"You can borrow my car if you like," said Kevvie. "I could get the streetcar. I'm just working on Russian Hill today."

"Can we talk about last night, Kevvie?"

"Can't I have fun like normal people? Don't get all judgmental. Just because you're so worried about your precious health. It was Klara's idea anyway. And what were you doing bringing that Yoke girl back here?"

"I wanted to show her where I live. We were over at Babs

Mooney's. I thought she'd like to see Calla's DNA and Derek's sculptures. And my blimps."

"I bet."

"I can't put up with just anything, Kevvie. The way you acted last night was really unpleasant. I'm sorry for you, but this isn't a way I want to live. I think—"

"Shhhh." Kevvie held her finger up to her lips. "Don't say something we'll regret. I've got to go to work now, so if you don't want the car, I'm going to take it. Get away, Umberto! Would you like me to drop you at the train station?"

"Okay."

"And, Phil, when you're down there today, be sure to watch the sky. For the flying saucers. The aliens are little gray people, you know. With slit mouths." Kevvie hunched her shoulders, squinted her eyes and held her mouth funny—Phil had to laugh.

It wasn't till he was on the train that Phil remembered he'd planned to try and stop by Babs's to see Yoke before leaving. It occurred to him that perhaps Kevvie had thought of this. Maybe that's why she'd been so quick to give him a ride.

In Palo Alto, Phil got a moldie to rickshaw him to his father's house from the train station. Willow said she didn't want to go near the tree again, so Phil borrowed her bike and rode over there by himself.

Some kids were climbing on the fallen tree branches. The tree was cracked and split; a full half of it was gone. There had been two trunks before, and now there was only one. But the roots were all there. There was a big hole where the roots had pulled out of the ground. Phil flopped Willow's bike down on the ground and, just to set his mind at ease, walked across the little crater to get at the fallen tree's roots. He pulled a dozen or so rocks out of the roots' embrace, scratching each of them to see if maybe, just maybe, it was gold. But none of them was.

Now Phil searched for the spot where he'd left the ring and emptied out the ashes; this took a minute, as everything was so plowed up. His father's last resting place was at the edge of the hole, right opposite the split, fallen remains of the tree. It didn't take too much imagination to think that the disturbance had spread out from there. Phil crouched down and dug at the loosened dirt. And, yes, there was the knotted ring, glinting up at him as if to say, "Hi, I've been waiting for you." Phil pocketed it and headed back to Willow's.

Willow prepared a little lunch of vegetables and noodles. They talked about Kurt. Phil told Willow he was sorry he'd argued with Kurt that last time. Saying this made him feel better.

Willow asked to see the ring once more after all, so Phil handed it to her. She examined it and then looked at Phil curiously.

"Didn't you notice that it's changed again?"

"What do you mean?"

"Look." Willow held up the ring with her long red fingernails. Phil studied it. And—well—maybe the ring was knotted in a subtly different way from before. Or maybe not. An overhand knot instead of an underhand? Would that make a difference?

"Look closer," said Willow. "Look at the inscription."

And then Phil saw that the writing was backward:

.wolliW morf truK oT

"Do you think Da's really dead?" asked Phil suddenly.

"I saw the wowo eat them up, Phil. First Friedl and then Kurt."

"Friedl! Your dog?" Phil recalled that Willow had owned a dachshund named Friedl. He hadn't consciously noticed the dog's absence, but, yes, come to think of it, the house was much quieter than usual. Friedl had been quite the yapper. "How come you didn't say anything about Friedl before?"

"Oh fuck, I guess I felt guilty. It was Friedl who got into the wowo in the first place. Kurt and I had been about to—we were in bed naked together and Kurt turned on the wowo to make a romantic light. And then suddenly Friedl starts carrying on like she's fallen into a salami slicer. And when I looked over there, the wowo was down by the floor and it had gotten all big and warped looking and Friedl was—I don't know, it was like she was stretched out over the wowo's surface. All blown up like a picture on a balloon?" Willow held her arms out, making a big round shape in the air.

"But a wowo's small," said Phil.

"Not when it ate Friedl and Kurt," said Willow. "Friedl was like *inflated*—except for her little head; it was sticking out barking like crazy. And I screamed for Kurt to do something and he grabbed at Friedl, and the stupid dog bit him—Friedl was like that—and Kurt couldn't get loose, she'd sunk her teeth into him and Kurt was yelling and then all of a sudden the wowo went over from Friedl to Kurt—so fast. And Kurt swelled up big like Friedl had been and Friedl was her own right size, but she still wouldn't let go of Kurt, she'd completely panicked. There was light inside Kurt, he had glowing eyes like in a monster viddy and he was yelling like—I didn't tell this before—he almost sounded like he was happy? *Whooping.* And then he got smaller and smaller, except for his hand sticking out trying to shake Friedl loose, the hand and the dog flopping in and out of the ball, half in and half out, and then—*pop*—Friedl and Kurt's hand exploded and blood spurted everywhere. After that I didn't see or hear Kurt anymore. There was blood all over me, and tiny little pieces of them on the floor. And the shit-ass wowo went back to pretending to be normal. I ran out of the room and uvvied the gimmie. The wowo wasn't doing anything more, so right before the gimmie came, I flushed the Friedl pieces down the toilet because I didn't want them to say it was my fault for having such a dumb dog." Willow stared at Phil, her eyes searching his face.

"It's not your fault, Willow," said Phil. "I'm not going to blame you."

"Thanks." Willow sniffed and blew her nose. "You should get rid of that ring fast, you know. Take it out onto the Golden

Gate Bridge and drop it down into the outbound tide. I bet the thing that blasted the oak tree is the same fucker that came through the wowo. And it could come a third time. Things always happen in threes. Get rid of that ring today, Phil. It would be too awful if something happened to you."

"I hear you," said Phil, pocketing the ring.

All the way up on the train Phil looked at the ring and thought about it. He remembered a math story that his father had told him about the legendary A Square, an inhabitant of an imaginary two-dimensional world called Flatland. A Square's eye was a dot at one corner, his mouth an inlet on one side. Whenever A Square was right side up, his eye was on his northeast corner and his mouth was on his east. But one day a Spacelander called A Sphere lifted A Square out of Flatland, flipped him over, and set him back down. And from that day on, whenever A Square was right side up, his eye was on his northwest corner, and his mouth was on his west. He was his own mirror image. A Square.

Something had pulled Kurt into hyperspace, had knotted his ring, and had later flipped the ring over in the fourth dimension. Maybe Kurt had only lost his hand—and no more than that. Maybe the hand had been crushed by the slam of a hyperdoor to hyperspace; and maybe Kurt was alive and healing—someplace?

Looking at the ring, Phil felt more and more fascinated. It was such a power object. The only remaining link to his father. And so what if the hyperspace thing did come for him? Was dying really so bad? No more work, no more hassles, no more trying to find the right girl. Phil recognized the insanity of the thought patterns, but for now he was too drained to do anything more than just let them run. He put the ring back into his pocket and stared slackly out the train window, thinking about death.

As soon as Phil got back to San Francisco, he went over to Babs's. He needed to see Yoke. But Yoke was gone. Worse than that, she was out of the country.

"That's right," Babs told Phil. "She and Cobb and Onar went to Tonga. Onar goes down there all the time for Meta West Link. And since Yoke is so eager to go diving in the South Pacific—why not? They got inside Cobb and he rocketed them there. So fine, good-bye all, but get this, Randy Karl Tucker still thinks he's welcome here." A smile played across Babs's lips. "I can't get rid of him. He has this ridiculous idea that I'm not completely revolted. He claims he has some ideas for my art."

"Yoke left with Onar?" Phil could hardly take it in.

"Onar's *wooing* the girl," said Babs. "Somehow he heard Yoke was here visiting me, and he got Saint to introduce them. Saint and Onar work together at Meta West, you know. Well, not exactly together. Onar's a tech and Saint's a maintenance manager. Just don't call him a janitor."

"I thought Yoke liked me," said Phil, his voice breaking.

"I'm sorry, Phil," said Babs. "Yoke thinks you're nice, and that you're cute, but she didn't want to break you up from Kevvie. She hates the idea of being the other woman. Maybe if you were single you'd have had a chance."

CHAPTER TWO

YOKE

═══   ■   ═══

February 20

"Rather snug in here," said Onar. "But I like it. Remarkable way to travel."

Yoke and Onar were packed in back-to-back, with Cobb's moldie plastic flesh wrapped all around them. They were streaking through space near the top of a long parabolic trajectory that led from San Francisco to Tonga. Cobb had an ion-jet in his feet, and the algae in his moldie body provided a steady flow of oxygen.

The moldie flesh near Yoke's face was transparent, like a faceplate. Looking down at the great fat curve of Mother Earth's body, Yoke could see the familiar black of space above the bright curving line of the atmosphere. Phil had called it Gaia's skin. Yoke felt bad about not saying a proper good-bye to him. But the scene with Kevvie last night had been too gnarly. How had a straight babe like Phil ended up with a bloblolly? "Bloblolly" was an insulting expression for "female merge user" that Yoke's twin sister Joke liked to use; Joke herself had gotten the expression from a loonie viddy show called *Kid Skid*. Occasionally Joke had dared to call their mother Darla a bloblolly to her face, and a fierce Darla tongue-lashing would ensue. Joke was brave. Yoke felt a sharp pang of loneliness as she thought of her sister and her mother; this was the longest by far that they'd ever been apart. Seeing the black of outer space was making her homesick for the Moon. Getting back to Phil, the fact that he lived with a bloblolly probably meant there was more wrong with him than met the eye. He seemed a little passive, almost paralyzed. No doubt bailing had been the best thing for her do. Still, there was something sweet about Phil. He'd been so eager for her to like his food.

"Did I tell you that I'm friends with King of Tonga?" Onar asked just then. "The Tu'i Tonga himself. He's a delightful fellow." His voice sounded fruity and intimate in the little cavity of air that surrounded his and Yoke's heads. Spongy little palladium filters in their nostrils eliminated Cobb's characteristic moldie smell.

"You did tell me that," answered Yoke. "Twice." She wasn't quite sure about Onar. "Why does Tonga have a King anyway?"

"It's the only Polynesian nation never to have fallen under the rule of a foreign power," said Onar. "Right, Cobb?"

"That's right," said Cobb, talking to them via uvvy. "Do you want to browse a guidebook, Yoke?"

"No. I like real things better than virtual things. I'm done with school."

Pretty soon they were arcing back into the atmosphere, heading down toward the multitudinous islands of Tonga, tiny dots in the vast Pacific Ocean, visible through the gaps in the clouds. The clouds were arranged with a surprising regularity, like cabbages in a farmer's field. Onar guided Cobb to the biggest of the Tongan islands, Tongatapu, on one side of which was Tonga's main town Nuku'alofa.

They landed in a sandy shell-strewn parking lot next to the city dock. Cobb split open to disgorge his two passengers and the two carry-on bags they'd brought. And then he formed himself back into his original old man shape, grown a bit beefy from the sheet of imipolex he'd gotten from Babs. Judging from the stature of the golden-skinned Tongans whom Yoke could see nearby, Cobb's new size would fit right in. For the moment the locals were just staring at them, too startled to approach.

"Here we are," said Onar. "This is the Queen Salote Wharf."

"It's quiet here," said Cobb. "I like it."

Besides the Bay Area, this was the only place on Earth that Yoke had visited so far. She was surprised at how primitive things were. Like in a travel viddy. A rusty Tongan Navy ship floated in the harbor; in addition there were a ramshackle ferryboat, a few motorboats and one or two yachts. That was it for the capital city's port. The rutted and potholed road along the waterfront carried a light traffic of battered electric trucks and cars, old models from the 2030s. A low shack across the road offered drinks and food; next to it was a "Guest House" that looked barely big enough to house the owner's family. Farther down the waterfront was a weathered white building like a Victorian mansion, and inland from it was what looked to be the town center, a dingy cluster of patched-up buildings.

"Welcome to da neighborhood," said a huge man with a horizontal wrinkle in his forehead. "*Malo e lelei.*" He was wearing a torn white shirt and a brick-red polyester skirt. "My name is Tiko."

"Greetings, Tiko," said Onar. "We've met before, no? I was down here six months ago visiting with HRH."

Yoke knew by now that Onar used "HRH" to stand for "His Royal Highness," meaning the King. Ugh. For whatever reason, Yoke hated all things British — with the single exception of Lewis Carroll.

"That's right," said Tiko. "Onar Anders. My wife Waloo is working at the New Beach Guest House. You gonna stay wid us again?"

"Yes indeed," said Onar. "We'll walk there from here. As you see, we traveled light." He nudged the two little bags at his feet.

"All the way inside dis moldie," mused Tiko, gingerly patting Cobb's shoulder. He leaned close to Cobb, sniffed him, and burst out laughing. "Low tide at da lagoon."

"I'm actually a human in a moldie body," said Cobb, drawing back. "Cobb Anderson. Perhaps you've heard of me?"

"No sir," said Tiko. "What are you known for?"

"I built the first robots for the Moon, sixty years ago," said Cobb. "The boppers? And then the boppers chewed up my brain and extracted my software. I've had a series of robot bodies since then. This one is the best. Look." Cobb flipped his wrist and his right arm split up into five thin arms, with a tiny hand at the end of each of them. He picked a different seashell up with each of the five minihands and waved them about.

"Most kinky," said Tiko. "And you can fly. Yes, I saw you three come shootin' down like a diving bird. Did you come in one jump all da way from America?"

"Never mind where we came from," said Onar.

A big handsome woman had joined Tiko. She wore a ground-length skirt and a yellow T-shirt with a picture of some kind of sea creature that Yoke couldn't make out. "Did Onar pay you?" the woman asked Yoke. Odd question.

"No," said Yoke. "We're friends. My name's Yoke. I'm from the Moon."

"I'm Oofa," said the woman. "That's my boat over there." She pointed to an insectlike hydrofoil boat with a quantum-dot-powered water-jet motor. "When you're ready to go diving, I'm the one to take you."

"I'm very interested in diving," said Yoke.

"I've got the equipment and the helpers," said Oofa. "I work with Sea Cuke Divers, right over there behind the guest house." She pointed across the street.

"I'm planning to use him for my dive-suit," said Yoke, nodding toward Cobb.

"Moldies are the only way," said Oofa. "But I think you better use a local. We've got moldies working out of Sea Cuke. I dive in them all the time. I'll engage two moldies and show you some very special things."

"Just get one for yourself, Oofa. I trust Cobb. Maybe we could go diving tomorrow. Is that okay with you, Cobb?"

"What?" The old man moldie's attention tended to wander.

"Okay if you and I go diving with Oofa tomorrow?"

"We'd better check our schedule with HRH first," said Onar. "It's possible that he'll have plans for us tomorrow. Or perhaps Cobb will have something he'd rather do."

"What's *with* you, Onar?" said Cobb. "Of course I'm taking her diving. I didn't get a new body and fly all the way down to Earth just to start kissing large Polynesian butt."

"No problem, no problem," interrupted Oofa. "We'll go diving in the morning. I'll line up two moldies just in case Cobb change his mind. Tashtego and Daggoo."

Tiko walked down to the New Beach Guest House with them; he insisted on carrying their bags. It was early afternoon and plenty hot in the sun. Down here, February was high summer. Onar pointed along the heat-shimmering road to the white Victorian building in the distance.

"That's the Royal Palace, Yoke. It burned down in 2010, but the Tongans faithfully rebuilt it. I think we may be having dinner there with the King tonight."

"Da King don't live in it no more," corrected Tiko. "He started livin' down by da lagoon."

"I can imagine why," murmured Onar, but Yoke didn't push him to explain. The sun made talking too difficult.

The New Beach Guest House dated back to the twentieth century; it was a quaint cinder-block structure with a wide concrete porch and many open doors. There were swaying palms. The shade was a palpable relief. Yoke flopped down on an ancient metal porch chair and caught her breath.

"Mrs. Yoshida?" called Onar, but no answer came.

"She not gonna answer," said Tiko. "Everyone resting till suppertime. Just pick an empty room." He waved a good-bye and disappeared off behind the house.

"Two rooms," said Yoke.

Onar looked at her with mild disappointment. "We won't

be sleeping together? It would be less expensive to share. Not that I want to presume on our brief acquaintance."

"I don't think so," said Yoke. It had been pleasant enough when they'd smooched a little last night—even if she'd only been kissing Onar to somehow spite Phil for Kevvie. But flying all the way here squeezed into Cobb with Onar had been a definite turn-off. And now Onar kept acting so—British.

"Quite," said Onar, with a little bow. "I'll wage a courtship for your favors, milady Starr-Mydol." Double ugh.

Yoke and Onar found two empty rooms on the ocean side. The New Beach Guest House was an incredibly casual place, with no locks on any of the doors. Some of the other guests were in their rooms napping or reading. While Onar made some uvvy calls, Yoke took a shower and put on her silvery summer dress.

"HRH is sending 'round a limo for us in half an hour," announced Onar when Yoke reappeared on the porch. "He'll be entertaining us at his country estate. It's on a little spit in the Fanga Kakau Lagoon." Onar sat calmly on a rusty chair, looking pleasant and relaxed. He really was very handsome. The breeze plucked at his long reddish-blond hair and rattled the leaves of the palms. "I suppose I should bathe."

"Where's Cobb?" asked Yoke.

Onar pointed, and Yoke noticed a shiny puddle of plastic on the ground near the guest house. Cobb was relaxing moldie-style, lying there in a patch of sun and letting his algae soak up the light.

Onar went off for his shower and Yoke got a bottle of soda from the kitchen fridge. She sat on the porch and looked at the ocean and the sky, with the endless puffs of cloud marching out over the Pacific forever. She picked up a handheld fan, a woven palm thing with feathery fringed edges. She waved it gently, enjoying the gentle pulses of air.

A vortex is like a boulder, mused Yoke as she played with the fan. If you hit a boulder, it breaks into smaller rocks; if you jolt a vortex, it decomposes into a pack of smaller vortices. The vortices coming off the edges of the fan would be interesting to model.

Overhead the light breeze rattled the leaves of the palms. It was so wonderful to be loose in the open air of this great living world. After a lifetime in the pawky corridors of the Moon, Yoke couldn't get over the oceanic dimensions of Earth's atmosphere. The lucky mudders walked around at the bottom of a very sea of air.

Around four o'clock the "limo" showed up, a tiny electric car like all the others, chauffeured by an enormous Tongan man named Kennit. He had generous Polynesian features, and his curly hair stood up in an Afro. He wore a shirt with a necktie and a blue serge skirt. Over the skirt he had tied on a tattered palm mat, some kind of ceremonial thing. He was formal, though with a cheerful twinkle. He had a funny accent; he said "yis" instead of "yes." Onar already knew him. Apparently Onar had once won a little money from Kennit in a pinochle game— and didn't want to let Kennit forget it.

Hearing Onar and Yoke preparing to leave, Cobb perked up and poked his head up out of the puddle. "Am I invited?" he wanted to know.

"You definitely should follow us down to the Foreign Ministry to register," said Onar. "But as far as dinner goes—I mentioned you to HRH's secretary, Cobb, and of course HRH would like to meet with you, but I'm afraid our little party will be for humans only."

"I'm human," protested Cobb, his plastic old man's head bulging out of the shiny patch on the ground.

"Maybe you should try making friends with the Sea Cuke dive moldies," continued Onar. "Or if you want to be with humans, you could go to a bar. The Happy Club is quite colorful. There's a lot of fakaleitis there." Onar looked over at Yoke and explained, "That's the Tongan word for transvestites. Boys raised as girls. It's not uncommon. They're quite promiscuous. Takes some pressure off the women, I suppose."

"The Happy Club's a dangerous place, Mr. Anders," put in Kennit.

"But isn't it true that moldies are welcome there?"

"Maybe a little too welcome," said Kennit, making an abrupt slicing gesture down his front.

"What's that supposed to mean?" asked Cobb in alarm. He'd grown himself back up into human form.

"That happens here too?" said Onar.

"Yis," said Kennit.

"*What* happens?" asked Cobb.

"Oh, you know," said Onar. "Sporeheads slitting open moldies to get all of their camote at once."

"God," said Cobb, looking down at his body. "If they want those little fungus nuggets so much, they only have to ask me. I gave some camote to my great-grandson just the other day. Randy Karl Tucker. He's a little that way. It comes from being a cheeseball. I just hope he's staying out of trouble in San Francisco. That boy." Cobb sighed heavily. "I better not go to the Happy Club."

"Whatever you like, Cobb," said Onar. "But right now you should follow us to the ministry so we can get you a chirper. According to Tongan law, moldie visitors have to be tagged. It's like an electronic visa."

"I don't need no stinkin' visa," said Cobb. "You go on without me. I think I'll fly around the island. See you here in the morning, Yoke. We'll go for a dive."

Onar shrugged. "I thought you might feel that way. Just as well if you don't come at all."

The elevator in the Foreign Ministry building had a marble floor. It was possibly the only elevator in Tonga, and it was manned by a dignified man dressed like Kennit: white shirt, tie, and blue serge skirt.

"Hello," Yoke said.

"*Malo e lelei*," said the elevator operator, kindly but firmly. "You must learn to say hello in the Tongan way. *Malo e lelei*."

"*Malo e lelei*."

A trim Tongan woman in a gray dress greeted them near the elevators. She was wearing an uvvy.

"Hello, Mr. Anders, I'm glad to see you. We are on the point of closing down for the day. Quitting-time is the one appointment that Tongans observe punctually! But I believe Mr. Olou is still here. And first we have our little business with your friend's visa."

"Excellent, Eleani," said Onar. "Let me introduce my friend Yoke from the Moon. Yoke, this is Eleani Matu. She's a Vice-Minister."

"Did Onar get you a contract from Meta West Link?" Eleani asked.

"No, I'm just a tourist along for the ride."

"Yes, yes," laughed Eleani. "Of course you are. Step into my office and I'll give you the visa." Eleani led them into a cool, dark room with elegant modern furniture. "Sue Miller," she said, nodding to Yoke. "It's all set."

"Huh?"

"It's your identity of record," said Onar. "Eleani's in charge of Tonga's interface to international ID protocols. Tongan counterintelligence, that is. She's setting up some one-month ID viruses for you and Cobb."

"Why?"

Onar looked cagey. "You'll find out later on tonight. When we go to meet the King. Suffice it to say that HRH wants you to help him with a mission that could lead to you getting hold of something extremely valuable, and he doesn't want any off-islanders hounding you for it. It'll be for your own good if nobody can recognize you."

Eleani looked hard at Yoke, then gazed blankly at the wall for a moment, off in the cyberspace of uvvy. "Yes," she said presently. "It's all here. Sue Miller died in a fire and shipwreck off Tongatapu last year and our navy recovered her body. She had a sailor moldie named Squanto who was also lost in the fire. We'll morph you into Sue and Cobb into Squanto, Yoke. I'm releasing the ID viruses now. They'll live till next month, and they're smart enough to actively search and replace any images of you two. That way if any person or moldie happens to video you, Yoke, the transmitted image is going to show Sue. This means that for the next month nobody's going to be able to take a picture of you. It'll look like this." Eleani uvvied Yoke an image of a skinny woman with short, dark hair.

"But isn't Sue Miller on record as being dead?" asked Yoke.

"No, no," said Onar. "In this day and age, an identity is a precious thing. When the Tongans find a body, they always incinerate it and base an ID virus on that person."

"This is creepy," protested Yoke. "You're not planning to murder me or something, are you?"

"Of course not," said Eleani. "Silly girl. This is for your protection, I'm sure! All right then, Yoke, I'm going to uvvy you the Sue Miller and Squanto identity codes now, in case someone directly asks you for ID. Very good. You have a registered Tongan visa in the name of Sue Miller for thirty days. Now let's see about Mr. Olou."

"If I have this fake ID," said Yoke, "does this mean I have to call myself Sue while I'm here? And have to call Cobb — Squanto?"

"Too much trouble," said Eleani. "On the islands nobody pays so much attention to details. My understanding is that we only need the fake ID for the rest of the world. In case someone takes your picture after you get hold of whatever it is you're supposed to get. With the ID virus nobody need ever know it was you. You'll be able to return home and live peacefully."

At the end of a marble hall they found a darkened office with a leathery Tongan man sitting in an armchair wearing an uvvy. All the blinds were drawn. The Tongan's eyes were closed, but he opened them when the three entered.

"Onar?" he said. "Very good, very timely. Put on your uvvy, if you would, and join me."

"Would this be of interest for my friend Yoke as well?" said Onar.

"She is most welcome," said Mr. Olou. "*Malo e lelei*, Yoke. Please take a seat, both of you."

They settled into a matching pair of chrome and leather Barcelona chairs. Eleani glanced at her watch and excused herself.

Yoke put on her uvvy and followed along as Onar joined Olou in cyberspace. The three of them seemed to be standing in a cartoon jungle, with bright colored vines stretching from the ground upward to—well, upward to nothing. No trees in sight, just lots of colored vines rising up forever above the simmie body icons of Yoke, Onar, and Olou. Glancing down at herself, Yoke saw that she was wearing her usual simmie, the Alice from *Alice in Wonderland*. The ground beneath her feet was soft black dirt with little beetles and sow bugs in it.

"The vines display the Cappy Jane sky-ray signal flow," said Olou. He looked like a grass-skirted, spear-waving Tongan warrior. "I've been improving the visualization, Onar. As you know, one hundred percent of our Cappy Jane signal flux is licensed to Meta West Link. The color spectrum codes from red through blue represent the various fee levels." The vines were glowing like rainbow neon tubes.

"Can you show me one of the bandwidth pirates?" asked Onar, whose body icon was that of a natty man in tails and top hat.

"Wait," said Olou, crouching with his spear at the ready. All at once he flung the spear at a purplish-white vine in the middle distance. "That's one of them," he said. "Bull's-eye. Now I've captured that signal into nonvolatile storage."

"I may be able to display it as a richer image," said Onar. "I have some rather wonderful virtual tools. They're in-house products of Meta West." He began pushing his way through the thickets of colored tendrils, closely followed by Olou. Yoke tagged along, wondering at the tingly feel of the vines.

Working quickly, Onar and Olou hauled down dozens of meters of the purplish-white pirate vine from where it disappeared up above. This preliminary task accomplished, Onar caught Yoke's eye and smiled confidently. He drew himself up and bowed as if beginning a performance. To begin with, Onar made some occult passes with his hands, and a beautifully inlaid, coffin-sized box appeared between him and Olou. It looked like a prop used in a "Disappearing Lady" stage-magic illusion. Then with an elegant snap of his fingers, Onar produced a scimitar from the air and proceeded to wield it like a homicidal maniac, slicing the vine up into a mound of two-meter segments. He did this with great theatrical flourishes and much mad rolling of his eyes. Yoke began to giggle and Onar glowed with pleasure. He stuffed the inlaid box with what seemed like many more segments than should fit—and perched himself on the lid, quizzically cocking his head to listen.

"Shroop!" sang the box. "Shroop, shroop, shroop!" The high, metallic sound reminded Yoke of an artisan's band saw cutting up slabs of moon-rock.

Onar hopped behind the box and started to open the lid, which faced roughly toward Olou.

"Careful there," said Olou, seeing something. He backed off so rapidly that he got tangled in the vines. For just that critical moment he was pinioned in front of the box. "Onar, don't!" he screamed.

It was too late. The lid slammed all the way open, and out rushed something quick and bright and overwhelming, something that leapt at Olou and crumpled him. This happened in an instant and then the thing was heading for Yoke, spreading itself out to an immense size. Yoke was already moving her arm to pull her uvvy off her neck, but the fast shiny thing got to her too quickly. It looked like a jellyfish, but with a smiling humanoid face that was somehow etched into its transparent flesh. It engulfed Yoke, and her overloaded uvvy sent out a stunning burst of pain. As if from very far away Yoke felt the slow-motion jolting of her body falling from the Barcelona chair.

When Yoke woke it was dark. Her head was throbbing. She was lying on the hard marble floor. The Foreign Ministry building around her was completely silent.

She peeled her uvvy off her neck; the skin underneath was raw and tender. She couldn't see if Onar and Olou were still in the room. Unsure where the light switch was, she went over to the window and opened the shade. The faithful Moon was a few handbreadths above the horizon, bright and full and tropical behind palm frond silhouettes. People were calling to each other, dogs were barking, and somewhere nearby an animal was grunting. Nuku'alofa came alive at night.

Looking back into Mr. Olou's office, Yoke could see Olou and Onar both lying on the floor. Dead? She paused, afraid. Her mind struggled to process the situation.

That jellyfish thing; the face on it had looked like—Onar? And it had said something just as it swallowed her, something important—but somehow impossible to bring to mind. She couldn't stop obsessively trying to remember it. As she circled around the memory, she found herself thinking about the day three months ago when some alien personality waves had taken over the bodies of a bunch of moldies at Willy Taze's house. One of the aliens had been a being called Shimmer, who came from a place where beings led zillions of simultaneous lives all at once in parallel time. Did the jellyfish have something to do with Shimmer? Yoke tried again to remember what the voice had said—but she couldn't bring it to mind. She grimaced, trying to shake off the memory.

"Hey Onar!" she called. "Mr. Olou? Wake up, veks! Please don't be dead . . ."

Onar stirred and sat up. Like Yoke, his first act was to take off his uvvy. But somehow he didn't look as if his head hurt. "God help me," he muttered, then looked up at Yoke against the moonlit window. "Are you all right?"

"Yes, but what about Mr. Olou?"

"Awful," said Onar, crawling over to the fallen Tongan. He leaned over Olou, thumping his chest and briefly attempting mouth-to-mouth resuscitation. "He's gone," said Onar presently. "It's my fault. I was showing off for you and I blundered. I'm a fool. A capering popinjay."

Mr. Olou's body lay utterly motionless, with a deep stillness that Yoke could somehow sense as that of a corpse. A sleeping person is only conditionally immobile; if you poke them, they'll arise. But Mr. Olou—Yoke could tell that no matter how much anyone bugged him, he'd never get up again. The stark moonlight made the dead man's mouth a ragged hole.

"Let's get out of here, Onar."

"I agree." He looked down at the body. "Forgive me, old friend."

The elevator was turned off for the day, so they took the marble stairs down. There were no lights. Onar caught Yoke's elbow and made her pause on the first landing.

"Before we go any further, Yoke, I have to ask you something." His breath was warm and pleasant in the darkness.

"Okay," said Yoke. She had a feeling they were going to kiss. It was hardly appropriate, but for some reason that's what she wanted. She'd felt a redoubled attraction to Onar ever since the jellyfish blast. A way to spit in the face of Death?

"Can I trust you to keep a secret?" asked Onar softly.

"Trust 'Sue Miller'? What is that about, anyway?" She put her hands on Onar's waist, trying not to think of Mr. Olou.

"The business I'm down here for—my business with the King—it's rather hush-hush. Can you promise me that you won't talk to anyone about what you see and hear? If you can help me out on this, there might be some rather substantial rewards for you. But you mustn't tell."

"Oh yeah?" said Yoke. Now that she was primed to kiss Onar, she was having trouble focusing on what he was saying.

"Not Cobb, not your parents, not Tre and Terri, no one," whispered Onar as he put his arms around her. "Not yet. Eventually, everyone will know. And they'll be glad. I promise you. It's a wonderful surprise."

"All right," said Yoke, and pressed her lips to his. It was romantic here in the marble Tongan dark. Onar smelled good and his body felt strong and lithe. It was pleasant to embrace him. They kissed for a minute, and then Yoke broke it off, feeling guilty about dancing on Mr. Olou's grave.

Outside they found Kennit standing in the street, talking with a couple of other Tongans. He walked over to Onar and Yoke.

"Good evening. You are ready?"

"There's been an accident, Kennit," said Onar. "Mr. Olou is dead. He suffered an attack while we were using the uvvy."

"So it comes to that," said Kennit, his face clouding over. "You left him inside?" He walked over to rattle the ministry door, which had locked itself behind Onar. Kennit called something in Tongan and the men he'd been talking to came over, opened the door and went inside.

"Poor Olou," sighed Kennit. "You can make a police report tomorrow, Mr. Anders. But now we must go to see the King."

"Why isn't Kennit more surprised?" hissed Yoke to Onar as they were settled into the back of the little car. "And what was that pale vine? What exactly is your job, anyway?"

"At Meta West they call me the anteater," said Onar with a little smile. "Meta West Link sells transmission time between the Earth and outer space. Mainly the Moon, but Mars and the asteroids too. My job is to keep cryps, phreaks, and ants from siphoning off free bandwidth." He opened his mouth and waggled his long, pointed tongue. "The ant's nightmare; the virgin's friend."

"Onar don't."

Kennit turned onto the main street of Nuku'alofa, a dirt road lined by high wooden sidewalks like in an ancient viddy of the Wild West. There was a traffic-jam of cars, pedestrians, moldies, and bicycles; it seemed that everyone on the island was out on the five-block main drag. Though it was early in the evening, a few of the Tongan men seemed extremely drunk. Recognizing the car as the King's limo, one of them leaned over to peer inside. The car was so small and the man so big that he had to bend practically double. One of his friends shoved him and he lost his balance and fell down. Great whoops of laughter.

"Tongans used only to go crazy on Saturday nights," said Kennit gloomily. "But now we do it on Friday as well. Evil times."

"Kennit doesn't drink," said Onar. "He's a Mormon. Although he does play cards. I've seen him."

"Very many Mormons in Tonga," said Kennit.

"I don't think I've ever heard of them," said Yoke. "Is that a religion?"

"Oh yes," said Onar. "And they own the world's largest asimov computer. A machine under a mountain in Salt Lake City."

"I've heard of that big slave computer," said Yoke. "Cobb's simulation lived inside it for a while."

"You're thinking of the Heritagists' asimov computer," said Onar. "Which is also under a mountain in Salt Lake City. I have a theory that the two are one and the same."

"I went to college in Salt Lake City," said Kennit, inching the car forward. "The South Pacific program at Brigham Young University."

"Do you dislike moldies, Kennit?" asked Onar.

"Yis."

"Will you stop changing the subject, Onar?" put in Yoke. "Finish telling me what you're doing here and what happened to Mr. Olou." Outside the window now was a Tongan food store, an open-air stand with shelves full of canned meat and muddy yams.

"Very well, Yoke. Let's do Telecommunications 101. For short distances, an uvvy signal hopscotches from one uvvy to the next. Completely decentralized. For longer distances, the signal zooms up a thousand miles to a cheap little saucer-sat and gets bounced back down. Ever since the 2030s the saucer-sats have been imipolex jobbies that fly up to space by themselves. There's millions of them by now. The size of dinner-plates, as smart as cockroaches, and easy to order around. You saw some of them on our flight here."

"Right," said Yoke. "Cobb ate one of them."

"That was a very moldie thing for Cobb to do," said Onar. "Moldies are such scavengers."

"So anyway," said Yoke. "Now you're going to tell me that since Meta West Link handles Earth-Moon signal transmissions, that means they have some really big saucer-sats, right?"

"Right-o," said Onar. "We call them sky-rays. Like manta ray or stingray? Big soft flappy things. They weigh a ton instead of a kilogram. And, unlike the little saucer-sats, they need a fungus-algae nervous system. Once you get that much mold-infested imipolex together, it's bound to wake up. And since we already know how to talk to moldies, it makes sense for the sky-rays to be made up of moldies. A sky-ray is twenty or thirty moldies stuck together to make one of those group creatures we call a 'grex.' You don't really own a sky-ray, it's a team that you hire. The moldies get paid in imipolex and they take turns working. Which is why you see so many of them hanging around Tonga. They come down here to breed, for one thing."

"And why Tonga?"

"The sky-rays stay in geosynchronous orbit; they circle the equator at some twenty-two thousand miles up. That's the altitude where the natural orbital speed exactly matches the rotational speed of the Earth. Geosynchronous means they're always above the same spot. Now, thanks to some clever international politicking by HRH's grandfather back before the millennium, the Kingdom of Tonga owns the best geosynchronous satellite slot for the South Pacific." Onar scrunched down and pointed up through the car window. "She's always right about there. Cappy Jane. Straight up, and a little to the north. She looks like a giant patchwork stingray. A harlequin. All of the Earth-Moon transmissions for this part of the world come through Cappy Jane."

"Mr. Olou mentioned her," remembered Yoke. "He said someone's been running pirate signals through her."

"Exactly," said Onar. "Cappy Jane's been losing some twenty percent of her bandwidth. The pirate signals go back and forth between Cappy Jane and a spot right near Tonga itself. So Olou called for the anteater!" Onar opened his mouth as if to display his tongue again, but stopped himself, thinking better of it.

Kennit was through the worst of the traffic now, driving rapidly past a series of small houses with showy tropical plants in their yards. "That's the Tongan cultural center on the left," said Onar, going off topic. "I must take you there, Yoke; they have a wonderful show. Everyone gets a chance to drink some kava before it starts. Gives a very nice buzz."

"So that pale vine was a copy of one of the pirate signals?" asked Yoke doggedly. Keeping his hand down in his lap, Onar pointed at Kennit and didn't answer.

Yoke's head was pounding, and Kennit was driving much too fast for comfort. Up in the cone of the headlights she saw a low black animal with floppy ears and a long snout, standing alertly by the road as if waiting for the car to pass. "What's that!"

"A pig," said Onar.

"They're not pink?"

"You've never seen a real pig before, have you? You're delightful, Yoke."

The car raced onward. It had adaptive DIM tires, and Kennit was going down the little roads at the electric car's flat-out maximum speed, perhaps sixty miles per hour. "Is it safe to go so fast?" asked Yoke plaintively. Nobody answered, so she tried another question. "How much further is it, Kennit?"

"We're almost there. This is the King's plantation."

The road was lined with tall coconut palms, and the headlights showed orderly fields of plants to either side. Up ahead were some colorful lights. "I understand that HRH moved out here because the people in town don't like to see him living with moldies," Onar said to Kennit. "Is it true that he's actually married one?"

"That's not my affair," said Kennit shortly, and then they were pulling up in front of a remarkable building resembling a mound of giant soap bubbles. Yoke could make out some ten or twelve huge transparent domes fused together, with colorful beings moving about inside. There was a shiny green figure in the driveway, a moldie in the form of a voluptuous woman. She made a gesture of welcome.

"Didn't you tell Cobb this evening would be humans only?" Yoke asked Onar.

"I lied," said Onar, "so he wouldn't come. Now remember what you promised me."

And then they were out in the fetid tropical night. Yoke recognized the trees around the gossamer palace to be banyans, though she'd never imagined they'd be so huge. The trunks grew up and down, splitting here and merging there, the giant trees' flesh like wax or honey. The green moldie stepped forward, splitting her thick green lips in a smile.

"Yo! I'm Vaana. The queen moldie you been talking to on the uvvy, Onar. And this must be Yoke from the Moon. Welcome to Tonga, sweet thing." Yoke recognized Vaana's distinctive style of speech as a black accent. Each moldie fashioned his or her own particular human speaking style soon after birth, drawing on the speech of family, friends, and nearby humans, not to mention the endless databases of the Web.

As the moldie turned to lead them inside the crystal palace, something dark and ragged came flapping down from one of the banyans. Yoke had a mental flashback of the attack of the cyberspace jellyfish; she shrieked and dove to the ground.

"Lordy-lord," laughed Vaana. "Yoke's scared of flying foxes. Don't get your undies in a twist, girl. Those things won't bite unless you a piece of fruit."

"A large bat," explained Onar, helping Yoke up. "One of the few endemic Tongan mammals. It's easy for them to travel from island to island. There's more of them here than on, say, Fiji, because the Tongans don't eat them. The flying fox is *tapu*."

"This is turning into a majorly long day, Onar," said Yoke shakily. She was wondering what the hell she was doing here, about to get mixed up in some kilpy plot. "I think I want to go back to the guest house and get in bed." She looked around for Kennit and the car, but they were nowhere to be seen.

"It won't take long, Yoke," urged Onar. "I know that HRH is eager to meet you. You'll feel better after a good meal. And then we can take a little boat across the lagoon to get back to the guest house. Just the two of us." He slipped his arm around her waist and squeezed her.

"Come on, Yoke," said Vaana. "Don't be a barbie."

Here in the jungle night the rank green moldie seemed like a figure of myth or legend, a Green Woman, an archaic personification of the Plant. Though Vaana continued to smile, Yoke knew full well how meaningless were the facial expressions of moldies. She wished she'd brought along the loyal Cobb. At least her uvvy still worked. Perhaps she'd uvvy Cobb to fly over here and rescue her soon, whether or not Onar liked it. But, yes, come to think of it, she was kind of curious about Onar's big secret. And deep in her girlish heart, Yoke felt a sharp hunger for that romantic boat-ride across the lagoon — just like in a viddy or a book, with air and water everywhere, and a handsome man at her side. It sounded so exciting. So, okay, she followed along as Vaana ushered them into the King's country palace.

The first of the palace's domed rooms was a great hall, filled with cool, oxygen-enriched air. A moldie waited within, this one red and crablike, a squat creature with pincer arms. A guardian.

"Lock the palace on up, Gregor," said Vaana. "Our guests be here." The crab raised his claws and scuttled past them toward the door, not bothering to answer out loud.

The next room was a conservatory, with blooming orchids fastened all over the curving walls. The room's air was pervaded by an intense, musty tang. A moldie like a giant yellow banana slug was sliming from plant to plant, carefully tending them. It was he, not the orchids, whose odor filled the room. Like the crab, he kept his silence.

The third room was a dimly lit sitting room, and in there they found the King, resting on a silk couch with a cup of hot tea. The air in this room was warm and rapidly circulating; the hidden fans swirled away any scent of the moldies.

The King was a big man with beautiful skin. His hair was

long and floppy. He was wearing a flowered silk shirt and white linen pants.

"Hello, Onar," said the King. "I got the news about Mr. Olou. Fill me in on how that went down."

Yoke was surprised to hear him sounding like a regular person. Somehow she'd expected a King to sound different, all "ye" and "thee" and "tally ho."

"Greetings, Your Majesty," said Onar. "Allow me to present Ms. Yoke Starr-Mydol from the Moon. Known in the records and all outgoing video as 'Sue Miller,' thanks to Eleani's work."

"Welcome to Tonga, Yoke," said the King. "And listen, Onar, I've told you before, just call me Bou-Bou. You too, Yoke. Bou-Bou!" The King humorously stuck out his lips as he pronounced his nickname. He leaned back on his couch and waited, favoring Yoke with a charming smile.

"Um, okay Bou-Bou," said Yoke, taking a seat on the other end of the couch. Onar sat in the middle. Yoke lolled back and looked up through the room's transparent ceiling at the banyans and the night sky. She thought she could see a flying fox hanging from a branch in the nearest tree.

"It's exciting to be here," said Yoke presently. "These domes remind me of the Moon. My family has a friend who built a big house out in a crater. An isopod, is what we called it."

The King nodded. "I know of the place. The Willy Taze dwelling. I studied lunar architecture at Stanford, among other things. How did Onar persuade you to come here, Yoke? Did he put you on the Meta West payroll?"

"You're the third person who's asked me that," said Yoke. "Am I missing out on something? I'm interested in diving the South Pacific, and since Onar had this anteater gig, he talked me into coming down here with him. I have a moldie friend named Cobb who rocketed us here from California, so it's not costing much of anything."

"Ah yes, Cobb the born-yet-again loonie moldie," said the King. "Thanks for not bringing him along tonight, Onar."

"But why?" protested Yoke. "Cobb's interesting. He built the first boppers, after all. And he's the first human to have his software installed into moldie flesh."

The King gave Onar a frank look. "You've talked to her?"

"Yes," said Onar. "She's promised to keep mum."

"Cobb's a wild-card, Yoke," said the King. "He has so many contacts. We're afraid about whom he might tell our secrets. Frankly, we'd prefer to keep him out of the picture."

"Oh come on," said Yoke. "Cobb's like my bodyguard. And he's a family friend. I don't care what I promised Onar just now. I wasn't thinking straight. If you tell something to me, I can't keep it from Cobb. He needs to know what's going on so that he can protect me."

The King looked questioningly at Onar and Onar said, "We don't really have a choice, do we?"

"I suppose not," said the King. "But please, Yoke, don't you or Cobb tell this to any of your loonie friends. The secret is that we've contacted an alien intelligence. A being named Shimmer. She's living deep below the ocean here, in what's known as the Tonga Trench. She knows you. She had an encounter with you and your parents just a little over three months ago, at the Willy Taze isopod you mentioned. November sixth, 2053. Your parents tried to kill her."

Shimmer! Yoke's stomach flip-flopped. She'd had a feeling this was coming. "She wants to get even?"

"Why would Shimmer be into that kind of kilp, honey?" said Vaana soothingly. She was standing behind the King's couch. "Shimmer's way too big for that. I bet she just wants to see you, Yoke. She probably digs your mind. When Shimmer was here talking to Bou-Bou she acted nice as pie."

Yoke felt frightened and angry. So Onar had been lying to her all along. She gave him a rough shove. "You deliberately lured me here! You don't like me for myself one bit. You fetched me like some bauble for your precious King. And I'm so stupid, I came for free."

"That's not the whole truth, Yoke," protested Onar. "I'm very attracted to you."

"And you killed Mr. Olou on purpose, didn't you!" Yoke's words popped out fast, and she saw something on their faces. She was getting in deeper every second.

"I think everyone could use some dinner," put in Vaana. "The table's set."

The King smiled and got nimbly to his feet, making a polite gesture for Yoke to follow him into the dining room, which was the next dome farther along. Following behind the big man, Yoke could make out his underwear through the thin fabric of his trousers. Purplish bikini briefs worn very low down on the crack.

"It's nice to finally meet you in person," said Onar to Vaana, as if trying to steer the conversation back to a normal mode. "How do you come to know HRH?"

"Well, my family nest was down in the flats of Oakland," said the womanly green moldie. "I got it together and landed a phat job in the wetware engineering labs at Stanford U. I met Bou-Bou when he was taking Wet E 202. I helped him invent a new kind of coconut for his class project. Less grease and mo' protein. Ought to been a miracle for the Tongan diet."

"Except the Tongans won't eat my new coconuts or even feed them to their pigs," said the King over his shoulder. "The flesh is a ghastly greenish hue. Wet E was never my thing. Here we are then, the royal dining room. Our main course will be Tongan lobster in a coconut cream sauce over steamed taro root. Nontweaked coconut, of course. I think we have some local melon as well. A glass of champagne, Yoke?"

"All right. Why not."

The three humans sat down at the dining table and Vaana discreetly withdrew. A kind-faced Tongan woman named Kika served them their food. Yoke and Onar were very hungry, and the King ate with a ready appetite as well. The first course of the meal was a green melon with tiny orange balls on it which were, the King informed them, the fruiting body of a special kind of Tongan seaweed. The second course was a curried pork broth.

"What was it like, Yoke?" Onar asked presently. "When all the moldies at Taze's isopod turned into aliens that day?"

"It was wavy," said Yoke. With the food and the champagne she was feeling a little more relaxed. "They were so interesting, so wise. Shimmer especially. Shimmer comes from a place where they have two-dimensional time. The extra time dimension is like possibility, of worlds that could be. That's why my parents couldn't shoot Shimmer. Even though the time in our part of the cosmos is only one-dimensional, Shimmer can see the ghosts of all the future maybes and she can actualize the right one. She's always where the bullet isn't." Kika removed the soup plates and began bringing in the lobster. Yoke was, on the whole, glad to be eating this meal. "But now you two answer some questions. Shimmer's the one who's siphoning off Cappy Jane's bandwidth, right?"

"Very clever, Yoke," said Onar. "Yes, the King gave Shimmer permission to gather and process data through Cappy Jane, so there's been a lot of traffic between those two. Cappy Jane's been winnowing out certain kinds of space signals that Shimmer's interested in. Not that Cappy Jane realizes who she's working for. Shimmer and the King have her convinced that Shimmer's a human scientist doing a study of high-energy cosmic rays."

"The Tongan Extragalactic Signal Survey," said the King, smiling.

"Moldies are even more leery of aliens than the humans," said Onar. "With good reason. Their computational architecture is very susceptible to invasion. If Cappy Jane knew this stuff was for Shimmer, she probably wouldn't help us no matter how much we pay her."

"Vaana knows about Shimmer," said Yoke. "And she's not objecting."

"Yes," said the King. "But Vaana expects to share in the benefits of helping Shimmer. Now that *you* know, Yoke, that makes five humans and four moldies who are in on the secret. You, Onar, me, Oofa, Kennit, Vaana, Tashtego, Daggoo, and

Turklee. Nine in all. And as soon as we get something from Shimmer, I'll have to tell a few more of my people. Secrets don't last on Tonga for very long. That's why we have to move forward so rapidly."

"Mr. Olou didn't know," said Yoke. "And instead of telling him the truth, Onar killed him."

"Mr. Olou was unreliable," said the King. "A loose cannon. He did know that some source in the Tonga Trench has been using up a large amount of the Cappy Jane bandwidth. He was very persistent in repeatedly bringing this problem to Meta West's attention. Too much so, and against my express wishes. Fortunately, I had a prior relationship with Onar, and I made sure that he was the anteater whom Meta West sent down here to deal with Mr. Olou's problem. I thought it would be a good idea to have Onar intimidate Mr. Olou within the framework of Olou's highly idiosyncratic visualization system."

"So what was in that pale vine signal?" asked Yoke.

"That was a red herring," laughed Onar. "I didn't really unpack the vine signal at all. Wouldn't know how to. What I did in cyberspace with you and Olou was just theater. The jellyfish thing, that was something I brought along stored in that inlaid coffin like a jack-in-the-box. I copied it off some phreaks who were using it to protect their clubhouse. I'd never tested it before, you understand, and I had no idea it would be lethal. The idea was just to frighten Olou and to impress you, Yoke. I was reckless and negligent, yes. But please don't think I'm a mind-assassin."

"So it really was you who killed Olou?"

"Don't blame me," said Onar. "It was the phreaks who made that stinging jellyfish." He gave a sudden giggle. "It talked Olou's ear off. More than his ear." He gave himself a playful slap on the cheek. "Sober up, Onar. It's not my fault at all. How was I to know that Olou had a weak heart? And he shouldn't have kept complaining about those extra signals."

"But what's in the signals?" demanded Yoke. "Can't anyone tell me?"

"Shimmer's been using Cappy Jane to download the personality waves of more aliens from her home world," said the King. "Isn't it obvious? Shimmer's specified a certain class of gamma ray burst events for Cappy Jane to record, preprocess, and transmit. And these signals are of course alien personality waves. Apparently Shimmer's been able to decrypt five or six of her fellows by now. That's what she wants to discuss with you, Yoke. Champagne?"

"Indubitably," said Onar, holding out his and Yoke's glasses. "Let's drink to the noble Shimmer! Oofa can take Yoke down into the trench to meet her tomorrow."

"We're supposed to be sitting here planning to help aliens invade the Earth?" said Yoke. "You two are xoxxed! Where's your sense of self-preservation?"

"It's what's happening, baby," said Onar. "There's no stopping Shimmer. If you want to blame someone, blame Gurdle-7 or Willy Taze. They're the ones who decrypted Shimmer's signal in the first place. But now she's here, and we're going to have to live with her, at least for a while. It's a new stage in history. Hop aboard or get plowed under."

"Shimmer's got good things for us," said the King. "She's promised to give us realware."

"What's that?" asked Yoke.

"It's some kind of magic or super science that Shimmer has," said Onar. "Direct matter control. We don't know much more than that. I think maybe when you dive down to see Shimmer tomorrow she's going to give it to you. She trusts you or something. You're up for this, right?"

Yoke sat quiet for a minute, thinking. She'd loved talking with the aliens that time on the Moon; she'd been sad and angry when her parents attacked them. Onar was probably right about there being no way to stop Shimmer now. And Yoke knew that even if she wanted to try and stop Shimmer, the only thing to do was to go farther in. "Okay," said Yoke slowly. "But I'm only diving if I'm safe inside of Cobb. And before we dive, I'm going to tell him every detail about what we're doing."

She held up her hand to stave off Onar and the King's protests. "I think I know why you don't want Cobb to know. He's a grandstander, a loudmouth. You're afraid he'll whip up a movement against the aliens. You're afraid everyone will react like Darla—like Darla would if she were still around." Her voice faltered as she thought of her dead mother. She caught her breath and pressed on. "But remember that Cobb Anderson is an explorer. A radical. The total opposite of those right-wing, moldie-hating Heritagists. If Cobb had a closed mind he wouldn't have built the boppers in the first place. Cobb loves change. And who knows, maybe his death experiences taught him something about the kind of world where Shimmer comes from."

"I could have you both silenced," mused the King. "Thanks to the ID viruses, it's like you're not even here."

"You wouldn't dare," said Yoke, deepening her voice and sounding more confident than she felt. "Shimmer would never forgive you. Don't you think she's already thought through the consequences of your talking to me? It's like we're dustboarding down an extreme slope, Bou-Bou. If you waver now, you'll fall. The only way to do this is straight and fast."

"Well said, Yoke!" Onar held up his glass. "A toast to Lady Yoke Starr-Mydol!" And the King toasted along.

"I expected as much from you, Yoke," said the King presently. "You have spirit. Yes, you're the one to bring back the realware. And that's the real reason I had Eleani put out the ID virus on you. Because if and when the news of the realware gets out, everyone's going to want to find the person who has it."

Yoke and Onar rode back across the lagoon in a wooden boat propelled by the yellow slug moldie, whose name turned out to be Topo. Topo fastened himself to the underside of the boat and beat the water like a long-tailed eel.

It was a clear, balmy night, with a caressing breeze of sweet fresh air flowing in from the sea. The full moon shone high overhead. Onar pointed out the pinprick of light that was Cappy Jane. Topo's underwater undulations left a glowing trail, and when Yoke let her hand dip into the smooth black water, it made a phosphorescent wake of tiny green sparkles.

"It's wonderful to share this with you, Yoke," said Onar, pulling his arm tight around her. "I love to see you smile."

"Liar," said Yoke, leaning against him. "I'm just a pawn in your scheme."

"Compared to Shimmer, we're plankton," said Onar, looking out over the lagoon. "The best we can do is glimmer in her wave. I won't lie to you again, Yoke. I care much more for you than I expected. You're so fresh and kind and good."

Onar kissed her then, and the boat ride turned fully as romantic as Yoke had hoped: the tropical lagoon, the champagne in her veins, and her arms around this handsome, raffish, not-quite-trustworthy man. When they got back to the guest house, Yoke made a snap decision that it would be a good idea to sleep with Onar after all.

But Onar turned out to be a poor lover, certainly the worst of Yoke's few partners thus far. Onar stinted on the foreplay, made a long messy fuss of his prophylactic preparations, and was up for at most sixty seconds of actual coitus. As a final turn-off, Onar said something British when he came, something like "Cor blimey," or "Top drawer," or "Bit of all right"—Yoke's outraged brain disdained to retain the phrase.

In the night, Yoke had a nightmare about her dead mother Darla, a dream of Darla desperately firing her needler gun at an endless attack wave of softly smiling jellyfish. She woke up in a sweat, feeling cramped in Onar's bed. She washed her face in the grungy guest house bathroom, then went into her own room to fall back asleep.

February 21

The next morning, Saturday, Yoke woke to the sound of a rooster crowing right outside her window. The first thing she thought about was Darla. And Phil's father. They'd been eaten by something from a higher dimension. And all of a sudden Yoke could remember what the cyberspace jellyfish thing had said when it came at her yesterday. "You love Onar," it had been saying. "Do what Onar says." The jellyfish had been quite thoroughly under Onar's control. Mr. Olou's death had been no accident. Onar was a killer. And now she was supposed to let Onar take her to meet Shimmer? What about Shimmer and the four-dimensional things that had eaten Darla and Phil's father? Was there a connection?

Oh, this was creepy. Yoke pushed on to other thoughts. The fat, polite King in his soap-bubble castle. The romantic ride across lagoon. The unpleasant, selfish groping in Onar's bed. Too bad she hadn't come here with Phil Gottner instead. That Kevvie didn't deserve to keep a boy like Phil. He was the cutest thing she had met on Earth so far. Phil would be perfect, if only he could learn to take hold of life and do something.

Before even getting out of bed, Yoke put on her uvvy, wincing a bit. Her neck was still tender from the jellyfish blast at the Foreign Ministry. She called for Cobb. His signal was faint and weird, so Yoke sent him an extra hard mind jolt. There was a thud right outside her window and then Cobb's face appeared out there.

"What? I was lying on the roof."

"Shhh! Come in here."

Cobb slithered through Yoke's window to perch on the foot of her sagging bed. He was nothing like so pink and shiny as usual. And he reeked of decay.

"I'm really spun," said Cobb, sounding satisfied. "Two of the moldies at the Bottom Club turned me on to this stuff called 'betty.' I rubbed it onto myself and whoah, Nellie. It's the first time I've found a way to use this body to catch a lift. 'Fine, fine betty,' my new friends call it. Tashtego and Daggoo. They work for Sea Cuke Divers. Tashtego's a moldie fakaleiti. I think maybe I had sex with him? Or no, wait, that was another moldie I did it with. A green one. Her name was V-something. She rubbed even more betty on me. Are we diving today?"

"Are you going to be okay, Cobb? You look way kilpy." Cobb's normally clean outlines were wavering and irregular, with small ripples darting about upon the surface of his skin. His rosy flesh was shot through with lines of gray.

"A shower would help," said Cobb. "I could open my pores and let the water flush out the toxins. But—not yet." He slumped against the wall. "I have too much slack. It feels good to be lifted." He held his hands up in front of his face, slowly moving them as if watching their motion trails.

"I'm not sure we should dive at all," mused Yoke. "There's more to it than you realize. Stop looking at your hands and pay attention! The biggest news is that there's an alien named Shimmer living down in the Tonga Trench. The King says Shimmer wants me to come see her. She's been decrypting more aliens out of signals from this Tongan Meta West Link satellite called Cappy Jane. Yesterday Onar killed a Tongan man who'd been trying to stop Shimmer from using Cappy Jane. For some reason Onar and the King don't want you in on this, Cobb. The King's a cheeseball by the way; his girlfriend is a moldie named Vaana."

Cobb stopped wiggling his fingers and looked past them at Yoke. "Killed?" said Cobb, not sounding so happy anymore. His motionless gray-streaked hands were in supplicating claw positions. "Vaana?"

"You better take that shower, Cobb. You want me to help you?"

"Help," said Cobb, and suddenly slipped off the bed onto the floor. He was more than lifted, he was poisoned.

Yoke dragged the stinking heavy moldie down the hall to the guest house bathroom. Another guest, a German woman, was just vacating it. She gave Yoke a disgusted look as she stepped over the inert Cobb. But she didn't bother to ask any questions. It was a very cheap guest house.

Yoke wrestled Cobb into the concrete shower stall and turned the controls on all the way, which produced a limp drizzle. The water didn't seem to be penetrating Cobb fast enough, so Yoke got into the shower and started kneading him with her feet. The shower wasn't exactly hot, but it wasn't freezing cold either. Out of reflex, Yoke picked up a stray sliver of soap and started washing herself, all the while jouncing around on the soft moldie flesh of Cobb. As she washed she thought about making love to Onar—which made her wash herself the more thoroughly. Triple ugh for Onar. Three ughs and you're out.

There was a shuddering beneath her feet. Yoke turned her attention back down to Cobb. Thanks to her trampling, the water was squeegeeing in and out of his flesh. The water coming out of Cobb was dark as if with dust or pollen. His eyes were open, glassily staring up at Yoke's body. She flipped him over with a deft motion of her feet and continued to tread on him.

The bathroom door swung open and in walked Onar, nude, with a morning erection.

"Cheerio, Yoke," he said. "Care if I join you? Missed you in bed this morning."

"It's pretty full in here," said Yoke. "Someone poisoned Cobb."

"What a stench!" exclaimed Onar, peering into the shower. "Don't tell me you're trying to save him? That'll never work."

"Why shouldn't I try?" snapped Yoke. "Do you want to just let him die? Don't bother to answer. And stop staring at me."

"You shouldn't waste your time," said Onar. "I've seen this kind of thing happen before. An overdose of betty. All of his fungus nodules are bursting out with spores, and the spores are going to poison him. Kiss the old duffer good-bye, Yoke. We'll find you another dive-moldie. Oofa's expecting us at nine sharp."

"Sure she is," said Yoke. "On the dot. Get out of here. It was a big mistake to sleep with you. Onar the one-minute wonder."

"Goood morning," said Onar, and left the room.

More and more of the dark dust, the spores, was coming out of Cobb. Some of the dust wafted up toward Yoke. She put a wet washrag over her face to keep from getting lifted. She kneaded Cobb harder and harder.

Finally the old man's moldie flesh was pink again. His tissues drew back into the shape of a human. He groaned and got to his feet.

"Man. What a burn."

"You're all right now?" asked Yoke. Even though Cobb smelled awful, she hugged him. His flesh was cool and smooth.

"When we go in the ocean I'll really clean myself out," said Cobb, hugging her back. "Thank you, dear Yoke. I think you saved my life. That green moldie woman, that Vaana, she smeared too much betty on me. Crazy. Like there was no tomorrow."

Yoke got out of the shower and began toweling herself off. "She was trying to kill you, Cobb. She's the King's girlfriend. She must have flown straight to the Happy Club after I left the palace."

Cobb remained in the shower stall, flexing his body to squeeze out a little more of the spore-darkened water. "So the King wants me dead," he said finally. "Did he mention why?"

"Last night I thought it was because he thought you'd talk too much. Now I'm thinking maybe it's because he didn't want you here to protect me when I dive down to see Shimmer today."

"Shimmer," said Cobb. He stepped out of the shower, looking vague. "Yoke dear, you're going to have to repeat what you told me in your room. Your words flew past me like a flock of— hummingbirds. Shimmer's an alien, right? And when you say alien, you mean an honest-to-God extraterrestrial?"

"Duh! Shimmer was one of the alien personality waves who decrypted into moldie bodies at Willy Taze's house in November. My parents killed all the others. And Shimmer got away. She's living down in the Tonga Trench. The King says Shimmer's bringing in a bunch of her relatives to live here. And for some reason she wants to meet with me."

"Real aliens!" exclaimed Cobb. "At last! I'd love to meet this Shimmer."

"You're in no condition."

"Hell I'm not. Buy me some quantum dots to get my energy up, Yoke, and I'll be good as new." Cobb stretched himself to an alarming height, then snapped back like a rubber band. "It's fuckin' great to be alive."

"I'm scared Shimmer might *get* me, Cobb. When I woke up this morning I started thinking about the four-dimensional things that ate Kurt Gottner and my mom. If that's what really happened, then maybe those things were from the aliens. Shimmer comes from a place where there's two-dimensional time."

"If Shimmer could kill Kurt in California and Darla on the Moon, then she could kill us right here and now if she wanted to," said Cobb. "So why not go and have a talk with her face-to-face? What does she look like?"

"She's in a moldie body. She has such a huge intelligence that her body's perfectly formed. It's like she's consciously aware of the curvatures of each square millimeter of her surface. She's inhumanly beautiful, Cobb. Like a glowing marble sculpture."

"Wow," said Cobb, visibly tweaking his body shape as if trying out the idea of making himself look divine. "Do I look good enough to meet her?"

"You look fine," said Yoke, even though Cobb only looked like a stocky, freckled white-haired old man pulling in his stomach. "Let's go back to my room. You stick with me before something else happens to you."

Yoke put on her new purple Santa Cruz bikini and a long chartreuse T-shirt. She and Cobb went out into the guest house common room. It was a bare old room, beautified by bowls of water with hibiscus blossoms floating in them. Mrs. Yoshida and her cook Waloo were serving breakfast: coffee, papayas, and toast. Mrs. Yoshida was a trim, no-nonsense lady with her hair in a black bun; Waloo was calm, smiling, and stocky. Onar was sitting at the table in a fresh clean sport shirt covered with satellite weather photos of the South Pacific, all blues and whites and grays.

"Feeling better, Cobb?" said Onar.

"Vaana dosed me," said Cobb. "Do you know where Yoke can buy me some quantum dots?"

Onar shook his head and began, "And I'm afraid that's—"

But Mrs. Yoshida interrupted him. "I can sell you some dots, Yoke. My husband, bless his soul, bought too big a supply of them for his boat and they're just sitting on a shelf in a magnetic bottle. You pay cash?"

"I'll do a transfer," said Yoke, picking up her uvvy. "How much?"

"Hold on," said Mrs. Yoshida, and disappeared into the kitchen, quickly returning with a shiny gray bottle. She shook the little bottle and held it up to the light. "The meter says there's half a terawatt left. You want it all?"

"Yeah," said Cobb. "If it's too expensive for Yoke, my grandson Willy can pay you back."

"Like he's really going to want to pay all your bills," said Yoke. "But sure, let's do it. Pop loaded up my $Web account for this trip. He'd definitely want you healthy, Cobb." She glanced at Onar, who looked to be bursting with objections. "You haven't met my pop, Onar. And you better hope you never do."

"Whitey's a bad-ass," agreed Cobb. "For true. By the way, Onar, why do you think Vaana tried to poison me?"

"I'm sure she didn't mean to," said Onar. "She's just wild that way. Ever since she's moved in with the King."

"I think it is a crying shame," put in Waloo, setting out some fresh toast and coffee. "HRH should be making a prince. We don't like our Tu'i Tonga to be a cheeseball." She favored Yoke with a frank, inquisitive gaze. "Are you that way with your moldie?"

"God no," said Yoke. "Only men are skanky enough to fuck plastic." The women laughed.

Yoke donned her uvvy and completed the purchase of the

quantum dots. Mrs. Yoshida handed Cobb the magnetic bottle. He grew a thick funnel shape out of the center of his chest and poured the quantum dots into it. They sparkled like iridescent dust and sank into his tissues.

"Spinach!" said Cobb, flexing like a bodybuilder. His biceps swelled to the size of hams; his legs grew sinewy as tree trunks. "Boing and a boing and a ya-yahoo! Should I torture loverboy till he tells us all his secrets?" He took a step toward the seated Onar.

"Can everyone calm down?" snapped Onar. "I still think it would be better for Yoke to dive inside of one of our local moldies today. In case something goes wrong. Get away from me, Cobb. You reek."

Yoke waited until Mrs. Yoshida and Waloo were out of earshot and answered Onar in an angry whisper. "You want to have Tashtego or Daggoo offer me up to Shimmer like a human sacrifice! Trussed on a platter with an apple in my mouth."

"We just don't want there to be any trouble," hissed Onar. "And Cobb's always spelled trouble. In all of his lives. We only want for today's meeting to go smoothly and for Shimmer to give you the realware."

"What's that?" asked Cobb, too loud.

"I don't really know," said Onar, stubbornly staring down at his cup. "Hurry up and eat your breakfast, Yoke. Cobb, why don't you wait on the porch so I can drink my coffee without vomiting."

And then they were out in the Sea Cuke dive boat: Oofa, Yoke, and Onar; Daggoo, Tashtego, and Cobb. Tashtego and Daggoo looked like cannibals, like fierce harpooneers from an old-time whaling ship, their imipolex skins intricately worked with tattoos. Daggoo was huge, coal-black with wild kinky hair; the imipolex of his earlobes swooped out into shapes like gold hoop earrings. His tattoos were raised white lines, seemingly of scar tissue. Tashtego was coppery in color, with long blond hair; his tattoos were polychrome fractals. Both of them had slim hips and muscular bodies. Though Tashtego was large, Daggoo was half again as big as Tashtego. Daggoo wore blue swimming trunks, while Tashtego wore a woman's red bikini with the bra-cups stuffed with two pairs of socks. The skin of Tashtego's face was colored to give the effect of orange lipstick and turquoise eye shadow. The crotch of his bikini bulged as if covering a large penis.

Yoke ended up sitting next to Tashtego in the bow of the boat. Behind them sat Cobb and Onar, and in the stern were Oofa and Daggoo. After leaving the Nuku'alofa harbor, the boat circled around to the south side of the island, there to rise up on its hydrofoils and speed southeast across the open ocean. They slowed down once to view a pair of spouting sperm whales. Yoke wanted to dive in and get a good look at them, but Onar urged Oofa on.

By eleven A.M. the sun was incredibly hot and bright. The water-jet motor was whisper-quiet; the only sound was the hissing of the hydrofoils through the sea. For no particular reason Tashtego was making a great show of combing out his matted blond hair—really just strands of imipolex, of course—and one of his undulating arms bumped Yoke on the shoulder. Hard.

"Why behave like a fakaleiti?" snapped Yoke. She felt anxious and irritable; the light breakfast had worn off. "It doesn't make sense. A moldie is whatever sex it decides on at birth. So you're a male moldie, fine. If you wanted to, you could shape yourself like a human woman. Why take on the form of a man impersonating a woman? It's stupid."

"Fakaleiti make happy thing happen," said Tashtego, archly looking down at his false breasts. As part of their images, he and Daggoo insisted on speaking a barbaric pidgin English. "Tashtego boom boom boy girl." He threw back his head and cackled. His teeth were as sharp and pointed as if they'd been filed. "You no dive in me today, Yoke? Me open up very good." Tashtego playfully split himself slightly open along a heretofore invisible seam down the front of his body. Like a clam cracking its shell open for a bit of water.

The appearance of the savage Tashtego's halved face was

deeply disturbing. Yoke shook her head and looked away. "I'm diving in Cobb and that's final."

"I'd like to dive in you, Tashtego," said Onar, who was eavesdropping over their shoulders. "I want to come along. More sunscreen, Yoke?"

"Thanks." It still seemed odd to Yoke to be bare beneath the sun. She was following the fair-skinned Onar's regimen of frequent applications of lotion. "How much further are we going?" she asked. "I don't see anything but open sea. We're going so fast that we must have come seventy miles by now."

"Oofa?" called Onar.

But Oofa was asleep, lounging back against Daggoo's sun-puddled body. Onar had to shake Oofa's bare foot to rouse her.

"No problem, soon come, the boat knows where to go," mumbled Oofa, rubbing her eyes and looking around. "We'll be near our dive-site when you can see 'Ata over there. And then you look for something like a lily pad." She waved her hand toward the starboard and relaxed back against Daggoo's smooth black flesh.

" 'Ata is the southernmost island of Tonga," explained Onar. "The deepest part of the Tonga Trench runs right past it. The Vityaz Deep. Better than six miles to the bottom. That's where Shimmer is."

Yoke felt a hollowness in her chest. "We're supposed to dive down six miles? I'd need a submarine for that. A bathyscaph, not a moldie wet suit."

"I be hard as you need, Yoke," leered Tashtego. Daggoo let out a carnivorous yelp of laughter.

"It's true," said Cobb. "We can switch our imipolex to a rigid form that's stronger than diamond. The loonie moldies taught me all the tricks."

"Why can't Shimmer just swim up to meet us?" wailed Yoke.

"She's shy," said Onar. "And, look, on the horizon over there, it's 'Ata! And here's Shimmer's antenna. Heave to, Oofa!"

The boat came to a stop and sank down to bob in the slow

ocean swells. Floating in the sea near them was a thick fleshy disk of silvery imipolex. Its upper surface was cupped like a parabolic dish.

"Ahoy, Turklee," called Tashtego, waving his snaky arms.

"Hello," sang back the lily pad. "Shimmer's expecting you."

"Is that thing a moldie?" asked Yoke.

"Sure," said Onar. "Her name's Turklee. I think the King mentioned her to you last night. The fourth moldie in the know. Turklee's working as a transducer for Shimmer. Radio waves don't travel well through water, you see. Turklee uses blue-green laser light to send signals down to Shimmer's lair. Shimmer needs a good link because she's pulling in so much bandwidth through Cappy Jane."

While Onar talked, Oofa rummaged in a cooler chest and took out a bunch of bananas and a bottle of water to pass around.

"I can hear Shimmer," said Cobb suddenly. "She's talking to us. Oh how strange. This is wonderful. Hello, Shimmer. Put on your uvvy, Yoke." Tashtego and Daggoo were grinning and nodding, enjoying Shimmer's signal too.

"What if she blasts me like Onar did yesterday?" asked Yoke.

"Be gentle, Shimmer," said Cobb. "The person you've been asking for is going to come on line. Oh yes, that's perfect. Try it now, Yoke."

So Yoke put the uvvy on her tender neck and right away she could hear Shimmer's voice, a sound like the piping of flutes, the whining of sitars, and the gentle resonation of a gong.

"Hello, Yoke. You were kind to me on the Moon. I'm grateful that you've come to see me. Let's plan your dive."

Now Shimmer began sending images of divers, figures against a dark undersea background, drifting down next to the blue-green shaft of Turklee's laser beam. In the images, Cobb was shaped like a sphere, with Yoke crouched within him like a tadpole inside a frog's egg. The pictures were clear and beautiful but with a curious multiplicity to them. Like seeing two or three or twenty things at once. In some of the images Onar and

Oofa were also present, riding inside Tashtego and Daggoo, and in one of those images, Tashtego bit a hole in Cobb's surface, causing him to collapse and to crush Yoke into bloody pulp.

"Yoke must come alone," said Shimmer.

"The King wants me and Oofa there too," protested Onar through the uvvy, his voice like the chirp of a persistent cricket.

Now one of Shimmer's images showed Onar and Oofa following Yoke. The blue-green laser beam intensified, twitched, burnt holes in Tashtego and Daggoo.

"You will stay on the boat," said Shimmer.

So Onar told the others that they wouldn't be going down.

"That's fine," said Oofa, settling back into her seat.

"HRH pay us imipolex all the same," said Daggoo.

"Bugger all," muttered Onar.

"Are you ready, Yoke?" asked Cobb.

She looked around at the sloshing sea, at pale angry Onar, at lithe Tashtego and massive Daggoo, at calm Oofa and pink old Cobb. The sunlight on the water was beautiful. It would be so odd to die here.

"Don't worry, Yoke," said Shimmer, as if sensing Yoke's thoughts. "You won't die at all. I'll help you find true happiness." She sounded so kind and wise that Yoke believed her.

"Okay," Cobb was saying. "Get on top of me now." The moldie had puddled himself out on the deck like a pancake with a little hump in the center like a footstool. Yoke fit her palladium filters into her nose and sat on the imipolex hassock. Cobb's flesh swooped up around her, sealing itself up to form a translucent sphere. Tashtego and Daggoo whooped, their voices muffled by Cobb's body, and then there was a jarring bump and a splash. Cobb's flesh held onto Yoke's body to keep her from being thrown about.

"I can't see anything, Cobb," protested Yoke. "Make yourself transparent!"

"I can't when I'm in this rigid mode," said Cobb. "But you can use your uvvy to see what I'm seeing. Just focus."

They were floating just beneath the surface. Yoke put her

attention into her uvvy, and now she could indeed see a remarkable view of the water's underside, all live and sparkling in the sun, a restless mirror. Cobb moved his gaze about in synch with Yoke's head motions; it felt like she was freely looking around.

Yoke could see the bottom of the Sea Cuke boat, also the heads of Daggoo and Tashtego, who were hanging over the edge to stare at them. Turklee the lily pad antenna was floating off to one side, a dark disk on the silver surface. A bright, narrow beam of blue-green light emanated from Turklee's underside. She had a ring of webbed duck-feet constantly paddling to keep her centered over Shimmer's location. A few good-sized fish hovered in the shade of the lily pad moldie, nibbling at whatever marine algae had begun to grow on her. Looking down, Yoke's gaze followed the crisp line of laser light to where it disappeared into the featureless depths. Six miles! Her stomach knotted like a fist.

There was a great splash from above. Tashtego and Daggoo were wrestling a huge weight over the edge of the dive boat for them; it was a massive pyramid of pig-iron with a handle at the apex. Cobb bulged out a hand to take hold of the dive-weight, the others released it, and then, as abruptly as stepping off a cliff, Cobb and Yoke were plummeting down into the abyss, slowly at first, then faster and faster, until soon they'd reached their maximum speed, with the downward pull of their weight just balanced by their friction with the water.

Their passage through the water made a low, thrumming sound. Cobb's flesh seemed to grow ever denser and more compact. Yet the pressure inside the spherical shell of his body stayed normal; Yoke didn't have to clear her ears as she'd had to during her Santa Cruz moldie wet-suit dives.

Quite soon it was pitch-dark in the Cobb bathyscaph. "Can you make some light for me?" asked Yoke. As she spoke, her teeth began to chatter. "And heat. It's getting colder every second."

"Here's heat," said Cobb, and immediately his flesh grew

pleasantly warm. "But I'd rather not light up. I don't want the denizens of the deep getting too curious about us. Just keep looking through my sensors. I'll dial my sensitivity down into the infrared."

Gazing through the uvvy, Yoke could see the featureless vertical line of laser light leading down as before. She stared into the abyss, searching for a sign. Time passed, perhaps as much as an hour. Now and then a flicker of small jellyfish flew past, and occasionally an angler fish or a big-mouthed gulper eel.

"We're at five miles," said Cobb. "I'm holding up fine."

Yoke felt oppressed by the sullen weight of so much pressure. The flecks of sea life sped past like snowflakes in a viddy snowstorm. Far far below was a hint of pale light. But before Yoke could ask about it, there was a distraction.

"Squid!" exclaimed Cobb, and, yes, all of a sudden there were squid everywhere. Big ones, small ones, and huge ones. The largest one looked to be some two hundred feet long. Its body was like an arrow, a great tapered cone tipped with two wild wavy fins. The fins fanned in rapid undulations, driving the squid toward them. Its immense round eyes looked frighteningly intent. Cobb had piqued its interest. Eight of the squid's ten tentacles were clenched into a tidy sheaf, but its two extra-long ones were reaching toward them like hungry arms. Cobb and Yoke plummeted past the giant squid, but it sped down after them, its fins flapping like flags. Now one of its fiendishly long arms slapped against them. Cobb's flesh shuddered.

"Oh no," said Cobb. "Brace yourself, Yoke."

And then the squid was upon them. Its bunched tentacles writhed apart to reveal a vile huge beak. Yoke could hear the scratching of the beak against the hardened rind of Cobb's outer skin.

"Oh, Yoke, I can't get loose without—" Cobb began, but just then the giant squid released them and jetted away fins first, propelled by a blast of water from the huge siphon next to its beak. A moment later Yoke could see why. A sperm whale went bucking past, its great flukes madly beating. The squid's speed was no match for the whale's. The leviathan opened its long, narrow, big-toothed lower jaw and clamped the squid crossways. The monstrous tentacles lashed about, seeking purchase on the whale's great blocky frame.

Cobb and Yoke continued to sink, and Yoke stared upward at the whale and squid as, incredibly, the whale swallowed the violently squirming squid whole, leaving only a few tentacles dangling from its mouth like live macaronis.

"We're here!" cried Cobb just then. Looking down, Yoke saw a wall of white light come rushing up at them. There was a clunk as they hit something, then a wild explosion of air bubbles, and then they dropped through a hundred feet of empty space to plop onto—a grassy meadow?

Cobb's body opened up like a blossom spreading its petals. Yoke stepped free to find herself standing in a diamond-roofed dome of air: a half-sphere dome like on the Moon, several hundred yards across, with the deep black sea outside. They'd fallen in through the roof, but whatever hole they'd made had instantly healed itself.

Cobb drew himself back into his old man form and stood by Yoke's side. Far from being ocean-floor ooze, the ground underfoot was springy green turf bedizened with wildflowers. The air was fresh and dry, though perfumed with tangy odor of moldies. The light seemed to come from all around. And Shimmer and five others of her kind were coming across the field toward them.

The aliens had shiny imipolex bodies like moldies, but iridescent, luminous, and shaped with infinite perfection. Two were formed like humans, and four like animals, with each shape an archetypal paradigm, a Platonic ideal, perfection incarnate. Shimmer resembled a marble Venus, and her partner was a bronze Apollo. The four animals were a unicorn with yellow-blond hair, a gem-like beetle, a muddy black pig, and a pale green python—each of them the correct size for the creature epitomized.

"Greetings, Yoke," said Shimmer, reaching out her hand. Her voice was sweet and resonant. "I especially wanted you to come, because you're the most reasonable and sympathetic human I've met. I'd like you to be the first to test out something we want to give your people."

Yoke took Shimmer's hand and squeezed it. The other aliens gathered around.

"Ptah," said the man, shaking Cobb's hand. His voice was a warm rumble. The four animal-shaped beings greeted them and named themselves: the unicorn Peg, the iridescent beetle Josef, Wubwub the pig, and the snake Siss.

"Where do you come from, Ptah?" asked Cobb.

"We're all from the same place," said Ptah. "All six of us. It's in a different domain of the cosmos. We travel as encrypted signals inside cosmic rays. Personality waves. They're like gamma rays but with a higher-dimensional component. Shimmer here's been decrypting us into moldie flesh one at a time. We had this idea that each of us form our body into a different shape. I was the first one she brought in. Josef's the most recent arrival—he talks a lot. He's just as smart as us, even though he's small. He found a way to miniaturize the moldie information representation."

"But what's the *name* of the place you come from?" pressed Cobb.

"You want one single name?" asked Ptah, smiling.

Wubwub made a sound like electric guitar feedback. Siss added a series of clicking sounds. Peg tacked on the sound of a gong being struck, and tiny Josef put in a clap of thunder. Wubwub stretched out his snout and made a sound like wind moaning in the trees. It was hard to be sure, but it seemed as if the aliens were making fun of Cobb's question.

"Oh, why not say we come from—from Metamars," said Shimmer. "And we can be Metamartians." She turned to Ptah.

"Cappy Jane's employer is called Meta West Link, you know. 'Meta' means 'beyond.' Like metaphysics."

"Yes, I am coming from very meta," said Josef, his voice loud and firm. For whatever reason, he chose to speak with a German accent. "And only just now have I arrived, as Shimmer has said." He lifted his wing covers and buzzed through the air to land lightly on Yoke's wrist. "This seems a very marginal place." His eyes twinkled and the little fans of his antennae waved. "From the little bit that I am able yet to see. It's so curious, this one-dimensional time. For your people I think death must be very frightening?"

"Duh!" said Yoke. "Death's not frightening for you?"

"In two-dimensional time death isn't so much of an issue," said Josef. "Yes, perhaps I die in one time-line, but I'm still alive in another."

"Not here you aren't," said Yoke. "I could squash you and that would be that."

"Now now, Yoke," said Shimmer. "I'd just been telling my fellows how kind you are. There's no need to be afraid of us. We don't plan to stay on Earth for very long. We're nomads and this is only one stop on our endless journey of discovery. How do you like these temporary bodies we've made ourselves? We're imipolex with algae and mold nervous systems like your moldies. We programmed our personalities right into the limpware."

"How many of you are going to come here?" asked Yoke. "Six is one thing, but six billion would be—"

"Too many?" asked Siss the serpent, then laughed. She sounded Chinese. "No worry, Yokie. Only one more of us going come. We form a family of seven, make a baby, help Om memorize all about your race, and then we move on and probably no Metamartian ever come here again. Your world not so very nice, I think. You know, Shimmer, I thinking perhaps we should be more small. Could we be ant, Josef? So tiny as germ?"

"I ain't gonna be no ant," interjected Wubwub, who'd been rooting in the sod. He used a kind of black rapper accent. He looked up at them, a few tubers hanging from the side of his mouth. "I'm too important for that, you know what I'm sayin'?"

"Too *fat*," put in Siss the serpent, striking at the pig's side.

"Me and Josef are the ones gonna help Cobb and Yoke out through the wall, ain't we?" said Wubwub, twitching the snake free. "Gimmie respect."

"Cease your soothsaying, O Swine," said Peg. "It's time for Lady Yoke to bleat her plaint." The unicorn spoke as if at a Renaissance Faire, with the speech mannerisms that Yoke and her friends called "swilly." With her flowing long blonde hair, the swilly unicorn reminded Yoke of a teenage girl enchanted by all things medieval. Her horn was shiny red like glossy lipstick.

"Thank you so much," snapped Yoke, not really understanding what they were talking about, but having a vague sense she'd been insulted. "What I want to say is that I hope Siss is telling the truth. And even six or seven of you could be a problem, frankly. If you start changing things, it could ruin our ecology. Your technology might overwhelm our civilization."

"Indeed it will," said Peg. "But is your way of life so fine? Dare to dream of more than grubbing in the mud. Yoke, we bring you the power to alter matter with a touch of mind. This is a power our god Om bestows upon us—a power she now sees fit to grant to you. You're lucky. Thanks to Shimmer's having been decrypted here, Om has noticed you. Your race will live as sorcerers."

"I suppose that sounds nice," said Yoke uncertainly.

"Give Yoke her *alla* now, Shimmer," said Ptah. He kept glancing around expectantly, as if someone or something else were about to appear.

"Yes," said Shimmer. "Om willing." She rubbed her thumb against her palm, and a little hollow gold tube appeared in her hand. It was almost cylindrical, with four smooth indentations like a hand-grip. "This is Om's gift through me to you," said Shimmer, and handed the object to Yoke.

The alla fit Yoke's hand comfortably. It had a live, vibrant feel to it. Looked at more closely, the substance of the alla tube was not gold—nor was it any other substance Yoke had ever seen. It felt smooth, even slippery. Another odd thing about the tube was that, rather than being a fixed color of gold, it was repeatedly flickering through a cycle of perhaps thirty subtly different shades.

As she held the alla in her hand, Yoke felt a link between it and her uvvy. "Greetings," said the alla. "I'm ready to learn your mind." Yoke uvvied her agreement to this—not that she was sure what she was agreeing to. The alla showed her an image for half a second and asked her to name it and give a memory association. The image was a circular pattern with colored patches.

"A chrysanthemum," said Yoke, thinking of the first flower she'd ever grown.

"Next," said the alla, and for a quarter of a second it showed an image of a crooked forked line.

"A crack in a wall," said Yoke, recalling the wall by the side of her childhood bed.

"Next." Each image was being displayed for half as long as the one before. This one was a uniform patch of rough texture.

"Moon-dust," said Yoke, though not out loud, as this was starting to happen faster than speech. She was thinking of a particular patch of moon-dust and how she'd gotten obsessed staring at it after she'd read a book on mineralogy.

More and more images came, each twice as fleeting as before—and at the end of a second Yoke felt as if she'd given the alla an all but infinite amount of information. She thought of the old Zeno paradox about fitting an arbitrarily large number of events into a unit of time: a half plus a quarter plus an eighth plus a sixteenth plus a thirty-second and so on—no matter how many terms you stick in, the sum is always a bit less than one. Each new step only uses up half of the remaining time. How many images had the alla just shown her?

"Now I'll learn your body," said the alla, and Yoke felt an incredible series of tingles and twitches—in her guts, in her chest, up and down her arms and legs, inside her head, and in the muscles of her face and fingers.

"You are now registered as my sole user for life," murmured the alla softly. "Feel free to select something from your catalog."

"Think of something you want," said Shimmer. "You think to the alla through your uvvy. Josef and Ptah made a human-style catalog for it. Oh, that's right, we have to copy the catalog to you. I hope you have a lot of clear memory space in your uvvy?"

"I should," said Yoke. "It's a yottabyte model."

"Here it comes," said Josef.

And then the alla catalog was stored in Yoke's uvvy. When she accessed it, the display showed an amorphous, featureless object, waiting for Yoke to tell it what to become.

"Ask for a sweatshirt?" suggested Cobb, who stood absently twining his fingers in the blonde mane of Peg the unicorn. "You look a little chilly."

Yoke thought of a fleecy white pullover she wished she'd brought along from the Moon, and now her uvvy formed a mental image of a somewhat similar sweatshirt, a precise, detailed image seemingly called up from its internal catalog. The image wasn't quite what she'd had in mind, but by mentally pushing at it, Yoke was able to slide about through similar catalog entries till she found something that was a very good match for what she wanted. And once she'd picked her sweatshirt design, the alla adjusted it to be a custom fit for Yoke's body.

"Now say, 'Actualize!' " said Shimmer. "You can say it out loud or just think it. That tells the alla to make a physical copy of the design."

Yoke said, "Actualize." A sudden mesh of bright lines appeared in the air in front of the alla, hanging there like a three-dimensional wire-frame engineering spec. A web of dark membranes appeared within the virtual sweatshirt, dividing and subdividing. There was a little puff of breeze, and then the bright lines disappeared and a fluffy white sweatshirt dropped to the ground.

"This must be what Onar meant by realware," breathed Cobb. "Direct matter control!"

Yoke turned the little alla so she could see through the length of its hollow tube, careful not to put it too near her face. Seen through the hole, the room seemed to be endlessly spinning around the alla's central axis. Whoah. Yoke looked away.

"Yes," said Josef. "What the alla makes is realware. You could call the alla a tool for realware engineering. Figuring out the designs for the realware takes some work. But the alla itself is a magical gift from Om."

"You got the alla from Om?" asked Yoke. "And Om's your god? Your god actually does things that are real?"

"Is your very world not real?" asked Peg.

"Well, yes," said Yoke. "But—"

"Om a medium-size god," said Siss. "Not like the big White Light that make everything. Om kind of curious. She like to learn all about different races of beings by giving allas to them. Long time ago, some other aliens bring Om and allas to the Metamartian race, and now we bring Om and allas to you. Pass it on. More is merrier."

"But what is an alla, exactly?" asked Yoke, looking down at it.

"The alla is part of Om," said Shimmer. "A vortex thread that loops out of her body to cross our space. When Om gives you an alla, she learns all about you—and you get to have a magic wand. It's a fair trade. Everyone benefits."

"One question," said Cobb. "Josef just said the alla transmutes matter. But when it made Yoke's sweatshirt out of air, there wasn't enough air inside that bright-line mesh. Not enough mass to match the sweatshirt."

"No problem," said Josef. "If there aren't enough atoms within the target region, then extra ones are drawn in. That's why one often feels a little puff of wind."

"Before we let the alla spread to all humanity, Om wants us to test it just with one person," said Shimmer. "And I picked you, Yoke. The alla has registered itself exclusively for your use."

"Shimmer chose you as a maiden pure of heart," said Peg. "Worthy of a magic wand. Nobler than that Tongan King."

Yoke put on her shirt. It was an exact replica of the preview image the uvvy had shown her. To get her arms through the sleeves, she passed the alla from hand to hand rather than setting it down.

"That right," said Siss, attentively watching. "Hang onto alla very careful. It no use to other people, but even so, they might try to steal. You should make pouch for it and wear at your waist."

"It's mine to keep?" said Yoke, staring down at the alla. She thought of orange juice, and her uvvy displayed a catalog image of a squeeze-bottle of juice. Without saying the word out loud, Yoke thought, *Actualize.* A pouch-shaped web of lines formed near the end of the tube; the pouch webbed over and cleared to produce the bag of juice. Yoke caught it as it dropped from the air; she held it to her mouth and sucked at it. Delicious. She gave a happy guffaw. "Hey, you've got *my* xoxxin' vote!"

The beetle Josef had flown off while Yoke was pulling on her sweatshirt. Now he flew back and perched on Yoke's breast like a brooch. He glittered many colors in the light.

"The allas will make your Earth a paradise," the man-shaped alien named Ptah was saying. He was jouncing back and forth excitedly. His eyes were wide and glowing, as if he were expecting some great event.

"But we do have a problem, Ptah," said Cobb. "What about those people who've been getting killed? Like Darla and Tempest Plenty and Kurt Gottner? Is there some connection between those things and your coming here?"

"Oho," said Siss. "Connection is Om. And don't worry, those people not really killed. You going see example right now. Om sometimes reach into space with her fingertips to take someone. Om fingertips have round shape we call 'powerball.' "

Just then Ptah let out a whoop. "It's time!" he sang. "Om's about to take me. Thank you, Josef! Farewell, Shimmer."

The Metamartians backed away from him. Wubwub pushed against Cobb and Yoke's legs, herding them along.

"I'm ready, Om!" shouted Ptah. He sounded ecstatic.

"Make a copy of yourself, Ptah," cried Shimmer. "We need one of you or we'll be back down to five!"

Just then something popped into the air next to Ptah, a spherical zone of warped space — something like a giant, airy lens.

"Look out!" cried Yoke, but rather than running, Ptah seemed to split himself in two. Or, rather, the air next to him shimmered and a fresh copy of Ptah was formed: another perfectly formed, bronze-colored, imipolex man. The new Ptah ran over to stand with Cobb, Yoke, and the other Metamartians, while the old Ptah stretched his arms up toward the mysterious ball of curved space.

"I envy him," the new Ptah said to Shimmer. "But I'm happy to help you reach the necessary seven to mate." He looked down at his new body approvingly. "I wasn't quite sure our replication procedure would work in this part of the cosmos." Ptah turned to Yoke, noticing her worried expression. "My original self will begin screaming now, Yoke, but don't worry, it's just a way to blow off a little physical discomfort. It'll look like he's being killed, but really he's just moving into a higher dimension."

The bright, shifting sphere darted to the original Ptah, and he became part of the round spatial anomaly. His beautiful, symmetric body puffed out as if inflated. And as predicted, he began to scream in pain. "Om kreet!" he shrieked. The great round anomaly of the powerball's space was inside of the original Ptah; his imipolex flesh was stretched out across its surface. A powerful glow emanated from his distorted face; his eyes were as lambent coals. "Om kreet, kreet, kreet!" A dreadful sound. His swollen form was starting to dwindle.

"Are you exactly the same as the old Ptah?" Yoke asked the new Ptah.

"Yes," said the new Ptah. "It's very easy for us to make realware copies of ourselves. We simply alla up an identical copy—each of us has an alla nestled within his or her body, you see. I'm used to seeing copies of myself go away. Remember that on Metamars we lead incalculably many parallel lives."

"What's going to happen to the old Ptah?" asked Yoke.

"Om wants to examine one of our Earth-style moldie bodies," said Josef. "The old Ptah will go to a kind of chamber inside Om, probably with the others. And then I imagine he'll move on. Into the Light."

Watching the old Ptah's apparent agony, Yoke wondered if this was what had happened to her mother. Was there any chance that Darla was anything other than dead? And what did Josef mean by the "Light"? Suddenly it looked as if the powerball might be drifting their way.

"No," groaned Yoke. She and Cobb began running across the grass floor of the dome. Shimmer, Peg, Siss, and the new Ptah fanned out ahead of them, with Wubwub following behind as if to protect them.

Soon they'd reached the diamond-hard wall of the dome. Wubwub sniffed at the ground and pushed himself against Yoke's legs, herding her a few yards along the curving edge of the wall.

"Stop it!" said Yoke. Across the meadow, the tiny shrunken powerball was darting about erratically, but it wasn't heading their way.

"Just a little to the right," said the black pig, insistently pushing Yoke with his snout. Finally he stopped. "This be the spot."

"Listen to me," said Josef. The lustrous beetle was still perched on Yoke's boob. "We are going to take down the dome now. The water will rush in."

"We'll be crushed!"

"Not if you get inside Cobb and stay at this precise spot," said Josef. "Wubwub will help push you in the right direction when the water comes. Remember that we can see a few minutes' worth of all the possible futures. Hurry, Yoke. Get inside of Cobb this very instant!"

Cobb flopped himself flat on the ground next to Wubwub, and Yoke sat down on him. She was still holding the alla. The old Ptah had stopped screaming. The five other Metamartians were standing by the dome's pure diamond wall as well, waiting.

"I will come with," said Josef, his legs clinging to Yoke's pullover. "And the others will organize a new node. Now that we've made contact with you, Yoke, we don't want the King to know where we are anymore."

The noble Wubwub stood firm at Yoke's side. He was lightly poised on his trotters, with his vigilant snout tracking the distant powerball's moves. "Rest of us movin' somewhere fresh. This place got bad juice now, you know what I'm sayin'?"

Cobb sealed himself up, and Yoke switched to viewing through Cobb's sensors. There was a *pop* and the last trace of Ptah and the powerball disappeared. Wubwub braced himself firmly against Cobb, pressing the bathyscaph against the dome's wall. The other Metamartians were braced against the wall as well, all of them ready to spring out into the sea.

And then the dome disappeared and six miles worth of water came rushing past them, crushing the air within the bubble into incandescent white light, illuminating for an instant, like the first flashbulb since creation, the dark ooze of the primeval ocean floor.

CHAPTER THREE

PHIL

＝　■　＝

February 21

Friday night Phil dreamed about his father again. In the dream he and his dad were sitting in a greenhouse full of orange nasturtiums and jasmine vines. Old Kurt was wearing his teaching clothes. His arms were missing. The jasmine smelled like musk, like rotten incense.

"The wowo took them off," said Kurt, his empty jacket sleeves flapping. "But they're healing fast." Blood was seeping through the shoulders of the jacket.

Made anxious by his father's wounds, Phil looked down at his own body. He was dressed in his sleeping outfit, a long T-shirt. He could see the individual hairs on his legs. One of his hands was clenched into a fist; when he opened it, the knotted, mirror-reversed wedding ring was there.

"I can't decide if I'm really dead," Kurt was saying. "Did I get a stuzzy funeral? Big tears? Bunch of drunks?" All the while the dusty orange nasturtium blossoms were singing in tiny, high voices, with the jasmine blossoms harmonizing a background.

"It was heavy, Da," said Phil, and the heavy gold ring tumbled from his hand.

"Gold from the roots," said Kurt. "Marry her."

The smeary music of the flowers was vibrating Phil's sinuses in a way he couldn't bear. He was crying. He tumbled off into jumbled dreams of mountain climbing.

When Phil woke, his father's knotted wedding ring actually *was* in his hand. He'd fallen asleep holding it. Was he crazy? He had to get rid of it today. Fuck this suicide shit.

It was ten A.M. and Kevvie was still unconscious. She didn't have to go in to work today because yesterday she'd gotten fired. Trying to get over the hangover from her Thursday night merge session with Klara Blo, Kevvie had stolen a bunch of Tendur painkillers from one of her lady clients, and the sharp-eyed old woman lodged an instant complaint. The geezer-sitter service had sent a dragonfly to sample Kevvie's blood on her way out of the client's building, and she'd failed the test big time. The service wouldn't stand for geezer sitters taking off their clients' drugs. So last night a resentful Kevvie had blown it all out on quaak and Tendur, and was completely twisted by the time Phil got home from work. He'd found her chasing after Umberto with a butcher knife yelling "Off with his head." Normally Kevvie was harmless, but when she was lifted enough she could get into a scary evil queen trip. This morning she looked like a nodded-out junkie, her mouth wide open and drool all down her chin. One of her hands was still soft from an ill-considered three A.M. splash of merge.

"It's over," Phil said softly to himself, and then he said it again, a little louder. "It's over, Kevvie. I'm not carrying you anymore." She snored on. Could he get her to move out? That would be hard. There was no formal lease, and Kevvie had been splitting the rent with him for the last ten months. Though Phil had built the birdhouse a full year before Kevvie moved in with him, she was likely to argue that by now it was hers as much as his. Which left only one alternative.

"I'm leaving, Kevvie," said Phil, trying out the sound of it. "I'm moving out." No reaction. "I'm moving out right now."

He dressed, put the ring in his pocket, picked up a duffel

bag and started walking around the room putting things into it. Another ending. He was trembling with emotion. What did he have here that really mattered? Toiletries, some clothes, some S-cubes, his quilt, a couple of books, and fuck the thrift-shop furniture. What else? His blimps! If he left them in here, Kevvie would trash them for sure. She'd never liked his flying machines. Phil used his uvvy to call his blimps down from the ceiling. Led Zep, Graf Z, the Macon, the Penile Implant, and the Uffin' Wowo. The blimps nuzzled against him like lonely puppies, their silky skins rustling.

"Come on, guys," Phil told them. "We're outta here."

Phil opened his arched door, maybe for the last time, and herded the blimps out into the open space of the warehouse. It was another gray day out the windows along the tops of the walls, gray clouds spitting rain. Derek was on the floor adjusting his green doughnut sculpture, Umberto squeezed up tight against his feet.

"Yaaar, Phil. Walking the blimps?"

"I'm moving out, Derek. It's Kevvie. I can't deal."

"You'd saddle Calla and me with that? Let's not forget that Kevvie got fired. How would she make the rent? Not to mention that last night she almost killed my dog. She's the one's gotta move outta here, Phil, not you."

"You can use my deposit to pay her rent till the end of March. Maybe she'll leave by then. I don't care anymore."

"Burn us is what she'll do," snapped Derek, his face hard. "I want her outta here by a week from today. *Before* March. Help me do it, Phil!"

"I can't be the one to put her out, Derek. And I can't live with her anymore either. I'm sorry, I—" Phil's eyes filled with tears. "It's too much, man. I just want to be quiet and not try, and it's not working. Burying my dad and dealing with Willow, and losing that Yoke girl so fast, and Kevvie's lifted all the time and I'm scared *I* could start using, and the wowo thing could come after me any minute and—" The tears were streaming down his face.

Derek softened. "Aw, Phil. If you gotta, you gotta. It'll be dense, but I can deal. On February twenty-eight Kevvie's outta here if I have to fuckin' change the locks. And I'm gonna keep Umberto safe over at a friend's till she's gone. Hear that, Umberto? You're gonna stay with Kundry." Umberto thumped his tail.

Phil wiped his eyes with his sleeve. "Thanks, Derek. You want to keep my blimps?"

"Feed them their helium and shit? No, man. The least you can do is take your blimps. Get outta here before Kevvie wakes up."

The wind was gusty outside, and Phil had to tether the blimps to his left arm lest they be blown away. The helium-filled imipolex DIM bags beat against him like balloons. It would be impossible to walk far this way, especially while carrying the duffel. Maybe he should let the blimps fly off into the wind? They were only toys. But still. He'd made them.

Just then one of the Snooks moldies accosted him. "Want a blow job, Phil?" It was Isis Snooks, a moldie curved into a fairly impressive female form. She had pouty lips and long, dark, slanted eyes.

"Would you like these blimps?" asked Phil in return.

"You want to trade blimps for a blow job? How much imipolex is in them?"

"I don't want a blow job, Isis. You know I'm not a cheeseball. I just need to get rid of the blimps. I'm moving out. Now, I don't want you to *eat* the blimps, I want you to take care of them. They'd be a nice decoration inside the *Anubis*. You have to feed them some quantum dots and helium every few weeks."

Isis cocked her head, studying the wind-whipped gas-bags. "Are the skins programmable?"

"I'll uvvy you the access codes right now if you promise to give them a good home."

"Fun," said Isis after another moment's thought. "I'll do it." So Phil uvvied her the control codes and handed her the blimp tethers. Something else occurred to him.

"Wait a second," he said. "This big one uses ballast." He took the knotted ring out of his pocket and pushed it in through the intake valve of his biggest blimp, the polka-dotted one named Uffin' Wowo. Perfect. "Enjoy them, Isis."

"Come by and visit anytime." Isis was smiling at the blimps, already uvvying new patterns onto them. Hieroglyphs. "Wavy, huh? Where you moving to, Phil?"

"I'm following a woman I met."

"Yoke Starr-Mydol," said the moldie.

"How would you know that?"

"Thutmosis saw you with her Thursday night. True looove."

"I'm goin' for it, Isis," said Phil. The moldie looked so smart and friendly that Phil regretted giving her the dangerous ring — but he couldn't bring himself to take it back and throw it into the ocean. "Make that one big blimp stay up near the ceiling," he obliquely warned. "It could hurt someone if it pops."

Phil headed for the closest haven he could think of: Babs Mooney's warehouse. The door was locked and he knocked hard and long. Finally it cracked open, revealing a man's pale face. Randy Karl Tucker.

"Haaah gaaah. Don't go runnin' out there, Willa Jean!" Randy Karl Tucker's plastic chicken appeared at the bottom of the door, staring up at Phil with its fixed little eye.

"Hi, Randy. Is Babs home?"

"She done took off for the art gallery. I spent all yesterday helpin' her make miniature worm-farms. Tryin' to earn my keep. I got my Master Plumber's certificate back in Louisville, you know. Yesterday I rented me a plumber's pipe-gun, a thing that pushes out whatever kind o' pipe or tube you want. I grew ole Babs some xoxxin' gnarly little mazes for her worms. What you call smart art."

"Babs is actually letting you stay here?" Normally Babs lived there all by herself. Her father, ex-Senator Stahn Mooney, had bought the place for her outright. Babs didn't need money and she didn't like roommates.

"Don't need to sound so surprised, Phil! I'm not as dumb

as I sound. And being a cheeseball don't make me a pervo right across the board. I think Babs is takin' a shine to me. Come on in if you like. Scoot, Willa Jean!"

"Thanks," said Phil. "I'm homeless."

"Hell, there's enough room in here for ten of us," said Randy, gesturing at Babs's immense warehouse with its bright, fabric-hung walls. "Pick yourself a corner and settle on in."

"Well that's kind of you to offer, Randy, but I do know that Babs likes her privacy. How long did she say you could stay for?"

"I'm expecting to be here till Cobb gets back from Tonga," said Randy. He threw himself down on a couch and Willa Jean hopped onto his lap. "Maybe a week? I'm pretty well burnt on Santa Cruz. San Francisco looks like a king-hell place."

"I don't mean to sound harsh, Randy, but Babs is bound to give you the boot. Maybe you don't know what she's usually like."

"I helped Babs a *lot* with them worm-farms, Phil. I'm more than just a plumber, I've worked as a process engineer. I'm a demon with the nanomanipulator. I helped Babs put sparkles in her worms. And to top it off, I'm gonna get her some leech-DIMs." Randy tapped the ragged purple patch that was merged into Willa Jean's back. "Illegal imipolex. Just for Babs to use in her art, you wave. We're thinkin' about a gallery show that's a whole henhouse of leech-DIM chickens. The viewers put on the control uvvies and it's *squawk-awk buk-puk*. Might could get some leech-DIMs from my ole bud Aarbie Kidd."

"Don't you get Babs in trouble, Randy," snapped Phil. "Take some time and figure out our scene before you start acting like a complete criminal. If you do anything to hurt Babs, Senator Stahn will take you down for true. Depend on it."

" *Tat tvam asi,*' " said Randy equably. "Means 'And that too' in Sanskrit. Did you know I lived in India for two years? I respect your concern for your friend, big gaaah. You think you'll be movin' in?"

"Well, no, my plan is to go to Tonga."

"You too? What all's in Tonga?"

"It's Yoke," said Phil. "I have to see her. For once I know exactly what I want to do."

February 22

So Phil ditched most of his stuff at Babs Mooney's warehouse and set off for Tonga with a few travel supplies in a knapsack. He took a conventional rocket-plane, with a change in Hawaii.

He arrived at Nuku'alofa early Sunday morning, Tonga time. The airport was old-fashioned and casual. He hadn't uvvied Yoke yet because he'd been scared she might tell him not to come. But now it was time.

The uvvy signal quickly found her, and Yoke picked up. She looked even better than Phil had remembered. Her calm eyes, her fine jaw, her wise mouth, her ivory-olive skin. She was wearing a purple bikini. She seemed to be sitting on a tropical patio eating breakfast. Alone?

"Hi, Yoke, it's Phil. I missed you so much that I flew to Tonga! I broke up with Kevvie."

Yoke took the news with aplomb. "Josef told me you were about to call," she said, tapping an imipolex beetle that was perched on her shoulder-strap like a tiny parrot. "He can see about five minutes into the future."

"Oh right," said Phil. "Did Babs blab? Where's Onar?"

"He and I are through. I think he's staying with the King. I'll tell you everything when you get here. I already asked Cobb to pick you up. You should wait somewhere obvious, like out in front of the airport? Cobb says he can get there in like fifteen minutes. It'll be wavy to see you, Phil. I'm glad you came."

A short while later Cobb plummeted down out of the sky and opened himself up like a mummy case. He looked considerably bulkier than before. Phil took the palladium nose-filters Cobb offered him and got inside the moldie-man, along with his pack. Huge acceleration and then they were arcing north across the Tongan archipelago.

"How's Yoke?" Phil asked Cobb.

"She's doing well."

"And what's with the beetle?" asked Phil.

"You mean Josef," said Cobb. "He's an alien from Meta-mars. A place where they have two-dimensional time. Apparently the Metamartians live a whole lot of parallel lives at once. They think our part of the cosmos is very odd!"

"Aliens! Are these the same aliens who were on the Moon back in November? There was one that got away?"

"Exactly. Shimmer's still here, and she's been decrypting other alien personality waves into imipolex bodies. Not just *any* aliens though, she only unpacks Metamartians. There's six of them now. This is like a bus-tour for them—or maybe an anthropological expedition. Shimmer, Ptah, Peg, Wubwub, Siss, Josef. Josef's taken a shine to our Yoke. He's a very useful individual to have around. Even though we only have one-dimensional time here, there's always a cloud of ghost futures around the next moment. And Josef's able to see the virtual futures and to actualize the best one. That's been making it easy to avoid hassles with Onar and the King."

"Tell me about Onar."

"Onar sucks," chuckled Cobb. "Just ask Yoke. She can't stand him anymore." Cobb did an imitation of Yoke's voice. " 'Onar's dishonest and a bad lover and he acts British and all British things suck. Except for Lewis Carroll.' "

"Who's Lewis Carroll?"

"Tsk, Phil. *Alice in Wonderland?* And your father a math teacher. Never mind. Onar and the King are so bummed about Yoke getting the alla. They want one of their own, but for now they have to be satisfied with Yoke making stuff for them. Mostly imipolex. She gave me some too." They'd reached their apogee, and now they were hurtling down toward the great blue sea with its tiny white-edged dots of green islands. "The alla makes realware; it uses direct matter control."

"Oh man, this is too much," complained Phil. "You've only

been down here two days and I don't know what the fuck you're talking about anymore."

"I haven't even mentioned the powerball yet," said Cobb. "The hand of Om. Om is the god of the Metamartians. She ate your father."

"You mean the wowo thing?"

"The wowo was what attracted Om. Like a flower for a hummingbird. Or a candle for a moth. Or a book for a scientist. And Om is—well, the Metamartians say she's God. Whenever the Metamartians go somewhere, Om shows up too. The powerballs are like fingers of Om."

"Cobb!" shouted Phil. The islands were rushing up insanely fast. "Stop the bullshit and pay attention! Slow down!"

"Aw, I'm getting really good at this," said Cobb, unfurling a bunch of wildly flapping imipolex ribbons. The ribbons flexed themselves, tearing at the air. Cobb continued to drop like a stone, but at least he'd stopped accelerating. They were fluttering toward a large, hook-shaped island with subsidiary islands scattered around it like appendages. It reminded Phil of a flea seen through a microscope, a big flea riddled with watery lagoons and intricate inlets, the island's harbor like a stomach. There were yachts floating in the harbor, and a small cluster of buildings beside it.

"The island of Vava'u," said Cobb. "The little town is Neiafu."

Cobb's ribbons fused into great wings, and he sailed serenely over Neiafu and across the harbor to home in on one of the tiny islands that peppered the harbor straits. Cobb's target island stuck out of the sparkling water like a verdant muffin; it had a high, round crown leading down to vertical, undercut sides. The summit of the island had been cleared down to the bare stone, and perched there was a single house, a sturdy yellow concrete building with a tin roof, much weathered. Beside the house was the aquamarine gem of a small swimming pool, seemingly carved right into the rock. Steps ran down the steep side of the island to a dock floating in the blue sea. Cobb touched down beside the pool, right next to a young woman sitting at a wicker table. Yoke.

"You're welcome," said Cobb, disgorging a shaken Phil onto the concrete pool apron.

"Thanks Cobb. Hi, Yoke!"

"Phil." Yoke was smiling so hard that her cheeks were bunched and her eyes were slitty. Phil sprang forward and hugged her; she hugged back. Now, finally, they kissed. But only briefly.

"You smell like moldie," said Yoke. "Let's take a dip."

Phil had a bathing suit in his backpack, and in a minute they were in the pool, swimming back and forth, laughing and splashing. Cobb wandered over to the house, which had a veranda shaded by woven mats of palm-leaves. There were two other moldies lying slack in the sun, and a few Tongans were sitting in the shade, some of them playing cards. Phil counted four big men and two women. All of them were staring, but Phil did his best to ignore them.

"It's beautiful here," said Phil, taking in the house, the palms, the ocean, the blue sky. "Whose is it?"

"It's the King's," said Yoke. "He's turned it over to me. I'm really important all of a sudden. Thanks to the aliens. You showed up just in time. I was starting to get lonely."

The jewel-like beetle that had been sitting on Yoke was buzzing around overhead. "*That's* an alien?" said Phil, pointing at it.

"Greetings, Phil," said the beetle, settling down to float on the water's surface. "I am Josef." His six legs twitched, sending off tiny ripples. "A Metamartian."

"Cobb claims you can see the future?" asked Phil. "Okay, what number am I thinking of? Between one and ten."

"You have not yet made a decision," said Josef. He had an odd, Germanic accent. "You are wavering between three, five, and seven. But now that I have given you this information, you are narrowing in on—"

"Four!" said Phil and Josef at the same time.

"Do you require further proof?" said Josef. "Try if you can touch me."

Phil reached out with his finger, but no matter how rapidly or abruptly he moved it, the little Josef was always where the finger wasn't. The beetle wasn't darting around or anything, he was just drifting this way and that, his legs mildly kicking. He had a preternatural gift of doing a zig whenever Phil did a zag.

"So I've got Josef's precognition going for me," said Yoke proudly. "*And* I've got a magic alla. Each of the aliens has one of these inside their body."

Phil had noticed that Yoke had a shimmering gold cylinder in a mesh pouch dangling from her waist. Yoke got out the alla and held it in her hand. "I'll turn some water into air," said Yoke. "Actualize!" There was a bluish glow underwater, and right away a big bubble came surging up out of the pool. *Fomp*.

"Like a fart in a bathtub," said Phil, not quite sure what was going on. The glow had looked like a spherical mesh of lines. "Do it again?"

"Yeah!" said Yoke. "But now I'll make a bubble of hydrogen and oxygen. And I'll put in a spark so it explodes!"

"Not so big!" warned Josef, buzzing back into the air. "Not too near! Remember that the alla's transmutation zone does not need to be immediately adjacent to the alla."

Yoke said "Actualize" again, and a bright glow appeared beneath the water at the far end of the pool, followed by a sudden, concussive jolt. Phil could feel the shock of the explosion all up and down his legs. A dome of water shot several feet up into the air.

"Yaaar!" said Phil. "How are you doing that, really?"

"Ready for another blast?" said Yoke.

"The housekeeper is going to come and scold you," said Josef, hovering fretfully above them.

"Do it, Yoke," said Phil.

Another explosive *fomp* and, sure enough, a glossy-haired Tongan woman appeared at the poolside.

"Don't you be cracking my pool, Yoke. And who is this man?"

"This is my friend Phil," said Yoke. "And Phil, this is Ms. Teta. Can you make up a room for Phil, Ms. Teta?"

"HRH doesn't want anyone here but you and me and the cook and the guards. The alla is supposed to be top secret."

"Yeah, and the King tells someone new every time he turns around. I'm not a prisoner! That was the deal. I can have a guest if I want to."

"I'll ask Kennit."

"Here's some more gold," said Yoke. She paddled to the water's edge and held her alla out over the patio. "Actualize twenty-five gold coins." A shimmering cylinder appeared near one end of the tube. The cylinder filled with a pattern like ghostly marmalade and then a pile of twenty-five gold coins fell jingling to the stone. Phil felt a little puff of breeze.

"This is too good to last," said Ms. Teta, stooping to scoop up the coins. "This is making me most uneasy."

"I could give some gold to Kennit too," said Yoke.

"He won't take it," said Ms. Teta. "Kennit is an upright man. Would you like some breakfast, Phil?"

"Sure."

"I'll tell the cook."

"Oh, let me make it with the alla," said Yoke. "It's more exciting."

"The devil's food," said Ms. Teta, shaking her head. "I don't know how this is going to end."

Yoke and Phil dried off and sat down at the little wicker table. Yoke grasped the alla and made, in succession, a hot cup of coffee, a sourdough roll, a ramekin of honey, and two halves of a papaya. The bread was a bit dense, but on the whole it was remarkably good.

"All right," said Phil, chewing. "Explain."

"I don't know how it works," said Yoke. "It's like magic. The alla has this virtual catalog that I can see in my uvvy. The aliens gave me that too. I pick something from the catalog and the alla makes it when I say 'Actualize.' "

"But you don't have to think of every detail of each thing?" asked Phil. "The molecules of the coffee, the air bubbles in the bread, the sugar-crystals in the honey?"

"No," said Yoke. "The aliens already programmed all that. But I think I can put the alla-catalog materials together in new ways. I haven't really tried that yet. I might be able to make some very complicated things, like by designing a program to put things together. That's a type of problem I enjoy. How to simulate Nature." Yoke nibbled at a slice of the papaya. "This is good. I've never had papaya before."

"But it's in the catalog?"

"Josef and Ptah said they made the catalog based on all the things they could find on the Web. First they figured out the materials, and then they figured out the things we make with them. A lot of research. The alla catalog combines all the existing human mail-order catalogs into one."

"Right," said the beetle, who was perched on the edge of the honey, dipping in his little legs. "While we were waiting for Yoke, I programmed a complete set of Earthly substances into the catalog. All of the chemistry and materials science that we could find on your Web. The formulae of molecules, the structures of crystals, the linkages of polymers, things like that. And then Ptah generated macros for essentially all human objects which are manufactured from these materials. Anything that's ever been advertised for sale is now free in our alla catalog. Ptah even ferreted out the limpware designs for the special DIMs that come in so many products. As Yoke said, our alla catalog incorporates the contents of virtually every human product catalog in existence. A big job—but remember that we're superhuman."

"How does the alla work?" asked Phil.

"With Om's power, it transmutes one kind of atom into another," said Josef. "And then it links together the atoms as specified. The breakfast you eat is of transmuted air."

"Air?" said Phil, hefting his coffee mug.

"A cubic meter of air has the mass of one kilogram," said Josef. "This is well-known. Air is very freely available."

"Can I have some avocado?" asked Phil. "With prosciutto and Emmenthaler cheese?"

"Yes," said Yoke, after a second. "I can find all of them. I'll make a special plate." She cocked her head and looked inward, then moved her lips and—*whoosh*—there was a fancy china plate with slices of Swiss cheese, prosciutto, and delicate sections of avocado. The topper was that the plate itself was glazed with a photographically accurate image of Phil: mussed, blond-haired, unshaven, smiling, bewildered, and with a palm tree in the background. Yoke leaned forward, admiring the plate. "That's exactly how you look to me right now, Phil. It came out perfect! It's the first alla thing I've really designed myself. My first piece of original realware!"

"Realware," mused Phil. "You can make anything you can imagine. What's going to happen if everyone gets an alla? Nobody will work anymore. They'll all have everything they need. What will people do with themselves?"

"Oh, one keeps doing things anyway," said Josef. "Even after one's material needs are filled, one wants to bloom and to create. Grow or die—it's in the nature of things. And don't forget that if one does something interesting, one has a better chance of having sex with a desirable partner."

"But even if I were to make something wonderful with an alla, something like a new kind of blimp maybe, then everyone could copy it," protested Phil.

"Ah, but only if they have the exact design," said Josef. "Remember that only what is in the public catalogs is free for everyone. If you invent something that has more to it than meets the eye, then you have the possibility to sell your invention's design to the individual alla owners."

"Can the alla make living things?" interrupted Yoke.

"It can," said Josef. "Haven't you noticed yet? There's a large section of plants and animals in your catalog. You can customize them to a limited extent—keeping in mind that reprogramming the wetware of a living biological system is difficult. Everything must be at extreme synchronization. Living systems embody a very deep fractal density of information patterns."

"And can the alla make a person?" pressed Yoke. "I'd like to make a new copy of my mother."

"The allas don't 'copy' things," said Josef. "They actualize instances of objects that have been completely specified in the catalog software or in user descriptions. To make a fresh instance of your mother, you would need an accurate representation of both her body and mind. Just knowing her DNA and having an S-cube personality backup aren't sufficient. So, no, your alla cannot make your mother without some further programming that is quite beyond your means."

"But it *could* make a person if it had the code?" pressed Yoke.

"Yes," allowed Josef. "And I may as well tell you, Yoke, that during registration your alla did in fact create and store an eidetic map of your body and mind. But Om doesn't allow an alla-owner to arbitrarily use this code. There is no magic command for instant self-reproduction. In order to use an alla to reproduce oneself, it's necessary to understand the working of one mind and body well enough to fully specify the design."

"And I guess you guys are at that high level already, huh?" said Yoke.

"In our first meeting, you have observed how Ptah copied himself," said Josef.

"Oh, right," said Yoke. "Well, let me try making an animal." She knit her brows and looked inward at her uvvy catalog. "Actualize." A scrap of space webbed over with bright lines, grew opaque, and a small writhing object fell to the tabletop.

"A slug?" said Phil. The slug oriented itself and began briskly sliming into the shadow under one of the plates.

"I'll try a jellyfish next," said Yoke. "They're so beautiful." She used the alla to create a little aquarium, then projected into the water a bright-line disk-shape that actualized into a clear bell of jelly—which began steadily beating. "Can I change its color?" wondered Yoke, and produced a shocking pink jelly-fish—which quickly dissolved into rags and tatters. She tried a series of variations on the catalog jellyfish, but none of them so much as twitched.

"Life is hard, Yoke," said Josef. "And so is wetware engineering."

The unsuccessful customized jellies were floating on the aquarium's surface. Yoke alla-converted them back into water and filled the tank with a selection of other standard catalog life: some more jellies, a shrimp, a clam, a scallop, and a few tropical fish.

"Can the alla make an alla?" asked Phil. "That's the biggest question of all, isn't it? Like in the fairy tale where someone wishes for more wishes."

"Yes," said Josef. "There is a way to use an alla to make another alla. And sooner or later one of you will learn the trick of it. But I am not intending to be the one to teach you. It is better that the knowledge should come to one of you directly from Om."

"Do you plan to give out more allas?" asked Yoke.

"As Om wills it," said Josef. "First we want to watch a bit what Yoke does. And then we'll test it with a few more individuals. And then I suppose Om will tell you how to spread the allas to everyone, human and moldie alike. I think it should work out for the best, but it's hard to be sure. We've never seen a place like Earth, you know. You can't imagine how really pathetic your one-dimensional time appears. I hope that the allas can really help you."

"Hoes for the savages," said Yoke. "Farming tools. What's in it for Om?"

"Om collects copies of sentient beings," said Josef. "By giving out allas and having the users register themselves, Om obtains the exact information codes of the users. As for your analogy to farming, perhaps an alla is more like a bulldozer than like a hoe. Restraint and caution will be called for. Especially for a race that's limited to a single dimension of time."

"You think there's a chance we'll kill ourselves off with the allas, don't you?" said Yoke. "Is that what you actually want? So that the Metamartians can take over the Earth?"

"Yoke, we already told you that we plan only for one more of us Metamartians to arrive here," said Josef. "Once we are seven, we will have reached the canonical family size. We'll conjugate to create a fresh Metamartian and then we'll move on—provided we can figure out the right direction toward a region with two-dimensional time. No Metamartian would want to stay here."

"We still haven't talked about the killer powerballs," interrupted Phil. "What's the story with them?"

"The powerballs are but manifestations of our god Om," said Josef. "Be assured that Om is no killer. Those whom Om touches are elevated, not destroyed."

Before they could press Josef any further, a large Tongan man came walking over from the veranda. He wore a white shirt, a necktie, and a blue skirt. He was squinting in the bright sun.

"Hi, Kennit," said Yoke. "This is my friend Phil. I want him to stay here with us."

"Yis," said Kennit. "I've just been in contact with HRH and he has no problem. Would you be willing to have Phil stay in your room? That way we won't have to wonder which shell conceals the pea."

"All right," said Yoke, looking down at the ground. She'd been making lizards and mice and rabbits. They were darting around under the table. On top of the table she'd alla-made a cheerful potted orchid. "The room has two beds. Can I make you anything with the alla, Kennit?"

"No thank you. HRH says the Tongan Navy ship will be arriving in the harbor today. We would like you to fill its hold with gold and imipolex during the night. Will this be agreeable?"

"Can we do it, Josef?" asked Yoke. "Does the alla have enough energy?"

"Quark-flipping is like jujitsu," said Josef. "As if to look at something and then to look at it in a different way. In and of itself, it costs nothing to interconvert protons and neutrons. But, yes, reassembling particles into different sorts of atoms can either create or absorb energy, even if one uses higher-dimensional shortcuts. Om acts as kind of bank for these transformations. Energies flow back and forth through the higher-dimensional vortex threads which connect Om to the allas."

"It sounds too good to be true," said Phil.

"Consider this: 'The world exists.' I think that also sounds too good to be true," said Josef. "Why is there something instead of nothing? Why is Om? We are only lucky."

"I want to take Phil snorkeling now," said Yoke. "All right?"

"Yis," said Kennit. "But if you should meet anyone, don't be showing off the alla. We don't want our people to become overly excited. Would Phil like to use Tashtego or Daggoo?"

"I only want to swim with a facemask today," said Yoke. "I don't want to bring along any strange moldies. Just Phil and Josef and Cobb and me. Cobb can protect us."

Ms. Teta found two sets of swim-fins, snorkels, and masks. Yoke and Phil walked down the steep steps to the water, followed by Cobb. Josef rode clamped to the strap of Yoke's bikini. The Tongans weren't interested in swimming. And the moldies Tashtego and Daggoo were content to remain puddled atop the island in the sun.

Phil and Yoke slipped into the water together, while Cobb and Josef swam off on their own. Phil felt as if he'd been transported to heaven. The bottom was white sand, and the water incredibly clear. The knobs of small coral heads dotted the bottom, each head surrounded by a school of luscious-colored fish. There were fluttering sea anemones as well, huge irregular pink ones quite unlike the small door-stop sea anemones of California. Striped clown fish idled in the tentacles of the anemones, darting forward as if to greet Phil—though when he looked closer, he saw that their smiling faces were split to reveal tiny rows of teeth. Far from greeting him, they were defiantly defending their turf.

Here and there on the bottom were giant clams, meter-wide behemoths with great, crenellated shells. They rested partly open, with the shell gap revealing an incredible fleshy mantle that was differently colored on each clam: some blue, some green, some purple, all of them wonderfully iridescent.

Rising up off the shell of one giant clam was a bumpy staghorn coral. The clam and coral made a marvelous, unbalanced composition, something nobody would ever think of designing, yet something with a beautiful inner logic. One single fish lived in the branches of the coral. Phil's soul overflowed like a wineglass in a waterfall. How to contain so much beauty?

He followed Yoke to perch on a big coral head, catching his breath.

"This is paradise, Yoke."

"Yes," said Yoke. "It's good to share this with you." They kissed again, this time much longer than before.

For the next forty-five minutes they paddled around, chatting and getting to know each other better. The more Phil talked with Yoke, the more he liked her.

Like Phil, Yoke was into being clean and sober. And she shared Phil's contempt for conventional goals. "It's like society wants you to be a machine," was how Yoke put it. "Programmed to ignore everything besides the one thing they use to control you. Money or clothes or drugs or group approval. People don't see that the real world is all that matters." But unlike Phil, Yoke's contempt for society made her invigorated, not paralyzed. "There are so many things I want to do."

"When I wake up each morning, I always think it's going to be a nice day," said Phil. "That's my basic take. Instead of thinking that I have to do something to make the day be good. It's already perfect. I don't have to do anything at all. In fact if I do anything, I'm likely to fuck up."

"Oh no, Phil," said Yoke. "We have to work on the world. It isn't perfect at all. What about the news on the uvvy?"

"Well of course I never watch news," said Phil. "News, commercials, mass entertainment—they're all the same. Buy and eat and shit and buy again."

"Yeah, all the ways to avoid being aware," said Yoke. "It's crazy. You think it's bad here, you should see the Moon. There's so much virtual reality there. On Earth you've got more Nature."

"Most people ignore Nature," said Phil. "Except for worrying about weather disasters. But, hey, we shouldn't be talking about 'most people.' That's a trap too. My goal is not to get sucked into anything. Just hang back and stay calm. I don't have to fix anything but myself. The rest of the xoxxin' world can xoxx itself some more."

They were standing in waist-deep water. Yoke splashed her face to reset herself. "I love the surface of the water, how the reflections make darker and lighter blues where it undulates. All this analog computation for free."

Phil accepted the change of subject and they looked at the water for a while. Now and then he glanced up at the island. Sometimes Kennit or another guard would be looking down at them, but not always.

Phil and Yoke waded over to the island's narrow beach to rest, out of sight from the people above. Cobb flopped down on the beach a little ways off to sun himself, and Josef busied himself crawling around at the edge of the water, investigating tiny forms of sea life. Yoke used her alla to make them a bottle of fresh water.

"This alla is such a powerful thing," said Yoke, passing Phil the bottle. "With some practice I could use it to model almost anything."

"Go beyond the catalog?"

"Yeah. The alla is the ultimate tool. I think I told you before that I'm into figuring out algorithms for natural processes, Phil? Like a coral reef. That would be so wavy to figure out how to grow one. The individual polyps swimming around and landing. I could make one with real coral polyps, and I could make another with imipolex DIM polyps. Sort of like the worms and fabricants that Babs Mooney designs. And, God, there's so much

I can do with plants. What a sea of bioinformation there is on Mother Earth." Yoke smiled, lost in happy thought.

"Speaking of Babs, I'm a little worried about that Randy Karl Tucker staying with her," said Phil after a while. "Right before I left, Randy was bragging to me that he was going to get Babs some leech-DIMs."

"That would be bad news," said Yoke. "But I know Randy a little. He talks tough, but he means well. Usually." She smiled at Phil and stroked his hand. "What's your dream of what you'd like to do? Own a restaurant?"

"No ambitions, no goals," said Phil. "I just want life hassle-free. No, I can't see running a restaurant. Feeding hungry cranky greedy people every day? Why? I guess deep down I feel like there should be something important I could do, but I don't know what it is. I'm scared there isn't anything at all. I did have these pet blimps I was really into. Kind of stupid."

"You were going to show them to me, but—"

"Kevvie," Phil winced. "Yeah, I built the blimps myself. You don't see many big blimps around because they're slow and they don't always go where you expect them to. Helium's pretty cheap, even without the allas. The real problem with blimps is that the wind blows them around. I keep thinking I might invent some way to beat the wind. And then maybe I could go into business selling my blimps. But I know that sounds dumb. Like all my ideas."

"No, it sounds floatin'," laughed Yoke. They kissed for a while, then got up and stretched. The sun was getting too hot.

"What now?" said Phil. "Go back up?"

"I think we should sneak off," said Yoke. "It bothers me for them to think they've got us trapped here."

"Where would you want to go?" asked Phil.

"Anywhere. I don't like the idea of spending the rest of the day sitting around that house with two maids and four body-guards watching me. This trip is my vacation. I want to look at Neiafu. Hey, Cobb, Josef, come over here."

Hearing Yoke's call, the two came over.

"Could you fly us over to Neiafu?" Yoke asked Cobb.

"They'd see," said Cobb, pointing upward. "Tashtego and Daggoo would come after us. I don't want to get in a fight with them. They're mean motherfuckers."

"We could go underwater like a submarine," suggested Phil.

"They could still see us," said Cobb. "This water's really clear. I'm sure they're watching that we don't move away from the island."

"They will not see you if you are not where they look," said Josef. "And this is what I know how to do."

So Cobb stretched himself thin enough to wrap around Yoke and Phil, with Josef on the inside with them too. Josef hooked into their uvvy connection and gave them a view of his odd way of seeing things.

Normally when Phil would imagine the future, he'd see a single mental movie of himself going ahead and doing something. But now, thanks to Josef, he was seeing his immediate future as—oh, a mansion with many rooms. In some of the rooms Tashtego and Daggoo zoomed down on Cobb and rousted them, but in a few of the rooms Cobb swam on undisturbed.

They zigzagged across the harbor from coral head to coral head. At one tricky point, Josef's vision showed them as apprehended in all the futures but one. So they picked the one, which meant that Cobb suddenly dove down to the bottom of the water and burrowed into the mud. A bit later the futures started opening up again. Cobb swam in close to the shore and lurked beneath one of the docks of Neiafu until there came a moment when nobody was looking that way.

Cobb disgorged Yoke and Phil, who scrambled onto the dock. Yoke used her alla to quickly make them some bland shorts and T-shirts. She and Phil walked up the dock's gangplank to Vava'u, looking like ordinary yachties come ashore for a bit of sightseeing. Cobb waited in the water, and Josef hung from Yoke's earlobe like a cunning gem.

They looked at the few small, utterly nontouristy stores,

closed for Sunday. Canned food, rope, straw fans, rubber thongs, pieces of cloth. The early afternoon sun was quite hot. A few Tongans walked slowly by, polite and handsome, dressed in their best clothes. Last night Kennit had told them that church could be an all-day proposition in Tonga. Phil could hear a congregation's voices lifted in song somewhere off in the distance.

"Let's go in here," said Yoke, indicating a small, blue-painted wood building: the Bounty Bar. They sat down by a window; at the next table were two tipsy wharf-rats, one a dark-skinned Fijian, one a pale New Zealander. Yoke ordered ice cream and Phil had a Coke.

"Listen," whispered Yoke after a minute. "They're talking about Onar!"

"Typical American, a loudmouth, always bragging," the New Zealand Kiwi was saying. "A real name-dropper, mentioned HRH. He was asking what's the most valuable and marketable element, pound for pound. What would you guess, Nuku?"

"Hundred dollar bills!" said the Fijian.

"Oh that's no good, you silly bugger. Every bank note has a DIM in it; each and every one of them is registered with the gimmie like a pedigreed dog. You can't just make up serial numbers for bills that don't exist. I said what's the most valuable *element*, meaning primitive chemical substance, don't you know."

"Carbon!" said the Fijian. "In the form of a very big, very beautiful diamond."

The Kiwi made a negative, fishlike face. "Bottom's dropping right out of the diamond market, it is. I hear Mbanje DeGroot's selling a bulk nanomanipulator that makes the price curve linear instead of exponential. No, my friend, the top four elements are rhodium, platinum, gold, and palladium. The market for palladium and rhodium's a bit thin and illiquid, and platinum's a shade high-profile. I told Onar that gold's the best bet. Metals are safe from all that nanotech fiddling, don't you know. There's no way to convert one kind of element into another, is there?"

"How about black people eating white people?" The Fijian grinned, showing his sharp teeth. And then their next round of drinks arrived.

"So where *is* Onar?" Phil asked Yoke.

"Well!" said Yoke. "When Cobb and I came up from meeting the aliens at the bottom of the ocean, I suddenly realized that I didn't have to deal with Onar anymore. I mean, here he'd gotten me to do something really dangerous, and like why? I don't owe anything to him. He was trying to get me to give him the alla, and I was all 'Go to hell.' " Yoke paused and looked at Phil round-eyed over a spoonful of vanilla ice cream.

"And then?"

"Cobb and I ditched Onar and flew back to Nuku'alofa. But I still wanted to look around Tonga, you wave. I mean I came here to do some diving. And I guess Onar uvvied the King, because the King called me up and said he'd let me use his island in the Vava'u harbor if I'd please just use my alla to make him some gold and imipolex. So I'm like why not. But it's not working out well. I might have to bail on Tonga pretty soon."

"Back to San Francisco?" asked Phil. "I just got here. The ticket cost a lot. There's still so much for us to do and see."

"Maybe back to the Moon," said Yoke. "I should show the alla to my family and friends back there. It's such a radical change. Too big to discuss on the uvvy. But you're right, Phil, I'd like to enjoy Tonga some more with you."

"If you leave, please take us with," said Josef out loud, his little voice deep and strong.

"I don't know about that," said Yoke. "Six aliens? Where's your new node anyway?"

"Oh, it's on Vava'u," said Josef. "Somewhere."

On the way out, Phil and Yoke asked the cashier about the local sights.

"You might like the singing at the church up the road that way," said the woman behind the counter "But that walk's all in the sun. And they're nearly done. If you go the other way it's shady, and in a mile you come to Mount Talau."

"How tall is Talau?" asked Phil.

"One hundred thirty-one meters," said the woman proudly.

"I can handle that," said Yoke.

They walked along under strange tropical trees, trees like Phil had never seen before: some with ferny leaves and masses of orange blossoms, some with purple flowers, some with doughy-looking trunks. Josef kept quiet, letting them enjoy themselves. They walked by a school and many little houses. The road petered out and became a dirt track. They passed a stripped, rusted-out car with a solemn goat standing inside it. A little farther on, a muddy trail led up a steep hill: Mount Talau. They scrambled to the top; there were a lot of trees up there and a bit of a view. The great open sea. They kissed for a while. Phil loved the smell and feel of Yoke. And her bold eyes. Looking around the hilltop, Phil found a giant bean pod hanging down from a tendril that vanished up above into some high trees.

"That's a *serious* bean," said Yoke. It was a lovely pale green and nearly three feet long.

Phil tried to snap the bean loose. He twisted the fibrous vine, bent it back and forth, but it wouldn't give. Finally he chewed the tough stem in two. The bean had a wonderful curve to it, and it bulged out in seven great pouches around its hidden seeds. It was like a bean in a fairy tale or a comic strip. Phil and Yoke laughed about it a lot.

On the walk back down, Josef suddenly told them to duck around behind one of the native's houses. Peeking around the corner, Phil saw a bronze moldie go racing by, running up the road on foot. He was a shaped like a muscular man, though he was wearing a woman's red bikini.

"Tashtego," breathed Yoke.

"*Malo e lelei*," said a voice behind them. It was an old man walking across the yard from another house. His shirt had several buttons missing, many of his teeth were missing as well, and he was carrying a small aluminum tub holding a big fillet of fish. He struck up a conversation with Phil and Yoke, talking about his sister in California. His name was Lata. Phil asked Lata about the bean he'd found.

"*Lofa* bean," Lata told him. "If you wait and pick when it's ripe, you can use the seeds for—dancing."

"I think he means castanets," said Yoke, clicking her fingers.

Lata invited Phil and Yoke into his house to look at his seashells. They took off their shoes, sat on his couch, and Lata brought out his trove, a little plastic bag containing shells wrapped in paper. The shells looked shiny and well-loved, as if the old man had gathered them and admired them over many years.

"Take some," he offered. "As many as you like."

"Oh no," said Phil at first, but soon it was clear that it would be rude to refuse the hospitality. Yoke picked out a big whelk, two brown cowries, and two tooth cowries.

"Right now is the good time to be walking back down," said Josef, using the uvvy this time. So they started saying good-bye.

"That was so touching, him offering us his treasure," said Phil back out in the shady street. Lata was still on his porch, kindly watching them. "Maybe you should make him something with the alla, Yoke."

"HRH said none of the Tongans is supposed to know," said Yoke.

"Look, you can do what you like, Yoke. See that rusty old bicycle leaning against Lata's house? Why not make him a nice new one? Make it out of titanium. Give it a basket and a bell."

"What do you think, Josef?" asked Yoke.

"I am content to observe," said the beetle.

"I'll do it," said Yoke, and took hold of her alla. She turned her back to Lata as if to hide the miracle—though it was kind of hard for someone not to notice a brand new bicycle being formed out of a shimmering web of magical air. In making the bike, Yoke tweaked the stored realware so that the frame had anodized gold cowry-shell patterns on top of the titanium. She wheeled the beautiful bicycle across the little yard and presented it to the old man. He accepted the gift with joy and dignity. In the grand scheme of things, a bicycle was, after all, a fitting exchange for his shells.

When they were halfway back to Neiafu, Lata rode past them, jingling his bell. And then things started to go crazy. Somehow everyone in every house they passed had heard of their miraculous gift. Men, women, and children streamed out, mostly in good Sunday clothes, offering presents. Shells, flowers, woven mats, even cans of beans and meat. It became hard to move forward. Just to get the people to back off, Yoke recklessly popped a dozen bouncy kickballs out of her alla, each with a different pattern, followed by gallons and gallons of ice cream. But the people were clamoring for something really good. Yoke made some gold bracelets and then—the biggest crowd-pleaser of all—a score of brand-new uvvies. Many of the Tongans didn't have uvvies yet.

By the time they got back to the harbor, a full-blown mob was squeezing in on them. Someone tried to grab Phil's lofa bean, but he hung onto it. He thought to uvvy for Cobb, and the old pheezer moldie came surging out of the ocean like Neptune come to rescue his children. Yoke created three dogs, who came into existence wildly barking—clearing out some space for Cobb. Cobb wrapped his arms around them and shot up into the air. But now Tashtego and Daggoo were homing in on them.

"Josef's gone!" Yoke exclaimed, touching her ear. "I don't know how to escape them, Cobb!"

Cobb dove down into the harbor water. He covered them over and fed them air. But now here were the coppery Tashtego and big black Daggoo, clamping tight bands around Cobb, Yoke, and Phil. The five of them swam back to the island together, staying beneath the surface so it wouldn't be easy for the agitated locals to pursue them. Phil still had his lofa bean and Yoke still had her shells.

"I hear you've started a riot in Neiafu," Kennit said frowning when they arrived. "On the Lord's day. You have done exactly what you were forbidden."

"So?" said Yoke. "What are you going to do about it?" And to that Kennit had nothing to say. Nobody quite knew how to deal with Yoke's defiance.

"The ship is going to be a day late," said Kennit finally. "We'll be asking you to create the imipolex tomorrow morning." And that was that.

Phil and Yoke had supper with the Tongans at a long table on the veranda, real Tongan food prepared by Ms. Teta. Fish, taro, and squash. Kennit didn't seem to carry any kind of grudge, and the other Tongans were friendly as well. They enjoyed teaching Phil and Yoke things about Tonga—the history, customs, geography, and language.

While they talked and ate, Cobb was hanging out with Tashtego and Daggoo off at the edge of the clearing. Despite old Cobb's misgivings about the Tongan moldies, the three of them seemed to be getting along very well. Indeed, from their hoarse cackles, it seemed likely that one of them had brought along some betty.

Soon it was full night, with an incredible clear sky. Phil was intoxicated by the stars, the full moon, and Yoke's low voice. And then it was time to go to bed.

"Now I am *not* going to do it with you tonight," said Yoke as they closed the door to her room. "I want that clear. I don't want to make a mistake and rush things. So no pushing, okay?"

"That's fine," said Phil. "I'm just happy to be with you, Yoke. We have plenty of time—I hope."

Phil took a shower and put on boxer shorts and a T-shirt for pajamas. Yoke was in a nightgown, sitting at a table playing with her alla. She'd just made a big rough prism of green glass with little whorled bubbles in it. The glass sat on one fat edge, rising up maybe ten inches. It had some funny little peek-through windows cut into it. The glass was smooth on one side, nubby on the other; it was something that Phil's hands instinctively longed to touch. He reached out to caress it.

"It's beautiful, Yoke."

"Thanks. This alla—it's the ultimate art tool. I can make

anything that I can think." She closed her eyes, looking inward. A control mesh of bright lines formed above the tabletop, a foot-wide knot of twisting curves. There was a whoosh of air, and a ribbon of smooth metal formed inside the cube, a Möbius strip with comical hieroglyphics of ants embossed all along it. Yoke cocked her head, critically examining her creation.

"Did you know we have ants on the Moon, Phil? They snuck up there. I should have made these guys thicker."

"Can't you revise it?" Phil asked. "My housemate Derek, he says that his sculptures do half the work themselves. Like he's talking with them. He keeps looking at what he's made and changing it. I do that with cooking too. Taste it, spice it, taste it, spice it."

"Good idea," said Yoke. She popped the same shimmering bright-edged control mesh out and positioned it around the ant Möbius strip which she then—*whomp*—turned back into air. Now she made the ant-shapes in the glowing mesh bulge out a bit more and said, "Actualize." The Möbius strip was back, but with its ants much more swollen, bulging out of the metal ribbon into high relief. "Yes," said Yoke, setting down the alla. "Thanks, Phil."

"Can I try using the alla now?"

"Shimmer said nobody can use this alla but me," said Yoke possessively.

"She's not here watching us, is she? Come on, Yoke, let me try."

"Don't break it." Yoke handed Phil the little gold-colored tube. It sat in Phil's hand, subtly flickering. Phil held it up and looked through it—and saw a dizzying view of the room eternally spinning.

"It's like staring down through a tornado," he said. "How do I make it do something?"

"You have to uvvy into it," said Yoke.

Phil tried, but the alla gave no response.

"I guess it's registered only to respond to my uvvy signals," said Yoke. "You'll have to uvvy to me and I'll pass your signals to the alla."

Phil tried for a minute to organize this connection but he couldn't do it.

"I hate this software bullshit," he muttered.

"Let me," said Yoke, and in an instant she had herself hooked in as an intermediary between Phil and the alla.

"Hello," the alla seemed to say in a squeaky cartoon voice inside Phil's head. It displayed an image of something that wasn't anything in particular: an amorphous gray glob, roughly spherical, floating against a white background.

"Think your target to me," said the alla voice.

Phil could think of nothing better than that he'd forgotten his toothbrush. The gray glob elongated itself and grew bristles at one end. Its color and dimensions remained—indeterminate. At the slightest push of Phil's velleity, the specific features of the toothbrush warped this way and that.

"Really sensitive, huh?" said Yoke.

"It's like I'm exploring toothbrush space," said Phil, finding more and more qualities to vary. Tuft stiffness, handle bend, transparency, bristle density—it wasn't like he was fully imagining the toothbrushes himself, it was more like surfing through an incredibly vast multidimensional online mother of all catalogs.

"Try and actualize one," said Yoke. "It might work."

"I want that one," said Phil to the alla, and a mental image of an excellent green toothbrush froze in place. "No wait, let me personalize it." With a special effort of will, Phil stamped his name on the image's handle and filliped its tip with a nonstandard kink. "Now make that sucker for me, little alla. Actualize."

But nothing happened. Wish as he might, Phil couldn't force the magical lines of bright mesh to appear.

"I guess I have to say it," said Yoke.

"That is correct," squeaked the alla. "I allow only one registered user."

"So actualize the toothbrush already," said Yoke, and Phil's toothbrush dropped into his lap.

Phil handed the alla back to Yoke, who quickly returned to revising her two sculptures. Popping out the old mesh, dissolving the existing version, adjusting the mesh, and making a new one. "The alla remembers the exact format of each of the things I've actualized," said Yoke. "So it's easy to keep changing them." She adjusted the bends of the metal loop, and shaved bits off the curved sides of the big glass prism.

Phil set his lofa bean down next to Yoke's sculptures and tried to get her to admire it some more. He didn't like for the alla to be getting all the attention. The bean was something remarkable that he himself had found. "What a beautiful green color our lofa bean is, Yoke." Yoke was tired of talking about the bean, but Phil kept on trying to riff on it, trying to get Yoke to look at him. "Could it be the larva of an alien centipede? The bean's vine was hanging right down out of the sky. *Jack and the Beanstalk!* What if it splits open and eats my brain tonight, Yoke?"

"It would get a small meal!" laughed Yoke. "Just kidding. I like your brain, Phil." She set down the alla, slipped into her bed and turned out the light.

"Good night, Yoke," said Phil, getting into his own bed. "It was a great day."

"I'm glad you're here, Phil. And, um, what I said when we closed the door—I didn't mean that you can't kiss me good night."

February 23

Phil dreamed about his father again, but when he woke Monday morning, the details faded out of his memory. Outside there were voices on the veranda, one particularly annoying voice the loudest: Onar Anders, saying something about tea, about the best way to make it.

Phil looked over at Yoke's bed; it was empty, the flipped-back sheets a gentle outline of her slender frame. And the lofa bean? It was sitting quietly on the night table, green and vegetal.

Phil put on the shorts Yoke had made him and a clean dark blue silk sport shirt that he found in the closet. It was quite a large shirt, patterned with suns and stars; perhaps it belonged to the King. Outside it was already mid-morning. Clear sky and a gentle breeze. Yoke, Onar, and the four Tongan bodyguards were at the long table on the veranda drinking tea and coffee. Cobb was also present, but Tashtego and Daggoo weren't around.

"*Ecce homo*," said Onar. He was wearing a white yachting cap with gold braid and a stiff bill. "Behold the man. Welcome to Tonga, Phil. Glad to see you could get some time off from your menial job."

"Xoxx you, Onar. Hi, Yoke. Man, I slept well. You've got a great room, Yoke. I found this nice shirt in the closet. What's happening?"

"The Tongan Navy ship finally got here," said Yoke. "I'm supposed to fill it up with goodies for the King. I like that shirt on you, Phil. It's—heavenly."

"Royal duds," said Phil, flapping the great garment. "Is filling up the ship going to take us long?"

"Well, I'll be making the gold and imipolex in slugs small enough for people to carry. So I'll have to make a lot of them. It might be a couple of hours. Do you want to watch?"

"I'm sorry, but Phil can't come aboard the navy ship," interrupted Onar. "Security, don't you know."

"Bullshit," said Yoke.

"HRH insists," said Onar. "And he promises not to lecture you about what you did in Neiafu yesterday. Some of the locals even took pictures of you, but thanks to the ID virus, all the images show Sue Miller. You can still be anonymous and keep your alla, Yoke. We've done all this for you. Be a sport, and help us. It's thanks to the King that you met the aliens and got the alla in the first place."

"What do you think?" Yoke asked Phil.

"Whatever you say," Phil answered, feeling himself slide into his old passivity. "I'll miss you, but I can keep myself entertained. I could do some snorkeling maybe. Or go to Neiafu and see what's down the road in the other direction. If you think you'll be safe."

"I'll bring Cobb along for protection," said Yoke. "And that's final, Onar."

"Let me check," said Onar, and silently consulted the uvvy he was wearing on the back of his neck. "Jolly good," he said a minute later. "Ms. Yoke Starr-Mydol and her moldie Cobb are cordially invited aboard His Royal Highness's flagship. Shall we go down to the launch? If you like, Phil, we can drop you off at Neiafu."

To avoid the danger of the locals coming after Yoke again, the launch dropped Phil at a deserted private dock rather than at the main Neiafu dock. Phil waved as the launch sped out to the big Tongan Navy ship floating in the harbor. Little Yoke. Maybe he should have insisted on sticking with her. But Phil knew he wasn't good at arguing. Oh well.

Phil strolled up to the main road and turned right. He passed a few locals. They all smiled and nodded, recognizing him, but there was nothing like the excitement of yesterday. Evidently everyone knew that although Yoke was the Queen of the Alla, he was only her Prince Consort. Nothing special.

Phil was intrigued by the thin black pigs he saw everywhere. All of the Tongans' houses were dirty on the outside from the pigs rubbing themselves on the walls. He tried to pet one or two of the pigs, but they were extremely wary. And some had tusks.

As he continued to walk, the houses gave way to trees and fields. In one field he noticed a hut as primitive as any he'd ever imagined—what the Tongans called a "fale." It had palm-trunk posts holding up a roof of palm fronds. The walls were woven matting, with a big gap in place of a door. Sitting on the ground in front of the house were the loveliest people Phil had ever seen, a man and a woman, the woman with a baby at her breast, the three of them looking supremely content. They noticed Phil, but didn't bother to wave. The Edenic family made

Phil think of Adam and Eve. Would it really be a step forward for them to have an alla?

He walked on and came to a field with a low wall around it. Within the enclosure were long mounds of gravel decorated with colorful patterns of pebbles and shells. The dimensions of the mounds and the faint odor of corruption told Phil this was a graveyard. A thin young woman with a pack of children was working on one of the graves; she was sweeping it with a stick broom and burning the rubbish in a small fire. Seeing Phil look at her, the woman made a gesture he hadn't seen before. She held her hand palm up, slightly cupped, with the fingers stiff and outspread, and then flipped the hand down toward him, a bit as if sowing seed. The gesture definitely meant "go away" rather than "come here." Could an alla have saved the life of the person whose grave she was tending? But why bother? thought Phil. There's always more people, and everyone has to die.

Phil's easy, callous thought stumbled over a fresh burst of grief for his father. There were always more people, but no more of Da. He'd been a jerk, but Phil missed him. Dead forever. Life was short. Phil wondered how Yoke was doing on the King's ship. Maybe he'd uvvy her in a little bit.

Now Phil came to a little village, a cluster of fales. Beyond the village was a low hill, and beyond that the ocean. Phil decided to walk through the village to the water. As he walked past the fales, a group of children came after him, shouting and laughing, three or four girls and a boy. "*Palangi*," they called him, which Kennit had said was Tongan for both "ghost" and "white person."

Phil asked the children to catch a piglet so he could pet it, but they wouldn't. Perhaps they were afraid of the tusks. The boy, about four, had fun poking at Phil's back with a long and disturbingly sharp stick. The girls asked Phil's name and had him spell it for them and then they danced around him saying, "Phil, Phil, Phil." Defining him here. It felt like being awake inside a dream. The border between life and dream seemed so elastic these days.

When he got to the top of the rise, the children went back to their fales, and Phil picked his way down to the rocky beach alone. Brittle sea stars were everywhere on the shallowly covered stones, striped snaky things, most with two or three arms in a hidey-hole and the other arms lashing about. Thank you, God, thought Phil as he looked at the calm waves coming in. Thank you for making the world.

Something nudged his leg. A pig?

"Yo, Phil," said the black pig. "I'm Wubwub. Hate to tell you, man, but I'm the brother what turned Om onto your Da. I found the wowos on the Web and told Om the news. But maybe there's a way you can help yo' da come back, you know what I'm sayin'? C'mon in here, see our new node."

The pig trotted down the beach and disappeared into a hole in the rocks, seemingly an entrance to a cave. Phil came along into the dark holding out his hands so as not to bump his head. The passageway twisted a bit; there was light ahead—and the rank smell of moldie flesh. Phil followed Wubwub around a last turn and found himself in a well-lit rocky grotto the size of a room. Six figures were in there; most prominent was a pale, nude woman—the famous Shimmer! In addition to her and Wubwub the pig, there was a handsome bronzed man named Ptah, the blonde unicorn Peg, a thick serpent called Siss, and Josef the beetle. All of them had moldie bodies.

"Good day, Phil," said Josef. "I present you the other Meta-martians."

"What are you guys really doing here?" asked Phil when the introductions were done. "What are you after?"

"We're like tourists on a road-trip," said Shimmer. "Except that we're never going home." She looked like a soft Greek sculpture, like Venus. Phil would have liked to touch her. "Like so many others, our race evolved to the point where we scattered out into the cosmos as personality waves, a bit like cosmic rays. It's rare that there's a—a 'radio' that can 'play' us. But we have an endless amount of time. Sooner or later one always gets lucky. Last November, as you must have heard, Willy Taze and the loonie moldies found a way to decrypt a number of extra-terrestrial beings into imipolex bodies."

"It was a disaster," said Phil. Though Shimmer's voice was mesmerizing in its musicality and beauty, Phil found himself wanting to argue with her. "One of you destroyed the Moon's spaceport. Hundreds of people died."

"Yes," said Shimmer curtly. She seemed to have adopted a beautiful woman's high self-regard and low patience. "But the single warlike alien who ran amok was no Metamartian. All of the *peaceful* extraterrestrials were indiscriminately murdered by humans—under the leadership of Darla Starr. I alone escaped. And it was I who eliminated the last vestige of that single warlike alien. But I don't ask for your gratitude—no more than you would seek praise from an ant. Or from a bacterium."

"We understand why y'all fought back," put in Wubwub. "But we be good guys, know what I'm sayin'?"

"I still don't get what you're doing here," said Phil.

"I said that we're tourists," said Shimmer. "But it would be better to call us nomads. We live in transit, and whenever we can, we form a little family and mate. Yes, whenever one of us manages to incorporate somewhere, we immediately try and build up a family of seven of our fellows. Bringing in more Metamartians is what I've been doing for the last few months, Phil, as you can see. There's six of us now, and soon we'll be seven. Seven provides the ideal resonance for reproduction, among other things."

"A bunch of nomads looking to get laid, huh?" said Phil. "Didn't I hear Josef say something about helping Om? You're really missionaries, aren't you?"

"Missionaries?" laughed Shimmer. "Every traveler is a kind of missionary, no? But, yes, it's true that our god Om follows us wherever we go. And, yes, we do help Om to give allas to the civilizations we discover. It's win-win. The alla-registration pro-cess allows Om to obtain software copies of the individuals who accept her gift—and everyone *does* accept. Receiving the power of the alla is the greatest gift a being can have. So now you know a Metamartian's entire agenda. First, to find a world where one can decrypt; second, to assemble a family of seven; third, to spread Om's allas; and fourth, to move on. There needn't be any problems at all when Earth is visited by the right *kind* of extraterrestrial, you see."

"What about my father getting killed?"

"We'll get to that in a minute," said Shimmer, the music of her voice gone a bit dissonant. "Can you please stop interrupting? I want to fill you in on what I've been up to, all right? Just very briefly. I flew from the Moon to the Earth and I made a deal with the King of Tonga to use his Cappy Jane satellite as an antenna to find some good personality waves. I picked up Ptah's signal first and then Peg, Wubwub, Siss, and Josef. And of course soon after I was decrypted, Om asked for a local being to examine. For my birth offering, if you will."

"Om is what you call the powerball, right?" said Phil. "Can you explain what happened when it got my father?"

" 'She,' not 'it,' " said the bronze Ptah. His body echoed Shimmer's perfection of human form. "Om is the God of Metamars. She lives in the higher dimensions. Our race first reached a working relationship with her some thousand of your years ago. Some other aliens brought her to us. Om lives outside of ordinary space and time. Whenever one of Om's people travels somewhere, a manifestation of Om comes there as well. Our god follows us. She can appear in various guises, but most commonly she shows herself as a four-dimensional hypersphere."

"Four-dimensional?" murmured Phil uneasily. He sensed the imminence of a batshit math-rap, bound to make him feel dumb.

"*Jawohl*," boomed the German-accented Josef. He was perched on Shimmer's lovely shoulder. "I am taking this question. Although I feel that Om is surely of an infinite dimensionality, she usually enters space as a powerball. Her surface is a bounded region of three-dimensional space that has no edges:

a hypersphere. Do understand that the fourth dimension of space is not to be confused with any dimension of time. If you doggedly wish to refer to your time as *the* fourth dimension, then the powerball can of course be called five-dimensional. But it makes an easier manner of speech to use 'the fourth dimension' for the extra dimension of space."

"I'm not going to touch that one," said Phil, momentarily distracted from finding out about his father. "Let me ask this instead. If Om can jump all around the cosmos, why do you travel as personality waves? Why not just ask Om to take you where you want to go?"

"We never know where we going in first place," said Siss. "What we do is to chirp into personality wave, let wave travel to place where it get decrypted into body, to find family there, to teach about Om, and then to chirp further. Travel is our way."

"But what does Om want?" asked Phil. "Why did she swallow up Ptah and my father?"

"Om is curious about everything," said Josef. "Your father caught her interest with his wowo display. Om thought this was a very interesting patterning of space. So one supposes that she had a curiosity to get a better acquaintance with your father. She could perhaps return him to the world at some time. As for why she ate the original Ptah—Ptah?"

"Om wished to see what kind of body a Metamartian on Earth might occupy, so one of us was selected," said Ptah. "The trip into hyperspace was painful for my original self, yes, but it was an honor. Om chose me at Josef's suggestion; Josef knows I come from the noblest Metamartian stock. The little beetle says he admires me—and I suspect that he envies me as well. His choice only heightens my glory. All must recognize that it was I, Ptah, who once led the most harmonious weave of lives in our two-dimensional time, and it is I, Ptah, who has been the first to travel from Earth to the bosom of Om."

"Well-spoken, Ptah," said Peg. The unicorn had a contralto voice and a theatrical way of talking. "Isn't it droll how one chains one's words together here? Like threading pearls upon a necklace. Phil wots not that the Metamartian mode of speech is as a fractally branching fan."

"Yadda yadda yadda," said Phil. "Why do you have to keep jabbering about math?"

"When she talk about a fan, she mean Metamars be in a place where time spreads out nice and fat," said Wubwub comfortably. "Like it supposed to be. In fat time, no one thing really matters, know what I'm sayin'? It's grim and down to live the way you do, Phil. One poor little time thread all by its lonely self. You folks deserve to have the allas."

"You said it was your fault the powerball killed my father," Phil said to the pig. "Tell me more about what happened!"

"He ain't dead," said Wubwub. "You got dirt in your ears, my man? Your daddy's in hyperspace. When Om sweep through your space it like someone's hand scoopin' up a water-strider bug. One second the bug on the water, second later it on the back of the hand. One second your Daddy in bed, next second he on Om's powerball. He probably just kickin' it. Om's powerball got light and air, and a built-in alla for food."

"My father's alive?" exclaimed Phil, finally getting it. As when Jane had uvvied him with the news of Kurt's disappearance, he felt a dissonant mixture of emotions. Joy that his father could be saved. Relief that the old man's forgiveness could still be obtained. An impatient weariness at having to deal with him all over again. And a primal horror of meeting the undead. "Up in hyperspace?"

"It's called 'ana,'" said Ptah. "Not 'up'. We've investigated your scientific literature, and 'ana' and 'kata' are the names of the directions of the fourth dimension."

"I know that," sighed Phil. "My father was a math teacher. I've been dreaming about him a lot. Do you think Om can affect my dreams?"

"I no know," hissed Siss. "Metamartians have no dream, Phil. Metamartians live in endless parallel worlds—no need dream world. Wubwub right, most likely your father alive, and is together with a few others Om take."

"Like my original self," said Ptah.

"And two women," said Wubwub. "Yes indeed. First thing Om did was scoop up that juicy Darla. Yoke's ma. Om got old Tempest too—and, let's see, got Tempest's dog, a toy moldie, and part of an oak tree. How I be so wise? Each time one of us get corporated here, Om ask the new Metamartian what be the most stuzzadelic sample she might scoop up. Om always do that. Likes to see the world through a spang fresh eye, know what I'm sayin'?"

"Would you like each of us to tell our story?" asked Siss.

"Not really," replied Phil. He felt dizzy and confused. Surely they were lying about Da. "I have to think about what you told me. It's too wiggly. I want to go back out onto the beach."

"Oh tarry in our sea cave just a bit longer," said Peg. She was in fact standing so as to block the passage where Phil had entered. Her horn, though red and swilly, was also quite sharp and long. "What does your poet say? 'Till human voices wake us and we drown.' Marvelous beads of meaning, each just so." She lowered the horn and fixed Phil with her great blue eyes. "Phil, you should harken to our tales while there's time."

"I'll tell first," said Shimmer, "Attention, please!" She drew herself up and laid her hand stagily upon her breast. "*My* powerball swallowed a miniature moldie from Willy Taze's isopod. What they call a Silly Putter; it's like a doll or a pet. Between a DIM and a moldie. This particular one was named Humpty-Dumpty. It happened to be the first living thing I laid eyes on—at least I thought it was alive—so I pointed it out to Om."

"And then Shimmer made me tell Om that—" began Ptah.

"The way you got here was as a copy of the original Ptah," Shimmer interrupted Ptah. "You didn't tell the powerball anything. So I'll tell the original Ptah's story." She cleared her throat, struck a new pose and continued talking. "When I decrypted Ptah, I was down in the ocean and there really wasn't much of anything around for Ptah to tell Om's powerball to

swallow. Ptah may think he's perfect, but he's not all that creative. So I suggested that Ptah tell Om to get Darla Starr on the
Moon. Space doesn't mean much to Om, she can spang out a
powerball wherever she wants. She's our god on Metamars, and
now we're way across the cosmos, but as soon as one of us is
born, why there's Om to greet us. Om can go anywhere. Praise
Om."

"Praise Om," murmured the other Metamartians comfortably.

"Why eat Darla?" asked Phil.

"Why Darla?" said Shimmer. "You might jump to the con-
clusion that I was angry with Darla for trying to kill me. But of
course no human could ever hurt a Metamartian anyway. And
I really wasn't angry. That's not a Metamartian emotion at all.
I just thought that Darla was the fiercest, most interesting human I'd seen so far. Yes. I was torn between suggesting her and
Stahn Mooney, as a matter of fact, but Darla seemed more spirited. And you don't have to look so impatient, Ptah, because
now I'm done. Peg?"

"When I was reborn on Earth, Om asked me what was interesting, and I knew not what to say," said the unicorn. "She
showed me that she already had Humpty-Dumpty and Darla.
Within our sea-dome I could only see Shimmer, Ptah, and the
grass. I humbly asked Om what she herself longed to behold
next. Om granted me the image of something she had seen in
Darla's room, a merry shape yclept a 'wowo.' Om coveted a
wowo. So I hastened to enter your Web, where I sought the
bravest wowo in creation. This wowo of all wowos I found upon
the greensward of a woman named Starshine, in the hamlet of
Santa Cruz, California. And thither did I direct Om's gaze. It
came about that Starshine's aunt, a crone named Tempest
Plenty, was tilling the earth there in the company of a dog
named Planet. Joyful at the girth of the wowo, Om took so bosky
a powerball scoop that she snared those two as well as the wowo
prize. I've told my tell, let Wubwub speak as well."

"Now Om just fascinate with that wowo; she asked me to

find the brainiac what dream it up," said the black pig. "And that be Phil's dad. So Om done gobble down Kurt Gottner and half of his wiener-dog Friedl—I say *half* because that wiener-dog fuss so much she got pinched in two. Old Kurt's hand got rotorvated as well, and the space-waves knotted his wedding ring, which leads straight into the next tale, you know what I'm sayin', Siss?"

"Om not really ask me what to do either," sang the pale green snake. "She already decide to go flip Kurt's ring to make another sign and see if any humans get excite. I do give her small idea to swallow some of oak tree so she can find out about plant."

"I'm last," said the iridescent beetle Josef. "And I told Om to swallow Ptah. It was time for her to take one of us, so why not the most perfect?" There was perhaps a hint of sarcasm in his voice.

"Who you think be next?" Wubwub asked Phil. "We wonderin' 'cause we 'bout ready to decrypt Metamartian number seven. And like we been tellin' you, every time there someone new, Om celebrate by eatin' something."

"Don't do it!" cried Phil. "She might get Yoke!"

"Cappy Jane has a nice new Metamartian personality wave prepared for us to incorporate, Phil," said Shimmer. "We're not about to waste it. It's important that there finally be seven of us. A complete family." The bland sweetness of her voice sent chills down his neck. "Sit back and watch."

Phil shoved Peg's horn to one side and tried to push his way past her into the passage, but Wubwub nudged the backs of Phil's knees in just the right way to make him fall down. Siss the snake was on the ground to cushion his fall—and to wrap herself around him.

Lying on his back, Phil noticed for the first time that the light in the cavern was coming from a small hole up above, a hole that opened to the sky.

Shimmer used her body's internal alla to project a bright-line cube that actualized itself into a knee-high block of imipolex. "All right, Cappy Jane," called Shimmer. "Beam it down." Some signal must have come to her from the satellite then, for as Shimmer laid her gracious hands upon the cube of plastic, the stuff began to twist and writhe. A figure formed and rose up in the shape of a man-sized bird, a black and white Indian mynah bird with yellow feet and a great yellow beak. Its dark head was decorated with a pattern of yellow feathers that made it look as if it were wearing a burglar's mask.

The mynah cocked its head and stared at them with its bright, inhuman eye. It made a preliminary cawing noise that sounded almost like "Hello." Phil felt like the bird was about to peck him. "Let me go!" he cried, struggling against Siss's tight coils.

"Not yet," said the snake. "We no want you go shit crazy."

Shimmer must have uvvied some information to the mynah, for now its demeanor grew less blank, a subtle effect achieved by a softening of the lines of its beak.

"Good afternoon," said the giant mynah. It cawed to clear its throat, whistled a few musical notes, listened to the echoes, and spoke again. "Something's badly wrong here, isn't it?"

"We're in a land with but one line of time," said Peg, gesturing with her red horn. "This is all there is. Seek as you will, you'll find no other time but the short woven threads of brief ghost futures. Praise Om that you've come, for now we are seven and soon we can mate."

"Who—Who is seeing this for real?" asked the mynah, tentatively stretching out its wings. "Why this very one thread?"

"Ain't got no notion," said Wubwub. "Could be the Light do it. What you gonna use for a name, mynah bird?"

"Call me Haresh," said the mynah. "An Indian name. I find it most oppressive here. It is jolly good that we are seven. We'll help Om, and mate, and then we'll chirp further." The bird twitched his head as if hearing something. "Om is speaking to me. It is almost time for her manifestation. I must pick something. She has already swallowed a Metamartian?"

"Yes," said Ptah. "Me. So don't do that again."

"This here is a 'human,' " said Wubwub, using his snout to nudge Phil's foot. "Om got three of those already, but might be she want some more."

"How soon is the powerball going to spang out?" asked Phil anxiously. "That's the word you use, right? 'Spang.' Floaty word. You guys are so brilliant. Let me go, Siss!"

"Not till powerball come," said Siss. "Om still looking things over, waiting for Haresh form some impressions of world. Since we see little bit of future, we going know just before Om decide. But until then very hard to guess what she going to do. Om follow odd kind of logic. Odd for you, not quite so odd for us. Logic of higher dimensions. Like human dream maybe."

Siss kept chattering, and Phil had a bad feeling about what she was getting at. He kept thinking about the sequence of what Om's powerballs had swallowed so far: a toy Humpty-Dumpty moldie near Shimmer on the Moon; Darla near a wowo on the Moon; Tempest Plenty and Planet and a big wowo in Santa Cruz; Kurt Gottner and part of Friedl in Palo Alto; half an oak tree near Kurt's ring in Palo Alto; Ptah; and—

"Yes, she going to take you, Phil," said Siss, suddenly slackening her coils. "Run."

"Praise Om," said Peg. "She calls Phil to be with his father."

"Don't wrassle with her, Phil," said Wubwub as Phil got to his feet. "If you wrassle Om, you end up like that wiener-dog, know what I'm sayin'? When Om come, you just ball yourself up and let her gulp you down. Look out fo' the churnin' when she break free."

"Will it hurt?"

"I think very much," said Siss. "Run, Phil, run! I no want powerball come near me."

"Thanks for nothing," snarled Phil, aiming a kick at Siss but—of course—the prescient snake flipped her body to where Phil's foot wasn't.

"You have but two more minutes," said Peg. "Pray use them nobly."

So Phil walked out of the cave to the beach and sat hunkered there, staring at the blank sky and the eternal waves, no different than before. And now he would probably die. So this is how it happens, thought Phil. It's not really so hard. Part of him felt weary, paralyzed, and almost glad.

But there was another Phil that knew he hadn't really started to live yet. He called Yoke on his uvvy. She picked up almost immediately. "Phil?" Behind her Phil could see laboring Tongan sailors and the great open hold of a ship. Vaana and the King were there as well.

"Hi, Yoke. The powerball is about to get me. I'm on the beach at the other end of the island. The aliens are holed up in a cave here. They just decrypted a new Metamartian, and Om's going to celebrate by swallowing me."

"Oh noooo!" Yoke's face bunched up and she burst into tears.

"I love you, Yoke."

"Don't die!"

"The Metamartians claim I won't be dead. That I'll be in a bubble in hyperspace. But I—I don't really believe it. The fourth dimension is bullshit. I'm just glad I met you, Yoke. I always said my life was good, but it wasn't really until I met you. At least we had one day together." Phil thought he saw something flickering out over the water. An isolated glint of strange perspective. "It's coming for me, whatever it is. And, Yoke, it was definitely Om that got Darla. Shimmer told her to. Stay away from the Metamartians, or they might kill you too."

"Wait, Phil, wait. How is it that you might not die?"

"Some crufty math fabulation. I'll find my way back if there's a way. Here it comes."

"I'll wait for you in San Francisco."

"I love you."

The powerball came in across the water, low down at Phil's level, flying straight at him. Phil braced himself, wrapping his arms tight around his knees. The powerball looked like a big, glowing crystal ball, reflecting and refracting light, though not so smooth as a glass ball, perhaps a bit more like a drop of water.

As it drew closer there was an odd effect on the rest of the world: things seemed to melt and warp, distorting themselves away from the magic ball.

Closer and closer it came, yet taking an oddly long time to actually arrive. It was as if the space between Phil and the ball were stretching nearly as fast as the ball could approach. The ball was like a hole opening up in the world. Everything was being pushed aside by it; the sky and waves were being squeezed out along its edges.

Phil looked back over his shoulder; there was still a little zone of normality behind him—the nearest section of the rocky cliffs looked much the same. But so strong was the space warping of the powerball that the beach to the left and right seemed to bend away from him and, as Phil watched, this effect grew more pronounced. In a few moments it was as if Phil stood out on the tip of a little finger of reality, with the glowing powerball's hyperspace squeezing in on every side. Back there at the other end of the finger, back in the world, Wubwub and Shimmer were peeking out of their cave entrance watching him, the cowards. He fought down an urge to run at them, and forced himself to turn back to face the engulfing ball. What could he see within the ball? Nothing but funhouse mirror reflections of himself: jiggling pink patches of his skin against a blue background filled with moons and stars—his shirt.

And then, like a mighty wave breaking, the warped zone moved over Phil. He felt a deep shock of pain throughout his body, as if something were pulling and stretching at his insides. His lungs, his stomach, his muscles, his brain—every tissue burned with agony.

"Phil! Phil!"

Phil didn't dare turn; he felt as if the slightest motion might tear his innards in two. But, peering from his pain-wracked eyes, he realized there was no need to turn, for with the powerball centered on him, his view of the world had changed. The entire world was squeezed into a tiny ball that seemed to float a few feet away from him like a spherical mirror the size of a dinner plate. And there in the little toy world, like animated figurines, were Cobb and Yoke. Running toward him. Phil instinctively reached out towards them but—*swish*—something flashed past his fingers like an invisible scythe. And then—*pop*—the little bubble that had been the normal world winked out of view, and Phil was alone in the hypersphere of the powerball.

Phil's guts snapped back to normal; the pain and its after-image faded. He found himself comfortably floating within an empty, well-lit space that contained glowing air, his body and seemingly nothing else. The Metamartians had been right, up to a point, but where were the others that had been swallowed? When the powerball finished examining him, would he dissolve?

"Hello?" called Phil. "Om?" No answer.

The space bent back on itself so that Phil saw nothing in any direction but endless warped barbershop images of himself, of his sunburned hairy limbs and his billowing shirt's blue field of moons and stars.

Phil remembered one of his father's stories about A Square stuck to the surface of the sphere, with all of his A Square light-rays traveling along great circles of the sphere's surface as well. In every direction, A Square sees only himself. Here in the hypersphere of the powerball, Phil could see the back of his own head, the blond hair shaggier than he'd realized. He wondered if he'd meet Da soon.

Since there were no other objects in the space with Phil, it was hard to tell if he could really move. But after a while he noticed that the space wasn't completely uniform. There was one particular spot up ahead where the images of himself were always fractured. He wanted to go over and look at this little flaw, but at first he couldn't think of any way to move. Finally it occurred to him to throw one of his shoes over his shoulder. Sure enough, the shoe-toss set him drifting forward in the direction of the flaw. Just as he got within arm's length of the special spot, his shoe came tumbling toward his face—the shoe had traveled clear around the little hypersphere of the power-ball. Phil moved his head to one side, and the shoe grazed his shoulder, which slowed his forward motion.

He stretched out his hand toward the flawed region. As his fingers entered the crooked space they disappeared. Phil convulsively pulled his hand back; there was no damage to it. He felt into the flaw again and wiggled his fingers. An odd sensation: his fingers couldn't find his thumb, and his thumb couldn't find his fingers. Just then the shoe came orbiting past again and caught him full in the chest. He drifted away from the anomalous spot with, *whew*, all of his fingers still intact.

A little later Phil started being hungry and thirsty. He wondered how long he'd been in here. He consulted his uvvy for the time, but its clock was stuck at 11:37 A.M.—presumably it hadn't received any update signals since he entered the power-ball. He made a halfhearted attempt to make an uvvy call to Yoke, but as he'd expected, it didn't work. Any signals he could send would circle around and around his hypersphere just like the rays of light. But then he noticed something new in the uvvy. It was showing him just the kind of amorphous mental image he'd seen when he tried to use Yoke's alla. It seemed as if Om had a built-in alla he could use!

Phil tried to nudge the alla catalog's grayish start-up image into a representation of food. But Om's catalog for this alla wasn't for humans, it was for aliens—presumably for Meta-martians? Though he was trying for the image of an apple, he ended up with a representation of a spiky red leathery thing that was—what? The alla catalog was multisensory, so Phil took a virtual sniff of the possible fruit; it had a faintly acrid odor, but maybe that was just the smell of the rind. Phil said, "Actualize." He wasn't sure if anything would happen; after all, Yoke's alla had refused to obey anyone but Yoke. But the powerball's intrinsic alla seemed willing to work for him. A brightly outlined alla mesh formed and—*whoosh*—the spiky pouch became real.

When Phil hungrily pulled one of the spikes loose, sick yellow cream dribbled out of the rip in the tough red skin, stinging his hand. A reek like ammonia assaulted his eyes and nose. Phil focused in on his uvvy and wished very hard for the alien pod to disappear. To his relief, an alla mesh formed around the fruit and it reverted to air, taking most of the corrosive smell with it. Maybe he wasn't hungry yet after all.

He gave up on food and wandered about in the mental maze of the alien alla catalog, marveling at wonderful baubles and bizarre forms. He even actualized three of the objects for himself.

First, there was something resembling a little pearl-handled pocketknife, but when he folded out the single "blade," it revealed itself as a waving broom of tiny metallic tentacles, each of them subtly articulated. Resisting the temptation to touch the metal fuzz, Phil folded it back away and pocketed the object.

Second, he actualized a golf-ball-sized sphere that resembled perhaps a goldfish bowl with luminous fish in it. Not that they were really fish; they were more like plankton. The little globe was velvety black with bright, glowing globules and disks within. The odd thing about the globe was that its image kept changing according to subtle cues that Phil could barely tell he was giving. Every time he moved his head, the bright little creatures inside the globe would swim to one side or the other. And every time he focused on one particular little denizen of the bowl, that "fish" would seem to swell up in size, and all the others would rush away from it.

Third, Phil picked from the catalog a necklace with a single large gem that seemed to embody an endless variety of possible formations. It was a ruby, emerald, diamond, sapphire — all of these, one after the other, and more. Not only did the gem's color change, the cut of its shape kept shifting as well. It was gorgeous. Phil vowed that if he ever saw Yoke again, he'd give it to her.

Though Phil still wasn't ready to try tackling any more alien food, he was getting seriously thirsty. He found his way to a part of the Metamartian alla catalog that seemed to be devoted to beverages. Using the uvvy's virtual odor feature to avoid drinks that smelled like gasoline or acetone, he was eventually able to actualize something that seemed to be a flagon of water.

Carefully he tasted of it, and it was indeed plain water, so he drank it down, then used the alla to turn the empty flagon back into air.

Phil looked around the alla catalog a little more, trying to figure out the appearance of the Metamartians in their home world—if indeed the catalog was for Metamartians and not for some completely different kind of alien. He couldn't find any pictures of intended users of the catalog, but he did stumble across an area with what seemed to be clothes. The aliens seemed to wear loose robes or caftans, things with a head hole and two arm holes. There was nothing like trousers and nothing like shoes.

After a while Phil tired of exploring the alla catalog, and he simply hung there doing nothing, looking back on his life. What had he made of his twenty-four years on Earth? He'd survived childhood, his parents' divorce, his overbearing father. He'd gone to UC Berkeley for two years, but when he was twenty he'd gotten sick of jumping through the hoops. The hoops weren't his, they were society's and his father's. Bogus. He'd dropped out, getting a series of kitchen jobs, eventually becoming the assistant chef for a top restaurant. Big whoop.

One other accomplishment was that he had stayed Straight Edge: clean and sober. But what else had he ever done? Was it really enough to be serene and balanced? Da certainly didn't think so. And deep down, Phil wasn't really so serene. Deep down he was frightened.

It would be nice to have a family and children someday; the worst mistake he had made along those lines was to hook up with Kevvie. At least that was over. And he'd almost had a chance at Yoke. But now his life was apparently done.

Phil let himself imagine what he might do if he got a second chance. Hang onto Yoke for sure. And what else? Stay sober, yeah. Cook for a day-job, but maybe finally try and move on. Dare to express himself. With blimps? Who could tell? Could be that now he'd never know. Phil sighed, making an effort to free himself of self-pity. He said a simple prayer: "God, please help me."

Usually a prayer like this would dissolve out into the glowing aether of the great buzzing world-mind. Phil would feel the better for it, but there wouldn't be any obvious response. It was just something he did, choosing to act as if there were a God who cared. The occasional prayers helped Phil keep his thinking clear enough to stay sober. He murmured the prayer again, felt more centered, and dozed off.

He hadn't slept for long when his prayer seemed to get a very literal answer. The hypersphere began talking to him. "So you're ready to move on?" came a rich, thrilling voice, the voice of Om. "Here we go." A dream: But then Phil woke to the sound of a *pop* near his feet.

When he looked down he saw a tiny ball with some people in it. Was he coming back to Earth? The little ball grew up toward him very fast, and as it engulfed him, there was another stretching sensation in his viscera, though not quite so violent or prolonged as before. And then the queasy pain was over. But Phil wasn't back to Earth. He was still in a hypersphere, only it was six or seven times bigger than before. Phil's hypersphere and a larger hypersphere had joined together like a pair of soap bubbles merging. Like two fingers of Om's "hand."

The new space smelled of dog, moldie, sweat, and alcohol. It held half an oak tree, and perched in the tree were a bony crone in overalls and a plump, nude matron. There was a big bright wowo, an egg-shaped moldie, and an orange and white collie-beagle dog as well, the egg with a colorful belt — or cravat? — around his middle. But all this was just a flash in the background, for right up in Phil's face was none other than —

"Da!"

"Phil! Oh no, you can't end up here too! Your poor mother." Phil's naked father gestured awkwardly. His left hand ended in a scabbed stump. "I'm scared about what comes next."

Phil spoke the biggest thing in his mind. "I'm sorry I was mean to you the last time we talked, Da."

"Oh hell, I started it by picking on you. What you said to me was nothing. I wouldn't have taken it so hard if I hadn't been drinking. Of course I forgive you! But, hey, you can't very well say the fourth dimension's bullshit anymore, can you?" There was alcohol on the old man's breath.

"Your poor hand," said Phil. "Jane says your wedding ring is already proof of the fourth dimension."

"What do you mean?" asked Kurt.

"You didn't know? When this ball chopped off your hand, your wedding ring got knotted. And then later it flipped into its mirror image."

"Gnarly!" Kurt looked ruefully at his stump. "It's healing up really well. Maybe it's like the way a corpse's fingernails grow fast. Old Tempest helped with it a lot. Let me introduce you. Darla, Tempest! This is my son!"

The two women scrambled closer through the oak tree, which provided a handy method of moving around in the hypersphere. Though Darla was nude and a bit overweight, she seemed unembarrassed about it. She had a wound on her foot; it looked like one of her toes was missing. Tempest was a lively old woman in overalls. She was carrying a half-empty squeeze-bag of wine. The woman greeted Phil with avid interest. Clearly everyone in here was getting cabin fever.

"Your old man's been telling me about you," said Darla. She talked like a hipster. "That's wavy that you've got alky-junky genes. I can really relate. And hats off for being Straight Edge. I'm gonna clean up too one of these days. Kurt and I were thinking it could be stuzzy if you met one of my daughters."

"I did meet Yoke," said Phil. "At Da's funeral. She came with Tre and Terri Dietz. In fact I was just now visiting her in Tonga."

"My funeral!" interrupted Da, totally into himself as usual. "Was it big?"

"I think I dreamed about you asking me this," said Phil.

"And maybe I dreamed about me asking you," said Kurt. "I've been having crazy, lucid dreams in here. It seems the whale talks to Jonah." He looked around, a bit wild-eyed. "I think this hypersphere is alive, and it comes into my brain when I'm sleeping. But now we're awake. Tell me about my funeral!"

So Phil told his father all about it. The part Da liked the best was how Phil had buried the ashes by the oak tree.

"You're a good son to have done that. I bet some of the ashes were Friedl's. That dog." He gestured at the great twisted trunk with its branches and dead leaves. "So this is our special tree? Small world."

"Too dang small," said Tempest in her Florida cracker accent. "Can I finally get past howdy and ask some questions? I happen to know Darla's Yoke too, Phil. Just before this here ball done gobble me up, I was a-visitin' my niece Starshine in Santa Cruz while Yoke was a-stayin' with Starshine's neighbor. You sweet on that little Yoke, Phil? She's a honey. Smart as a whip too."

"I like her a lot," said Phil. "We were about to have a really great time in Tonga."

"What's Tonga?" asked Darla.

Darla was so nude and female and voluptuous that Phil was embarrassed to look directly at her—but Da was staring at her all the time. And now Da put his arm around her waist as if to steady her. Gross.

"Tonga's a cannibal island," said Tempest. "Don't you know nothing, Darla? Go on, Phil. Tell about you and Yoke in Tonga. Were you two shacked up?"

"Back off!" said Phil, desperate to change the subject. This was turning into real torture. And there was no way to escape. Desperately he fixed his eyes on the hypersphere's other two occupants. "You got a dog and a Silly Putter in here?"

"That's Planet and Humpty-Dumpty," said Tempest. "Planet's my good boy. Come here, Planet, come to Auntie Tempest." Clumsily the dog clawed his way through the branches of the oak tree, finally losing his footing and flying through the air to bump into Phil, tongue and tail wagging. Phil and the dog drifted around the whole hypersphere, coming to rest back at the splintered base of the oak tree with the others.

"What were you and Yoke doing in Tonga?" asked Darla as soon as Phil caught his breath.

"We've only just met," said Phil. "We were getting to know each other, and snorkeling, but then I ran into Shimmer and some other Metamartians."

"Metamartians?" spat Darla. "Is that what they call themselves?"

"Shouldn't there be one of them in here with us?" asked Phil, continually avoiding looking at Darla. "A Metamartian named Ptah?"

"Darla and me done chased his ass outta here!" cackled Tempest. "I got the magic wisher to make us some grain alcohol to set him on fire." She patted the uvvy on the back of her neck. Phil noticed that Da and Darla didn't have uvvies. They'd both been abducted at night. "Couldn't catch him nohow," continued Tempest, "but he got so sick of it that he done took off out the hole. P-tah said p-fuck it!"

"There's a hole up there where you can stick your head out," explained Da, pointing toward the other end of the tree. "Into raw hyperspace. Very creepy."

"You said you dreamed this hypersphere talks to you," said Phil. "Does she call herself—"

"Om," said Kurt, just as Phil said it too. "Yes, she calls herself Om."

"The Metamartians call her that," said Phil. "She's their god. Wherever they go, Om comes too. She scooped you up because she was curious about the wowo."

"So it's true?" said Kurt. "I hadn't been sure. Om only talks to me when I'm dreaming. But it's slow going because I'm always drunk. Hard to think logically. The shock. I keep thinking we're all dead."

"Pass around the wine, Tempest," said Darla. "It's time for a drink."

"I'm half in a bag already, Phil," said Kurt apologetically. "I should explain that we've been partying hard. Tempest figured out how to make wine. Well, it's similar to wine, anyway. We've been drinking enough of it."

"Could you make me some food?" asked Phil. His stomach was rumbling. "I haven't figured out how to find it."

"These things are tolerable good," said old Tempest. She made a gesture and a bright alla mesh pattern formed to whoosh out a big crisp golden shape, fat in the middle and pointed at both ends. Phil nibbled at it. It seemed to be something like a deep fried sweet potato. Fibrous, oily, not too bad. He took a big bite, and then another and—*crunch*—hit something like a vein of wiggly cartilage.

"Like a rubber bone in there, huh?" said Tempest. "Reminds me of a hog snout."

Phil peered at the greasy object he'd been eating. "What is it?"

"Hell if I know," said Tempest. "I call it a yam-snoot. You should of seen some of the other vittles we tried. Alien food, I guess." She took a pull from her sack of liquid and tried passing it to Phil. "Hope you ain't a tight-ass, Phil," she said as he refused the sack.

"No, no," said Phil, though his heart sank at the thought of being in here with three drunk pheezers. "Da, tell me more about that hole?"

"It's a kind a flaw, a place where the space of this sphere has an edge. According to my reasoning, when you stick your head out there, your head is in four-dimensional hyperspace. I've only tried it for a few seconds. It's cold and you have to keep coming back for breath. And there's this freaky light. I wouldn't try it, Phil. But if, God forbid, you do stick your head through the hole, be very sure to hang onto the tree so the rest of you doesn't slide out." Da squirted a stream of wine into his mouth, and then some into Darla's. A rivulet dribbled down her chin and onto her big breasts. "Don't stare at us like that, Phil.

I know I shouldn't be getting fucked up, but I'm far enough into this run that I've got to finish. After I sleep it off, I'll get myself together and we'll talk about our chances of getting you back to Earth."

"Hey, Da!" said Phil. "This is xoxxed. Can I at least make you and Darla some çlothes?"

"Oh bless his heart," cackled Tempest. "Hear that Darla?" Darla responded by striking a coy pose with one hand over her crotch and one over her boobs. Phil realized she was quite drunk.

He quickly found the clothing area of Om's Metamartian catalog and actualized two of the colorful loose caftans. He made Darla one with a pattern of unearthly biological shapes that might have been purple flowers; Da got one with flickering red shapes like flames. The fabric was some unknown material that was slippery but not sticky. A bit like silk, but with no sign of threads.

"Give me one too," said Tempest. "A blue one."

"All right," said Phil, and made Tempest a Metamartian robe that resembled a waterfall. "I'm outta here for now, losers."

He pulled himself toward the other end of the oak tree, pausing to study the glowing holographic knot of the oversize wowo. It was a roughly doughnut-shaped pattern of steadily changing mathematical curves and surfaces. Tre Dietz may have turned off all the wowos he'd sold, but he hadn't been able to reach this one. It was going strong. Phil liked to think a wowo looked a little like a glass pelican continually crawling farther and farther up its own butt, while at the same time emerging from its own beak, somehow changing into its own mirror image in the process. Mind-boggling and gnarly.

Phil proceeded onward to the other end of the tree. The toy Humpty-Dumpty was sitting there, clamped onto a branch like an owl. Phil gave him a gentle poke, and the egg smiled ingratiatingly. A low husky laugh floated up from Darla at the other end of the tree. Fortunately there were enough dead leaves between them that Phil didn't have to see what the old folks were doing.

Just as Kurt had said, right beyond the end of the tree was a flawed spot like Phil had seen in his own little hypersphere. He took a deep breath and stuck his head through it.

CHAPTER FOUR

YOKE

━━
━━ ■ ━━
━━

February 23

After dropping Phil at the dock in Neiafu, the navy motorboat ferried Yoke, Cobb, Onar, and Kennit to a big aluminum ship anchored in the harbor. The flagship of the Tongan Navy. Its rounded lines made Yoke think of a beer keg. Amidships was a tower of cabins surmounted by the bridge; aft was a flexible whip-cannon poised like a cobra head.

The King was waiting for them on board. He was wearing a white coat and peaked cap for this nautical occasion. His green moldie girlfriend Vaana was at his side.

"Good morning, Yoke," said the King. "And it's an honor indeed to meet the famous Cobb Anderson. Welcome aboard." He glanced around the deck. "We can speak quite freely. The sailors barely know English, while Kennit and the bodyguards are completely to be trusted. Greetings, Onar! Anyone need a coffee? Champagne? No?" He led them aft to stand by a big open hatch in the deck. Above the hatch was a crane mounted on a high triangular brace. "You've brought the alla, Yoke? Ah, it's that little tube thing. Excellent. I look forward to seeing it in action. Slugs of gold and imipolex all morning long. Yum

yum!" He smiled and rubbed his hands. A dozen Tongan sailors were sitting around, ready to start work. Kennit joined two of the King's bodyguards, who were ensconced up on the bridge, playing a game of cards with a Tongan man in a captain's hat.

"Won't the ship sink if it gets too full?" Yoke asked the King,

"Oh, I'm not so inordinately acquisitive," said the King, a cheerful twinkle in his eye.

"Captain Pulu gonna keep an eye on the tonnage," said Vaana, waving toward the bridge. "And Yoke, child, I want you to make twice as much imipolex as gold."

"You owe me an apology, Vaana," interrupted Cobb. He'd been staring fixedly at the sexy green moldie since they'd come aboard the ship. "You almost killed me with that betty the other night." Yoke recalled that Cobb had also mentioned having sex with Vaana.

"Ain't my look-out," said merry Vaana. "You was partyin' with the best. We do it again sometime, hey? You a lift, old Cobb."

"A man your age should have the maturity to own the consequences of his self-destructive behavior, Cobb," said Onar primly.

"You're a devil, Vaana," said the King. "Let's get started with our day's work, shall we, Yoke? I'd suggest your rhythm be to create a pair of hundred kilogram cylinders of imipolex followed by a single hundred kilogram ingot of gold. One-two-three, one-two-three, and so on. The sailors will load them onto pallets and lower them into the hold."

"I forget," said Yoke. "Why am I doing this for you?"

"It's thanks to HRH and me that you have the alla in the first place," said Onar.

"I thought it was Shimmer who gave it to me," said Yoke.

"Yes, but we guided you to her," said the King. "Be a sport, Yoke. Just one day's work. And then you're perfectly free to go."

"But Cobb and I could leave right now, if I wanted to," said Yoke. "Right?"

"You should know that HRH's bodyguards are well-armed,"

said Onar. "And this is, after all, a warship, complete with a whip-cannon that can shoot a sea gull out of the sky."

"No need to take that tone, Onar," said the King. "As you and I discussed earlier, our policy is persuasion, not force."

"Speaking of bodyguards, where are Tashtego and Daggoo today?" wondered Cobb.

"They'll be here in a bit," said the King. "They flew over to Fiji very early this morning. They're looking into the imipolex market for me."

So Yoke grasped her alla and started turning air into gold and imipolex at a rate of one pulse every second or two. The sailors stepped lively, stowing the booty. With each transmutation, a hundred kilograms worth of air would rush into a bright-line alla control mesh, making a big *whoosh* and *thud* that caused the ship to bob. Yoke figured out in her head that a hundred kilos of air took up about as much space as an apartment's living room. The cumulative rocking effect of the repeated gusts became a little sickening after three-quarters of an hour. Yoke took a break and alla-made herself a glass of fresh orange juice.

The King was sitting in a deck chair smoking a cigar. Vaana lolled on the deck beside him, looking like a thick, sexy serpent. Cobb stood behind the pair, discussing something with Onar. Now Onar patted Cobb on the back and took a chair next to the King. Cobb remained stiffly erect, his face gone oddly blank.

"Are you all right, Cobb?" called Yoke.

"Yes," said Cobb shortly. Perhaps he and Onar had argued?

"Captain Pulu's estimates make it that you're one-third done, Yoke," said the King, squinting up at the man on the ship's bridge.

"What are you going to do with all this stuff?" asked Yoke.

"Refurbish Tonga's credit in world banking circles!" said the King happily. "I'm going to ship this load straight to Suva in Fiji and sell it. Tonga will be in the black for the first time this century. Not that our debt is all that large, mind you; it's well under a hundred million dollars. We've been prudent, but we can never quite get onto the good side of the ledger. This will make me a hero to my people."

"You're going to give every bit of it away?" asked Vaana. She sounded surprised. "I thought you said half the imipolex would be for the Tongan moldies."

"Strictly speaking, there are no 'Tongan moldies,'" said the King. "Only a native-born flesh-and-blood Tongan can be a citizen. This isn't the U.S. with its quixotic Moldie Citizenship Act. I have to take care of my own people first. You moldies are only our guests." He held up his hand to stave off Vaana's anger. "You of course can have all the imipolex you require for your personal needs at any time, dear Vaana. And I promise you that once I've taken care of the Tongan national debt, I will try and do something for our very honored guest moldies."

"A promise ain't enough," snapped Vaana, standing up in her full womanly form. "My people been counting on me to get us a fair deal."

The King shook his head. "My local standing is already shaky due to the gossip about our relationship, Vaana. For my own political survival, I can't be put in a position of seeming to give a too preferential treatment to—"

At this point Yoke lost the thread of their conversation because a nightmarish call came in on her uvvy. It was Phil, standing on a beach looking desperate. He'd encountered Shimmer and the aliens in a cave at the end of the island. The powerball was about to eat him.

When Yoke sprang across the deck and pulled Cobb around her, the old man moldie was maddeningly sluggish in his responses. "Faster, Cobb," urged the frantic Yoke. "You have to fly me to the far end of the island!"

"Why?" drawled Cobb. "You're not finished filling the ship."

"The powerball is about to get Phil! Oh, hurry! Maybe we can save him."

"One certainly hopes not," said Cobb with unexpected venom. His voice sounded all different. "But, very well, I'll take you there. It should be amusing."

"What is *wrong* with you?" cried Yoke, but Cobb gave no answer. Silently he flew Yoke to the island's end as directed.

When they landed on the beach, Yoke quickly popped herself out of the moldie. It was too late. A big warped ball of space had slid onto Phil, and his form was swollen up like a balloon. Even though she knew it was hopeless, Yoke ran toward Phil, calling his name, with Cobb trotting along behind her.

The warped sphere of the powerball snapped loose from normal space—and Phil was gone. A nauseating ripple of distortion passed through Yoke's body. And then nothing. The world going on the same as before. With no Phil. Right at the end he'd said he loved her. Yoke realized that she could have loved him too.

Cobb was standing just behind Yoke, looking sarcastic and unhelpful. And down the beach a ways was a hole in the cliff with some of the aliens watching. Yoke could make out the pale glow of Shimmer and the dark snout of Wubwub.

"We have to get back to HRH and the ship," said Cobb. "We're not nearly finished there."

"What*ever*," said Yoke, striding down the beach toward the aliens. "Shimmer! You have to help bring them back. I want Phil and I want my mother!" On an impulse, Yoke used her alla to create a flaming wooden torch. "Moldie flesh burns, Shimmer!"

Calmly the pale woman and the dark pig stared out at Yoke. Did she really have any chance against these superhumans? Not likely. But she held her little torch up high. "Help me or else!"

Before the scene could play itself out, Yoke was tackled from behind. By Cobb. The old man moldie knocked the torch from her hand and flowed forward, enveloping and immobilizing her.

"We really must be on our way," said Cobb. "HRH wants us back immediately."

And then they were rocketing up from the beach, arcing back across the island to where the roly-poly aluminum Tongan Navy ship waited. Yoke tried to talk to Cobb, but it was no use. It was as if he'd been hypnotized or turned into a zombie.

"I put a leech-DIM on him," explained the smirking Onar when Cobb split open to disgorge Yoke back onto the deck of the ship. "As long as Cobb's wearing it, he's an extension of me. I slapped it on him while you were busy making the gold and imipolex. I let Cobb take you to watch Phil get eaten because I was curious too. Too bad about that, really. Phil was a decent sort. No mental giant, though. In any case, it's time to get back to work, Yoke. Break's over."

"You heartless prick." Now that she knew what to look for, Yoke could see the leech-DIM on Cobb's back, knotted into his pink flesh like a purple scar. She reached out to see if she could tear it loose, but Cobb's body twisted away.

"Do as Onar says," said Cobb, his voice a slavish replica of Onar's.

"That leech is comin' off right now!" yelled Vaana. She'd become very agitated as soon as Onar pointed out Cobb's leech-DIM. She gave the King's shoulder a shake. "Bou-Bou! You can't sit here and let this skanky white dook put a leech-DIM on a moldie. Tonga's a free zone!"

"Yes, but a free Cobb might take Yoke and her alla away from us too soon," hissed Onar. "Surely even you can understand that, you fat, stinking sex-toy."

"Understand *this*," said Vaana. Her arm lashed out snake-fast to strike a concussive blow against the side of Onar's head. Onar collapsed like a rag doll, and so did Cobb.

"Oh, you shouldn't have done that, Vaana," said the King, very upset. "I'm sorry about the leech-DIM. Onar talked me into it. Greed, don't you know." He waved both arms, making a broad "calm down" signal to his bodyguards on the bridge. "The guards may think they have to defend the Tu'i Tonga, Vaana. They're obsessed with the notion that you might harm me."

But Vaana was too agitated to pay proper attention. "You actually gave Onar the okay, Bou-Bou? You told him he could use a leech-DIM?" She grabbed the King and gave him another rough shake. "I thought you loved moldies!"

Up on the bridge the bodyguards were frantically conferring with the captain, and now the whip-cannon at the rear of the ship twitched into life. Yoke dove onto the deck next to Cobb to get out of the way. The whip-cannon snapped like a huge towel. A heavy puck of metal flew into Vaana, cutting her completely in two. The puck punched through the deck and the side of the hull—fortunately above the waterline—and plunged violently into the sea.

"No!" screamed the King. "Vaana!"

With what seemed like her dying effort, Vaana opened her mouth and made a cracked warbling noise. And then both halves of her were still. Kennit came pounding down the companionway from the bridge. "Are you all right, Your Majesty?" he shouted. "Thank God we saved you."

Onar began twitching, starting to wake back up, and Cobb was twitching too. If Yoke waited any longer it would be too late. Quickly she made herself a knife with her alla and rolled Cobb over so she could cut the purple scar of the leech from his back. But Kennit darted forward to take the knife and the alla from her.

"Don't hurt the girl!" shouted the King. "You've done enough damage."

"No weapons near the King," said Kennit. "I'm going to handcuff her till I figure out what's happening." And then he yanked Yoke's hands behind her back and snapped some tight bands of plastic around her wrists. Kennit pushed her down into the deck chair next to the King, then threw the knife into the ocean and handed her alla to Bou-Bou.

"I'm sure Yoke's no danger," said the King, taking the alla. "She was only trying to help her friend. As was Vaana, you were glad for an excuse to kill her, weren't you, Kennit? You and the guards have been waiting for—for—" The King's voice broke and he put his hand over his eyes. "You can't understand this, Kennit, but I loved her."

"Yis," said Kennit.

There was a minute of silence. At Yoke's feet lay the two halves of Vaana, inert in a reeking puddle of straw-colored moldie ichor. Onar was sitting woozily upright on the deck next to the dismembered moldie. It seemed as if the bad guys had won.

"If I give you back your alla, will you finish your work for me now, Yoke?" the King asked. He was fiddling with the alla as if desperate for a distraction from the sight of the shattered Vaana. "Curious," continued the King. "Just an empty tube, though if I look through it the world seems to be twirling." He knitted his brows as if willing something to happen, but nothing did. "It won't make anything for me. Yes yes, it really is keyed to you, Yoke. You're the goose who lays the golden eggs. A fine role."

"No eggs if the farmer mistreats the goose," said Yoke. "Unshackle me so I can take the leech-DIM off of Cobb. Until then I'm not making you anything more. Once you free us, I'll still keep my promise to fill your ship with imipolex and gold."

"Oh, but we can make her do much more than that, Bou-Bou," said Onar, his voice slurred. He squeezed his eyes shut and rubbed the side of his head, gathering his forces. Moving slowly and carefully, he got to his feet and sneered down at Yoke with something like his old energy. "Yes, Bou-Bou, I have another trick up my sleeve. I can make little Miss Snooty Britches do anything I want her to. Look." Onar pulled a twitching piece of imipolex out of his pants pocket, a fat dark red slug of a thing.

"Be careful, that's a thinking cap!" exclaimed the horrified Yoke, who'd been warned about them many times before. "A moldie can make it crawl up a person's nose to take over their brain!"

"Yes, my dear," said Onar. "Up *your* nose. I'll use the leech-DIM to run Cobb, and Cobb will use the thinking cap to run you. A baroque little chain of command, no?" He paused and giggled. "I have an idea, Bou-Bou. Why don't I smear Yoke with Vaana's ichor and get her to have sex with you. Little Yoke's a rather good shag, don't you know."

"How revolting," said the King coldly. "I'm shocked at you, Onar. Set the girl free, Kennit. She's perfectly willing to finish filling our ship. And do something about having poor Vaana's body stored away. I'm going to give her a proper funeral."

"But Yoke was holding a knife, Your Majesty," said Kennit. "I have to protect you."

"Do you presume to disobey my direct command?" said the King, rising to his feet. Kennit temporized by continuing to talk, and the two of them went to stand over the remains of Vaana. Meanwhile Yoke was still sitting in the deck chair with her hands cuffed behind her back.

While Kennit and the King continued debating, Onar handed the nastily twitching thinking cap to Cobb—who had no power to do anything but accept it. At the activating touch of Cobb's moldie fingers, the thinking cap bloomed like a blob of ink in a glass of water, sending out long, greedy feelers. Now Onar darted around behind Yoke and held her by the shoulders. The enslaved old Cobb shuffled forward, holding the excited thinking cap out toward Yoke's face.

"Help!" said Yoke, but her voice came out small and squeaky. Stupid Kennit and the King weren't even looking at her. It was like a dream where you try to run and your legs are knee-deep in molasses. Onar had her shoulders pinned in a grip of steel. The dark red thinking cap was coming closer. This was happening too fast!

It occurred to Yoke that perhaps she could control her alla even when she wasn't holding it. She reached out for mental contact with her alla and—yes! She alla-made a quick hydrogen-oxygen explosion at waist level between Kennit and the King.

The blast was encouragingly loud. The King bellowed, Kennit roared, and Onar and Cobb were so startled that Cobb dropped the writhing thinking cap onto Yoke's lap. Yoke quickly exploded a much bigger sphere of hydrogen and oxygen in a spot that she guessed to be behind Onar. He came tumbling onto her from over her right shoulder. The chair collapsed.

With a quick twitch of her legs and torso, Yoke maneuvered Onar's head to be near the thinking cap. The thinking cap crawled onto Onar's face and shimmied into his left nostril. Onar screamed for Cobb to catch it, but he was too late. With a last filthy wriggle, the thinking cap had disappeared all the way into Onar's nose. Onar's limbs twitched as if in an epileptic fit.

And now Cobb began twitching too. He and Onar were in a feedback control loop. Onar's leech-DIM was controlling Cobb, but Cobb's thinking cap was controlling Onar. They sprang together like wrestlers, like magnets. The Cobb-directed Onar tired to claw the leech-DIM out of Cobb's back and the Onar-directed Cobb probed into Onar's nose in search of the wily thinking cap. Yet at the same time, Onar was directing Cobb not to direct Onar to tear out the leech-DIM, and Cobb was telling Onar not to tell Cobb to try and get the thinking cap. Not to mention the fact that Cobb both was and wasn't trying to choke Onar. With all the contradictory impulses in the loop, nothing was accomplished, and the two could only flail about in chaos, their spastic motions cycling through a Wrestle-mania strange attractor.

Meanwhile Kennit had placed the muzzle of a pocket-size rail-gun against the side of Yoke's head. "If you make one more speck of trouble," he growled into her ear, "I'm going to blow off your head."

Now a new complication arrived. Moldies were flying in from every side, seemingly drawn by Vaana's distress cry. Up on the bridge the captain began using the whip-cannon to flail out metal pucks in every direction, and the two other bodyguards opened up automatic weapons fire. Kennit let go of Yoke and began firing his gun at the moldies as well. But there were too many moldies and they were too fast. A half dozen of them homed in on the whip-cannon and cut the thing off at its base. Yoke watched all this, sitting handcuffed on the deck. She'd scooted herself away from the flailing Onar and Cobb. The King still had her alla, and after Kennit's threat she was scared to use it again.

As the whip-cannon fell into the sea, Tashtego and Daggoo suddenly arrived. They came running across the deck, teeth bared like joyful pirates.

"Hold your fire!" the King called to his bodyguards. "These are my best agents! Tashtego, Daggoo, can you revive Vaana?"

Instantly taking in the scene, the great Daggoo bent over Vaana, his rapid fingers beginning to splice the halves of her body together. Tashtego disappeared into the ship's hold.

There was a steady thud of more and more moldies landing on the deck. Each of them went immediately belowdeck and moments later flew back out of the hatch, two or three times as big as before. Most of the ship's crew had jumped overboard. Cobb and Onar continued to wrestle.

"Who dealt this mess?" said Kennit, looking around despairingly. He gave a shrill whistle and the two other bodyguards came down the companionway. "We're taking HRH back to the secure island," he told them. They started across the deck.

"Let's not leave quite yet, Kennit," implored the King. "I want to see if Daggoo can fix Vaana." Tashtego reappeared from below, much fattened, and carrying a spare slug of imipolex that he gave Daggoo to use on Vaana. From the water came the sound of the ship's motor launch starting up. One of the bodyguards yelled down that they should wait for the King.

"Take off my handcuffs," called Yoke. "And give me back my alla. I can use it to save Cobb."

"Do it, Kennit," said the King. He handed Yoke's alla to the big Tongan.

Kennit crossed the deck, holding his rail-gun out at the ready. He removed Yoke's plastic handcuffs and pressed her alla into her hand. "Just remember, Yoke, if anyone comes near HRH, my boys and I will waste them." He went back to the other side of the ship.

Now that she had her alla, Yoke realized she didn't need a knife to take the leech-DIM out of Cobb. She could simply alla it into air—if she could place the control mesh steadily over the leech-DIM, that is. She explained the situation to Tashtego and Daggoo, and the three of them knelt on Cobb to hold him still, with Daggoo fending off Onar with one long arm. At the last instant Onar managed to lunge in and push his hand in as if to protect the leech-DIM. When the alla turned the contents of its control mesh into air, it took a chunk out of Onar's thumb too. He started bleeding profusely from the wound.

But the main thing was that the leech was gone. Cobb got to his feet and with one glance made Onar crouch down motionless. With no leech-DIM to counter the commands of the thinking cap, Onar was Cobb's slave.

"Good show!" called the King. "And how's Vaana doing, Daggoo?"

"She almost back," said the huge, black moldie, who'd turned his attention back to his injured comrade. "Yaaar." And indeed, the sinuous green shape of Vaana was lazily beginning to shift about.

"That's twice you've saved my life," said Cobb, hugging Yoke. "And now I own Onar? I'd sooner own a rabid baboon."

"I'll take him," said Vaana, sitting up and rubbing her eyes. "Thank you, Daggoo. I'd like to do something special with you soon." She flowed up Daggoo's body like a vine growing up an oak, then twirled free. Even as Yoke watched, Vaana's body was continuing to heal. "Hi, Bou-Bou," called Vaana, waving to the King.

The King waved back a little uncertainly, but when he saw Vaana's smile he tried to come over. His bodyguards grabbed his arms to hold him back.

"How would I give Onar to you?" Cobb asked Vaana.

"Let me uvvy into you and I can grep your thinking cap control code," said Vaana.

So Cobb and Vaana did the info transfer, and right away Vaana set Onar to dancing a jig like an organ-grinder's monkey, the blood freely dripping from his hand. Onar's jaw was pumping, but Vaana wasn't letting him say anything. His eyes were coals of fear and anger. His forced capering was a ghastly, melancholy sight.

"Oh stop," said Yoke. "Don't torture him, Vaana. We should bandage that cut."

"I've got a better idea," said Vaana, turning so she faced away from the bodyguards and the King. "A way to finish it. Come here, Onar, I want to ask you to do something." Onar stood before Vaana, tense but obedient, oblivious of his bloody hand.

Before Vaana could speak, Yoke interrupted. "Onar, did you kill Mr. Olou on purpose? Make him answer, Vaana."

"Yes," said Onar, his voice strained and cracked. "It was my idea."

"Go git HRH," said Vaana softly. "Don't slow down for them guards. Go git Bou-Bou."

Onar charged across the deck as if hell-bent on attacking the King. At this, the bodyguards reached their flash point. Moving as one, the three of them raised their weapons and blew off Onar's head.

"Takes care of the thinking cap too," said Vaana.

Onar fell heavily and lay still, his neck spurting. Yoke retched. Three days ago she'd made love to this man; his body had been warm and strong, turgid with the same blood that was puddled on the aluminum deck. What a waste, what a pitiful end.

And then the sky seemed to fall in, as something big came crashing into the ocean next to the ship. The object came down so fast that there was an ear-splitting sonic boom. A great wave rolled the ship far to one side like a tin toy, tossing Yoke and the others into the sea.

By a happy accident, Yoke and Cobb ended up next to each other, along with Vaana and the King. The ship, now some distance off, had righted itself. The other moldies and the bodyguards were out of sight. And floating between Yoke and the ship was the great object that had caused the splash. What the hell? It was a flattened disk—a couple of centimeters thick and ten meters across—with two dozen lively beaked heads sticking out of it. Yoke thought of the nursery rhyme about four-and-twenty blackbirds baked into a pie. A pizza pie.

"It's Cappy Jane," said Vaana, noticing Yoke's wonderment. "The Tongan geosynchronous satellite. Hi, Bou-Bou, looks like we're together again." She wrapped her arm around the King, who was struggling to stay afloat.

"Dear Vaana," said the King. "I was devastated when that fool of a captain shot you. Thank heavens you recovered."

"Don't let it happen again," said Vaana. "One more thing, Bou-Bou. You got any more leech-DIMs?"

"I don't!" cried the King. "It was all Onar's idea. He got what he deserved. Disgusting person. I never should have befriended him." He was dog-paddling hard, weighed down by his heavy clothes. "I'm sinking, Vaana."

Vaana sucked in volumes of air and positioned herself between the King's legs like an inflatable sea horse.

"I hope Kennit and the boys don't start shooting again," fretted the King. "With Cappy Jane here they must be going mad. I never should have given them guns."

Vaana grew her neck up twenty feet to have a look. Her head snaked around for a minute up there like that of a slender green sea serpent. "They're way over by the ship. The launch circlin' around to pick everyone up. We cool for a while. Man, when I chirped for help, I didn't expect Cappy Jane to come. Twenty thousand miles in twenty minutes? She must have curled up like javelin for the trip down."

"Remember that it's important that the moldies don't find out who Yoke and I are," Cobb whispered urgently to Vaana and the King, using his voice rather than the uvvy. "Or they're going to be hounding us for Yoke's alla. That's why you set up the Squanto and Sue Miller ID viruses for us, right?"

"That's right," said the King.

"Here, Cobb," murmured Yoke. "I'll uvvy you their identity codes."

"Beautiful," whispered Cobb. "I'll put those out for the Cappy Janes to see. We don't want them and their pals to follow us home for more free goodies."

"Where's our imipolex?" squawked one of the bird heads sticking out of the big disk of Cappy Jane. "Yeah, Vaana," said another of the heads, clacking its beak. "You called for help and promised us more imipolex than we've ever seen, so where the fuck is it?" A third head craned toward the aluminum ship. "Is it in the hold of that tub?"

"The local moldies done cleaned us out," said Vaana. "Nothin' left in there but gold."

"Ah, the superstitious human worship of rare minerals," said one of the Cappy Jane heads bitterly. "Too bad they don't know what it's like to have to buy the flesh to make their children." A different head eyed Yoke and piped, "Is this the girl who's supposed to have the magic wand? Who is she?"

"I'm Sue Miller," said Yoke. "And this is my moldie Squanto. How much imipolex would you like? How about a thousand tons!" She felt gay and reckless from so many crazy events. If things kept up as weird as this, maybe Phil could come back too.

Yoke gripped her alla and grew a large bright-line box in the water, keeping it a safe distance from her and the others. She could sense the location of the alla box through her uvvy, as if from a phantom limb. How big could it get, anyway? Though she tried to push it farther, the cube seemed to max out somewhere between twelve and thirteen meters on each side. About forty feet. Well short of touching the sea floor.

"Get ready for a jolt!" she cautioned the others. "I'm going to turn that big cube of water into imipolex. Actualize!"

Sproing!

Something like an enormous cube of gelatin was now bobbing in the sea, just barely afloat. A giggly, shuddery gelatin, alive with pulsing colors. Truly something for nothing. What was that Josef had said about the working of the alla? "Quark-flipping is like jujitsu. As if to look at something and then to look at it in a different way."

"Yow!" exclaimed one of the Cappy Jane bird heads, eyeing the imipolex.

Ordinarily, moldies reproduced in pairs, each acquiring half the necessary imipolex for new scion and each contributing about half of the newborn's nervous system and software. But given an opportunity like this, a moldie could reproduce all alone. If you gave a moldie a seventy kilogram chunk of imipolex, it could replicate itself in seconds—provided it hadn't done so within the last six months.

The six-month condition had to do with the fact that, when reproducing, a moldie's system generated a growth hormone that spurred its mold-and-algae nervous system to speed-grow a fresh nervous system into virgin imipolex. Six months was how long it took a moldie's body to generate a sufficient amount of its reproductive growth hormone.

The big Cappy Jane pie undulated over to the cube and began madly pecking away. Minutes later there were two pies. Due to the growth hormone limitation, the Cappy Jane moldies couldn't reproduce any further than that, but for a while they kept pecking, bulking up their bodies with additional imipolex. Each of them grew to as large a size as his or nervous system could handle, and then they pooped out, leaving most of the gnawed imipolex cube still floating in the water.

"*Urp,*" belched the nearest Cappy Jane beak. "What a blow-out. A clone-fest. I wish I had enough mold in me to breed over and over and over. Where did you get that terrific tool, Sue?"

"From some aliens," said Yoke, not thinking to lie.

"*Yeek!*" screeched the pie-bird. "Aliens! Find them! Kill them! Emergency!" The pie lifted awkwardly out of the water, little take-off jets firing out of its underside. It was slow and heavy from having incorporated as much imipolex as it could possibly hold.

"Being a grex down here sucks," cawed one of the birds in the flying pie, and twitched itself free. The disk broke up into pieces then, into twenty-four awkward-looking moldies. For now the other pie kept its integrity, floating there in the water. The freed Cappy Jane birds looked like featherless pelicans. Or maybe pterodactyls.

Back beyond the pie and the squawky birds, Yoke could glimpse the navy launch trying to circle around toward them. A figure was standing in the bow, tiny at this distance.

"The Metamartians are our—" Yoke had been about to say "friends," but then she remembered Phil's last warning. About how Shimmer had deliberately told the powerball to swallow her mother. But if the Cappy Janes wiped out the aliens, that might scotch any hope of getting Phil and Darla back.

"What?" croaked the closest Cappy Jane bird. "What did you say about the aliens, Sue? Metamartians you call them?"

"I'm not sure they're enemies," said Yoke lamely.

"Who knows where the Metamartians are?" screeched one of the birds still in the pie. "I want our grex to be the one to get them! Let's test some poofballs, guys!" Like a flock of pistons, the birds in the pie rose and fell, successively belching out little balls of imipolex that burst into flame once they were well up into the air.

"Yee haw!" crowed one of the birds raucously. "Follow me to kill the Metamartians! I just found out their location from Squanto!"

"Ooops," said Cobb.

"Oh, Squanto," said Yoke.

"It's hard, dammit," said Cobb. "That Cappy Jane kept nosing at me and asking stuff about Vava'u and somehow an image popped out. I showed her the aliens looking out of that cave on the beach. But that's all. I'm sorry. Anyway, you're the one who really blew it. 'Where did you get that wonderful tool, Sue?' "

Rather than probing any further, the Cappy Jane creatures lifted off in hot pursuit of the aliens. The leathery birds spread out their rumpled new wings. The great wobbly pie launched itself on steamy jets and, once airborne, began flapping like a stingray.

"I hope they find 'em," said Vaana. "Aliens mean trouble, Bou-Bou. Especially for moldies. They can move their minds right into a moldie's body. They talk about freeware, 'cept *we* the ones that get taken for free. It's just as well if things get back to normal here."

"I suppose so," said the King. "And we're still lovers?"

"Sho'," said Vaana. "And the rest of the imipolex here, that's for my people, right?"

"We already had a lot of your 'people' clean the imipolex out of our ship, Vaana. It was—daunting. I think it best to get rid of this. We've already had too much attention."

"Let me fill up," said Vaana, and assimilated as much of the imipolex as she could hold—swelling to perhaps twice her usual size. "I'm not quite ready to reproduce yet," she said. "But Lord knows when the time comes I'll be ready. You say all the other locals got some plastic too?"

"I don't know about all, but it sure seemed like a lot of them," said Yoke. "I think the King's right about getting rid of this evidence."

"Okay," said Vaana.

Yoke sent her control mesh out over the sullenly floating imipolex cube and turned it back into seawater, complete with an assortment of local diatoms and plankton.

"Cobb and I are ready to leave, aren't we, Cobb?" said Yoke.

"Okay," said the old man. "Did we finish doing whatever we came here for?"

"Diving," said Yoke. "I came here to dive. And Phil came to find me. We did have one good morning of snorkeling. I saw a wonderful little fish in a staghorn coral. And a giant clam."

"Don't forget the whale and squid," said Cobb.

"Do you think the Cappy Janes will kill the aliens?" asked Yoke.

Cobb's answer was drowned out in the roar of the navy launch that pulled up next to them. Aboard were Kennit, the two bodyguards, four sailors, and Tashtego and Daggoo.

Kennit and the bodyguards were grinning ear-to-ear, obviously thrilled at finding their king in good shape. It didn't look like they cared one bit anymore about seeing HRH so cozy with Vaana. There were no guns in sight. "We got a ladder in the rear," said Kennit. "Watch your step, Your Majesty. I think we ought to haul ass out of here. There's some sharks in a feeding frenzy on the other side of the ship. Finishing off Onar."

"Let's bail," Yoke said to Cobb. "Before everyone starts in on me again."

"Okay," said Cobb.

"Thanks awfully," said the King, still bobbing on Vaana's back. He extended his hand and Yoke shook it. "Do come visit Tonga again. Could I ask you one last favor?"

"You want more gold," groaned Yoke.

"Just, you know, as you're flying away, buzz the ship and put a few more tons in the hold? I'll tell the captain not to fire on you. It would be so lovely to have our budget balanced. I did get you the alla, you know. You're fixed for life now, Yoke. You're a golden goose."

"Honk honk," sighed Yoke, looking down at her alla. "Though I may end up throwing this thing into the ocean. So all right, one last favor. And in return, Bou-Bou, I want you to do whatever you can to block any publicity about me and the alla. Don't tell anything to the Cappy Janes. Stick to the Sue Miller and Squanto cover-up. And I hope the Tongan moldies don't know too much?"

"Tashtego and Daggoo know more than the others," said the King. "But so far I've been able to trust them as much as Vaana. The moldies who came and stole all the imipolex from the ship didn't know who you were or where it came from. And the local people won't talk much — and if they do, nobody will believe them. Nobody listens to Tongans. Let's do our best to consider this entire interlude expunged from the historical record. Deny, deny, deny. It's best this way for all of us. I wouldn't want the Fijians to know I'm selling fairy gold."

So Cobb and Yoke cautiously buzzed the navy ship, Yoke averting her eyes from the avid gray sharks who'd eaten Onar.

Captain Pulu waved a friendly go-ahead. They landed long enough for Yoke to outdo herself by making a perfect one-meter gold cube, weighing in at just under twenty tons. The cube was quite the elegant objet d'art.

But, in the event, making so massive an object out of thin air was fairly drastic.

As Yoke later calculated, if one kilogram of air takes up a cubic meter, twenty tons of air takes up a cube some twenty-seven meters on a side. A volume the size of a ten-story office building. Fortunately, she thought of making herself a pair of earplugs before she did it.

The whirlwind of so much air being sucked into the alla-cube made a thunderclap that knocked Cobb and Yoke off their feet. The ocean sloshed sullenly and some loose debris blew off the deck. But nobody was hurt, and the ship's hull didn't burst, and the captain didn't shoot at them, and Yoke and Cobb flew on up into the sky, leaving the Tongans with nearly one hundred million dollars worth of gold.

"But wait, Cobb," said Yoke as the ship began to dwindle below them. "We have to stop by the place where we slept last night. I want to bring my souvenirs."

"What souvenirs?"

"Oh, just some little things. Come on, Cobb. We'll do it fast."

Ms. Teta, the housekeeper with the glossy bun, greeted them. She was dozing in the shade with the cook and the maid. "You want lunch today?"

"We're going home," said Yoke. "We're all finished."

"You been back for a while?" asked Ms. Teta. "I thought I heard you in your room."

"No, I've been out on the ship with the King all morning."

"Well, maybe it was your boyfriend."

"Um, maybe?" said Yoke, her heart beating faster. She opened her room's door with a mixture of hope and fear. But it looked the same as before, except that the beds had been made.

"So what are we taking?" asked Cobb.

Yoke picked up her glass sculpture and the looped metal band with the ants embossed on it. Phil had been with her when she'd made them. She spotted Phil's dirty shirt from the day before, picked it up and sniffed it. His smell. She wrapped it around the sculptures. And there was the big green bean Phil had been so proud of. Of course, that had to come too. Yoke's eyes filled with tears. Last night had felt like the first of an endless series of similar nights—hard to believe it could have been the only one.

"Let's go, Cobb."

As they arced up into the sky, Cobb used telephoto vision to peer down at the beach where the aliens had been. Yoke shared in his vision via the uvvy. It looked like a pelican rookery and UFO landing field down there, with all the Cappy Jane birds and the giant disk. And—

"Oh Lord, they caught them," said Yoke. "Why didn't they run away!"

Cobb's telephoto vision had a nearly unlimited zoom ability; Yoke was able to dial it up to see that the Cappy Janes had captured all seven Metamartians down there. They had Shimmer, Ptah, Peg, Siss, Wubwub, a new one that looked like a man-sized bird and—dialing up the magnification a bit more—Yoke could even see that one of the Cappy Jane birds was holding the little beetle Josef. The Cappy Janes kindled a fire in which the seven unresisting aliens were consumed.

"It's hard to believe," said Cobb.

"Maybe it has something to do with coming from two-dimensional time," said Yoke. "They might not have much of a survival instinct? But that's not how I saw Shimmer acting that time on the Moon. It's weird. But, oh Cobb, with the aliens gone, how can I ever get Phil?"

"I don't know," said Cobb. "Could be you'll have to give up on him. There's more fish in the sea, Yokie." He powered up for a bit longer, finally reaching a point where he could cut off his jets and let them coast along their trajectory.

"I just noticed that the Cappy Janes are locked onto our location," Cobb said. "They're tracking us. Unless we do something, they'll track us all the way to San Francisco. And eventually hunt us down."

"Can you make yourself invisible?"

"I can block the Squanto ID locator signal I'm putting out, but then they might want to follow us in person. One of them might tail us."

"Why don't we send off a decoy? I can alla you some imipolex and you can copy yourself just like the Cappy Janes did."

"Two—two of me?" said Cobb hesitantly. "I'm not sure I'm in a mood to reproduce."

"Can you just make a dumb minimal clone that sends out your Squanto signal and flies—I don't know—out into space or something?"

"I could do that. In fact we can send Squanto on a trip to the Moon. That'll make sense to them, even if the 'Sue and Squanto' cover breaks down. The Moon is exactly where you might expect Cobb and Yoke to go. Tell you what, Yoke, use your alla to customize a piece of imipolex shaped exactly like me. And I can put a partial nervous system into it. The air's very thin up here. Anything you make will just coast along next to us. Can you stick your alla out through my skin?"

"I don't need to stick it out. I can move the control mesh to wherever I like. There it is." A bright-line copy of Cobb's form appeared next to them, and then—*whoosh*—it was virgin imipolex.

Cobb stretched out a mold-filled tendril and began programming his dummy. "Something else, Yoke," he said after a minute. "I think you should make a big piece of human flesh that we can seal inside him so he looks like he's still carrying you. In case the Cappy Janes really focus in on him."

"There's no human flesh in the alla catalog. The Metamartians didn't want it to be easy for us or the moldies to try and use the alla for reproduction. But, hmm, they do have a human skeleton. Remember, it's like every possible catalog in the world got folded into the master alla catalog. And this skeleton I'm looking at is like what you buy to use for anatomy classes. I guess it's kosher for the alla, since dead bone doesn't have living cells. And, oh wow, of course it's tweakable. I can make it just the same proportions as me!"

"Do it."

"I'm getting it ready in my head. The way you do realware, Cobb, is you completely get your image all together before you make the mesh and actualize it with the alla. Instead of just making a naked skeleton, I'm going to wrap the skeleton up in something of about the right density. I could use bologna but—" Yoke suddenly giggled. "How about tofu! Sue Miller as the ultimate vegan!" Another *whoosh*, and there was a tofu-and-bone fake Yoke flying along next to them.

The fake Cobb opened up and sealed itself over the fake Yoke. Cobb turned off his own locator ID signals and brought up the dummy's signals at the same time. And then the fake Yoke and Cobb—or the fake Squanto and Sue Miller—blasted on up away from them, presumably tracked by the Cappy Jane's surveillance signals.

The flight back to San Francisco was uneventful; Yoke slept most of the way. She woke as they plummeted down toward the thumb of the San Francisco peninsula. The sun was setting and the buildings of San Francisco looked lovely and gold.

"Back to Babs's?" asked Cobb.

"Yeah," said Yoke. "I like her. And she seems to have a lot of room. I hope she doesn't mind putting us up."

"She talks tough, but she's a soft touch," said Cobb. "Hell, she's even letting my great-grandson Randy stay there. I like Babs too. Wait till she sees your alla!"

"We should keep that quiet for now, Cobb. I don't want to end up in the middle of another feeding frenzy."

Nobody paid much notice when they landed on the dead-end street with Babs's warehouse. There was a homeless woman fishing in the bay, some kids working on an ancient old truck, a woman bent over her garden, a long-haired boy sitting on some steps strumming his guitar, a man walking down the street with a bag of groceries. And now here were Cobb and Yoke again, back in the thick of it.

They walked in through the open garage door to Babs's warehouse. The little plastic chicken Willa Jean cackled a warning. Randy Karl Tucker looked up from a nanomanipulator, surprised to see them. "Shit howdy! I thought you'd be gone till next weekend, Cobb."

"Well, we—um—"

"We pretty much did everything in Tonga already," said Yoke.

"Did Phil come back too?" asked Randy.

"Not yet," said Cobb after a quick glance at Yoke.

"I hope you ain't gonna try and rush me off to that dang Moon," said Randy. "I'm lovin' it here. Hey, Babs! They're baaack! Quiet down, Willa Jean."

The little chicken walked over and pecked at Cobb's foot. And Yoke and Cobb's gaze fell upon the twisted purple leech-DIM embedded in Willa Jean's back. With a grunt of anger, Cobb lashed down with an arm suddenly grown long. He caught hold of the wildly squawking Willa Jean, formed his other fingers into scissors, and excised the offending strip of limpware. And then he dropped the chicken and cut the leech-DIM into teensy tiny bits.

"God damn you to hell, Cobb!" Randy picked up the wounded plastic chicken and cradled her to his chest. "Willa Jean's been my special pet since India!"

"She'll live," said Cobb. "You got any more of those xoxxin' leech-DIMs around here?"

Randy sullenly refused to answer, and Yoke got right into his face. "Phil told me you were bragging about leech-DIMs, Randy. If you have any, cough them up. I wasn't going to talk about it, but down in Tonga we saw some shit that—"

"What's all the psychodrama?" asked Babs Mooney, ambling out from the warehouse's colorful, fabric-hung depths. "You sound like a bunch of snap-heads!"

"Did Randy give you any leech-DIMs yet?" asked Yoke.

"Tomorrow Aarbie Kidd is supposed to—"

"Call it off, Randy," said Cobb. "Or I'll tell Willy to disinherit you without a cent. Frankly, he'd love the excuse."

"Oh, fuck my ass and call me Barbie," said Randy. He sighed and made a voice connection with his uvvy. " 'Sup, brah? No, that's why I'm calling. No can do. Problem at this end. Yeah yeah, a shitty diaper. Reet. Later." He glared over at Yoke and Cobb. "Satisfied?"

"What excitement," said Babs, sitting down on a sofa. "Tell me what came down in Tonga. The way you two look, it must have been savage."

Yoke so much wanted to pour out her heart. She'd been meaning to uvvy her twin sister Joke on the Moon, but Babs was right here, and she was cozy and easy to talk to. And even Randy, in his oddball way, was comforting too. "Can you really really promise to keep a secret, Babs? Randy? Not tell a single soul outside this room?"

"I'll close the front door if you like," said Babs.

"You should," said Cobb. "If we're going to spill everything. And then you'll understand why I got so upset, Randy. I'm sorry about Willa Jean. I bet we can rig up a safe workaround. You don't need a full leech-DIM to remote-run a chicken, for God's sake. I'll help you design something simpler."

"Okey-doke," said Randy. "Hell, it's just as well not to be startin' up again with Aarbie Kidd."

So for the next two hours Yoke and Cobb told Babs and Randy the whole story of what had happened in Tonga. As they talked they made a supper of what Babs had around her kitchen: half a loaf of bread, a green pepper, jack cheese, old salsa, hibiscus tea, a liter of beer, and a gnawed Hershey bar. Cobb, of course, didn't eat anything, and he decorously held his pores closed so as not to exude an unappetizing smell.

"Show me how you make something with the alla," asked Babs when Yoke finished talking. It was dark outside and the kitchen was lit with candles.

"I don't want to," said Yoke. "Not today. I did it way too much this morning. The cubic meter of gold. Did I mention that I put Andy Warhol's signature on it?" She smiled and yawned, then got out the two sculptures wrapped in Phil's shirt. "These are more the kind of realware I'd like to get into." They looked good to her: the chunk of glass glinting in the candle-light, the ants shiny on the band of metal.

"Those are great, Yoke," said Babs, handling them. But Yoke could tell Babs wasn't all that impressed. Babs only liked art that did things.

"There's so many possibilities," said Yoke, running her hand over the embossed ants.

"Realware," said Babs. "I'd love to make some."

"I'd like to meet Shimmer," said Randy thoughtfully. "I bet she escaped the Cappy Janes. Shimmer can give an alla to most anyone she wants to, right? I wonder what I'd make with an alla?" Randy looked at the healed up Willa Jean in his lap and gave a country chuckle. "Maybe a sexier chicken."

"Randy!" said Babs.

"After Tonga, I think the best thing to make would be allas for everyone," said Cobb. "So people don't beg you and hassle you for things."

"*Can* you make an alla with an alla?" asked Babs.

"Josef said it was possible, but that the Metamartians don't want to tell us how," said Yoke. "And speaking of chickens, they put living things into their preprogrammed alla catalog too. Everything but moldies and people. I want to make a real reef and then try to limpware engineer an imipolex reef to copy it."

"I'm starting to think being a moldie is better than being flesh and blood," said Cobb. "By the way, Randy, you would have gone bananas over Vaana. Did I mention that we fucked?"

"How do moldies actually do it, Cobb?" asked Randy, his voice turning low and husky. "When it's just the two of you, one on one."

"I'm outta here," said Yoke, getting to her feet. "Can I sleep in the same place as before, Babs?"

"Sure. And I'm so sorry about Phil."

"Me too. Thanks." Yoke found her way to a foam mattress on the floor in a corner of the warehouse, next to a giant red and purple wall-hanging. She took off her clothes and put on Phil's shirt to sleep in. She set Phil's funny big bean pod next to her bed. The bean had seven odd shiny spots on it, a little patch near the summit of each bulging seed.

February 24

"Yoke?" "You're going to wake her?" "Shh!" "What's she going to say?" "This feels fine, doesn't it?" "I don't like being small." "Will she help us?"

Yoke woke to the sound of mutterings, of squeals and hisses and a few very clear notes of tiny bird-song. Her eyes flickered open. For an instant she flashed back to a Christmas morning when Whitey and Darla had left her and her twin sister's new toys on the floor right by their beds. Today seven tiny live action figures were set out: a woman, a man, a unicorn, a beetle, a snake, a pig, and a mynah bird. Cute.

Yoke sleepily closed her eyes, drifting back toward her dreams.

"Did she see us?" "She's asleep again." "I thought she'd be scared." "I want to get big." "Wake her up!" "Where are we?" "Yoke!"

Yoke opened her eyes again. The seven little figures were still there. The Metamartians?!

"Good morning, Yoke," murmured little Shimmer, half the size of Yoke's thumb. The miniature woman, man, and five animals were crawling around on Phil's bean, which looked somewhat the worse for wear. There was a hole in each of its seven bulging seeds. Evidently the seven little figures had tunneled into the seeds like weevils, sealing their entry holes over with plugs of green imipolex.

"You stowed away," murmured Yoke.

"I knew you'd keep the bean," said Josef the beetle. Of all

the Metamartians, he alone was the same size as before. "I showed the others how to make copies of themselves as small as me. And I copied myself too. We're the copies. We flew to your room and got inside your bean."

"Go away," said Yoke. "I don't want the powerball to eat me too."

Wubwub answered. "Aw, we not gonna decrypt any more Metamartians. Seven's all we need for a complete family, you know what I'm sayin'? We got the family now, we gonna look around a little, make a baby, maybe help Om spread the allas, and then we move on."

Yoke sat up, fully waking. "I thought the Cappy Janes killed you. Cobb and I saw them burning you on the beach."

"We're copies," said Ptah. "Like Josef said. We left before the Cappy Janes got there. Our original selves died; they let themselves get killed so the Cappy Janes would think they'd won. We're seconds; well, actually, I'm a third. Like I told you when Om ate my first self, Yoke, losing a life isn't a big deal for us. Every day, every minute of my life on Metamars, I saw one of my time-lines end. Letting the Cappy Janes kill versions of us was a small price to pay so that we can observe your people in peace. Do you mind if we settle in here?"

"I don't want to help unless you can bring Phil and Darla back."

"Are you not grateful for the boon of your alla?" asked the little unicorn Peg. She was the Metamartian Yoke liked the least. Such a tacky-looking thing, with her swilly, corny style of speech.

"I could live without it," said Yoke airily. "It caused me nothing but trouble in Tonga. I went there to do some diving and I ended up being a golden goose. In fact, here, you can take it!" She pulled the alla tube out from under her pillow and tossed it at the little figures, who hopped about in kind of a cute way. "I'm not grateful one bit," continued Yoke. "As far as I'm concerned, you can turn yourselves back into personality waves and find a different world to xoxx with."

"She a tiger," said Siss admiringly.

"It's too late to stop it now," said Ptah. "How this all comes out is up to Om."

"Are you talking to yourself, Yoke?" said Babs, suddenly appearing in Yoke's field of view. "Oh my God, what are those wavy little figurines? And they're moving! Did you make them with your alla?"

"Hi, Babs. These are the aliens I was telling you about. Okay, Metamartians, this is Babs. And Babs, this is Shimmer, Ptah, Wubwub, Siss, Peg, Josef, and—the seventh one's new. The little bird that looks like he's wearing a yellow mask."

"I'm Haresh," said the bird, his voice loud and melodious even though he was but one centimeter long. "An Indian mynah. I am very pleased to be meeting you, Miss Yoke and Miss Babs."

"Did you tell the powerball to eat Phil?" said Yoke accusingly.

"Yes, but it was Wubwub's idea that I so do. I am very sorry about this. Can you help us find shelter?"

"They're so little," said Babs, leaning over the Metamartians. "They're really from another world? Oh, I'd do anything for them. Do you guys want to live in one of my cupboards? Or I could find a dollhouse."

"It's too risky, Babs," said Yoke. "As soon as people—or the moldies—find out about them, they're going to want to kill them. The place could be bombed. We'd all die and the Metamartians would escape as usual."

"I ain't livin' in no dollhouse," said Wubwub "I'm gonna alla me a right-size body." There was a sound like a loud handclap and a bigger copy of Wubwub appeared, knee high and pig-sized. "I'm gonna get more respect if I'm this size," said the fresh Wubwub. "You know what I'm sayin'?"

"I want to be large as well," said Shimmer. Ptah, Peg, Siss, and Haresh chimed in too. "I'm no insect." "The floor is vile with dust." "Someone might step on me." "I'll be tall, not small."

There were five more explosive sounds as the necessary volumes of air were converted into patterned imipolex. And now Yoke's sleeping corner was crowded with a marble woman, a bronze man, a blonde unicorn, a green python, a black pig, and a giant bird with a yellow mask around its eyes. This made thirteen Metamartians in all: a single Josef, still the size of a beetle, plus big and small versions of each of the six others.

"Praise Om," said the new Metamartians.

"This is insane," said Babs. "What happens to the little guys now?"

"We feel it's ecologically unsound for one of us to have more than one body in a given time-line," piped the tiny Shimmer. "Farewell." And the six small Metamartians dissolved into poofs of air—effectively killing themselves.

"I don't think people could ever act that way," marveled Yoke.

Josef buzzed over to perch on Yoke's pillow. "I'm happy to see you again, Yoke," he said.

"What happened to you on Vava'u?" asked Yoke. "You disappeared when I needed you. When all those Tongans were crowding in on me."

"There was no way out for you," said Josef. "You'd painted yourself into a corner, as one says. Remember that we can see a little way into the future. I didn't want to be there when Tashtego and Daggoo arrived to deliver the great scolding."

Babs was all agog, smiling at and touching the aliens. "I don't know what to ask first," she laughed. "Where you're from, what you want—this is wonderful. At first I thought you were just Silly Putters, or moldies."

"Our essence is energy," said Shimmer. "We can incorporate ourselves in various ways. The moldie form seems to be convenient. For now." She glanced up at the sunlit windows high in the warehouse walls. "I'm ready to get out and about and see some things. To be a tourist! Our plan for now is to blend in and mingle. And then Om will spread the allas, and we'll mate, and we'll move on."

A warning gong sounded, meaning that someone had just entered Babs's front door. "Maybe that's Randy and Cobb," said Babs, looking upset. "They went out last night and they never came back." She hurried off.

"Great day in the morning!" came Randy Karl Tucker's voice. "You're all paisleyed up there, Babs. Checkerboard paisley everywhar!"

Cobb's deep voice murmured something. And then there was a crash of someone knocking over a chair.

"You gross cheeseball, Randy!" cried Babs. "And you're lifted on camote? Here I thought we might start a relationship and you act so — so disgusting! You're a sporehead *and* a cheeseball. I wish I'd never seen you! And, no, you can't go back there."

The low rumble of Cobb's voice came again, and then Randy's voice lifted in incoherent ranting that segued into words. "Hiiigh as a kite tail! Babs don't want me to head this-a-way, José? Well that's whar I'm a-goin'!" Another crash, followed by snorting sounds and more yelling. "Fee-fie-foe-fum, I smell *fuck plastic*!" A pile of books tumbled over, and then Randy appeared, followed by Cobb and Babs.

Yoke had never seen Randy like this. Instead of his usual timid, introverted self, he was wild and expansive. For his part, Cobb looked the way he had after all that betty in Tonga. Quivery. Evidently the two of them had spent the night on the *Anubis* getting lifted and having sex with hooker moldies. Like great-grandfather, like great-grandson. Icky, sad, and kind of funny. Yoke felt sorry for Babs. She'd obviously had hopes for Randy.

At the sight of the aliens, Cobb hiccuped and sat down on the floor, his skin rippling with rapid wrinkles. Randy made a beeline for Shimmer, shoving Peg the unicorn to one side.

"Dog with an antler, what the hell. Look at this milky mama." He lurched forward, throwing his arms around Shimmer's neck and sniffing deeply. "Hey thar. Want to make twenty bucks the hard way?"

"Greetings, Randy. I am Shimmer from Metamars."

"Whoah!" said Randy. "I'm in looove. Sex with an alien!" He ardently embraced Shimmer, and instead of pushing him away, the alien lowered herself down onto Yoke's bed with Randy on top of her. Yoke sprang up, getting well out of range. "If we do it, can I have an alla too, Shimmer?" Randy was saying. "I'm the natural man to show you the facts o' life."

Even though Shimmer was making a noise that could have been laughter, Ptah and Wubwub dragged Randy off of Shimmer, Ptah pulling Randy's legs and Wubwub pushing his chest with his snout. Siss wrapped herself around Randy's body, strapping down his arms. Haresh the giant mynah bird strutted over to peer at Randy's face.

"Is this typical human mating behavior?" asked Haresh, cocking his head.

"Don't even," said Babs. "He is so far from any semblance."

"Randy's a cheeseball," explained Yoke. "He likes to have sex with moldies. He thought you were a moldie, Shimmer."

"Who says she ain't?" said Randy, trying to raise his hand to his face, seeming not to understand that his arm was held down by Siss's coils. "The nose knows." Randy kept on trying to move his arm, soddenly struggling against Siss.

"Let him go," said Shimmer. "He's harmless."

"I wouldn't trust him," said Ptah. "What if he somehow pollutes your plastic?" But Siss went ahead and uncoiled.

"Once I git naked, I'll do some harm on you all right," said Randy, crawling forward to rest his head facedown in Shimmer's lap. He inhaled deeply. "The nose knows." This time Randy managed to lay his finger against his nose, but in the process he rolled off of Shimmer's thighs, bounced off the edge of the bed, and clunked his head on the floor. "Ow," said Randy, and fell asleep.

"What a colorful individual," said Shimmer.

"I pick the absolute worst men," said Babs.

"I hope you have some other prospects," said Yoke.

"There's always Theodore," said Babs. "I'm going to do a mental reset, Yoke. Like 'Randy is just a friend and I have no feelings for this man.' Reset, reset, reset. Yes, I'm going to call Theodore today. He's been wanting to take me out to a brain-concert."

"You go, girl," said Yoke. "I wonder if I'm going to have to wash Cobb again."

"What do you mean?" asked Babs.

"He's high on betty. Last time he got like this he almost died. I had to knead him with my feet for ten minutes in the shower."

"Betty's bad," said Babs. "My mother took it once and—ugh." Yoke recalled that Babs's mother Wendy Mooney was a human/moldie hybrid. That is, Wendy had a tank-grown human body that was run by a scarf-shaped moldie that did all the actual thinking.

Now Babs went back to marveling at the aliens. "Randy's right," she said, petting Peg's mane. "You seem just like moldies. But—prettier. I don't mind if you stay here for a while. I don't really mind the moldie smell, you know. It reminds me of my mother. Tell me more about where you come from. It's called Metamars?"

"Yes," said Josef. "That's where we began. But now we travel forever. Our near-term goal when we depart is to get back to a zone of two-dimensional time." He flew from Yoke's pillow to Babs's shoulder, and started talking to her about higher dimensions, with Haresh and Siss listening and adding comments.

While they talked, Yoke crouched down and touched Cobb. He didn't seem nearly so shaky and blotchy as he'd been in Tonga. Presumably this time he hadn't taken an overdose. So she left Cobb to sit there, grinning and shivering.

Yoke needed fresh clothes. The alla was still lying on the floor where she'd thrown it; she picked it up. She popped out black tights, silver boots like Phil's, a shrimp-colored skirt, and a thick black wool turtleneck.

"So you do enjoy the miraculous alla," said Peg. "And our superb catalog."

"They're okay," said Yoke casually.

"Can I have an alla?" asked Babs, interrupting Josef's science lecture. She'd been closely watching Yoke make her clothes.

"Well . . ." said Shimmer. She was sitting on the edge of Yoke's bed, keeping an eye on Randy.

"You barged into my house and stole my man," said Babs, not entirely joking. "It's the least you can do."

"Oh *ja*, let's give Babs an alla," said Josef. "Om wants us to. Yoke's alla has worked out well enough and Om feels it's safe to try more."

"I'm down with it," chimed in Wubwub. "Allas for the people. Why not one for this Randy-neck too? That could be kinky, you know what I'm sayin'?"

"Here, Babs," said Shimmer, rolling her thumb against her fingers. A subtly flickering silver tube appeared in her hand. "Om made it look different from Yoke's so you don't get mixed up. Take it. You're wearing an uvvy? Good. That's what the alla uses for an interface. An alla registers itself as owned by the first person who picks it up. It'll show a rapid-fire series of images so Om can learn your personality, and then it'll feel around in your body to teach Om your physical form. Once that's done, it's registered."

Babs held the tube in her hand, eyes closed to better see the uvvy visions in her head. "Cathedral window, tree-branch, sand," she murmured, each word faster than the one before, and then she was going too fast to talk out loud. The descriptions sounded familiar to Yoke; probably the alla was showing Babs the same images it had shown her. Yoke could tell when the body-mapping part of the alla registration happened, because Babs briefly twitched all over.

"Stuzzy," breathed Babs, opening her eyes and looking down at the little alla tube. "I've been memorized by Om."

"Now I'll transfer our human-oriented alla catalog to your uvvy, Babs," said Ptah. "Josef and I made the catalog, and it's quite complete. We got it by combining every existing catalog we could find on the Web. Basically, I figured out how to make everything. Here it comes."

"Once you get the hang of it, Babs, you can design original realware of your own," added Shimmer. "And now for Randy's alla."

"Nay, nay!" protested Peg. "That youth is base and foul. His crafting will be full unsavory."

"Peg's right," said Ptah. "I realize that you don't need for me to defend you, Shimmer, but I really feel that this kind of degenerate individual is a serious threat."

"It good practice to include deviant in test population, I think," said Siss. She listened into herself as if silently conversing with something. "And, yes, Om agree."

"I'll do it," said Shimmer. She rolled her thumb against her fingers again, producing an alla tube in gently fluctuating shades of copper. She gracefully leaned over to tuck the vibrant tube into the sleeping Randy's shirt pocket. "Let's wake him up so he can register it," she urged.

"Don't wake him now," said Yoke. "Not while he's still lifted. I'll make sure he registers it later. And I'll uvvy him a copy of the catalog."

"Whu-Whu-Whu about me?" said Cobb, shuddering away on the floor.

"No," said Wubwub. "We ain't ready to start in with moldie allas too."

"I'm nuh-not a moldie," protested Cobb. "I'm human." It was just like back in Tonga, when Onar had told Cobb he couldn't come to the dinner at the King's because it was for humans only. It made Yoke sad to hear Cobb insist he was human. Why not face the truth? As far as Yoke was concerned, being human meant being made of flesh and blood. And poor old Cobb hadn't had a human body since 2020.

"If you want something, I'll make it for you, Cobb," said

Yoke gently. "But for now, you don't get an alla. Especially not when you're lifted. Maybe you should go get in the shower. Wash those spores out."

"Yeah," said the old man moldie. "I gotta shake this betty shit." He shuffled off towards Babs's bathroom.

Meanwhile Babs had been sitting silent on the floor, uvvying around in her alla catalog. And now she produced a bright-line shape that became a cup of coffee in a ceramic mug shaped like the head of an ant. Babs liked ants as much as Yoke did.

"Oh. My. God!" said Babs. "I love it!"

"Don't get so grateful that you let the Metamartians stay here," cautioned Yoke. "If they don't kill you, someone else will by coming after them. I like Shimmer's idea. The Metamartians should go out and blend in. You don't have to look like *exactly* a pig, do you, Wubwub? And Peg, could you possibly bag the unicorn thing? I mean why not pass yourselves off as regular moldies? Unless you just want to be birds or insects. Nobody cares about them. Nobody would notice if a bird is plastic."

"I am proud to be a bird," said Haresh. "From scanning through your Web, I am learning very much about them. The only small cloud is that to be called a 'birdbrain' is by no means a compliment. Nevertheless there is a very famous poem of this name. *Birdbrain!* by your immortal Hindu bard Allen Ginsberg. So I am even proud to be a birdbrain. But I do not accept your suggestion to be a small plastic bird which nobody notices. I too would like to be freely mingling with humans and moldies on an equal basis. I want to be accepted as a full-sized moldie."

Cobb came ambling back from the shower, looking pink and fresh again. "That did me a world of good."

"What kind of look do a moldie generally have?" asked Wubwub.

"Here in the city they look like people," said Babs. "Approximately. Like caricatures. It's considered dooky for a moldie to look too exactly human, though Shimmer and Ptah are so over-the-top that they'll be okay. No humans are that beautiful.

And the way they look like marble and bronze makes it clear that they're not trying to pass for people. Now you, Wubwub, you can be a pig-man. A person with a face like a pig. Keep your snout and ears, but change your body and legs. That's good. Legs a little longer. You need more than two fingers on your hands, try three, no, four counting the thumb. All right. And, yes, keep the tail, in fact make it bigger and curlier. Like a corkscrew. Wavy. Now your mouth — it's too scary. Here, let me — " Babs stepped forward and began molding Wubwub's face. Wubwub generated dancing bright alla-lines to effect the changes as fast as Babs suggested them. "We'll curve the lips up at the end, put in a smile wrinkle, make the snout a little shorter, shorten those snaggle teeth, arch the eyebrows, fold that one ear over, and, oh, how about a big white spot around this eye? That's perfect. You look darling. Look at yourself through my uvvy. You don't like the white spot? Oh, all right, get rid of it, then. Fine. You look handsome but tough."

"Come to my aid, Babs," said Peg, elongating and taking on a womanly form. "What think you of my horn?"

"A unicorn horn is more of a guy thing," said Babs. "It's a dick symbol. You'd do better to have, um, two little horns."

"Like a cow?" asked Peg. There was a flicker of bright mesh-lines and her face grew broader.

"Oh yes, Peg," put in Yoke unkindly. "Be a cow."

"Don't listen to her," said Babs. "You want to be a devil-girl. Sexy and with curvy red horns and reddish skin. Yeah, yeah, okay, but make your T and A bigger. That's good — if only it were so easy for everyone. And, um, fine, keep the blonde hair. Usually devil-girls are brunette, but you can be a Val devil-girl. Better make your skin more pink like sunburn instead of that coppery Native American hue. Oh, and don't forget to make your tail all leathery and with a little arrow at the tip. That's a dick symbol too, but on a devil-girl it's hot. Like a strap-on dildo. Oh, you've got it now, Peg, you're moanin'. Next?"

A few minutes later six of the Metamartians were the shape and size of well-proportioned humans resembling, respectively, a marble Venus, a bronze Apollo, a pig-man, a devil-girl, a snake-woman, and a bird-man. For his part, Josef stayed resolutely the same.

"I'll observe," said Josef. "A deep participation is not my style. I'll be the fly on the wall. The beetle."

"Haresh looks like that Egyptian god," said Yoke. "Thoth." The Metamartian had left his head exactly in the shape of a bird's. "What a birdbrain."

"Zoom!" exclaimed Babs. "Egyptian! You Metamartians can go join the Snooks family on the *Anubis*. After last night, Cobb here must know those moldies pretty well. Right, Cobb? You can tell Thutmosis and Isis Snooks that these six are friends of yours just down from the Moon and that they're looking for work."

"Work doin' what?" asked Wubwub suspiciously.

"Oh, the Snookses are into all kinds of things," said Cobb. "You can tell them you're a—a burglar, Wubwub. Just secretly actualize things like liquor for the *Anubis* bar and say that you stole it. And that can be your contribution to the family. You don't necessarily have to fuck the cheeseballs, if that's what you're worried about."

"*I'm* not worried about that," said Shimmer, staring down at the sleeping Randy Karl Tucker. "It might be fun."

"I'm going to call Theodore right now," sighed Babs, walking off toward the front of the warehouse.

"Babs likes Randy," Yoke explained to Shimmer. "It makes her unhappy to think of him having sex with you. So don't do it, please."

"Oh!" said Shimmer. "I hadn't realized."

"It's not our affair if the vile youth lacks wholesome passion for Babs," said Peg snippily.

"What kind of sex system do you Metamartians have?" asked Yoke. "Do you have any kind of clue?"

As usual, Josef wanted to be the one to answer the question, but Siss made as if to swat him.

"I the one who sexy, Josef. You let me speak."

Siss had a face of pale humanlike skin with large, almond-shaped eyes. Her nose was little more than two flattened holes and her mouth was immensely long and thin-lipped. Instead of hair, she had a skull-fitting hood of shiny green snakeskin that flowed down to join the snakeskin which covered the rest of her body, save her hands, which had humanlike skin and long green fingernails. The hood had a dramatic widow's peak in the middle of her forehead. Siss looked decadent, Asian, androgynous.

"We have something like boy/girl too," she explained. "One got stick, one got hole. Each of us is 'stick' in some lives, 'hole' in others. Many lives across two-dimensional time. Stick to hole, hole to stick, like big crocodile sex zipper." Siss showed her fangs and made a gentle biting motion, her long curved fangs sliding into matching sockets in her jaws. "Everyone both girl and boy."

"But there's more to it than that," piped up Josef. "We zipper together in loops of seven. Why seven? It has to do with a feedback resonance in the strange attractor of our metagenome. In ancient times we mated only on Metamars, but now we've chirped out into the cosmos. When seven of us nomads can meet and mate—it's a wonderful thing. Seven of us landed here, but eight of us shall leave."

"I for one am eager to be getting on with our adventures," said Haresh. Other than Josef, he looked the least human. "Can we go and meet the Snooks family now?"

"Stay uvvied in with me," said Cobb. "If they ask you any hard questions, I can feed you the answers. Now is a good time to show up. Most of them are going to be asleep or hung over. Remember, you guys come from the big Nest on the Moon. And you're going to promise to give the Snookses half the imipolex you earn, in return for them letting you join their family."

"Let's do it!" said Shimmer.

They waited by the warehouse's front door until they could see a time-line in which no passersby would notice them. Cobb and the six big Metamartians jumped out onto the street with little Josef buzzing along above them.

"Look at them go, Yoke," said Babs, just ending her uvvy call with Theodore. "What a sight."

"*Anubis*, ahoy!" said Yoke. "We better not stare after them. We don't want it to be totally obvious that your warehouse is where they came from. How was Theodore?"

"Oh, fine. Thrilled that I called. We made a date, not a dinner date, a meet date. We're going to meet at the Fillmore and see Larky's brain-concert. Larky's this guy who uses really big sheets of imipolex for his audio and video. Sort of like Saint and Onar were doing the other day, but more professional. I like Theodore—I guess."

"I told Shimmer to leave Randy alone," said Yoke.

"What? I don't believe you, Yoke. What'd she say?"

Yoke put on her Val voice. "Shimmer was like, 'Oh I didn't know.' And that swilly Peg is all 'It's not *our* problem.' And I'm like 'Do you have any clue about sex?' And Siss goes, 'We're bi.' But then Josef says they do it by sevens."

Babs laughed and gave Yoke a hug. "Whatever. Randy is pretty skanky. Let's get our allas and do art!"

"What about Randy's alla?" said Yoke.

"Maybe we should take it away?" said Babs. "Maybe give it to someone else?"

"At least hide it for now," said Yoke. "He might do something really gnarly with it if he's still lifted when he wakes up."

So they tiptoed back to Yoke's sleeping corner. Willa Jean had perched herself on Randy's chest, as if guarding him. Though Cobb and Randy hadn't yet fixed up a new DIM link between Randy and the plastic chicken, Willa Jean was still quite loyal to the Kentuckian.

Yoke held Willa Jean's beak shut while Babs took Randy's alla out of his pocket.

"This is what happens to stoned rednecks," hissed Babs, pocketing Randy's alla. "Their powers disappear." Willa Jean let out an outraged cackle when they released her, but Randy slept on unperturbed.

And then Yoke and Babs went out to the front of the warehouse and started making things.

February 26

"I'm kind of waiting to see what's going to happen next," Yoke was saying. It was two days later, Thursday, February 26, 2054, about two in the afternoon. Yoke was on the uvvy with her twin sister Joke on the Moon. The to-and-fro response time for a message was about five seconds, due both to the large Earth-Moon distance and to the intricate diffusion-encryption software they were using for the call. Diffusion-encryption sent each byte of the message along a different path — to prevent there from being any traceable signal binding the speakers together. It took a lot of computation.

With the five-second lag, the best way to converse was to take turns sending long blocks of speech and images. It was more like a fast E-mail exchange than a normal conversation.

Yoke continued her turn: "Babs and I have been making the best things. I already showed you some of my static sculptures, but now let me show you one that moves." The uvvy transmitted the images direct from Yoke's vision centers. She was looking at a sweeping loop of shiny wire with bright shapes sliding along the wire. "I made this on Tuesday. The rail is chrome steel and there's a linear induction field in it. The power comes from a quantum-dot generator embedded right inside the rail. The shapes are the Platonic and Archimedean solids, remember them?" Two of the polyhedra collided and reversed directions. They swooped along the track's twists and loops, rising and falling. The beautiful, shiny polyhedra were tinted crystal, grown around magnetic metal cores. "It's a magpie kind of thing. And I keep making myself more clothes. Look at my outfit." Yoke stepped in front of a fancy full-length wood-framed Art Nouveau mirror to show off her latest clothes, a short thin red leather jacket over baggy shin-length pants and a white

T-shirt inset with lace spirals. "And Babs made a bunch of furniture. Like this mirror for instance. It was from a Sotheby's auction catalog. And she made a silk couch with ants embroidered all over it and a canopy bed. I made myself a bunk bed like we used to have on the Moon, only big enough this time. The thing Babs is proudest of so far is over here, check it out. Like a glass bowl of living spaghetti." Yoke pointed her gaze at a cubical quartz box holding a wriggling mass of imipolex worms of every color and thickness. The sharp edges of the square box contrasted with the lively antics within. "Babs could never have afforded this many plastic worms before. I think there's two hundred thousand of them, all custom made by her—well, you can tell the alla to make a whole lot of copies of something in a row, but I guess that's still custom. Custom mass-produced? Anyhoo, see how the same-colored ones band together and flow along like gouts of lava? I love it. Okay, now you talk."

Joke's message started coming in: "Your clothes are floatin', Yoke. I have so many clothes ideas I want you to make. Like polka dots with the dots being cutouts. Look." The signal showed Joke's hands quickly sketching a girl with an outfit. Beyond Joke's hands was a lunar workshop crowded with equipment for making Silly Putters: shelves and shelves of chemicals, a hulking injection molder, and a workbench with imipolex-machining tools such as a piezomorpher and a volume-filling airbrush. Joke was living with her somewhat gnarly artist boyfriend, Corey Rhizome, who was visible at the other end of the workshop. A few of Corey's Silly Putters were hopping around; they were plastic pets a little like Willa Jean, but smarter and more autonomous. Yoke recognized two of the Silly Putters: the small green pig of a "rath" and the football-shaped, orange-beaked "Jubjub bird," the two forever engaged in mutual battle. Joke set down her pen and continued talking. "I hope you bring that alla back here really soon! Oh, and your sculptures are terrific. I never knew you could be such the artist, Yoke. That wire thing with the sliding blocks is sooo weightless. I guess you could make a really big one? I mean, like as big as a carnival ride, with each of the sliding thingies hollowed out so that a person could ride inside? I'm wondering if there's any limit to the power of the alla. I mean, could you hollow out a huge biosphere under the Moon's surface and fill it up with dirt and rivers and lakes and an atmosphere and maybe even a little fusion sun? There's no end to what people might ask you for. So you're right that it's really important to figure out how to copy the allas so that it's not just you and Babs being golden geese when everyone finds out. I'm glad that the people and moldies from Tonga haven't tracked you back to San Francisco. I guess the King is keeping quiet and the Cappy Janes really fell for the decoy. The tofu Sue Miller! We knew a girl just like that, remember Simmie Lipsit? I wonder if one of the Cappy Janes has chased down the tofu Sue by now. You know, I'm going to ask Emul and Berenice to check on the moldies' chat lines right now. While I do that, tell me what's up with Cobb's great-grandson. Did you ever give him his alla?"

Yoke: "Oh, that was so wild. All afternoon Tuesday, Randy was moping and dragging around all hung over while Babs and I made wavy stuff. He was wishing he had an alla and wondering where the aliens went, and we were like, 'Serves you right for getting so trashed.' But then after we alla-made a bunch of soup and bread and cheese for supper, Babs finally gave Randy his alla and it registered itself to him. That's a trip in itself, it's like the alla is memorizing your body and your mind—your wetware and your software—the whole package. I was for holding out on Randy, but Babs keeps wanting to be nice to him. Or get his attention or something. And then as soon as she *had* Randy's attention, Babs did a head-trip on him by going out on a date with this new guy Theodore. I have a feeling she's using Theodore to make Randy jealous. Anyway, Randy and I were alone together Tuesday evening. I showed him how the alla works, and the very first customized thing he did was to make a safe DIM control patch for his plastic chicken, Willa Jean. Willa Jean is sort of the same thing as a Silly Putter, except Randy has a control feed into her, and she's not as smart. Randy was using an illegal leech-DIM before, and he got Cobb to approve the new one as safe around real moldies; in fact Cobb helped him design it. Hey, there goes Willa Jean now." Yoke trained her vision on Willa Jean wandering across the floor, ostensibly pecking for stray crumbs of imipolex. "I'm surprised that plastic chicken's here, because Randy's gone out on his new motorcycle. I wonder if he's using her to eavesdrop on me. If so, you're a geek, Randy." Yoke swung her alla through the air to launch a buzzing, bouncing spark-machine that frightened Willa Jean off into the far corners of the warehouse. "But I still haven't told you the best part. After Randy fixed Willa Jean, he was tired, so he made himself a good bed and lay down on that and started creating all sorts of little samples of every kind of material he could think of, each sample in the shape of a Lego block, and he was snapping them together and then—this is the rich part— Randy fell asleep while he was wearing his uvvy, and he ended up hooking into his alla and making something that he'd been dreaming, God you should have heard him scream. The screaming started at like three in the morning and Babs wasn't back yet, so it was just me and Cobb to deal. Randy's realware dream thing was a giant snail with his mother's face. It was chasing him. A giant imipolex snail actually crawling around the warehouse at three in the morning, knocking things over, and I mean a snail this big." Yoke stretched both arms up high, shaking with mirth. "I really shouldn't be laughing because it's very sad, his mother died at the end of November and Randy had totally been neglecting to stay in touch and he missed the funeral and apparently he has these recurrent guilt nightmares about a giant snail, it has to do with being too late. It was crawling after him all around the warehouse and wailing 'What taahm is it?' in this bewildered, Kentucky-accented voice. 'You goin' be late for school if you don't hurry up, Randy Karl. When is Tuesday?' Except it said 'whiyun' instead of 'when.'" Yoke was struggling to keep her voice level, but now and then letting out shrieks of laughter. "It had a silver-frosted black shell, like a middle-aged lady's hair. And there was some incest thing in there too. It wanted to sit on his face. I heard it say 'Ah'm real hot to crawl on you, Randy Karl.' Randy was just completely freaking out. And finally he was cornered and the snail really did crawl onto him, right across his body and up onto his face, I think it must have weighed four hundred pounds. It moved a lot faster than you'd expect. Randy would have suffocated if Cobb hadn't been able to drag it outside; Cobb can be really strong. We burned the imipolex, but the shell's still there. I'll show it to you in a minute."

Joke: "I can see where you'd think that's funny, Yoke. Not everyone would. But that's why we love you. It sounds like Randy could run amok, a gunjy dook like that. You're going to push him too far. Not everybody appreciates your sense of humor. Though Corey's loving it. I'm telling him some of the stuff while it's coming in." Joke's view showed a greenish-skinned man with square vertical goatee and the sides of his head shaved, grinning and leaning forward as if hungering for information. "No, Corey, you can't uvvy in. This is totally diffusion-encrypted. Emul customized some cryp code just for this call. Yes, Corey, you heard me right, a giant snail with his mother's face wanted to crawl on him. Back off-ski! Okay, Yoke, while you were telling about Randy just now, Berenice did an anonymous search of the moldie chat-lines and found out a few things. The aliens' sacrificial clone trick went over; the moldies really think they killed them all. But they're suspicious about Squanto and Sue flying to the Moon. The dummy is halfway here and nobody wants to bother chasing it down, but they're doubting it's real. They've posted the Sue Miller information all over the place, along with one of the Cappy Jane images of you. But it isn't you. Look." Joke flashed the Sue Miller ID sheet with the photo image of a short-haired hollow-cheeked girl with black hair. In addition, there was a holographic still image of Yoke and Cobb floating in the Vava'u bay, with the giant cube of imipolex just behind them. But Yoke's face was replaced by Sue Miller's, and Cobb looked like a plastic American Indian.

"The moldies didn't notice you searching, did they, Berenice?" Joke paused, looking into her head, which was partly inhabited by the wetware-coded personalities of two old-time boppers called Berenice and Emul. Quickly receiving her answer, Joke continued talking. "No, you're safe for now, Yoke, but you better believe the shit's going to hit the fan one way or another. You didn't say where Randy went on his motorcycle. And what about Babs?"

Yoke: "Well, yesterday was pretty calm, and we were nice to Randy and made things together, so don't worry too much about him going amok. He made the motorcycle this morning. A really tough machine, all big and black and loud, though of course it's electric. Like I say, he's out riding it now, but I don't know where. Babs was so impressed with Randy's motorcycle that she made herself a car, look, you can see it out in front of the warehouse." Yoke peered out the warehouse's big square door at an incredibly decorated dune-buggy outside. It was covered all over with drawings of girls, done in a casual sketchbook kind of style, and its fenders were curled up in funny squiggles. It looked like a live cartoon, bright in the afternoon sun. Standing by the buggy was Babs herself, talking to a burr-cut man with little round glasses. "That's Babs's new friend Theodore. He slept here last night. Believe it or not, Randy's jealous of him. As if he had a right. I think that's why he took off on his big bad motorsickle this morning. And then Babs made herself the car just to show she's still on top. She thought about it for a couple of hours and when she was ready she alla-made it real fast when nobody was looking. She transmuted some heavy garbage instead of just air, so that there wasn't this like big thunderclap. Theodore and our neighbors don't know about the allas yet, thank God. If the word gets out, it's going to be a zoo. I'll go ahead and step all the way outside so you can see down the street. Hi, Babs, I'm talking to my sister Joke on the Moon. See Cobb lying in the street next to the car sunning himself, Joke? It's the third sunny day in a row. Say hi to Joke, Cobb, you lazy old slug." Cobb stuck a head and arm out of his puddled form and waved. "And see the giant, charred snail shell across the street by the water, Joke? Isn't that too much?"

Joke: "Keep looking, I want to sketch the shell for Corey. He wants to make a Silly Putter pet Tucker Snail. And then look down the street so I can see the *Anubis*, Yoke. I'm getting really nice image quality. And also I want to talk about how soon you're coming home. I don't want to lose you. You should leave before the heavy kilp starts happening."

Yoke stared at the shell and the *Anubis* for a minute, then wandered back into the warehouse. It was two in the afternoon. "Phil's the big issue to me, Joke, and of course Ma too. I'm sorry, but I don't want a clone with a Happy Cloak for my mother. According to the aliens, Phil and Darla and the others are off in the powerball hyperspace bubble, maybe not so far away. In the fourth dimension. I told Phil I'd wait for him here. If I hang here just a little more, maybe he'll come back. Oh, and look, I didn't show you yet what Randy, Babs, and I made yesterday." Yoke gazed at a chest-high aquarium filled with delicately shaded plastic jellyfish. "These are imipolex, like Babs's worms. It's very easy to program an artificial jellyfish, at least it was with Randy helping. See how we put a different mandala onto the surface of each one? The kind of realistic ones are Babs's and the more abstract ones are by me. I think Babs is right that moving art is better than art that just sits there. Next I want to make some simulated polyps that build a coral reef. I wish I knew more limpware engineering. Randy's good at it, believe it or not. Of course, playing with real life would be more exciting, but the aliens say it's going to be impossible for us to use the alla to really program biological life until we completely figure out all of the wetware engineering for ourselves, and who knows when that'll be. They don't want to tell us too much, because they don't want it to be easy for us or the moldies to actualize a billion instances of ourselves and instantly over-populate the planet. They think we're that dumb."

Joke: "Too true. I wish you'd come back home, Yoke. Those allas—they could be dangerous. What if someone were to turn one against you? It sounds like things could so easily get out of control. Does Randy Karl Tucker realize that the aliens are in bodacious moldie bodies just down the block?"

Yoke made a little marble head with her alla, an image of how she felt. An open-mouthed face: excited, anxious, aware. "We didn't tell him yet, no. But I think we might go see them tonight."

CHAPTER FIVE

RANDY, PHIL, BABS, PHIL

═══ ■ ═══

Randy, February 26

Randy steered his motorcycle south out of San Francisco, taking Route 1 down along the coast past Pacifica. Though it had been sunny over at Babs's warehouse, it was foggy and cold on the coast. He pulled over and alla-made himself gloves and a set of biking leathers. Awesome what the little coppery tube could do. It had been great making things with Babs and Yoke yesterday. That Babs was really something. And now, just when he was starting to go for her, she was slipping away from him, which was majorly depressing. Maybe it was time for him to change.

Randy tucked the alla tube inside his right glove just in case he needed it all of sudden. He'd never ridden a motorcycle before, and he had a notion that if he were about to collide with something, he might be able to use the alla to turn the obstacle into thin air. Just project a bright-line cube on out there and zap whatever it was: a rock, a tree, or even another vehicle. Though if he couldn't have Babs, then why bother? Randy caught himself and pushed that feeling away.

Riding the bike proved quite easy. Randy had picked a top-of-the-line model out of the alla catalog, and it was very stable.

It had a big quantum-dot electric motor and imipolex DIM wheels. South of Half Moon Bay, Randy decided to stop and make himself a snack. Not seeing any official beach, he simply drove his bike across a field of dead brussels sprouts to the edge of a hundred-foot bluff at the edge of the sea. The smart wheels had no problem picking their way across the furrows.

Randy parked his bike upright on its stand, then used his alla to make himself an energy bar and a can of Bharat Jolly Zest soda, an anise-flavored Indian soft drink he'd become fond of in Bangalore. He was pleased to find it in the truly exhaustive alla catalog. After eating, he kept sitting on the bluff, amusing himself by designing a series of little realware glider airplanes and flinging them out into the eddying winds. He couldn't stop thinking about Babs Mooney.

Babs's sudden relationship with Theodore was bothering Randy a lot more than he would have expected. Up until a few days ago he'd been thinking of Babs as basically an easy mark whom he could sponge off of, as well as being a pretty good person to kill time with. It's not like she was knock-down gorgeous or anything. But now all of a sudden things were getting complicated, the way women were said to like them to be.

Randy's experience thus far with women was very limited, one might even say stunted. The sum total was this: in high school he'd had a hot and heavy affair with a bisexual older woman named Honey Weaver who—it later developed—had really just been using him as a way to get at his mother, with whom Honey also had an affair. It was Honey who'd gotten Randy interested in cheeseball sex. She'd had two memorable moldie sex toys: the dildo Angelika and the versatile rubber sheet Sammie-Jo.

The day after Randy graduated from high school—lordy lord, that was nearly four years ago—Honey had converted to Heritagism and cut him off without so much as a kiss good-bye. "All them things you and me did was wrong, Randy Karl," she'd said. "I'm through bein' the goddamn Whore of Babylon. It was only because of your mother that you was important to me."

Honey had used him and ditched him, and then the same thing had happened again—only this time with a moldie named Parvati. Randy lived with Parvati while he was working for an imipolex fab in Bangalore, India. In the end it came out that Parvati really and truly only wanted him for the imipolex he could give her. There'd been a bad last scene involving poisoning and knife-play; Randy ended up in possession of one of Parvati's buttocks, which had become none other than Willa Jean.

Randy didn't tell anyone that particular story because it was too ludicrous, like so much of his sorry-ass life. From the inside, of course, his life didn't feel funny one bit. Just because most people's lives worked out so goody-goody bone-normal, did that make him a Bozo clown that anyone could take a shot at?

He sighed, staring down at his bright-line alla mesh and tweaking the wing shape of another glider. No way to deny that it was his fault Babs thought he was a fool. First of all, he'd come in loaded on camote on Tuesday morning. He had a painful memory of trying to hump one of those aliens, just like a dog getting on someone's leg. His eyes all rolling back to show their whites. Ow. Since then he'd been too ashamed to talk about the aliens, or even to ask Babs where they'd gone.

And then there'd been the second thing. Tuesday night, before he had any kind of chance to reestablish his credibility, Babs had left for a date—a date!—and in the night he had his godawful recurring nightmare about the snail that followed him everywhere, the snail that would always catch up no matter how fast or how far he ran.

Sitting alone on the bluff, Randy writhed in agony, remembering the raw terror of waking up in the night with everything *not* okay, with the nightmare snail big and real and truly after him, dragging its realware shell through the sad real world, the snail talking like his poor dead mother, its voice loud and clear so that Yoke and Cobb could hear it, could hear all about how the snail wanted to sit on his face so nasty. "Ah'm real hot to crawl on you, Randy Karl."

He was no motherfucker, he didn't deserve this kilp, but try and explain it to Babs after she heard all about it from that little loonie twist Yoke; Yoke laughing her ass off about it every time she brought it up, twenty times so far if it was one.

And this morning Yoke had told that slick Theodore about the snail. Since they were keeping the allas secret, Yoke had to talk all around everything to avoid spilling the beans. She'd made it sound like he had hand-built the monster while he was lifted or sleepwalking or something.

So who was Babs gonna go for, Bozo the hillbilly or Theodore the smooth-talking California scene-maker, always with the right opinions about the right things—shit, the dook even worked at an art gallery, which had to be Babs's perfect wet dream. Theodore had slept over with Babs last night. The guy was already gettin' on her. Randy felt a sick rush of self-loathing. All the twisted, rotten things he'd done over the years—how could any regular woman love him?

Randy set the next glider on fire and watched as it warped and burned, spiraling down into the pounding surf. "That's me," he muttered, and damned if he didn't half feel like jumping off the cliff himself. Get it the hell over with. The way he was, nobody could ever love him. He was better off dead. Randy inched closer to the cliff's edge, watching as some dirt crumbled under his weight. Better off dead? All because of that noisy, plump-cheeked little Babs Mooney? "Come on, Randy boy. *Tat tvam asi.*"

He thought of a better thing to do, reckless enough to slake his death-wish without being sheer suicide. He found the alla-catalog image of his motorcycle, located an image of a full-size glider plane, and mentally attached the titanium-braced imipolex wings of the glider to the bike. He studied the image, adjusted the bends of the wing, and said "Actualize." The alla projected a bright-line wire mesh near the edge of the bluff, then filled it in with Randy's newly designed fly-bike.

The ocean wind beat at the twenty-foot wings, threatening to push the motorcycle-glider over on one side. Randy bulked up some dirt mound supports for the wings and added a rocket-pod to the rear of the bike. And then he took another look at the ocean. The restless waves were gray and cold, utterly heedless of human comfort. It would xoxx to fall in. Fuck death! He didn't have to die; he could change! It wasn't too late yet. There had to be a way. Randy decided to launch the fly-bike in an *unmanned* test-run. Whether or not it worked, it would be easy enough to alla up another, and while he was doing all this he could think about how to make himself more lovable.

So as to properly weight the trial vehicle, Randy alla-made a mannequin of—why not polished madrone wood? That was one of the nicest materials he had seen so far, a fine-grained reddish wood nearly as dense and heavy as flesh. The lustrous madrone figure looked very floatin' sitting on the motorcycle-rocket-glider. Yaaar. Give it green glass eyes and a shit-eating grin. Randy fired up the rocket to launch the combine off the cliff. One of the wings twisted; the bike spun into the cliff and tumbled out of control. Meanwhile the rocket was blasting and—*splash*—the bike punched into the water at easily forty miles per. The crouched wooden rider floated facedown, the waves beating the figure against the rocks.

"That's the old me," laughed Randy, relieved not to be down there. "This boy's startin' up a new leaf." He still had a chance with Babs. He'd stay away from camote, stop fucking moldies, and quit doing deals with sleazebags like Aarbie Kidd. Yaaar. Better straight than dead.

The wrecked motorcycle-glider looked bad down in the ocean, so Randy sent his alla control-mesh down there to surround it. It was stuzzy how you could just wish the mesh out to wherever you wanted it to be.

Once Randy had the mesh around the smashed motorcycle, he had to tweak the mesh, as the smashed-up machine wasn't shaped the same anymore. The alla hookup was intense enough that Randy had a direct sensory feeling for the contents of the mesh; there were some rocks in there, a couple of little fish, lot of mussels—would have been a shame to wipe out all those things. He tightened the mesh in on the busted fly-bike and turned the machinery into water. But he left his wooden man to keep bumbling about in the rocks and surf. The bad Randy.

"One more taahm," muttered Randy, and made a new motorcycle with wings. This time, though, he gave it some wing-flexing controls hooked into the handlebars, plus a better rider, one more likely to steer the test vehicle in a helpful way. He actualized an imipolex figure and equipped it with camera-eyes, an uvvy, a rudimentary niobium wire nervous system, and a control patch like he'd given Willa Jean. Like a ventriloquist throwing his voice, Randy put his awareness out into the imipolex rider, looking through its eyes and twitching its limbs and fingers. The more of this he did, the less he felt like dying.

Vooden-vooden, screeched the fly-bike's electric engine, and *kkkroooooow* went the rocket. Out into the air the jury-rigged machine flew. Fully into the virtual personality of his stand-in, Randy felt himself to be riding it. He twitched the wings, adjusted the rocket, gained some altitude, but then—damn!—a gust of wind crimped down a wing and he was flying straight back at the cliff. Frantically he manipulated the wings and—yes!—he was turning, he was going to make it, but—double damn—there was one jutting rock that was just going to catch the tip of his right wing—quick, alla-blast it out of the way!

Randy got the uvvy on the plastic rider to send his alla a direct signal that—*boom*—turned a protruding knee of rock into thin air but—uh-oh!—turning so much rock into air made a shock wave that threw the fly-bike further off balance. The bike rocketed downward. So as to make the cleanup simpler this time, Randy snapped an alla mesh out there and turned the machine and its plastic rider into air just before they crashed into the rocky shore. He was seeing out through the eyes of the rider right up to the instant when it dissolved, which was a very strange feeling. Somehow the experience made him think of that poor moldie Monique whom he'd kidnapped and sent off to her death last fall. "I'm sorry, Lord," said Randy out loud, not that he'd ever been a praying man. "Please forgive me." And that was the moment when Randy felt that change was really going to be possible.

He'd been a fool too long. It was time to go back and talk to Babs. He'd abandoned any thought of riding a fly-bike. They'd served their purpose now, they'd kept him from killing himself.

He was thirsty again, but when he uvvied into his alla to make another soft drink, a strange thing happened. Instead of producing a control mesh, the alla began talking to him.

"Greetings," said the alla. "Shall I actualize a new Randy Karl Tucker or shall I execute a fresh registration?" As it spoke he felt a series of tingles in his body, as if the alla were checking him out.

"Hey," said Randy, confused. "We already done this before. I *am* Randy Karl Tucker."

"Original user identity is ninety-eight percent confirmed," said the alla, as if not even listening to him. "The Randy Karl Tucker actualization option is withdrawn. For full confirmation and reactivation, we must now execute a fresh registration. Please give a name and thought association for each image." And then it showed Randy the same series of images it had used before to learn his mental software. The first three flicked past: a symmetric circular pattern of colored lights, a crooked forked line, and a uniform patch of rough texture.

Just like the first time, Randy said they were like a mandala he'd seen the first time he got high on camote in Bangalore with Parvati, like a dried up creek-bed out at the London Earl Estates trailer park south of Louisville, and like the skin of a dead moldie he'd seen in a jar at a Heritagist church fair.

After the dizzyingly rapid and thorough quizzing came a series of tingles throughout Randy's body, and then the alla said, "You are registered as my sole user for life. Feel free to select something from my catalog."

And at this point Randy realized what had happened. The complicated hookup through the imipolex dummy had temporarily tricked the alla into the belief that it was the real Randy who'd been alla-converted into air. The alla thought it had killed him.

Once he was dead the alla could either—what had it said?—"actualize a new Randy Karl Tucker" or "execute a fresh registration." Had the first option, so quickly withdrawn, meant that the alla could make a duplicate of him, a second Randy identical in mind and body? That would be floatin'.

"Go ahead and make that copy of me," Randy told the alla, not really thinking through the consequences. His pulse was pounding with excitement. "Make a Randy Karl Tucker Two."

Again there came a series of tingles in Randy's body. "Ninety-nine point nine eight seven confirmation that you are Randy Karl Tucker. Request to actualize multiple instances of yourself is denied."

Oh well. Come to think of it, if there were a Randy II, he'd be competing with Randy for Babs. Theodore was already trouble enough. Still, it would have been nice. Randy had grown up an only child; he'd always wished he had a sibling who understood him.

Just about then another thing about the alla's behavior struck Randy. If he really had been dead and some other guy had picked up the alla, then maybe the alla would have actualized a fresh Randy, but more likely the new guy would have chosen to register the alla to himself.

Randy looked around, suddenly anxious that someone might be watching him. But he was alone at the edge of the bluff. There were a couple of liveboard surfers out in the ocean, but they were quite far away. Nobody was watching him. But what if someone saw him use his alla and became maddened with the lust to own it—what if someone saw this wonderful tool and killed him to take it away?

The alla would offer the murderer a choice like, "Do you want to bring back the sap you just killed, or do you want to enjoy the endless power of this magic wand?" And of course the killer would choose the second option.

The alla would go ahead and register a new "user for life,"

probably forgetting the old Randy Tucker body and mind pattern entirely.

This meant that once the news of allas and their transferability got out, owning an alla would become seriously hazardous to your health. To his health, and that of Yoke and Babs. There was a slight chance the "new you" option might still save your ass—but someone would have to like you enough to ask for it and, truth be told, it was hard to believe it would really work.

While he was thinking all this, Randy sent out a control mesh to alla-make a plug of sandy yellow rock to fill in the smooth square hole he'd punched out of the cliff. It was starting to get dark. He got back onto his original motorcycle and rode across the field toward the narrow track of Route 1, his electric motor loudly purring.

When he'd started out this morning he had a vague idea of visiting Aarbie Kidd down in Santa Cruz to look up some fresh hell to raise. But that would have been the vicious, self-destructive old Randy, the same guy who'd been using leech-DIMs to kidnap moldies. And from now on, that Randy was history. He was going to make amends and do right by moldies and people alike. There was no reason to see Aarbie at all. Hell, if Aarbie saw his alla, he might kill him for it—and be able to start using it as his own. No point in him getting killed just when it was time to start a new life! The only place the new Randy wanted to go was back to San Francisco.

Randy tooled along northward, with the winter sun setting off on his left. The thing to do was to go right back to the warehouse and make a serious play for Babs. Tell her that she was the nicest woman he'd ever met. Tell her he was sick of being a heartless crouched-over piece of wood. What would Babs say? It did seem like the girl was kind of sweet on him, at least it had at first. He just had to undo the damage of his camote trip and the realware snail. And, hey, yesterday had been pretty mellow, what with him, Babs, and Yoke making those plastic jellyfish. Maybe if he flat out spilled his heart, Babs would kick out Theodore and let him into her canopy bed.

Which led to a new problem. If it got down to the dirty, would he be able to have sex with a normal girl his age? Fella wouldn't want to come up limp for a dynamo like Babs. That would be a real strike three for Bozo the country clown. Now, if Babs could see her way clear to her and him layin' on a moldie rubber sheet, there'd be much less chance of a problem. And, you know, Babs had said something about not minding the smell of moldies. Her mother Wendy was supposed to be part moldie in some way.

Randy got kind of excited thinking about him and Babs on a Sammie-Jo. Yaaar. Just put some moldie-flesh in the picture and there'd be no doubt about what would occur. Not that he wanted to fall back into his old ways.

He was motoring in through the city now and it was dark. He had an intense desire to get laid. As he rolled into Babs's neighborhood, he saw the lights of the *Anubis* by the side of the road. The great beached ship was alive with glowing moldies and capering revelers. Maybe he should pull on in there and rent some time with a moldie? He'd had quite a session with Isis the other day—but, no, that wasn't the way he wanted to act anymore. With Babs he had, for the very first time, a real chance at a real woman. "Don't lose it, Randy Karl," he said aloud, motoring past the *Anubis* and toward Babs's warehouse.

Just as he pulled into her street, he saw a funny-looking cartoon car go driving by. Babs in her new electric dune buggy. And next to her was that goddamn Theodore. Babs smiled and waved—and kept on driving.

"Babs!" said Randy, reaching out to her with an urgent uvvy call. Not wanting to lose sight of her, he swung his bike through a tight U-turn and began following her.

"Hey, Randy," came Babs's cozy voice on the uvvy. "Where've you been all day?" She turned a corner and drove in toward the city down Third Street. She didn't realize yet that he was right behind her.

"I was cruising the coast. I was gonna see Aarbie Kidd, but I decided not to. I'm gonna change. I feel like I got off on the wrong foot with you, Babs. Are you coming back to the warehouse soon?"

"I'm just giving Theodore a ride to work. He has the evening shift at the Asiz Gallery. What's on your tortured mind?"

"I figured out two things today, Babs. The first thing is about the—the 'toy' I got. I found out that if I die, the 'toy' will either make a copy of me or work just as well for the next person that picks it up."

"Bizarre." A long pause while Babs thought it over. "Good news and bad news, isn't it? But I don't think we should be discussing this on the uvvy." Randy saw her glance into her rearview mirror. "Hey, is that you following me?"

"Right on your sweet tailfeather, baby. Look, I gotta tell you the second thing in person. Pull over, would you?"

"Okay." Babs pulled her funny car over to the curb and hopped out. Theodore stayed in the car, looking anxious and annoyed. Randy parked his motorcycle and held out his arms to Babs. Babs took a few uncertain steps closer and spoke to him without benefit of the uvvy.

"What is it? I hope you're not lifted again, Randy."

"You're—You're not like any gal I ever met, Babs. I didn't realize it at first, but I could really go for you."

Babs blushed, glanced back at Theodore, took another step closer. "Are you serious?" A little smile played across her lips.

"I know I been acting screwed up. But you're the only woman I could care about, Babs. I had me kind of a peculiar childhood. The cheeseball thing—well, I was thinking that your ma's part moldie so maybe it's okay. I mean if you and I was to—I'm just worried I might need some—well, if you wouldn't mind layin' on a moldie rubber sheet is—"

Babs's voice was loud and hurt. "What do you think you're talking about!"

"I'm gettin' ahead of myself, sorry," said Randy. "Just a-thinkin' out loud. Don't sweat the details, right? You and me, Babs, we got a future, huh? It'll work. You're the best gal I ever met. I'm just a-scared I'll blow it."

"Are you all right, Babs?" called Theodore, getting out of the car.

"Yes yes," said Babs. "Just a second."

"Don't go off with Theodore now, Babs," begged Randy. "We gotta talk some more."

"How did you find out about what your alla does if you die?" whispered Babs. "Is what you said really true?"

"You're going to make me late," said Theodore, walking over. "Hi, Tucker. Seen any giant snails today?"

"Oh, leave Randy alone," said Babs. "Look, Theodore, you just take my car for now. In fact, keep it overnight and show it to Kundry Asiz tomorrow and see if she'll take it for the gallery. I talked to Kundry on the uvvy about it already, and I think she's interested."

"But—"

"Something's come up," said Babs, and gave Theodore a peck on the cheek. "Bye. I'll uvvy you tomorrow."

So Babs got on the back of Randy's motorcycle and rode back to her warehouse with him.

"One thing," she said as they got off the bike. "I am not going to fuck you on any gross moldie sheet. Not that I'm saying I'd fuck you at all. Hi, Cobb."

"Back so soon?" Cobb was slouched in the warehouse doorway, sort of guarding the place. "Yoke was just saying maybe she should go back to the Moon. Talking to her sister made her homesick. Hi, Randy, good to see you. You don't want to go to the Moon yet, do you? There's too much happening down here, don't you think?"

"Yeah, I feel like things are just starting," said Randy. "Hey, come on inside, Cobb, we four oughtta have a little talk. If Yoke can lay off raggin' me."

"Help," hollered Yoke, seeing Randy in the doorway. "The attack of the giant snail!"

"I'm gonna whomp your butt!" shouted Randy, charging after her. He was tired of drag-assing around and being humble. Yoke shrieked and ran, firing off a few hydrogen-oxygen air-bombs in her wake. Randy alla-made a big cushion right in front of Yoke, and she stumbled over it. He stood over her, with Willa Jean loyally at his side. "You've teased me enough, Yoke. I know I done acted like a clown, but I'm gonna be different now. You hear that, Cobb and Babs? I'm gonna be a new man. Worthy of my great-grandpa, and worthy of the woman I love."

"Huh?" said Yoke.

Babs walked over and put her arm around Randy's waist. "I think Randy's cute. So be nice to him."

Randy smiled and kissed Babs's cheek, then went ahead and threw both arms around her to give her a full-body hug. As he hugged her and inhaled her warm fragrance, he realized that, if he ever got her into bed, he wasn't going to be needing any sex-aids.

"Okay," said Babs, worming away. "But now we better talk about the alla thing you mentioned before."

So Randy told the other three about how he'd learned that an alla would freshly re-register itself to whoever next picked it up after its last owner died—although there was supposedly a possibility that it could instead actualize a fresh copy of you.

"So in this fairy tale, the greedy peasant who kills the golden goose gets the goose's powers," said Yoke. "Xoxx it."

"Unless he chooses to actualize a fresh, live instance of the goose," pointed out Babs.

"Me, I've known my share of peasants," said Randy. "Ain't no peasant in the world would ever wish that goose back."

"So either we keep the allas secret forever," said Babs. "Or we get murdered. Or we throw our allas away. Or we figure out how to give one to everyone in the world. Four possibilities. And the first one's impossible. Secrets get out. Especially with the aliens hanging with random cheeseballs and lifters all day long."

"They're on the *Anubis*?" said Randy. "That's where, isn't it? Why didn't anyone tell me?" He was sitting next to Babs; Willa Jean had nestled in between them.

"We assumed that if you knew, you'd instantly run over

there to try and fuck Shimmer again," said Cobb. "I, for one, wanted to see my great-grandson's poor bod get a few days rest."

"I—" Randy's voice cracked. "I ain't doin' that no more. Not while I got a chance with Babs."

"How touching," said Yoke in a voice that struggled to stay level. She paused to clear her throat. "Let's think. What Babs said boils down to this. If we don't want to get killed, we either get rid of our allas or we figure out how to give an alla to everyone. I'm for everyone getting an alla. We just have to find out how to tell an alla to make an alla."

"I'm not sure about that," said Babs, absently petting Willa Jean. "People are too stupid. If everyone gets an alla, every square inch of the world will be full of—crap. It's been fun making art with the alla, but I was an artist before I got my alla, and I'll be an artist when it's gone. Maybe I'd rather just throw it away than have idiots use it."

"Well, that's great for you, Miss High and Mighty," said Yoke. "But I'm an artist too. Only there was never an art-form I felt really good at till the alla came along. Does that make me a clumsy peon? I'm not giving up my alla, Babs."

"You're great with your alla, Yoke," said Babs soothingly. "And I didn't mean to sound like I don't think you're an artist. But actually you *could* do art even without the alla, you know. I was just saying that most people aren't artists at all."

"Most people are dumb shits," said Yoke, still feeling feisty. "But if everyone has an alla, then what a fool does is fixable. If one person does something stupid, someone else can undo it."

"Are you sure?" said Babs. She projected a mesh over a potted African violet and turned it into an ugly plastic flower jabbed into a chunk of Styrofoam the shape of a cat. "This is what people will do. Can you fix it?"

"Yeah," said Yoke slowly. "The alla can make plants. Here you go." And a new African violet appeared. "I had the alla give it standard potting soil complete with bacteria, bugs, and worms, though I admit I don't have any way of knowing exactly what was there before."

Babs leaned over the plant examining it. "I'm impressed," she admitted. "I like it. This gives me hope. And you know, come to think of it, I can't bear the thought of losing my alla. I was just scared to admit it before. This could really work." Babs laughed happily. "Yes. I have this image of some dook turning a beautiful woodsy hilltop into a gross puffball Mc-Mansion with three stories and forty thousand square feet. And then his greenie neighbor turns the house back into a woodsy hilltop. Back and forth all day long. Maybe the dook would only put up his house at night."

"There'd still be zoning laws in any case," mused Yoke. "That would put some limits on the houses. If the gimmie could enforce them. And there's a limit to how big a volume the alla can transform at one go. A cube something like forty feet on a side."

"But even so, everyone would build out to the legal max," said Babs. "They'd alla up their giant houses one section at a time. And homeless people would pitch houses for themselves just anywhere, even though they don't own any land. But that's actually good, isn't it? No more homeless."

"Squatters deluxe," mused Randy. "They wouldn't need no plumbing hookups. Use the alla to fill your bathtub, and use it again to make the dirty water go away. Wouldn't be so bad. You could put up a house anywhere. Use the alla to make batteries for any electricity you needed."

"But what kind of kinky kilp would psychos make?" said Babs. "A thousand ton turd in the middle of Union Square! A *statement* turd, you wave? And of course there'd be giant crucifixes everyplace. And just imagine solid, three-dimensional graffiti. You try to open your front door and there's a fifteen-foot solid chrome freestyle 'Yuki 37' in the way." Babs laughed again. "Actually I can't wait to see it."

"People could alla that kilp back into air," said Yoke. "If everyone did it as a matter of course, then cleaning up wouldn't have to be anyone's full-time job. It wouldn't be as hard as picking up litter, you wave. You'd only have to look at something and wish it away. You said turds, crosses, and graffiti? You forgot porno and political ads. Uh-oh, I'm seeing another problem. What if someone allas something that *you* like into air. Like your new car, Babs—someone could vaporize it because they don't like the way it looks. Just like you'd get rid of a giant turd."

"If she saved a software map of her buggy, she can alla it back whenever she needs it," suggested Randy. "Parkin' is hell in this city anyhow. Just turn your car back into air instead of parkin' it. Long as you got the alla and the software map, you only need to bring back your realware when you actually wanna use it. In the end, the allas should be good for Nature. We won't have to manufacture nothin'. You want paper or lumber, you alla it up, 'stead of cuttin' down a live tree. Alla up oil instead of drilling for it. No more factories!"

"This is making me dizzy," sighed Babs, putting her hands to her head. "It's like a beautiful dream. If only people can— oh, wait, what about nuclear explosions?"

"That could be the biggest problem of all," said Cobb. "It would be easy to alla up a twenty-five-pound ball of plutonium. A supercritical mass. Instant atomic bomb."

"Shit," said Babs. "There's got to be a way out. Will the alla actually make plutonium? Let's check."

Randy, Babs, and Yoke uvvied inward, examining their alla catalogs, and sure enough, plutonium was listed.

"Don't try making any of it," cautioned Cobb. "It's highly poisonous, even in small amounts."

"We have to get the aliens to talk to Om," said Yoke. "To tell Om not to let the allas make nuclear fuel. Uranium, plutonium—no evil heavy metal. Om ought to be able to control what the allas can do. They're all connected to her, you know."

"Yes," said Babs. "And then everyone gets an alla."

"Here we are gettin' all worked up," said Randy. "And we don't know how to copy no alla in the first place.

"The Metamartians do," said Cobb. "Remember, Yoke? Josef said they know how to use the alla to make an alla. We should ask them how to copy the allas and at the same time get them to tell Om to not let allas make uranium or plutonium. Let's go to the *Anubis* now!"

"Have you ever been on the *Anubis* before, Babs?" said Yoke.

"My brother and I went there right before I moved in here," said Babs. "Just to look it over. It seemed kind of sad. Lots of xoxxy people. If we go over there, I think we should have a plan. We're supposed to beg the aliens to tell us how to make an alla with the alla? And to block plutonium?"

"Begging is about all we *can* do," said Yoke. "We can't really threaten them or anything. I mean, they have built-in alla power, and they can see a little way into the future. No way we can hurt them."

"Maybe I can get Siss hot for me," said Cobb. "When Randy and I got onto Kleopatra and Isis the other night, Kleopatra said I was good. I think Siss is kind of interesting."

"Who knows, Babs, if we beg, maybe the Metamartians will help us," put in Randy, eager to move the conversation forward. "From what Yoke and Cobb say, Om does plan for everyone to get the alla. And it's not like she's out to destroy the planet. All Om wants is to memorize us each and every one. It's like the allas are the ultimate reward for filling in your questionnaire."

"Do you think you can handle being on the *Anubis*, Randy?" asked Babs. "Without going on another sporehead cheeseball rampage?"

"If you with me, girl," said Randy sticking out his hand. "You all I see. We'll leave Willa Jean here to watch over things."

Phil, February 23–25

Phil spent four days in the powerball—from the Monday when Yoke flew back to San Francisco through the Thursday when things came to a head on the *Anubis*. The first three days went as follows:

MONDAY

While his dad guzzled wine with Darla and Tempest, Phil pulled himself to the other end of the oak tree. Right near the last branch was the flaw in their hyperspherical space. Things looked funny near the flaw. Goaded on by the inane chatter of the drunk pheezers, Phil got a firm grip on the branch, took a deep breath, and pushed his head out through the hole.

His viewpoint swung about with uncontrollable rapidity, like the view from a video camera left running while it dangles from a wrist-strap. Phil saw an endless landscape of curved pink surfaces—it was a bit like an ant's-eye view of a million-mile tall woman's body, not that the surfaces had the order and symmetry of a human form. Awed and dizzy, he let his eyes follow along six metallic tendrils that led out of the cosmic pink form. The tendrils eventually ran into a great circular expanse of rock and mud that wavered and became a disk of water. When Phil turned his head a bit farther, he saw blinding bright light. Around then, Phil's face began to feel frostbitten and he realized he was desperately out of breath. For one panicked instant he couldn't figure out how to pull back his head—so formless and disorienting was hyperspace. It took a special effort to remember to bend the arm belonging to the hand holding the branch. This quickly brought his gasping head back in through the hole. Anxiously, Phil patted his face, but the skin wasn't frozen, just very cold.

He needed something like a limpware bubbletopper spacesuit if he were going to explore out there. But it seemed futile to try and find a human spacesuit in Om's Metamartian alien alla catalog. The "yam-snoot" Tempest had fed him—had that even been food? His mouth felt greasy and nasty.

Phil's eye fell on the Humpty-Dumpty doll, big as a watermelon. It was made of good moldie imipolex and could, in principle, serve as a spacesuit. But would he be able to get it to stretch itself over him? It didn't look very intelligent. Silly Putters weren't exported to Earth from the Moon, so Phil had never actually handled one before. They were said to be poised half-way between DIMs and moldies in intelligence. Supposedly, the famous inventor Willy Taze had developed an algorithm to keep them from unexpectedly tunneling into ungovernable moldie consciousness.

"Come here," he said, beckoning ingratiatingly to the Humpty-Dumpty. The fat egg smiled uncertainly. Phil decided to try uvvying into it. The mind of the Humpty-Dumpty was what one would imagine the mind of a dog to be: a simple, affectless reflection of the passing scene. "Come here," repeated Phil. "I need for you to help me. Come on, Humpty. Come to Phil." Slowly the egg inched closer along the branch.

"Can you wrap me up?" asked Phil, forming a mental image of a man in a bubbletopper. "Can you act like a spacesuit and give me air?"

Humpty-Dumpty's face split in a big smile, and it uvvied back something that sounded like prerecorded ad copy. "Yes, Humpty-Dumpty can act as a spacesuit. Every genuine Corey Rhizome Silly Putter doll is usable as an emergency bubbletopper. It's just another reason why every loonie family should own at least one!"

The egg waddled closer, opened its mouth wide and gently bit onto Phil's arm. And then its plastic flesh liquefied and flowed all over Phil, sealing him up inside a full-body suit. Cheesy-smelling air trickled out of an indentation over Phil's nostrils, and the imipolex over his eyes became a transparent visor.

Grabbing the branch again, Phil stuck his head out into hyperspace for a second time. Again, the first thing he saw was a great expanse of pink—it had to be the body of Om.

In an effort to keep his viewpoint from thrashing about, Phil made every effort to hold perfectly still, even though he was holding onto a drifting tree with a dog and three drunk old people at the tree's other end. Phil tried to compensate for the jiggling by turning his head this way and that, but he couldn't quite put it together. No action seemed to have the expected consequence; it was like trying to do something with his hands while watching them in a mirror. Everything was upside down, backward, and maybe even inside out.

Even so, he was able to get a better look at some of the things he'd seen before. He found that when he unexpectedly lost sight of something, he could wobble his head to scan back and forth to find it. Wobbling had the additional effect of sometimes showing him a series of views that his mind could integrate into a solid whole. Some of the endless pink surfaces were spheres that seamlessly blended together—surely these were views of the hyperspherical powerball finger of Om whose hypersurface enclosed the rest of his body. And the pink curves beyond the spheres? Further sections of Om's body—Phil got the feeling she was astronomical in size.

When Phil glanced down at himself, he discovered a truly gnarly sight. Where he'd expected to see his chest and shoulders, he instead saw a cross section of his body. One part of the image was regularly twitching, and the twitches matched the beating of Phil's pulse, clearly audible in the hush of hyperspace. The twitching thing was his heart. But in this odd view, his heart appeared not as a whole organ, but as a cross section, a muscular ring filled with surging blood.

Next to the heart were cross-sectional views of his flexing lungs, which looked like ovals of fractal broccoli. And arranged outside his innards were layers of muscle inset with circlets of bone—rib sections. The pink curve of the powerball's hypersphere blocked any view of his stomach and its contents.

Now one of the geezers heavily bumped the tree, and Phil completely lost his orientation. The same intense bright light as before glared in his eyes. Phil squinted against it, trying to make out some detail. As he looked into the light, he picked up a sense of serenity and grandeur. Wobbling his head to scan the adjacent environs of hyperspace, he made out a flickering around the light, as if things were swarming into it. What a fine thing it would be to fly ana into the Divine Light.

But now heavy hands grabbed Phil's waist and pulled him back in. It was Da, drunker than before. Phil felt like hitting him. Stupid old man.

"You have to be more careful or you might fall out," Da was saying. "Good thing I thought to check on you."

"I was doing fine," said Phil, pushing the cowl of Humpty-Dumpty off his face. The Silly Putter assumed its duties were over and crawled off, firming itself back into its original form. "Leave me alone, Da," continued Phil. "We'll talk after you sleep."

"I'm tired of sleeping," said old Kurt. "That's when Om always comes for me."

"Just get away," said Phil, and pushed himself off from the tree, floating out into an empty region of the hypersphere. It had been a long day, and he was exhausted. He used Om's invisible alla to make himself a cup of water, and drank it greedily. That lightened the unpleasant load of the yam-snoot in his gut. He closed his eyes and let his limbs go slack, missing Yoke and thinking about the new things he'd seen. Before long he was asleep.

TUESDAY

Tempest woke Phil by tapping his mouth with one of her greasy food-spindles. "It's a new day, Junior. Hope you ain't still mad at your Dad. Here's a naahce yam-snoot for your breakfast."

"Xoxx it, Tempest, I can't eat this scuzzy kilp. Show me where in the alla catalog you found it. There's got to be something better." Though Phil was quite hungry, his queasy stomach categorically forbade any further yam-snoot.

"Hyar 'tis," said Tempest, and she uvvied Phil a bookmark into Om's alien alla catalog.

None of the objects near the yam-snoot seemed to be food at all; indeed, Phil soon got the impression that the yam-snoot was in fact a Metamartian cleaning product. "God help me," he sighed.

And the instant he said that, the catalog altered its display to show a veritable buffet table of pleasant, normal-looking breakfast food: fruits, breads, cheeses, and pouches of juice.

"Actualize," said Phil quickly, and the cornucopia of food floated around him and Tempest. "Thank you, Om."

Phil listened for an answer, but he couldn't seem to hear Om while he was awake. The dream conversations with her last night had been intense. Yes, Om had been talking to him most of the night, avidly going over all of the memories and impressions that she could dredge out of his twenty-four years of life. It was like the time he had tried camping out with Kevvie, and she'd stuck a methedrine-patch on herself for the hike and then forgotten to take it off. Though unlike Kevvie, Om had wanted him to do most of the talking. Tell me this, tell me that, and when you said that other thing, what exactly did you mean? No wonder he still felt tired.

But the breakfast foods were delicious. Tempest, Darla, Kurt, and Planet the dog joined in. And afterward, when everyone skulked off to relieve themselves, Om turned their waste right into air. Phil could pee, and the stream would just vanish into breezy nothingness a few inches from the tip of his dick.

"No drinking for me today," intoned Da solemnly when they drifted back together. "My son and I have to talk."

"The fourth dimension," said Phil. "It's real."

"That was a good idea of yours to use Humpty-Dumpty for a spacesuit," said Da. "I didn't think of that. I've only grabbed two quick peeks out of the hole so far. It scares me shitless."

"But it's what you've been talking about your whole life," said Phil. "Hyperspace! Some of the things you taught have been coming back to me. I was seeing cross sections of my body, and I saw a whole lot of different spheres that must have been sections of this hypersphere."

Kurt looked uneasy. "I—I don't remember if I brought this up yesterday, but—don't you think it's at least possible that we're dead? That this is an antechamber before we go on into the Light? That's why I can't get too enthused about anything. You know I hate religion, Phil. It's not my bag. I thought that when I died everything would be over. And now it looks like I might end up facing the fucking God of the rednecks."

"The Metamartians say Om is God. So maybe we've already met God. In our dreams. She talked to me all night long. Asking about life on Earth."

"You too, huh?" said Kurt. "In my worst moments I think Om is St. Penis-at-the-Pearly-Gates's assistant, deciding whether or not to send me to Hell. But mostly Om's been picking my brain about mathematics. It was the wowo that got her attention. Advanced as they are, the Metamartians never happened to make this particular model of the Klein bottle. It reminds Om of her — childhood? That's not the right word. Origin, maybe."

"She didn't tell me anything about her origin."

"She says there's a higher-level God that she comes from. And that's the God I'm worried about. He's supposed to be made of Light. I think maybe I saw Him when I peeked out into hyperspace. Light with a capital L."

"I saw that Light for a long time yesterday," said Phil. "There were wonderful vibes coming off it. I'm not scared of God like you, Da. I even pray. It helps me stay sober."

"You're a better man than me, son. I wish I could be more like you. But I'm too old to change."

"It's never too late."

Kurt put his hands to his head. "What a hangover. So the Light didn't dart over and grab you when you looked at it? Let's go stick our heads out and have a good look around. I'll try using Humpty-Dumpty like you did. If there's any way for us to get back to Earth, it's got to be through that hole."

So Kurt and Phil got hold of Humpty-Dumpty and took turns looking through the flaw in the hypersphere. Kurt finally agreed with Phil that the Divine Light had good vibes.

"It doesn't feel like a judgmental God," allowed Kurt. "It feels like a God of Love. Like the Light cares and wants to help me. Weird."

"I think we get to decide what our God is like," said Phil.

"God is so different from us that any of our notions is inadequate. So why not assume God is good and loving? All right, Da, I see your expression, I'm not going to harp on this, I don't want to sound like the usual bullshitting religious pricks. Next topic: Do you have any ideas about that big disk of rock and mud that sometimes looks like water?"

"Those are slices of the Earth," said Kurt. "It's good they're so detailed. That means we're not at a very great hyperspace distance from home."

"Earth!" exclaimed Phil. "Teach me some math, Da. I need a refresher course. Why do Earth and my body look like cross sections? Talk about A Square."

Kurt smiled. He loved to talk about A Square. "All right! So think of A Square on a sphere floating above the plane of Flatland. We're the same, with every dimension one notch higher. We're on a hypersphere floating ana the space *we* come from. A Square's sphere has a little ledge on it, a place where he can slide his eye corner off. That's like Om's flaw. When A Square wags his eye back and forth, what does he see?"

"Weird shit," said Phil.

"Indeed. Let us analyze. When we look at the world, we see little 2D patches on our 2D retina, and we use these to build up a 3D image of a world. A Square sees little 1D patches on his 1D retina—imagine that his retina is a line at the back of his 2D eye—and he uses those to build up a 2D image of a world. But when he's up above Flatland looking down, he doesn't see Flatland as a whole. Instead he sees what's in the particular 2D world of his eye plane. The plane of his eye intersects the plane of Flatland in a 1D line. A cross section of Flatland. And if the cross-section line intersects some Flatland object, then A Square is seeing the innards of that object. In the same way, the 3D space of your eye intersects the 3D space of our ordinary universe in a 2D plane. And that's why you're seeing slices of innards."

"Whew," said Phil. "It's easier to see it than to talk about it. I saw a cross section of my heart. Did you look down at your chest, Da?"

"I did. Right down into my tired old ticker. And when we look down at Earth, we see cross sections of the Earth. We see these giant disks of dirt or water. It depends where our eye's 3D cross section of 4D hyperspace happens to intersect the 3D Earth in a 2D plane."

"Yaaar," said Phil. "But why is the inside of my heart lit up? You'd think it would be dark in there."

"That must be because there's a four-dimensional light in hyperspace," said Kurt. "From that divine Light we saw."

"The SUN!" exclaimed Phil. "Cobb Anderson talked about it at your funeral. I asked him what it had been like to be dead. The God Light must be what Cobb called the SUN. Capital S-U-N."

"The SUN," said Kurt. "That's a good name. As long as you understand that the SUN has nothing to do with our regular Sun."

"The SUN's light is inside everything," said Phil slowly. "It's like our world is made of stained-glass pieces with the God Light shining through. A cathedral window lit by the SUN. How can you be scared, Da?"

"You know," said Kurt after a long pause, "I have this feeling I should fly into the SUN. Maybe if I sacrifice myself, then Om will let you go."

"Oh man, with you getting so wrecked all the time, you don't know what you're talking about anymore," said Phil. "Put that shit away. I'm gonna look at the Earth again. Crawl on me, Humpty-Dumpty."

With his father hanging onto his legs, Phil leaned way out of the flaw in Om's hypersphere. He flopped around until he saw a huge disk of rock and dirt; this time he noticed a glowing region at its distant center. The Earth's core. Now Phil began delicately wobbling his head to make the cross-sectional disk smaller and smaller. Right before it disappeared it became a great lake of water. He moved back the way he'd come, and this time he could see that there were some bumps off on one side of the water, some circles of dirt and—yes!—some angular shapes that must have been the cross sections of buildings. He studied it for ten or fifteen minutes, minutely adjusting his angle and focusing all of his attention down into the squares. There were moments when the image bore a more than passing resemblance to a map of San Francisco. Yoke had said she'd wait for him there. Oh, Yoke.

Da pulled Phil back inside and took another turn with Humpty-Dumpty. He said he wanted to get a good look at the SUN. After a few minutes he came back inside the hypersphere looking very jangled.

"I do believe it's happy hour," said Kurt. "God, I wish I had some pot."

Sure enough, three minutes later Tempest and Darla floated over with fat reefers burning in their lips.

"Looky what I just found in the catalog!" twanged Tempest. "It's like Om's learnin' herself to make ever'thang we need. This is Heaven, ain't it?"

"Or Hell," said Phil, and pushed himself away.

WEDNESDAY

Phil woke up earlier than the others. He put on Humpty-Dumpty and got to work trying to see San Francisco again. This time he took closer notice of the six metallic tendrils leading kata from Om toward Earth. The tendrils seemed to be in pairs: two were golden, two silvery, and two copper-colored. All six led down toward the grid that seemed to be San Francisco. Was there any chance he might glimpse a slice of Yoke? Phil asked Om for help.

"Can you move us closer, Om?"

There was no audible answer, and Phil expected none. In last night's dream conversations, Om had explained that she was accustomed to talking only to Metamartians, to beings who lived in endless layers of parallel time. Om's utterances were so diffuse that a human needed to be asleep in order to achieve a state of mind subtle enough to hear her voice.

But even though the waking Phil couldn't hear Om's answer, he could see that his request had been noted, for now the grid pattern of San Francisco began to expand. The crazy, shifting angles of the cross-sectional buildings were no more than a few thousand yards off. Phil felt sure Yoke was down there. What if he jumped kata toward her? This might work—or it might not. He might end up like an animated sidewalk painting of a man with all his innards on display. Or fall through Earth-space entirely. Or not intersect it at all.

Someone was tugging on his legs. Da. Last night had been way gnarly. Tempest had gone on to find snap and gabba in the ever expanding catalog and then, though Phil managed not to witness it, the maddened Da and Darla had probably fucked. Ironic, that. All Phil and Yoke had managed so far was to kiss and to lie briefly in the same bed. Kid stuff.

This morning Tempest was nodded out on gabba, but Kurt and Darla were wide-awake on snap, very wired, very lifted. Why did people do this to themselves? "I've got it, Phil," chattered Da. "I'll go into the Light, and Om will be satisfied. Sacrifice Abraham instead of Isaac. And then Om will let you and Darla go back to Earth."

"Calm down, Da." Humpty-Dumpty slid off of Phil, but Phil kept a good hold on the fat egg, lest Da try something rash. Today was going to be xoxxy. This was definitely Hell—or at least that's what these pheezers were making it into.

"He's right," said Darla, her eyes looking glazed and jittery. She was naked again, with Planet at her side. "Kurt and I have been fabbing about it all night. Om must want one of us to jump all the way out of that hole. She's like curious to see what happens. And if Kurt does the deed, then Om will put us back. Why can't you wave it, Phil?"

It occurred to Phil that—duh!—he hadn't yet thought of directly asking Om to return them. So now he tried.

"Dear Om, please put us back on Earth. Please take us back."

Kurt and Darla were quiet for a minute, looking around, but nothing happened.

"I'm going out now," said Kurt, tugging at Humpty-Dumpty.

"Stop it!" said Phil.

"Give it to him!" said Darla, prying at Phil's arms. "It's the only way!"

"You guys are too spun to know what you're talking about," said Phil. "Forget it."

But then Kurt and Darla set upon him in earnest. The excited Planet began wildly barking. It was hard for Phil to fight back, to strike out at his father and at the plump, nude mother of the girl he loved. But he managed to stave them off—until Darla woke Tempest.

"We need to get the Humpty-Dumpty doll," Darla told Tempest after jabbing her into wakefulness. The old cracker woman's eyes were goofball pinpoints of instant rage. "Phil won't give us the doll," hissed Darla. "Work out on him, Tempest." The lean Tempest joined battle with a streetwise savagery.

A minute later Phil's face was bleeding from where Tempest had clawed him, and he was doubled over from being kicked between the legs. And now Darla had managed to bind his wrists with a knotted loop of material from her discarded clothes. Tempest looked like she was ready to beat up on him some more.

"No, we're done now, Tempest," said Darla, shoving the vicious crone away. "We've got the Humpty-Dumpty doll. See? Kurt's putting it on. Time for you to get weightless, Tempest. Take another hit of gabba. That's a girl. Curl up with Planet there, yaaar, nice furry dog. Wavy dreams, sistah." And then Tempest was asleep again.

"I hope you're all right, Phil," said Darla, dabbing at his wounds. "I didn't viz that Tempest would come at you so giga nasty."

"I'm sorry, son," said Kurt. "And don't worry, I'm not just doing this for you. My life's garbage, has been ever since I left

Eve for Willow. I don't want to go back to Earth. They've already had my funeral! I'm moving on. Into the SUN. Can't be any worse than this. And maybe Om really will set you back down."

"Da—"

"And one other thing, Phil. I'm sorry I ever dumped on you for not finishing college. It doesn't matter. You'll do fine, whatever you do. You're a good man. You have heart and soul. And you're every bit as smart as I ever was."

Hearing that made Phil feel wonderful. Like a weight falling from his shoulders. "Thanks, Da." He smiled. "You're good too. Now please take that suit off and tell Darla to let me go."

"Sorry." And with that Kurt pushed himself out through the flaw and disappeared.

"Set me loose, Om!" cried Phil. And the knots around his wrists slipped free. Phil peered into Om's ever-expanding alla catalog, and there, just where he needed it, was a bubbletopper spacesuit. "Actualize," he said, and when Darla snatched the first spacesuit, he made another one. And then he was halfway out the hole in Om's hypersphere, peering out through his imipolex visor to look for his dad.

At first he couldn't find him. He saw a cross section of the Earth, the mountainous pink curves of Om, the six shiny tendrils leading from Om kata toward Earth, and the great SUN ana everything.

And then way out there, silhouetted against the Divine Light, appeared the brave little figure of his father, moving steadily ana.

It would have been nice to end like that, but now something shocking happened. A jagged beaklike form streaked across hyperspace toward his father. Wobbling his head this way and that, Phil could make out a few more sections of the intruder—each view was fierce and angular, like shark jaws, like a heraldic predatory bird. And then the beast struck at his father and ripped him in two.

Phil groaned in agony, as did Darla, who was next to him now, watching as well. Phil had been wondering if he might retrieve his father, but he now knew there could be no restoration. The hyperspace monster tore his father to bits. It was too sad. Da would never make it to the SUN.

But wait—now Phil glimpsed a final resolution. A form like a tattered butterfly lifted out of the torn fragments of Da's body. Gently beating its wings, the gossamer shape continued ana, ever closer to the final Light.

Phil passed the rest of the day grieving, looking through the alien alla catalog, and praying for Om to take him back to Yoke in San Francisco. He avoided Tempest, but he had a pretty good conversation with Darla, who was supertalkative from all the snap. Finally he was tired enough to go to sleep.

Babs, February 26

Babs and Yoke alla-made themselves some nice new outfits for the evening's outing. Yoke made herself a plush green crop-top and black leather pants with elastic along the seams. Babs made herself a form-fitting red dress with a low décolletage, a white cashmere cardigan, and a funny little red flower-bud of a hat.

Outside it had turned cold, and the wind was picking up. Babs, Randy, Yoke, and Cobb picked their way down the street to the *Anubis*.

To Babs's embarrassment, Thutmosis Snooks recognized Randy from thirty feet away. Thutmosis was, as usual, working the street out in front of the *Anubis*, acting as doorman and barker, inchworming his bulk back and forth, flaunting his stylized pharaoh beard and his striped blue and gold headdress.

"Randy Karl Tucker," bellowed the shiny gold moldie. "Got some more money from home? Isis is booked solid tonight, but—you're gonna need your sperm for this, my man—we've got six new moldies, three female and three—"

"Hey, damp it down there, Thutmosis," said Randy. "I ain't

into that kilp no more. This here's my lady friend, Babs Mooney."

Babs gritted her teeth, smiled and bowed.

"Babs Mooney?" said Thutmosis, peering closer at her. "I'm
terrible at recognizing fleshers. Except for the egregious few like
our Kentucky Fried Randy Karl Tucker. It's an honor to have
you visit us, Ms. Mooney. Give our very best regards to Senator
Stahn. I'm going to comp you and your party." He gave Randy
a soft shove toward the ship. "That means no charge, country
cousin, so go right in. Enjoy yourself. And ah, here's old Cobb
again too. Kleopatra's been talking about you, you dog. What a
stellar company this is! And, hmmm, last but not least is little
Yoke Starr-Mydol, isn't it? The moon-maid. No leech-DIMs tonight, I trust? Where's your friend Phil? His ex recently joined
our staff."

Some passersby were hesitating as if wondering whether to
come in, so now Thutmosis started in on them. "Yes, noble
pilgrims, you've found the good ship *Anubis*. Come aboard!
You'll be beamed, steamed, dreamed, reamed, and triple-
creamed. We got the biggest, juiciest, gnarliest camote nuggets
in town. The toughest moldie dicks and the tenderest moldie
janes. Take a walk on the Egyptian side. Are any of you gawking
fleshapoid hicks experienced? Wonderful. Guess what, my floatin' friend, we've added six, yes six, moldie staff members! And
an amazing new lady performer as well. Hurry on in and you
can catch our all-new stage show featuring the meltingly human
Kevvie in a uniquely personal encounter with the bird-headed
moldie Haresh. This evening's second performance is just starting. Pay once out here, friends, and the rest of the evening is
cost-free plus standard gratuities."

"Like your brain and everything you own," muttered Babs
as she and Randy walked up the gangplank, which flowed with
a million colored lights. "You're lucky you didn't pick up a
thinking cap here Monday night, Randy."

"I know all about that," said Randy, pulling something out
of his pocket. Two transparent, flexing pieces of plastic, a bit

like limpware dental appliances, capable of adjusting themselves to fit. "These are titaniplast nose blockers. I brought the two along so's you could use one too."

"Can't we just avoid getting too intimate with any moldies?" asked Babs. "I hope you're not planning to—"

"All I'm here for is to ask the Metamartians about the allas," said Randy. "Swear to God, Babs. And to show you a good time. But wearin' a nose blocker in this kind o' place is what I'd call a reasonable precaution."

Babs was intrigued by Randy's low-life expertise. They stepped off to a quiet corner of the ship's deck and she let him show her how to put on the nose blocker while Yoke and Cobb watched. You had to half swallow it and then use your tongue and breath to push it up over your dangling throat thingie— over your uvula—and into the back of your nose. And once it was there it settled itself into place. It made your voice sound funny, and for a minute Babs and Randy stood there making honking noises at each other and laughing.

"Hey," interjected Cobb. "I'm going on down below to look for the Metamartians. See you three later."

"Thanks a lot for not bringing *me* a nose blocker!" said Yoke to Randy after Cobb left.

"Like I'm gonna be doin' *you* favors," said Randy. "Little snip. Alla up your own nose blocker, why don'tcha. Ain't nobody watching us."

"Incorrect," said a small, deep voice.

"It's Josef!" exclaimed Babs. "I recognize his voice. That cute little beetle? I don't think you noticed him the other day, Randy. He's one of the aliens. Where are you, Josef?"

"Here," said the beetle, and buzzed down from the ship's rigging to land on Babs's shoulder. "It's safe to use your alla, Yoke, almost everyone else is belowdecks for the performance." So Yoke popped a small glowing mesh into the air and made herself a nose blocker.

"Is that skanky Kevvie really doing a moldie live sex show?" asked Babs.

"That's what Thutmosis meant?" said Yoke in a strangled voice. She'd just put the nose blocker in her mouth.

"This must be Kevvie's new job," said Babs. "I hear she has to move out of Derek and Calla's place by March first. She's hustling to get money for a new room."

"Yes, Kevvie and Haresh have been performing together," confirmed Josef. "But they already did it once this evening, and Haresh is questioning the validity of repeating such an act. We're about to leave the *Anubis* in any case."

"Hell, I think this tub's got a primo buzz to it," said Randy. "Sex and drugs and moldies and aliens. Something waaald about a party boat, even if it is stuck in the mud. Have you ever tried camote, Babs?"

"I did all that in high school," said Babs. "Drugs make me uptight. I try to see God, but I end up in a loop of neurosis. That's just how it is for me. I'm fine with beer, wine, and loud music." She let Josef crawl onto the tip of her finger. "Anyhoo, Josef! We want you guys to tell us how to make allas. Because today Randy figured out that when one of us dies, our alla registers itself to the next person who picks it up. Which means, since people are such greedy pigs, that when the secret gets out, we're dead meat."

"Interesting," said Josef, and fell silent for a while. "This had not occurred to me," he said finally. "And I've just uvvied the others, and they hadn't thought of it either. You must realize that death for us is a very minor thing, what with our two-dimensional time and many lives. In your merely one-dimensional time, death is —"

"You gonna tell us how to copy allas or not?" demanded Randy. He swept his hand like someone catching a fly, trying to snatch up Josef, but the prescient beetle eluded him by sliding down Babs's finger at just the right instant.

"Force will get you nowhere, Randy," said Josef from Babs's palm. "It's not our decision as to when you humans can have the power to make an unlimited number of allas. But I'm sure

Om will give you the knowledge soon. Om likes for beings to use her allas."

"Who is this Om?" asked Babs. "You guys said 'Praise Om' the other day."

"Om is our god," said Josef. "She follows us around. Now that the Metamartians are on Earth, Om is present."

"Om has something to do with the powerball as well as the allas," added Yoke. "What about Phil, Josef? Can you ask Om how Phil's doing? Or can Om talk to me directly?"

Josef was quiet for a moment. "Om says Phil is fine. And that he'll be back soon. But, no, Om can't easily communicate with humans due to the one-dimensionality of your time."

"Shitfire," exclaimed Randy. "All this bug can do is bitch about our *time*? What kind o' bullshit is that? He's wastin' *our* time, what it is. I say we go downstairs and see the show. I missed it on Monday."

"Wait," said Yoke. "Don't forget that we want Josef to tell Om to prevent allas from making plutonium."

But Josef had already flown off.

Babs, Randy, and Yoke headed across the deck to the companionway. There were a few others grouped here and there on the deck, many of them well into trips on various kinds of drugs. Their faces made Babs think of people sitting on the john. Listening to their bodies.

Down below there was an Egyptian-looking bar decorated with lotus-stem columns, a hieroglyph mural, and an overhanging textured plastic Sphinx head. Hieroglyphs covered the other walls as well, and there was a music mix going, a combination of notes and sound samples. Not all that great, thought Babs. But of course people didn't come here because of any wonderful artistic ambiance—they came for the illicit things they could do. The room reeked of moldies, of corruption and decay.

A Snooks moldie who resembled a partially unwrapped mummy was busy behind the bar, serving up whatever concoctions were requested. Now and then he plucked a camote nugget out of his windings. Randy got beers for himself and Babs, but Yoke didn't want anything. She just wanted to run around looking for the Metamartians. Babs suggested they meet up again inside the big show room.

As she drank her beer Babs noticed that there was a sound-DIM stuck to the side of the bottle, and that when she moved the bottle, a little bit of the music changed. When she wiggled the bottle back and forth, for instance, there was a *skritchy-skritch* sound, and when she moved it up and down there was a loop of black rapper saying, "Yubiwaza!" She played with that for a minute. "Yu-Yu-Yu-Yu-Yubiwaza!" When Babs got her second beer, she kept the first bottle. The second bottle's DIM could trigger a guitar riff—*whang*—and a woman's deep voice saying, "Space cowgirl?" With a bottle in either hand, Babs began tweaking the web of sound. "*Skritch sk-sk-skritch-itch* yu-yu-yubi space cow-ow-ow-*itchy-itch*-owgirl? girl? *Wha-whang* girl? girl? girl? *Whang-a-whang* yubiwaza cowgirl?" Once you were part of it, the music sounded good.

Randy noticed what Babs was doing, and was smilingly dancing along. And there were three lifters dancing too, doing the flat-footed sporehead newt-dance. One of them was a musician, he had about a hundred sound DIMs stuck all over himself. Each of his gestures made audible trails of tasty media-sampled noise. There were a couple of Egyptian-looking Snooks moldies dancing too, with gracefully undulating arms grown impossibly long.

The people in the booths nearby weren't really into the music, at least not in any obvious way—they were mostly just sitting there sucking on soft bags of juice and wearing that inward look of "When does my lift come on?" or "When do I come down?" A few of them were peaking, and *their* expressions were more like a cartoon image of something missing: a white void with alternating long and short surprise-lines radiating out from a central lack. Like, "Huh?"

Babs saw one of the dancing Snooks moldies snake her arm

down behind a really zoned man. A lump moved up the moldie's arm like a rabbit inside a python. Probably the guy's wallet.

One of the other Snooks moldies had split himself or herself up into an archipelago of body segments, shaped like egg-sized two-legged eyeballs carrying swords and shields. There were maybe two dozen of them, a few with wings as well, the eyeballs running all over the room chasing each other, having little sword fights, jumping off of things, and all the while piping their high voices into the sound mix.

In the far corner of the room was a big transparent-walled love-puddle with a bunch of people in it merged together. Hard to be sure how many. Four, five, six? You could see the faint outlines of their limbs through the sides of the merge tank; the limbs were temporarily fused, but there was still a kind of wrinkle where one person started and the other left off.

Right next to the merge tank, some moldies were sitting around a big round table getting high on betty, rubbing each other with ointment from a little jar shaped like a pyramid. The lifted moldies were growing their bodies into really odd forms. It was like they were trying to outdo each other—though none of them was really as good as the fighting eyeballs, who kept running across the betty table as if to playfully hassle them. One of the lifted moldies was made of nothing but long, wagging, spitty-looking tongues; a second was shaped like the Book of Mormon, with Urim and Thummim stones dangling to one side; and a third was a lacy hollow form a bit like wrought-iron lawn furniture. Babs danced closer, studying the lace moldie's pattern, trying to remember it so she could copy it later, but just then a teenage girl vomited on the floor right next to her, spattering chunks of camote all over her shoes.

"Gettin' a little rough," said Randy. "Let's go into the big room, Babs."

They pushed through the sound-canceling imipolex curtains that separated the bar from the big room. It was a vast echoing space, formerly one of the ship's holds, with steel deck and slanting steel walls. Dwarfed in the center of the cavernous volume was a little round stage, lit by an overhead spotlight. Slowly gyrating at stage left was a pale purple Snooks moldie with a fat stomach and a nose that grew out like a long trumpet. Babs knew him from sight; his name was Ramses. Ramses was fingering his nose horn, playing soft Egyptian music. The note progressions were hypnotic, a whole different world from the bar's chaotic munge. Babs took a few deep breaths and peered around, getting a look at the crowd.

There were no chairs; people and moldies were either standing or sitting on the steel deck. There were maybe a hundred spectators in all—far too small a crowd to make this enormous cold room feel properly inhabited. It was easy to pick out the few moldies in the crowd because they glowed. Of the humans, it looked like there were a lot more men than women. Babs had never known anyone who had even met any woman who was a cheeseball. But men liked to imagine that such women did exist—to imagine, in other words, that some women could be such indiscriminate hump-anything horndogs as men.

Now Babs noticed some objects moving about overhead, repeatedly passing through the spotlight's bright cone like great, bumbling moths. Phil's blimps! He must have given them to the moldies when he left town. Babs knew them well, as Phil had always brought them to their block parties. She pointed out the blimps to Randy, telling him some of their names. "That little one is the Graf Z," she whispered. "And there's Led Zep, and the big fat polka-dotted one is the Uffin' Wowo. And, oh look, its dots are Egyptian cartouche patterns now."

"Pssst!" said Yoke, sidling up out of the darkness. "Most of the Metamartians are in here. See over there? Peg the devil-girl with the proverbial drunk businessman. I asked her if she could help us, but she said the same thing as Josef. 'It's up to Om.' What a bitch. I didn't talk to any of the others yet. See Wubwub over by the wall? With the beautiful woman on his arm? Can you even believe?"

"That's a trannie," whispered Babs. "Look at her hips."

"Oh, too true. And Shimmer and Ptah are sitting together

right beside the stage, someone said they were about to perform."

"I don't see Siss or Haresh," said Babs.

"Siss went off with Cobb," said Yoke. "Maybe he can get her to talk? Like if he fucks her?"

"What's Siss look laahk?" interjected Randy.

"Like a snake-woman," said Babs, giving Randy's leg a big pinch. "Bite! Uh-oh, Shimmer and Ptah are going onstage."

Babs had been around moldies for most of her life; she'd been five when her father sponsored the Moldie Citizenship Act of 2038, and there had been a steady stream of grateful moldie visitors ever since. And of course Babs's mother herself was part moldie; that is, Wendy Mooney's personality lived in a moldie Happy Cloak that had a symbiotic relationship with Wendy's human flesh. In the natural course of things, Babs had seen moldies having sex a number of times — moldies weren't modest. It excited her even less than seeing two dogs fucking, which was not at all.

But Shimmer and Ptah certainly did give a spirited performance. They bounced up onto the stage, began embracing each other, and, just for the goof of it, Shimmer pushed her body right through Ptah's, his bronze flesh forming itself back together on the other side of the marble Shimmer. Ptah did the same to Shimmer, and then they corkscrewed themselves together so tightly that they looked like a candy-cane or a barberpole. To top off the foreplay, Shimmer divided herself up into an archipelago of separate globs, and Ptah juggled her. While continuing to juggle, Ptah began pinching off more and more globs of himself, until all that was left of him was a pair of hands down on the platform of the stage, incredibly keeping some two score white and bronze balls aloft. And then the bronze hands became balls as well. Before the balls could all tumble out of the air, two of the white balls stuck to the ground and formed themselves into hands — and took over the juggling. At each round another white ball stuck to the hands, and the hands grew into arms, into a torso, and finally into all of Shimmer, juggling bronze globs of Ptah, and then Shimmer stepped aside and Ptah's globs somehow sprang together in midair, reassembling the grinning bronze superman all at once.

Even Babs had to applaud for this. But now the inevitable had to happen. Ramses's music took on an urgent, throbbing tone, and Shimmer and Ptah swooned to the ground. They softened their flesh to a near liquid state and pasted their bodies together, opening up their pores enough to exchange wet flows of imipolex that carried along cells of their algae and their fungal mold. The mold nerve magic took over, and they shuddered in a mutual orgasm. A musty, cheesy reek came drifting down from the stage.

Babs peeked over at Randy. His eyes were wide and his mouth was open. Emboldened by her two beers, Babs couldn't resist letting her hand steal over to gauge the state of Randy's excitement.

"Oh yes, Babs," moaned Randy. "Please touch it."

Well, why not? Just for a minute, anyway. She slipped her hand under the waistband of Randy's baggy pants. Hmmm. A girl could definitely do something with this. But no point letting him come. After a few quick caresses, Babs took her hand back out.

"Later!" she whispered. "Can you get me another beer?" Randy hurried off.

"What's up?" said Yoke, who was standing on Babs's other side.

"Never mind," said Babs. "I bet Kevvie's next." Ramses picked up the pace of his music, managing to sound like several instruments at once: drum, oud, tambourine, and flute.

And now, surging out of the darkness behind the stage, there came a big bird-headed moldie carrying a robed woman in his arms.

"Oh puke, it really is Kevvie," said Yoke. "I don't want to see this."

"Hold on," whispered Babs. "I want to see how it starts." After living near Kevvie for a year or so, Babs didn't have much sympathy for her. "We'll leave as soon as it gets too rank. Oh thanks, Randy." He was back with her beer.

Haresh was doing a little Egyptian dance, his arms held out in that funny hieroglyph way. Kevvie sat on a low bed on one side of the stage looking kind of amused. She slid out of her robe with broad, theatrical gestures. And now she put her hand between her legs, supposedly gazing at Haresh as if he were a huge turn-on. She kept losing her focus and zoning out, then suddenly remembering to keep the act up. But now things got serious. Haresh turned toward Kevvie, with a stiff dark penis shape rising from his midsection. Kevvie feigned surprise and placed one hand over the O of her mouth.

"Don't do it, Kevvie," called Babs, but Kevvie went ahead and lay down on her back with her legs wide open. She gave her pelvis an encouraging wriggle.

"Go for it!" shouted a man off to the right.

The Egyptian bird-god took another step toward Kevvie.

"Stop it, Haresh!" shouted Yoke. "You're too good for this!"

At that, Haresh turned his head, peering out at the crowd and spotting them. "I am agreeing entirely, Ms. Yoke," he said, his penis going soft and then disappearing back into the mass of his belly. Ramses's nose horn went limp and his music drooled off into silence. "This show is nonsensical," continued Haresh. "Kevvie and I have already simulated a sex act today. I find it ridiculous to repeat our unnatural congress in search of some unlikely satisfaction. If your shoddy Earth time were properly parallel, then we could have explored every variation within the span of one single act, but—"

"Oh maaan," moaned the frustrated Randy. "Goin' off about our *time* again?"

"Put it to her!" shouted another man. Kevvie had lifted her head up and was looking around. She drew her knees together. More people were yelling. Kevvie sat up and began putting on her robe. "Don't go!" someone else shouted. "You're supposed to fuck the moldie!" Kevvie smiled, shook her head, wrapped the robe around herself and stepped down off the back of the stage. Haresh joined her, and the two walked off into the darkness together, laughing and talking like good friends.

"We'll take an intermission now," said Ramses from the stage, talking loud to drown out the grumbling. The curtains to the bar pulled away, letting in light and music. The spotlight above the stage stayed lit. "And feel free to ask any moldie you see for a 'date,'" continued Ramses. "The next round of refreshments is on the house, and meanwhile enjoy the zany antics of our buffoon blimps." The five blimps drifted down to about twenty feet above the stage and began circling around each other like clumsily flocking birds. "I'll have a talk with our performers," promised Ramses. He hopped off the stage and set off after Haresh and Kevvie, just now disappearing through a little door in the hold's far side. Most people began drifting to the bar, and all the Snooks moldies headed in there too.

"Those are Phil's," Babs told Yoke, pointing to the blimps. "Those are the ones he wanted to show you last week."

"Before Kevvie ruined everything," said Yoke. "She's really something, isn't she? What could Haresh possibly find to discuss with her?"

Just then Ramses came flying back out of the door at the far side of the hold. Someone had shoved his head up his ass so far that he looked like a wowo. It took him a minute to get himself unknotted, and when he did, he took off toward the bar, probably looking for support.

"Looks like Haresh is on strike," said Yoke. "We really should talk to him. Or to one of the other Metamartians. We have to get them to tell Om not to allow plutonium." Now the Metamartians were all following Haresh toward the far door— Peg, Wubwub, Shimmer, and Ptah.

"Did Josef say they're leaving tonight?" said Babs. "Maybe they're worried the Snookses are going to hassle them. You're right, Yoke, we should talk to them about plutonium. But maybe first we need another beer." Babs was feeling merry. She gave Randy her biggest smile. "I loved the juggling, Randy."

"You got me in your spell, Babs," said Randy gamely. "How soon we goin' back to your place?"

"If you're not going to talk to the Metamartians, then I will," said Yoke, about to take off after the aliens. But suddenly her face changed. "Look—"

"Oh God" said Babs.

Up above the stage the air was looking oddly warped. And the Uffin' Wowo blimp—good lord, it was swelling up to the size of a refrigerator, the size of an automobile, the size of a house! It wobbled hugely down and then—as in some fabulous stage-magic illusion—the spotted blimp split open to reveal a dog, a thin woman, a plump woman, and—

"Phil!" screamed Yoke, running toward the stage. "Ma!" The air above the stage rippled, and then the space of the room was normal again. The shock of the miracle made Babs feel hollow inside. Or like it had shaken loose some deep part of her. Without really knowing why, she was weeping. Randy seemed equally overcome. He threw his arms around her.

"I love you, Babs," he said into her ear.

"You do?" said Babs. "You do?"

Phil, February 26

Phil woke up late Thursday morning, at peace with the world. Da was dead, yes, but in the end his death seemed to make sense. Phil's dreams last night had included Da. Da was happy. He was inside the SUN, yet still flying toward it, as if the center of the SUN were unreachable. In Phil's dream, the SUN was a point of light inside a cloud of glowing butterflies.

Phil's dream conversations with Om last night had been the best yet. He'd learned to understand the way that Om spoke in glyphs, in concept blocks, expressing many variations of a thought at the same time. He was bursting with new information. Today was going to be a good day.

For once Tempest and Darla seemed sober, and Darla was even dressed—wearing the purple caftan he had made her.

"I dreamed Om said she's putting us back today," said Darla. "Did you dream that too? Tempest can't remember."

Seeing Tempest reminded Phil of what she'd done to his face, but when he felt around his eyes, yesterday's scabs were gone. As well as remembering the dream Darla was asking about, he remembered that in one layer of his dreams Om had been healing him.

"Yes, I did dream Om is going to put us back," Phil answered Darla. "She had us inside her so she could figure out our circuitry—and now she's done. She said from now on she'll just watch people through their allas. She's going to set us back down."

"Anywhere she drops us is faaahn with me," mewed old Tempest. "Why you lookin' at me so funny, Phil?"

"You don't remember trying to claw my eyes out?"

"We—We was fightin' over a doll?" said Tempest, glancing around for Humpty-Dumpty, who was, of course, nowhere to be found. Tempest looked strung-out and querulous. "Young fella like you shouldn't of been pickin' on a naahce ole lady like me."

Phil didn't bother answering that one. "Om said she'd home in on Da's wedding ring," he told Darla. "She likes to have a specific thing to go for."

"Kurt's wedding ring?" said Darla. "He wasn't wearing any in here. You know where it is?"

"I do," said Phil. "It's inside a pet DIM blimp I made. I called it the 'Uffin' Wowo,' not that it really is a wowo, it's just a blimp. It's aboard the *Anubis*, which is beached in the mud at San Francisco. A bunch of moldies use the *Anubis* for a night-club."

"Stuzzy," said Darla. "I've never been to San Francisco. Your father's wedding ring, huh?" She paused for a second. This morning her expression looked composed and intelligent. "You know, Phil, there's something we should fab about, especially since you're such a good friend of Yoke's. It's—the gunjy way I've been acting in here—I mean with your father and everything—Phil, you have to viz that I flat out thought we were dead, so—"

"I can forget it," said Phil.

"Especially don't tell Yoke," said Darla. "She'd flame me. My little darling does have a temper on her. If she found out that when I met her boyfriend I was lifted and naked and—" Darla broke off, laughing. "I'm glad we fabbed about this."

"And you say good things about me to her too," said Phil.

"You *are* good," said Darla. "But, no, I won't praise you to Yoke or it might turn her against you. I've always had to handle that girl with kid gloves. You know how it is. Your dad felt a little the same way with you. He was wonderful. His sacrificing himself like that—I bet that's what turned Om around."

"Where *is* Kurt?" wondered Tempest. She was sitting on the oak trunk holding Planet and tremulously trying to light a cigarette.

"He jumped out of Om's hole to fly into the SUN yesterday," said Phil flatly. "You helped him."

"Don't blame *me*. Hell with you." Tempest clammed up and looked away, squinting her eyes against her tobacco smoke.

Phil turned back to Darla. "I had so many dreams last night, Darla. I saw Da, and then Om was talking to me about him. She says she didn't urge him to jump at all, that you and Da just found that idea in your own heads. But, yes, in a way, Da jumping really did make Om decide to set us down. It impressed her, and made her feel sorry, and—I don't know—it was such an intense moment that now Om feels like she knows what makes us tick."

"Whiyun we supposed to land?" whined Tempest, hunching over something in her lap.

"I think tonight," said Darla. "It's just coming back to me. Om showed me this previz flash of how we'd come down. Something about a dark room. A stage? And don't you be getting spun again today, Tempest, I see that wine. Give it here, cruster. That's xoxxin' right, I'm pouring it out. Whirl, whirl, whirl, Om's magic rays are turning it into air. We're not gonna come knuckle-walking out of here tonight like Shasta ground sloths, you wave?"

While Darla kept an eye on Tempest, Phil went to peer out of Om's flaw again. Sticking his head out, he remembered something else Om had told him. The flaw was one of Om's "fingernails." A shelf sticking out of the smooth curve of the powerball fingertip that contained them.

Phil looked ana past the vast, curved pink forms of Om's body, visualizing the SUN's bright orb as a cloud of winged souls. Da in there too. *Hi, Da*. Looking kata, Phil once again studied the three pairs of tendrils running from Om's body kata to the Earth. Two gold-colored, two silvery, two coppery. He and Om had talked about those tendrils in his dreams last night. What Om had said about the tendrils had been esoteric, but Phil had been able to follow it. Having Da say Phil was smart had loosened up Phil's old mental block against mathematics.

The tendrils were in pairs because they were loops. Each pair was a loop like the handle of a coffee cup—with Om the cup, and the loop a handle that had been stretched like taffy, stretched all the way kata to touch the space of Earth. The tendrils were "hypercylindrical vortex threads"—like four-dimensional smoke-rings or tornadoes. The big new insight was that where these threads intersected the space of Earth, they looked, to the Earthlings, like cylindrical tubes: one gold, one silver, one copper. And these three tubes were allas: Yoke's gold alla and, according to Om, two additional allas that she'd recently allowed the Metamartians to make. A silver alla for Babs and a copper alla for Randy Karl Tucker. The vortex threads carried energy and information back and forth between Om and the allas.

Most important of all, now that Phil understood what the allas were, he knew how easy it was to split one in two. And with this new knowledge, he was quite sure he could use Yoke's alla to make one of his own—Om willing.

Phil squinted kata toward where the alla-threads met the cross section of Earth. Slowly, slowly, Om was moving them closer. Closer to Yoke. He prayed for their landing to come soon. As he was watching, a new pair of alla-threads appeared, purple ones. Someone else on Earth had just gotten an alla. He wondered who, but the only way to ask Om would be to fall asleep and dream. And he wasn't tired.

Phil had lunch with Darla and Tempest, played with Planet, looked out the flaw some more, showed Darla and Tempest his alien "fishbowl," examined Starshine's old wowo, thought about flying machines, and carved a little on the oak tree with his fuzzy alien pocketknife. The way the knife worked was that its little metal tentacles would pick away at something to carve out the shape you wanted. It didn't have any kind of DIM hookup; you controlled the little feelers by turning the knife this way or that. Phil carved "Yoke" and then started on a bas-relief of her face, as best he could remember. The carving wasn't coming out all that well, but learning to use the knife was a pleasant enough way to pass the time.

And then, finally, there was a *pop* and a dark ball appeared in the midst of their hyperspherical space, off to one side of the oak. Phil pushed off from the oak, drifting toward the black ball. "Come on, Darla," he called. "This is the exit. You too, Tempest. Bring the dog."

The women hauled themselves up the trunk and pushed toward the black sphere as well. Nobody doubted that this was their salvation.

As they entered the dark ball there was a hyperdimensional switcheroo. The space inside the dark ball became their space, and the Om space they'd come from became the inside of a small bright ball behind them.

As they switched spaces, there was a stretching and pulling in Phil's guts again, but he didn't mind. Anything to get back home. Darla and Tempest thumped into him; Tempest was carrying Planet. Phil was worried the women's impact might knock him out of the dark space, but he stayed well within it.

It wasn't completely black in the new space, there was a dim yellow glow, with spots. The bright ball of the space they'd come from was shrinking. Still visible within it were the warped tiny images of the oak tree and Starshine's wowo. Now that they were inside the dark space, it seemed ever brighter, and no longer so round. It was longer than it was wide, and dim yellow with spots on it—

"We're inside my blimp!" exclaimed Phil, and then—*pow*— the spotted blimp burst. Phil clearly heard the *ting* of his father's wedding ring falling to the platform of the stage they landed on, and then Planet started barking. There was a spotlight shining down on them and a few people staring up, very surprised, but where was—

"Phil!" screamed Yoke, running toward the stage. "Ma!"

"Yoke!" Da's wedding ring was right down there by Phil's foot, the ring finally unknotted by this last disturbance of space, and Phil scooped it up before Yoke jumped onto the stage. He hugged her and kissed her, and before Yoke could say much more of anything else, he put the ring on her finger and said, "I want to marry you, Yoke, I never want to lose you again," and Yoke kissed him some more and said, "Yes, yes, me too."

And then Yoke began to hug Darla. There wasn't really anyone for Tempest to hug, but Randy Karl Tucker hugged her anyway. Babs Mooney was right at Randy's side, clinging to his arm; it looked to Phil like they'd grown closer while he'd been gone, which was kind of surprising, though it made sense in a way.

Phil felt into his pocket where he had the fuzzy knife, the black "fishbowl," and the necklace with the big gem. He put the necklace on Yoke for good measure. Yoke was all smiles, squeezed in between Phil and Darla. The gem looked amazing, continually changing between looking like a ruby, an emerald, a diamond, and a sapphire. And Da's gold ring was shining on Yoke's finger. Phil felt like his heart would burst. They were on the stage of the nearly empty show room in the *Anubis*, with most of the few remaining people wandering off to the bar rather than pressing forward with questions; they seemed to think this miraculous appearance had just been some kind of hokey, over-blown magic trick.

Cobb came across the dark room from the little door on the far side, his pink skin looking a little rough and blotchy.

"Phil's back!" Babs called to Cobb. "Along with this dog and two women! Yoke's mother."

"I know," said Cobb. "Hi, Darla. Hi, Tempest."

"Kin you flaaah me and Planet down to Tre and Terri's, Cobb?" Tempest wanted to know. "I bet they been worried sick."

"Worried sick that she'll come back," Yoke giggled to Phil.

"I'm gonna stay here, Tempest," said Cobb. "There's, um, too much going on. And frankly I'm a bit lit. I was trying to talk to Siss, but before I knew it I'd rubbed on some betty and started conjugating with her. What a session. I've got to learn to lay off this stuff. Whew. It's too much fun. Hire a Snooks moldie to, um, take you to Santa Cruz, Tempest. Ask one of those dancers in the bar."

"Ah don't have that kind o' money."

"Here," said Yoke, pulling a big bill out of her purse. "Now scram, Tempest. You can't be the focus. We've got Phil and my mom here, we've got seven Metamartians disguised as moldies, we've—"

"Seven aliens?" cried Tempest. "Kill them!"

"Shut your pie-hole, Tempest," said Cobb. "They're leaving anyway. Go the hell home."

"And don't blab," cautioned Yoke. "No need for the Snookses to get worked up."

"You were so dumb to tell her, Yoke," put in Babs. "She's such a redneck."

"Xoxx all of you," said Tempest, and stomped off, dragging Planet after her.

"You're lifted, Cobb?" said Babs. "How lame. Did you find out how to make an alla? Did you get the message about the plutonium to Om?"

"I'm not really lifted," said Cobb. "Just buzzed. And, yes, I told Siss to tell Om to please not let us make plutonium or uranium. Siss was surprised that we thought instant atomic bombs would be such a big problem. Weird. It's the two-dimensional time thing again. On Metamars it doesn't matter all that much if a city gets blown up; it'll still be around in all the other time lines. But, yeah, she passed the word to Om. Check in your catalog and see if you can still make plutonium. And, um, as far as copying allas goes, Siss told me that Phil already knows how to do it. Is that true, Phil?"

"Yeah," smiled Phil. "Om told me. We can make allas for everyone. Everything's going to change."

"Yes!" exclaimed Yoke.

"And Om really got the message!" exclaimed Babs, who'd been focused inward on her alla. "I just checked, and plutonium is like grayed out in the catalog. Uranium too."

"So maybe I'm not so lame," said Cobb proudly. "More news. The Metamartians are leaving here tonight because, um, the seven of them are planning to make a new baby. It takes them about three months. Sweet Siss is gonna be a mommy."

"They're leaving Earth?" asked Yoke. "We're off the hook?"

"Not quite," said Cobb. "They're not ready to leave Earth entirely. Like I say, they have to finish mating and, um, gestating and all that. And they want to kind of keep an eye on things too. To make sure we aren't ruining everything with the allas. Did I say that they're planning to travel around in a flying saucer?"

"A saucer?" said Phil. "Have they been talking to Kevvie?"

"You hit the nail on the head," said Cobb.

"You're kidding!" said Phil.

"He's not," said Yoke. "Kevvie's been working here on the *Anubis* with the aliens since you left. She and Haresh are—"

"We have been coworkers," said Haresh, suddenly reappearing from the far side of the hold with Kevvie at his side. "Kevvie has been giving me insights into your race's mental archetypes and into the rawer forms of human emotion. Om suggested that we give her an alla to test in practice what such a person might do. I must apologize in advance for what is about to occur. This is a necessary test."

Kevvie was striding along with her head held very high and her lips moving. She was talking to herself and making little gestures with her hands. Phil had seen this mental state before; when Kevvie got really lifted, she turned grandiose as a spoiled child playing Queen—and mean as a killer robot.

"Kevvie's a crazy, skanky slut," snapped Yoke. "Can't you see that, Haresh, you xoxxin' birdbrain?" Yoke said this quite loud. Kevvie heard her.

"The man-hungry little moon-maid has a nasty mouth," said Kevvie regally. Her eyes were unforgiving. "I don't tolerate it. Begone!" She raised her hand as if she held a scepter. And now Phil glimpsed the purple tube of an alla in her hand.

It was over as soon as it started. Phil was turning to get in front of Yoke, Randy was leaning toward Kevvie, Yoke's mouth was opening to say something—but Kevvie's wish was fast as thought. In the same instant when Phil saw Kevvie's alla, a bright-line control mesh had already sprung into tight relief around Yoke's body and—*poof*—Yoke was gone, transmuted into a puff of air.

Yoke's gold alla clattered to the stage and rolled to one side; it was the only sign of her that remained. Numbly, Phil picked it up. He couldn't wrap his mind around what had just happened. It was impossible. He'd just given Yoke Da's ring. They were going to be married. Everything was—Phil pawed softly at the air that had been Yoke. Could she really be gone?

"See, Phil!" shouted Kevvie. "See!" Randy was trying to wrestle her to the ground.

"Kill her!" screamed Darla, and she, Tempest, and old Cobb moved forward to exact blood-vengeance. But Haresh didn't want any further violence. The alien sent Randy tumbling across the stage. And then Haresh picked up Kevvie and ran across the great hall, disappearing again through the far door.

"What's the use?" muttered Phil, as Darla tried to muster their forces for further pursuit. "Yoke's gone."

"Siss warned me something bad would happen," said Cobb, his body sagging. "But she said, um, Randy would know how to fix it."

"Where's Yoke's alla!" Randy was yelling, frantically crawling around on the stage. "Did anyone get it?"

"I got it," said Phil listlessly. "It's in my pocket."

"Well don't despair, old son." Randy's voice cracked with an odd jubilance. He looked around and lowered his voice. "Her alla *remembers* her. Body and mind both. Let's go back to Babs's where it's safe. We'll see if we can't whomp up a new realware Yoke."

"I—I want *my* Yoke," said Phil wretchedly. "I gave her Da's ring."

"Gonna be the *same* Yoke, Phil," said Randy, putting his arm around Phil's shoulder. "That's all we are: information. Come on."

"But we're not just information," murmured Phil brokenly, as Randy led him toward the door to the bar. "There's souls. I saw them in hyperspace. I had so much to tell everyone. Ow!" Ramses Snooks had just slammed into him.

"Where are those new moldies!" Ramses was shouting. He had a phalanx of twenty Snooks moldies behind him. "That old woman said they're aliens! We have to exterminate them!" He and Isis were carrying serious-looking flamethrowers, and most of the other Snookses were packing O. J. ugly-stick rail-guns, each of them capable of shooting a thousand fléchettes per minute. They surged into the ballroom, with Tempest following along, looking bloodthirsty and vindictive.

"They've gone up the back stairs to the deck!" called Kevvie, suddenly appearing from the far door again. "Someone stop them! They mustn't leave without me! I'm—I'm their Queen!"

"Keep goin', gaaahs," Randy murmured to Babs, Cobb, Phil, and Darla. They were already out in the bar. "Don't go after Kevvie. Might just get another of us killed. Only thing we gotta do now is get back to Babs's and fix Yoke before something happens to her alla. Up the stairs and out!"

So Phil stumbled up the stairs with the others. They got up top before the Snookses did, and sure enough, the seven Metamartians were on the deck, standing in a circle holding hands — or *legs* in the case of tiny Josef, who hung suspended between devilish Peg and sinister Siss.

Jostled by a knot of bewildered lifters, Phil was seized with a sudden terror that he'd lost Yoke's alla. He dug out the contents of his pocket. His fuzz-knife, his "fishbowl," and, yes, Yoke's alla. Wubwub happened to look over at Phil just then, and did kind of a double take, as if he was surprised at the stuff in Phil's hands.

But then the Snookses had arrived. At the very last moment before they opened fire on the aliens, the air around the Metamartians flickered, and a silvery disk-shape formed to enclose them. The supersonic fléchettes from the rail-guns bounced off the silver disk like hail off a tin roof; the hot tongues from the flamethrowers licked against the disk as harmlessly as water on a stone.

The flying saucer lifted slowly into the sky, gave a twitch and shot off toward the heartland at an incalculable speed. Kevvie stood in the center of the deck, stretching up her arms and screaming that she wanted to come along.

Tempest and her dog got into a Snooks moldie and headed for Santa Cruz.

And Phil and his friends hurried down the gangplank toward Babs's warehouse, not looking back.

CHAPTER SIX

YOKE, BABS, RANDY, YOKE

═══ ■ ═══

Yoke, February 26

"Pig!" is what Yoke had been about to shout—defiant to the last. But the sound never made it to her lips. As soon as Kevvie said "Begone," Yoke felt the alla-mesh tingling on her skin, and the next instant she was air.

There was an uncanny moment of transition when Yoke was still materially alive—her old flesh patterns fleetingly preserved as worming, ionized air. But the currents and charges quickly dissipated, and then every physical remnant of the pattern that had been Yoke Starr-Mydol's body was gone.

I'm dead, thought Yoke. I'm a ghost!

She could sense the people who'd been all around her just now, not that she could see them anymore, but she could feel their presence: her mother, and Babs and Randy, and Phil—had she really said she'd marry him? Kevvie's vibe was out there too. Triumphant.

Yoke convulsed in a spasm of stark hatred. It was disorienting, and when she tried to find Ma and the others again, she couldn't. It was like being blindfolded and feeling around in a china shop with baseball-bat arms, everything getting smashed and falling apart, oh no this was the end—but, wait, what about her alla? Randy had said her alla could remember her, which meant—what? Yoke couldn't seem to think logically, there was dark slush all around her and something was coming for her, something making a sound that wasn't a sound.

Krunk krunk krunk.

It was prying at her—ow—scraping at her like she was a stain on a piece of cloth—*krunk krink krunky*—oh this felt bad. And then she was drifting out into some other level, she was out of normal space entirely and—yes!—she could see something bright.

It was a light, a White Light. Yoke was flying gladly toward it. God. There were others flying with her. Yoke flashed a vision of someone driving a car in a snowstorm with the snowflakes flying into the headlights, not that Yoke had ever seen snow in real life, but now she did see it, she was the driver, tasting coffee in her mouth, and then she was one of the snowflakes, rushing through the cold black toward the car, yet never reaching it, as if the path to the Light were being stretched.

Yoke was a flat little thing endlessly tumbling after the Light. It felt good to do this, she was happy, getting good vibes off that Light but—*zow!*—now something shot past in front of her, a thing like a Bardo demon, gulping down a bunch of the snowflakes, danger danger—*zow!*—another one going by with something like a beak, but, oh well, nothing to be done, once you're dead the worst has already happened, right, and once you're born you're in for it too—*zow!*—"Hi, there!"

Yoke kept flying on toward the Light and kind of laughing at the Bardo demons, they made it interesting was all, the demons were woof shuttles for this tapestry, with Yoke and the other souls the world-line warp threads on the White Light loom, it was good and—*zow!!*—why worry, the Light would take care of all things.

And then all of a sudden it was like in a flying dream when your dream self remembers you can't really fly—and you fall, pulled down from the heavens by reality's anchor-rope—

"Aaaaaaaaaaaaaauuugh! Aaaaaaaaaaaaaauuugh! Aaaaaaaaaa-aaaauuugh!"

"It's okay, Yoke!"

"She's back!"

"Oh, Yoke! Dear little Yokie!"

"It's me, darling!"

"Hold her, she's going to fall!"

"Aaaaaaaaaaaaaauuugh! Aaaaaaaaaaaaaauuugh! Huh?"

Yoke could see! She was back in good old three-dimensional space, her mother and her friends all around her, yes, Ma and Phil, Randy and Babs, Cobb squeezing in too, even Planet and stupid Willa Jean, all of them touching her, oh dear life. Yoke slumped to the floor sobbing. There was something hard and rubbery in the back of her throat; she coughed it out; it was the nose blocker.

Half an hour later she felt like her old self again, sitting on Babs's ant-patterned silk couch talking with the others. Phil and Darla sat on either side of her, and Babs and Randy were on another couch. Cobb was flopped down on the floor, his head sticking out of a formless puddle. A huge green brocade fabricant tapestry covered the nearest wall.

"What happened to your foot, Ma?" asked Yoke. "Your little toe is gone."

"It happened when Om's powerball swallowed me on Christmas Eve," said Darla. "I tried kicking my way out."

"Poor Ma. You were in there for a long time. Thank God you're back."

"I don't matter that much, Yoke. I'm old. Thank God *you're* back."

Yoke kept testing her thoughts and looking down at her body, her precious flesh, touching herself, her leg, her stomach, her face, yes, all of her was back, even the same clothes that she'd been wearing—her new stretch leather pants and plush green shirt—and even the gem necklace Phil had given her, as well as his father's gold ring, loose on her finger. She was going to have to think about that one.

"Did you see the SUN?" asked Cobb.

"The White Light," said Yoke. "I saw it." If she looked within herself, she could still see feel the Light. A savor of serenity, a sense that everything was okay.

"I saw it too," said Phil. "When I was peeking out of Om. Da flew into it."

"It had good vibes," added Darla. She was wearing a shapeless dress with purple patterns on it. Not like something she'd normally wear.

"The best vibes ever," said Yoke. "It's wonderful to know that God is real. And then you guys brought me back?"

"Slick as snot on a doorknob," said Randy. "All I did was hold your alla, and it goes, 'Shall I actualize a new Yoke Starr-Mydol or shall I execute a fresh registration?' And I go, 'Yaaar, make me one o' them Yokes.' And then here you come, screamin' your head off."

"It was quite a shock," said Yoke. "I was already in heaven, I guess." The impossibly bright memories were fading. "And now I'm back to—this." Though life was wonderful, it was hard. There were so many things to see and feel and think about. Phil kept putting his hands on her, for one thing, and it was a little bit annoying. Was he serious about that marriage thing?

Babs leaned forward, staring at Phil. "What was that you said before about knowing how to make more allas? Is it really true?"

"It's about time I got an alla!" interjected Cobb. "Fuck this 'humans only' bullshit. Anyway, I am human. I'm the same damned information I always was."

"I'm starting to see your point," said Yoke. "Now that I'm made of realware. Stop touching me every second, Phil."

"I want an alla too," said Darla on Yoke's other side. "Just think what I could do to our cubby, Yoke. We could have a swimming pool. Can you really make me one, Phil?"

"Yes, I think I know how to get us as many allas as we want," said Phil. "As long as one of you guys with allas will help."

"Tell me what to do!" said Babs. "It's important that we start handing out allas before people start wanting to take ours away from us."

"Om told me you can split up an alla," said Phil. "You have to understand that an alla is part of a vortex thread. Like the central line down the throat of a whirlpool? Both ends of the alla's thread are connected to Om. The thread is a loop, and the alla is where the loop dips into our space. Just barely skims in. Now, it's hard to create a brand-new vortex thread, but it's easy to split one lengthwise. That's how you make more allas."

"I can split this in two?" said Babs, holding her silvery alla in her palm. "How?"

"You only have to ask," said Phil. "You can't ask an alla to make an alla, but you can ask it to split. A subtle distinction." He sounded oddly professorial.

"I ask it, and it splits in two, and both allas will work?"

"That's what Om told me. The alla-thread divides itself up like strands of yarn coming untwined—and then the split moves ana along the loop back to Om. You end up with two loops of vortex thread and two allas. Or three, or four, or anything up to seven. The most you can split an alla into at once is seven. Om and the Metamartians are big on sevens. One of the allas will still be yours, the same as before, and the others will be blank slates, ready for someone's registration."

"So you understand all about Om now?" asked Randy.

"I've been inside Om for the last four days," said Phil. "Om's the god of the Metamartians. She's a huge, higher-dimensional intelligence."

"Is she like that light Yoke saw?" asked Randy.

"No," said Phil. "Much more concrete. Om reminds me of a giant, pink woman. A woman the size of the solar system. You'd probably try to hump her leg, Randy. Except that she's four-dimensional or, come to think of it, maybe five. That would explain how she could have disjoint hyperspherical fingertips."

"You a math-freak all of a sudden?" snapped Randy, hurt by Phil's dig. "I thought that was just your dad."

"Phil made peace with his father," said Darla. "It was beautiful. I helped them, Yoke."

Yoke glanced sideways at Darla. There was something in her mother's face that made Yoke suspicious. "You met Phil's father, Ma? Was he nice?"

"They got along very well," said Phil quickly. "Try and split your alla now, Babs. I want one too."

"Okay," said Babs. "I'll make one and you three decide who gets it." She clenched her alla in her hand and focused inward on her uvvy. "Split in two," she said.

Though Yoke was staring at Babs's hand, the transformation was hard to follow. There was a moment of fuzziness, a kind of double vision around Babs's alla, and then there was a second silver tube that passed through Babs's fingers and clattered to the floor.

Phil shot out of the couch and managed to pick it up before Cobb or Darla could, and now he was into his alla registration process. "A face," said Phil, naming the first three images the alla showed him. "A path. Yoke's skin." And then the images were coming too fast for him to talk.

Once again it sounded to Yoke like the alla's series of images were the same ones she'd seen: a disk of colors, a crooked line, and a patch of texture. It was sweet that Phil automatically thought of her skin.

"Show me your alla, Phil," said Babs when Phil's registration was complete. "My alla's paler than it was before, don't you think, guys? And Phil's is the same pale color as mine. Almost platinum. Let's see if mine still works. Here we go." Babs popped a little imipolex DIM dinosaur out into the air. It capered around in circles like a windup toy, now and then pausing to let out a tiny roar. "*Skronk!*" said Babs, encouraging it. "*Gahrooont!*" She made three more dinos, each one a different shape. They started fighting with each other. "Collect the whole set!" crowed Babs. "You want my catalog, Phil? It's the one the Metamartians made, but with additions by Randy, Yoke, and me. We've been pooling our designs. Randy's good with DIMs."

"What about an alla for *me*?" said Darla. "Split yours, Yoke."

"I want one for me too," clamored Cobb. Yoke eyed him critically. He didn't seem lifted anymore.

So she uvvied into her alla and said, "Split in three." Simple. There was a momentary vibration in her hand, then a kind of breeze passing through her fingers, and then two pale gold-colored tubes dropped to the floor, ringing like chimes. One rolled over to Cobb. Darla leaned forward and picked up the other one, which was next to her injured foot. Yoke's alla was the same pale gold color as the two new allas.

"Earth," said Darla, doing her registration. "A vein. Cereal."

"The SUN," said Cobb. "A wrinkle. Television."

"Zap me that catalog?" Darla asked Yoke. "I want to get some bitchin' threads like you."

"Here you go, Ma," said Yoke. "Now think about clothes, and the catalog will show them to you. You can customize things too. Where did you get that purple muumuu, anyway? You look guh-roovy."

"Too true," said Darla. "Phil made it for me, poor thing. When he showed up in the powerball I was—um, so yeah, I think I'll make some black leather moon-boots and sparkly gold leggings, and a kicky black skirt and—"

"He saw you naked, Ma? Were you drunk?"

"I was cooped up in there for eight fucking weeks, Yoke," snapped Darla. "A lesser woman would have gone crazy. Now stop grilling me and let me look for my new clothes." She stood up and marched off, holding her alla. She had only the slightest limp from her missing toe.

"You know what I'm going to do?" said Cobb, fondling his alla. "I'm going to invent a bacteria that eats the stink right off the moldies. It's high time. Call it the stinkeater germ. Hey, Darla, I'll come sit with you. You can be the test-sniffer." Darla made a face, but Cobb followed her across the room.

"Good thing Randy didn't hear Cobb's plan," Yoke said to Phil. "Randy likes the way moldies smell right now." Babs and

Randy, on the other couch, were deeply engrossed in a personal conversation.

"I'm surprised that your alla remembered the necklace and the ring, Yoke," said Phil, scooting even closer to Yoke and touching the gold band around her finger. "It must update itself all the time. And you got all of your memories back too? You remember right up to the last instant?"

"I remember," said Yoke, bracing herself.

"I meant what I said," said Phil. "I'd like to marry you."

Yoke slipped the ring off her finger. "This is too big for me, you know. And it's your father's."

"But I want you to have it," said Phil. "That is, if—"

"Oh, I don't know, Phil. Yes, I like you very much, but what's the big rush? Don't pressure me. It's all too much for one day. And you keep this ring, I don't want it, it's kind of creepy." She peered down at its inscription. "The writing's still backward."

Phil took the ring and read the engraving. " 'wolliW moıf tɹuʞ oT,' " he said. "At least it's unknotted." He pocketed it. "The necklace looks really good on you. You notice how the shape of the gem changes as well as its color? Dynamic Meta-martian realware. You'll keep it, won't you?"

"Okay," said Yoke, glancing down. "And now let's stop ne-gotiating. I'm tired. But I'm afraid to go to sleep. Being dead wasn't all sunny and nice, you know. There were bad things too. Things like demons. I'm sure I'm going to dream about them."

While Yoke and Phil were talking, Babs and Randy finished their tête-à-tête and now they were standing up.

"Good night, guys!" sang Babs. "We're going to hit the hay. We'll start handing out allas in the morning." She and Randy disappeared behind a floor-to-ceiling curtain of red and yellow moiré silk, presumably to share Babs's canopy bed.

Darla and Cobb were over in the kitchen part of the room chatting. Darla was sipping at a split of champagne and alla-making outfit after outfit, asking Cobb's opinions about each one. Cobb was screwing around with some cryptic biotech ma-

chinery that he'd alla-made. Each time Darla would ask Cobb about an outfit, he'd ask her what she thought of the smell of some fresh sample of gene-tailored mold.

"Let's get in bed together?" suggested Phil.

"In here?" said Yoke, rolling her eyes toward her mother.

"We can alla-make ourselves a nest. Like what I used to live in at Calla and Derek's."

"Where Kevvie probably is right now. That pig. What happened to her after she killed me?"

"Haresh kept us from getting to her. But then the aliens took off in a flying saucer. Kevvie wanted them to take her with them, but they didn't. We didn't try to do anything to her yet because we wanted to hurry back here and make a new realware you. We just left her there on the *Anubis*."

Yoke felt a stab of fear. "What if she comes to get me again? Shouldn't you call the gimmie?"

"Oh, not the gimmie," sighed Phil. "And then everyone finds out about the allas? I'll do something to Kevvie myself tomorrow morning. Maybe I'll take her alla away. But I don't think we have to worry right now. If I know Kevvie, she's back at Calla and Derek's, trying to snort her way to the bottom of an alla-made mound of gabba. Saint and I'll go over there tomorrow morning and we'll take her alla while she's still passed out. Okay?"

Yoke found Phil's calmness maddening—but it was contagious. "Okay," she said, leaning against him.

"Now let me make us that nest." Phil gazed thoughtfully at the girders supporting the warehouse roof.

"Not up there, Phil. Put it where Ma won't be staring at us. In fact let's put it outside. In the alley."

So they stepped out the warehouse's side door into a deserted, dead-end alley. It was raining. Phil held out his pale gold alla and formed a control mesh in the air. Raindrops fell through the mesh, twinkling in its light. It took Phil a minute to get the structure fully imagined. Finally he said, "Actualize," and a cozy-looking box was resting on the alley's cinders; it was

pentagonal like a shingled wren's house, with a big round door on hinges and a triangular window next to the door.

"I had the alla put rubber cushions under it, Yoke, so we don't get cold. See?"

"Don't come a-knockin' if this nest's a-rockin'." Yoke giggled, feeling relaxed for the first time since she'd popped back. "Looks like Babs and me are gonna scooore!" She stuck her head back into the warehouse. "Hey, Ma, good night!"

"You're sleeping outside?"

"Phil made us a little house. You can use my bed. Just for fun I made it a bunk-bed like Joke and I used to have at home. It's in the corner over there. Cobb will show you."

"How cute. Well, good night, dear. What a scare you gave me today. Thank God you survived. I'm going to uvvy Whitey in a few minutes."

"Don't whip him up too much about Kevvie. Just say I'm fine and tell him hi from me. The big news is that *you're* back, Ma. He's going to be so glad."

"I hope so." Darla's face hardened a little. "I might just blow Kevvie's head off tomorrow morning. And as for your father — he better not be with one of his little chippies." She held out her arms. "Give me a kiss."

So Yoke walked across the room and kissed her mother good night, and then went back outside to get into the little nest-house Phil had made them. Phil had put a bed in their nest, and three lit candles for light. They lay there cuddling for a long time, talking a little, and then, finally, they made love.

"That was even nicer than I expected," said Yoke when they were done.

"Me too," said Phil. "I love you, Yoke."

"I love you."

"June wedding?"

"Maybe." Yoke found herself smiling uncontrollably. "We'll see. What's going to happen to everything in the meantime? After everyone gets an alla."

"We're really going to give them to everyone?"

"We were talking about that while you were gone," said Yoke. "If other people can't get allas, they're going to kill us to take ours away."

"Does getting killed matter? If your alla can bring you back?"

"If someone shreds you with like an O. J. ugly-stick, and then your alla asks them if they'd rather actualize a new Phil or register the alla for themselves, they're not going to make a new you."

"And—*myoor!*—I just thought of something," said Phil, running his fingers through his blond hair. "When your alla brought *you* back, Yoke, it made a realware copy of you just the way you were before you died. And that was fine—since you were in perfect health right up until the instant Kevvie turned you into air. But if I bleed to death from an O. J. ugly-stick attack, then when the alla actualizes a fresh Phil, it's gonna be me lying there all trashed and bleeding to death—and I die all over again."

"Gnarly! It would be torture!"

"Actually, I have a feeling that recorporation only works if it was an alla that killed you in the first place," said Phil. "It's probably a kind of fail-safe feature to keep the allas from becoming a weapon. I think the aliens would have told us if an alla also had the effect of making its owner immortal."

"Why don't you ask Om?" said Yoke. "Didn't you say she'd been talking to you?"

"Yes, I could hear Om when I was inside her, up there in hyperspace. But even there I could only do it when I was dreaming. I don't think I'll be able to hear her at all down here in regular space."

It was raining hard now, and the drops were drumming on their little roof. The window was open a little to let air in, with a red silk curtain over it for privacy. Yoke alla-made herself an orange.

"Want some?" she said, peeling it by the warm candlelight.

"Thanks. This is such fun. I've never been so happy. It was good to see my dad."

"What was that like?"

"He was nice to me," said Phil. "And I told him I was sorry I'd been mean to him. He told me I was smart."

"I knew that already." Yoke smiled and touched Phil's cheek. "Are you going to use your alla to make blimps?"

"I have been thinking about it. I have an idea how to keep blimps from getting pushed around by the wind. People are always looking for new ways to fly. Getting a moldie to carry you isn't that pleasant. I mean, then you have the moldie to deal with. It's like taking a cab instead of driving."

"I don't understand why people don't use DIMs to make big brainless flapping things that aren't moldies. Kind of like Randy's giant snail?"

"The problem is that safely flying a person takes enough mass and enough computational ability that you'd have to give a flapping thing a fairly elaborate mold-based nervous system. And then it would end up turning into a moldie and not being willing to work for you. A blimp's brain can be a lot simpler. My secret is that I'm going to give my blimps a kind of *hair*. But what giant snail of Randy's are you talking about?"

Yoke was expecting to start laughing about Randy again, but her recent contact with the White Light had sapped the meanness right out of her. The story ended up coming across as something pathetic that had happened to a friend.

"Poor Randy," said Phil when she was done. "What a story! If all the snail needed to do was to repeat things and to crawl on him, it could perfectly well be a wad of dumb imipolex with a DIM. Like those little dinosaurs Babs just made. The mind boggles at the kilp that's gonna come down when everyone gets an alla. What was all that talk about plutonium on the *Anubis*?"

"Cobb told Siss to tell Om to not let people make atomic bombs," said Yoke. "Just in case. We feel like everyone on Earth should get an alla—and there's bound to be someone who would make an atomic bomb on purpose. And even if there weren't, somebody might worry about it so much they'd end up accidentally making an atomic bomb themselves while they were dreaming. Having a really bad dream."

"Isn't there a way to turn off your alla before you go to sleep?" asked Phil.

"You just take off your uvvy," said Yoke.

"Oh, right. Which of course I always do."

"Once I forgot and slept with my uvvy on and people were coming into my dreams. Pervs. Some of them make a point of sleeping with their uvvies on."

"Bad news. Are you tired yet?"

"Almost," said Yoke. "I'm looking at my necklace." She'd set it down next to a candle. The gem was lazily cycling from square ruby to round diamond and back.

"Oh, let me show you the other two things I brought back," said Phil, reaching out to get his pants off the floor. He took out a pearl-handled pocketknife and a black ball with bright spots in it. "The knife has a fuzzy blade, it's pretty nice," continued Phil. "I already carved your name on a tree with it, Yoke."

"Good boy. What's this little ball?"

"I think of it as a fishbowl with luminous tadpoles," said Phil, handing it to her.

"They're more like brine shrimp and flat little jellyfish," said Yoke, peering in. "Funny how they jump around when I look at them. I mean—how can they tell?"

"Alien tech. Who knows? But I like it. I think I'll keep it in my pocket for good luck."

"I know what it is!" exclaimed Yoke after studying the toy a bit longer. "It's an alien star map!"

"Oh, I like that idea," said Phil. "I bet that's why Wubwub seemed interested when he noticed me holding it."

They played with the star map a little longer, and indeed, the bright spots were like stars and galaxies—and once or twice Yoke thought she recognized one of the constellations.

"So far, so good," said Yoke, yawning and handing the star

map back to Phil. "We still haven't figured out what's gonna happen next."

"Let's trust God."

Phil pulled the nice smooth quilt over them, and Yoke fell asleep in his arms, lulled by the patter of the rain.

In the middle of the night something made her wake up. Phil talking on the uvvy. He sounded upset. Yoke woke just as the conversation ended.

"What?" asked Yoke, lighting a candle so she could see. Phil was sitting on the edge of the bed. He looked beautiful, his hooded eyes thoughtful, his strong chin covered with whiskers.

"That was Derek. He found Kevvie in the bathroom. Dead of an OD."

Yoke hated to ask the next question. "Can—Can he bring her back with her alla?"

"Derek didn't say anything about Kevvie's alla offering to recorporate her. It looks like that really only happens if it was an alla that killed you. Kevvie's alla went ahead and registered itself to Derek."

"Are you sad?"

"Yes. But I'm glad you're safe."

Babs, April 1

"Well *I* think it's worked out fine," said Babs. "And it's going to get better." She was sitting in the living room of her parents' fine Victorian mansion on Masonic Avenue above Haight Street. Her gray-haired father, Stahn, was lounging in a soft, low armchair, and her mother, Wendy, was doing aerobic exercises with a little set of dumbbells. Wendy's personality lived in a Happy Cloak moldie attached to the neck of her flesh body. Of course the Wendy 'Cloak could have taken off on its own, but, for whatever reason, the 'Cloak was in love with Stahn, and chose to live with him, driving around a blank-brained tank-grown flesh body. The Wendy 'Cloak had in fact gotten herself a new tank-grown flesh bod just before Christmas. Babs was still getting used to having a mother who looked not much older than herself. But that wasn't the issue today. The real issue was the big news that Babs had come to tell her parents. But it would have to wait till they were done talking about allas. The main thing on everyone's mind anymore was allas.

It had been a little over a month since Babs and Yoke had driven around San Francisco distributing allas, telling each person to split their alla into seven and to pass them on with the same instructions. It had worked like a chain letter. After a dozen cycles there were billions of allas, one for every person and moldie on Earth—and that was enough. You couldn't register yourself to more than one alla. Darla had gotten Cobb to ferry her back up to the Moon—so the allas were all over the Moon as well, though news from the Moon was spotty. It was harder and more expensive to uvvy the Moon these days. Many of the sky-ray satellite moldies like Cappy Jane had quit work. Fortunately there were still a handful of moldies interested enough in money to keep a couple of the big communication satellites going. Not that moldies needed to buy imipolex anymore. It was free now, like everything else except real estate and personal services. Things were different everywhere. Real different.

"Sure, there's been some initial problems," said Babs, "but—"

"I think it sucks," said Stahn staring out his window. He was almost sixty now, and it showed.

"Medical advisory, Da," said Babs. "Your rectum's showing."

Wendy tittered, set down her dumbbells and walked over to pat Stahn's head. "Poor curmudgeon. He's upset about our view. We used to be able to see a little bit of the bay."

Looking out the window, the only thing Babs could see now was pieces of other houses, all fresh and pastel in the sun of a mild spring day. It seemed like most of the people in her parents' neighborhood had tacked on extra stories, cupolas, widow's walks, minarets, and sky-decks. Farther up the hill, Babs saw an entire three-story house suddenly appear on what had been a vacant lot. The big house went up in pieces—*pop, pop, pop, pop.*

"There goes another one," said Wendy. "It's like a sped-up movie or something. Some people have been changing their houses every few days. See the big tower across the street on the Joneses' house?"

"The one that blocks your view. What are all those boxes in the Joneses' yard?"

"They keep alla-making themselves new stuff," said Wendy, shaking her head. "Kitchen appliances, furniture, luggage, recreational vehicles, sports equipment, home entertainment consoles, on and on. You can see from the writing on the boxes. They've been doing this nonstop for a month and their house is completely full and they can't figure out where to put everything, but they won't just turn the extra stuff back into air. People are so ridiculous. Speaking of ridiculous," continued Wendy, "yesterday your father went over to their yard and turned their big tower back into air—you would have thought he was drunk, the way he was acting, but it's just the real Stahn coming out. Of course Mr. Jones allaed his tower right back into place again. And then Stahn scuttled home, and Mr. Jones came pounding on our door and told Stahn he'd kill him if it happened again. He was carrying the most amazing gun. At least Stahn didn't zap the tower while one of the Joneses was inside it."

"I wish I had," grumbled Stahn. "And there's no use complaining to the zoning board. They've totally punted. They can't begin to deal. And it's not just the yuppie greedheads that chap my ass, it's the stoner yurts everywhere."

Some homeless freak in the Haight had passed a stuzzy Tibetan hut design on to all his brahs, and now every sidewalk, alley and parking spot in the neighborhood was cluttered with the muffinlike little people-nests. In a hurried emergency session, the city had approved the use of temporary sleeping shelters up to a certain size, with the proviso that the squatters removed their structures between 9 A.M. and 9 P.M. But of course people got attached to their little homes, and most of the yurts were starting to look permanent, with walls ever more bedizened with stick-on alla graffiti. Amazing stuff, really. Babs liked it.

"And more and more people keep showing up," said Stahn. "Nobody has a job anymore, and everyone wants to be in San Francisco. We're being invaded by the fucking scum of the Earth." Given that people could use their allas to make whatever they needed, most factories were going out of business. And the few people who could have kept their jobs were quitting work. You could pretty much live anywhere you wanted.

"That's probably what someone in a big house said when *you* showed up, Da," said Babs. "Maybe you're so uptight because you're off drugs. Not that it isn't wonderful. Are you still going to your N.A. meetings?"

"Yeah, yeah," said Stahn. "The meetings help. More people in the program all the time. The ones that don't OD. Can you imagine junkies with allas?" He chuckled briefly, his mouth spreading in his long, sly grin. "Some of these kids are going through twenty years worth of addiction in three weeks. There's definitely some learning taking place. Do you think that if I asked Mr. Jones to move his tower a little to the left he would?"

"Don't even," said Wendy. "If you care so much about the view, why not put a high deck on *our* house."

"I don't want to be part of it."

"Why not a tree house?" suggested Babs.

"We don't have any trees except our avocado," said Stahn. "It's only twenty feet high. We'd need more like a *hundred* and twenty feet."

"Then alla up a redwood!"

"A redwood," mused Stahn. "You can make a plant that big?"

"It can be done," said Babs. "Phil figured out that the maximum size of an alla control mesh is four pi meters on each side. About forty feet. I don't know what pi has to do with it, but there it is. You'd have to make your redwood in pieces.

That's okay for a house, but it's tricky for a plant. For it to work, you have to make all the pieces at exactly the same time. Otherwise the cells at the seams die off and it doesn't join up and the sections fall apart. I know about this because we put some big palm trees in front of my warehouse."

"Phil—you mean Phil Gottner?" said Wendy, sticking to the personal level. "How are he and that cute little Yoke doing?"

"They're engaged! And—" Babs broke off, still not quite ready to tell her news. She jumped to another topic. "Speaking of building, Yoke and Phil made themselves a nest in my alley. They keep adding to it; it's grown up the side of my warehouse and onto the roof. Like a shelf-fungus. Yoke's busy designing artificial coral and Phil's trying to invent the perfect personal flying machine."

"And what about you and Randy?" pressed Wendy. "Is it true love?" Even though she looked like a twenty-year-old, Wendy still had the personality of a nosy old mom.

Now would have been the moment for Babs to make her announcement, but Da spoke up before she could.

"The other day I talked to the man who was Randy's boss in India," said Stahn. "Sri Ramanujan. He called Randy a 'degenerate bumpkin.' "

"Why do you always have to dump on my boyfriends, Da?" snapped Babs. "Is it a Freudian thing?"

"You of all people can't be prejudiced against someone who likes moldies, Stahn," put in Wendy.

"Sorry, I'm just telling you what Ramanujan said. He's a snothead, a scientist mandarin, I'm not saying I agree with him. If Randy makes you happy, Babs, that's the main thing. I wish you'd let me meet him for myself."

"Why don't you introduce him to us, dear?" asked Wendy. "There's not something you're hiding from us or from him is there? Uvvy Randy to come over right now! He could help us put up Da's redwood. With four of us using our allas at the same time we could get sixteen pi meters, which is, um, 164 feet and 10.95 inches." Wendy's moldie brain could effortlessly crunch any calculation. "We need that much because at least thirty feet are going to get used up by the roots. Three of us wouldn't be enough to make a proper-sized tree. Randy will be happy that we need him."

"Well—I'd like to," said Babs. "It's high time. As a matter of fact Randy and I rode over here together, but he was scared to come in. He's wandering around looking at the Haight. I told him I would uvvy him if it looked like Da could act normal. Can you, Da?"

"Of course I can. I'm sure he's a fine boy. I won't scare him off."

So Babs uvvied Randy and a few minutes later he walked up the front steps. He was pink with self-consciousness and his Adam's apple was bobbing. He was wearing a new T-shirt with an incredibly intricate stippling of colors. Babs thought he looked so cute that she planted a kiss on him when she opened the door.

"Come on in, Randy. Ma, Da, this is Randy. Randy, this is Stahn and Wendy."

"Hey," said Randy, shaking their hands. "It's an honor. I've heard about you two all my life. The Heritagists back in Kentucky are still squawkin' about that Moldie Citizenship Act."

Babs noticed Randy's nostrils flaring as he sampled Wendy's odor. Wendy had successfully infected her Happy Cloak with Cobb's new stinkeater bacteria last week, so the smell was quite mild. But Babs didn't want to tackle the topic of Randy and the smells of moldies. "How were things down on Haight Street today, Randy?" she asked.

"Waaald. Is it always that crowded? Or maybe it's on account of it bein' April Fool's Day. It's like a street festival, people alla-making shit you can't believe."

"I haven't been on Haight Street in weeks," said Stahn. "I always go around the back way. And, yeah, All Fool's Day is very big in the Haight. What did you see?"

"Some of the stores have their windows painted over and you have to pay the owner to get in. Thanks to the individual

Web address on each dollar bill, people can't alla up counterfeit, so money's still real anyway. Not that you need it for most things."

"I noticed those stores," said Wendy. "What do you get if you go inside?"

"Well, I paid one fella to find out," said Randy, looking a little embarrassed. "Guess I thought he'd have something pretty racy behind them painted windows. But it was just a goddamn T-shirt store. He lets you pick out a T-shirt you like and then you alla yourself a copy. Can't hardly sell objects no more. All you can do is sell ideas."

"Exactly!" said Babs. "That's what I've been trying to tell Da. Intellectual property is all that matters now. It's wonderful."

"Yeah," said Randy, looking down at his T-shirt, which had subtle patterns like faces embedded in its fractal swirls. "Notice how much detail this shirt's got? I never could have seen it all in time to make a copy just from lookin' at it. The store-guy uvvied me the design. Reason he keeps the store windows covered is some folks will just eyeball one of his shirts and alla-make a half-ass knockoff of it. There was a gaaah right outside the store, matter of fact, who looked me over and made a copy of my new shirt, then turned around and sold it to a tourist. All smudged and blurry, though. Look over here on the sleeve, I just noticed this line o' little elephants. No way the pirated street copy picked that up."

"I think I'm too old for new ideas," sighed Stahn. "Don't want to buy, don't have to sell. What else did you see on Haight Street, Randy?"

"There was some folks in old-time metal armor with imipolex power hinges. Jumpin' around like silver jelly beans. I saw a guy givin' away jeweled Easter eggs, all diamonds and rubies, and when you took one, he'd make it disappear. April fool! Another fella was walking down the sidewalk poppin' out a concrete lawn dwarf every step he took. Skinned my knee on one of those suckers, and allaed a bunch of 'em back into air. Some hairfarmers made themselves a pizza ten feet across and didn't eat but a corner of it, then just left it on the sidewalk so you had to step around it. Wasn't nobody bothering to clean it up, and when I went to turn that one into air, one o' the hairfarmers yelled at me not to waste food. One gaaah was standin' around naked doin' his laundry in the middle of the street; he had a washin' machine hooked to a quantum dot battery and he was usin' his alla to feed the water into it. He was just lettin' the wastewater spill out on the ground. He shoulda alla-made it back into air, but I didn't feel up to hasslin' him. There was a peck of musicians playin' electric guitars hooked to batteries, and a bunch of women doing brain concerts on sheets of imipolex hangin' off the lamp-posts—right confusing, all the noise. One gaaah had a swarm of maybe a hundred dragonfly cameras buzzin' all over gettin' in everyone's face and he was mixing their video so you'd just about go crazy lookin' at the output—it was runnin' on an imipolex billboard he'd pasted to the wall. Lots o' cars and custom motorcycles. One of the choppers had a bathtub for the driver to sit in, and it wasn't just a tub, it was a merge love puddle. Can you imagine drivin' a hog while you're merged? Your eyeballs stickin' up on little stalks?" Randy laughed and shook his head. "I love this city. First place I ever felt normal. The craziest thing I saw in the Haight was two stoners taking turns zapping each other into air. And then recorporatin' the aired-out gaaah from his alla."

"Ow," said Babs. "I wouldn't do that for anything. Yoke said there's a real chance of not being able to come back."

"I hear there's been a lot of people getting 'aired out,'" said Wendy. "And not for fun. People trying to kill each other."

"Yeah, but remember that it hasn't been working," said Babs. "Seems like Om's got it set so that a dead person's alla starts beeping after a day. An alla is indestructible, and someone always finds it. And if it was an alla that killed you, your alla offers to bring you back."

"Like in *The Telltale Heart*," said Stahn. "That Poe viddy where the murdered man's heart under the floorboards is beating so loud that it shakes the room. So what else did you see on Haight Street, Randy?"

"Did I mention that it's crawlin' with moldies down there? It's a good thing they can't reproduce themselves but every six months. Even if the average moldie don't live but two years, that makes three times as many moldies every two years, less somethin' makes 'em cut back. Lord knows I'm the last one to say anything against moldies, but they could run us outta room! They don't hardly smell like nothin' anymore. I can tell you got that new stinkeater bug too, Ms. Mooney."

"Oh, call me Wendy," said Ma. "Yes, Cobb brought some over here before he left with Darla. He said since I'm a public figure, I should be an example. So I went ahead and infected myself with stinkeater. It's not an infection, really, it's more like a symbiosis. I benchmarked my computation rate before and after the stinkeater, and there's an eleven percent enhancement. So I'm telling all the moldies to do it. Stahn likes it and I do too."

"She's moanin', huh?" said Stahn, admiring his wife. "But I'm with you on what you said about too many moldies, Randy. We three were just fabbing about it. Too many people, too many moldies, too much *stuff*. I think the allas suck. Look out there right now. My moron neighbor Jones is up on his roof again. I bet he's planning a second tower for his house. I can't fucking believe it. And see the house right down the hill from him? Used to be a beautiful madrone tree there, and now Ms. Lin has a garage. For what? For her brand-new fucking electric-motor-retrofitted vintage 1956 Rolls-Royce Silver Shadow with twenty-four-karat-gold trim. A garage to protect her car that she made out of air and could replace in one second."

"Don't make yourself sick, Stahn," said Wendy. "Let's go out in our backyard and build the tree. Randy, we were thinking we'd make a redwood with some kind of tree house in it. And we figured out that if each of us alla-makes a section at the same time, the tree can be a hundred and sixty feet long from top branch to bottom root. Come on, we go out this way."

"Maybe it should be two hundred feet," said Stahn when they got outside. He was starting to get excited. "A monster tree. That'll show 'em." Their yard was maybe fifty feet on a side.

"Let's call Saint," suggested Wendy. "He should be here for our little get-together. With five allas, the tree could be two hundred six feet and 1.69 inches. Call your brother, Babs, I don't want to always be the one to bother him."

Saint answered Babs's uvvy call right away. " 'Sup, sis?" He sounded cheerful and lively.

"I'm over at Ma and Da's with Randy," said Babs.

"Yaaar. Did you tell them yet?"

"There hasn't been a good moment. Da's all uptight about the neighbors. We're going to help him put up a giant redwood."

"Make a sequoia instead." Saint had a contrary streak.

"A big tree," said Babs. "I don't really care what kind, but now Da's fixated on redwood. Anyway, that's what right for this climate. If you were here, there'd be five of us and the tree could be two hundred feet tall instead of a hundred and sixty. What are you doing anyway?"

When Saint had gotten his alla, he'd quit working at Meta West. Recently he and Phil and Randy had been talking about starting a business. But for now he'd been spending most of his time riding his bicycle and playing uvvy games with friends. And he had a new girlfriend.

"I made a bicycle that I can ride on the water," said Saint. He patched in a view of where he was: out on the bay, near the Golden Gate Bridge. He glanced up at the people-nests encrusting the underside of the bridge, then turned his attention back to the water. There were exceedingly many recreational watercraft around him. Everyone who'd ever wanted a sailboat or DIM board had one now. And you didn't need an expensive dock for your boat—when you finished using it, you just turned it back into air. Saint abruptly veered to avoid a collision. "This is too much fun to stop right now. And I'm supposed to meet Milla later. Whoah, here comes another boat. Just say hi for me.

It's enough if Da's tree is a hundred and sixty feet. Tell him not to be so greedy. And to make it a banyan."

" 'Bye, Saint."

"Good luck with Randy and the rents."

"He doesn't want to come," Babs told the others. "He's out bicycling on the bay. And then he's going to see *Milla*." She stressed the last word as bait for her mother.

"We haven't met Milla yet," complained Ma. "You children are so secretive."

"You two are so hard to talk to," said Babs.

"Let's make the redwood," said Stahn. "I'm stoked."

Babs found a redwood in her alla catalog, and scaled it up to 160 feet, including the big fan of roots at the bottom. She jiggled around four bright-line maximum alla cubes and readjusted the image until everything just fit lengthwise. There was still room to spare on the sides, so Babs enlarged the redwood some more, then lopped off the parts that stuck out. This gave the effect of a really big redwood that had been topped. The trunk was thick all the way up.

"Floatin'!" said Stahn when Babs uvvied everyone the pattern of the tree overlaid with the four alla cubes. But then he paused. "What if it falls over? Then we lose our house as well. We end up with nothing."

"We could alla-make a new house if it came to that," said Wendy. "I've been thinking of all sorts of improvements."

"I want a real house, not a realware house," insisted Stahn.

"But just think," said Wendy teasingly. "If it falls, maybe it'll reach clear across the street and crush the Joneses!"

"Yaaar," said Stahn. "Tree good, house bad."

"It's not going to fall," insisted Babs. "Like I said, Randy and I made a bunch of big palm trees from two pieces each. If two pieces work, so will four. Now, Da, you make the roots and the bottom of the trunk, Ma can make the next piece, Randy will do the piece above that, and I'm going to make the top. Oh, and we better wear earplugs."

They placed themselves in four different corners of the backyard, made themselves earplugs, and carefully aligned their alla control meshes.

"Hold on a minute," said Babs, and privately readjusted the design of her section. "Okay, now I'm set. On three. Let's count together."

"One, two—actualize!" said the four.

Ka-whooomp! The ground beneath their feet shuddered, filling up with the roots. Jones across the street shouted in surprise at the noise. Above them towered 120 feet of fluted trunk, garlanded with swaying branches whose needles shivered in the breeze. But then—

"It's falling!" screamed Stahn, streaking across the yard. "Run!"

From across the street Jones echoed Stahn's shriek. Frantically Babs stared upward, projecting her largest cubical alla control mesh, ready to convert the tumbling behemoth into air before it crushed her. The tree was so big that it was too late to run. But—

The tree wasn't falling.

"April fool," said Stahn, his long smile an icon of utter delight. "Gotcha."

"Phew," said Randy, with a loose grin. "What a lift."

"Zerk," said Wendy, poking Stahn. "We're not always this hard to be around, Randy."

"Hey, I'm havin' a good taaahm. But what are those holes up in the top?"

Stahn glanced up, worried. "Don't tell me there's something—"

"I put a room inside it," said Babs. "Just like in that book we read when I was little. I put a nice room with a door and three windows. And a deck."

"The Little Fur Family," remembered Wendy. "How sweet."

"Is it strong enough, hollowed out like that?" wondered Stahn.

"Sure," said Babs. "Redwoods have hollow spots in them all the time."

"How do we get up there?" was Stahn's next question.

"Anemone boots and Spider-Man gloves," said Randy, quick as a flash. "Me and Babs found 'em when we wanted to climb our palm trees. I'll show you in the alla catalog. They used to be made by a company named Modern Rocks out to Colorado. Guess they outta business now—like all the other folks with goodies in the alla catalogs."

Stahn alla-made himself a set of the bulbous yellow plastic boots and gloves. "Stuzzadelic! I never would have bought them."

"See, he's finally getting the picture," said Babs. "With an alla you get all the wavy stuff you'd never buy. And then you turn it back into air. Consumerism isn't wasteful anymore." She and Randy made themselves Spider-Man gloves and anemone boots as well. "I'll go first. Watch how I do it, Da." Babs stared at the first branch she wanted to get to, then spread the fingers of her right hand. Her Spider-Man glove shot out a thick, sticky rope of imipolex—a bit like a frog's tongue. The glove had a DIM linking it to Babs's uvvy, and it knew to shoot its tongue at whatever Babs was staring at. Now Babs relaxed her fingers. This gesture told the strand of imipolex to slowly contract, pulling her up. Meanwhile the toes of her anemone boots had split into a zillion pseudopods that walked their way along the bark like the legs of a millipede, preventing too much strain on Babs's arm, as well as ruling out any chance of her being yanked around uncontrollably. Babs smiled down from the first branch, securely anchored by her anemone boots. "Come on, Da, it's easy."

"I'm supposed to do this every time I want to visit my lookout?"

"You can figure out an easier way if you like. That's the fun of having an alla. It lets you try all sorts of new things, and if something doesn't work, you get rid of it."

"Or you pile it in your yard like the Joneses."

"Sooner or later they'll realize they don't have to hoard. Matter doesn't matter anymore."

Stahn shot up a tongue of imipolex with each hand, and gingerly hauled his way up to stand beside her. "This is easier than it looks. Thanks, Babs."

Now Randy climbed up to join them. Babs took off fast, closely followed by Randy, the two of them scampering up the tree like a pair of squirrels. *Splat* kick kick, *splat* kick kick. What fun! Babs could see Stahn far below them, creeping along. And Wendy? There she was, swooping around the tree like a sea gull. She'd unfurled her Happy Cloak into a huge set of wings. She reached the top before Babs and Randy.

"Oh, this is beautiful," she called down. "There's a cute, round room."

The trunk was about ten feet across up here. The room was carved right into the living heartwood of the tree, with two polished bucket seats, three little porthole windows, and an arched door. The widest part of the floor was maybe five feet across. A plump burl of the redwood bulged out to make a deck in front of the door, with four more seats carved into it. Once they were all up top, they tried out everything, and then Ma and Da sat on the deck, while Babs and Randy sat cozily in the little room.

"This view kicks ass!" exulted Stahn. "I can see the whole city and both bridges! I can even see the Farallon Islands!" He leaned over, chuckling with satisfaction. "Jones looks like a bewildered gopher. Should I give him the finger? Alla down a bucket of piss?"

"Don't goad him," said Wendy. "He might turn us all into air. That's been happening quite a bit, you know. I hear there's been too many killings for the gimmie to even keep track of. And not everyone's been able to get recorporated."

Stahn winced at the thought. "You're right. I have to be nice to Jones. Maybe I could convince him to replace his tower with a tree. This is where it's at, no lie. Is it stuzzy in that room, Babs?"

"You want to trade places?"

"No no, the cozy nook should be for the lovers. Ma and I can try it when you're gone. Hey, Wendy, can you viz letting me bone you up here? Tarzan and Jane. But our feet would stick out of the door."

"You could alla-carve bigger rooms lower down in the tree," said Babs equably. She was accustomed to her father's gaucherie. Maybe that was why she was so comfortable with Randy. Babs patted Randy's hand, and he smiled at her. The redwood room had a nice, fresh fragrance. Tendrils of late afternoon fog were drifting by.

"We could live in a tree like this, Babs," murmured Randy. "Maybe we oughta put one up by your warehouse. Or once I get my consulting business goin' I can buy us a lot down in the Santa Cruz Mountains and we can live in a tree out there."

"What kind of consulting do you want to do, Randy?" asked Wendy. Her hearing was preternaturally sharp.

"Nose much, Ma?" said Babs, implicitly daring her mother to ask the question that was really on her mind.

"And you're planning to live together? That's nice . . ." Wendy's voice trailed off, begging for more information.

"We're engaged," said Babs, finally springing her news. "We're going to have a double wedding with Yoke and Phil on the first of June."

Randy, May 1

To Randy's relief—and slight surprise—Babs's parents gave his marriage proposal their blessing. He settled in at Babs's, waiting for the big day and working on some projects with the others.

It seemed important to try and do good things with the allas, all the more so because the world news was bad. Savage conventional wars had broken out in Africa, Central America, Quebec, and the Balkans. There was sporadic gang fighting in parts of the U.S. too, mostly near Boston, Dallas, Atlanta, and Los Angeles. Needless to say, there were almost no women doing it, and the moldies were staying pretty well out of the fray as well. It was just men fighting men. Everyone had all the food and

shelter they wanted, so there was no logical reason to fight—
but men were doing it anyway, using all the great new weapons
they could alla up for themselves.

It turned out that Phil was right—the allas wouldn't undo
the ordinary kinds of deaths. If someone shot you or blew you
up, your alla wouldn't save you. The alla recorporation feature
was indeed designed only to undo any killings that had been
done by an alla itself. Even so, there were men who used the
allas to make themselves weapons so they could beat and rape
and torture and kill at will, growing more cruel and brutal every
day. The killers were killing each other off, but still there
seemed to be no shortage of them. And the innocent were dying
as well. The only thing keeping the wars down was that the
Metamartians' flying saucer kept appearing at the goriest battle
scenes. First the saucer would call for peace, and then it would
beam down rays to destroy everyone's weapons, and if the men
still kept on fighting, the saucer would incinerate them. But the
Metamartians couldn't be everywhere.

Babs was in a frantically creative mode, as if trying to prove
it hadn't been a mistake to distribute the allas. In mid-April,
Theodore helped her put on a show at the Asiz Gallery. Theodore was being a good sport about losing Babs, which surprised
Randy, who kept expecting some Kentucky-style sneak attack
from the guy: a stolen vehicle, a midnight beating, an arson fire,
a tip-off to the gimmie. But it never came. Instead Theodore
got Babs gallery space and wrote a great little catalog for her.
Randy was unable to comprehend such behavior.

Babs's show was called "Realware Worms," and it featured
twenty of her worm-farms. Some were the ones she'd been making before she got the alla: mazes of plastic tubing filled with
soil and a mixture of real and imipolex DIM worms. Just to play
with the categories a little, Babs had also made some new versions of these, using alla-made realware biological worms in
place of "wild" biological worms. In addition, she'd alla-made a
half-dozen large transparent shapes filled solid with writhing
DIM worms. There were cubes of plastic worms, some big

doughnut shapes, and even a mounting, squiggly spiral like a moonshiner's "worm coil" condenser. That last one had been Randy's suggestion, he was proud to say. To fill out the show, Babs hung a lot of her lace on the walls and alla-made seven variations on her cartoonlike dune buggy, giving them hard "kandy kolors" that marched up the spectrum: red, orange, yellow, green, blue, indigo, violet. Babs put smiling worm logos on the car doors so they'd fit the show's theme, and parked the "worm buggies" in a cutely angled row on the sidewalk outside the Asiz.

The title of the show was a good idea, as everyone was still in the process of trying to assimilate what "Realware" might mean. There was a big crowd on opening night—decked out in freaky S.F. outfits like never before seen—but the sales were disastrously weak. The potential customers seemed to want to go home and make their own copies of Babs's works with their allas. In fact, one woman with a beehive hairdo and a skirt made of dangling transparent dildos stood out on the sidewalk staring really hard at one of the worm-buggies for half an hour and then—*whoosh*—used her alla to make her own version, using the same base-model Metamartian alla catalog dune buggy that Babs had used. The art on the knockoff worm buggy wasn't quite the same, for it came out of the dildo-skirted woman's head and not Babs's, but it seemed to suit her well enough, and maybe better. She hopped in her new car and drove off, with Randy running after her down the street shouting empty threats.

The situation with the lace was a bit different. The decorations of the worm-buggies were big and easy to mentally represent, but the lace simply had too much pattern, produced as it was by colonies of interacting DIM-based fabricants. No casual gallery-goer would be able to mentally specify the twists and turns of all the lace knots for his or her alla. Even so, Randy did catch a tipsy man in orange leather leaving the gallery wearing a mantilla of crude knockoff lace on his shoulders. Rather than being knotted, the copied lace's threads were simply fused at the crossings. And the overall pattern repeated itself every four inches, instead of subtly varying all along the mantilla's length.

The plastic worms were the least susceptible to copying, as it was their living behavior that made them art. Their flocking, their wriggling, their subtly oscillating hues—all of these were based on limpware DIM designs that Babs had invented for them with Randy's help. And there was no way to "see" these microscopic code designs just by looking at the worms. Yet everyone was in such a do-it-yourself frenzy with their allas that they seemed to overlook this fact.

The sole person to offer to purchase one of Babs's works was a sleek banker named Chock Fresser. Fresser wanted to acquire the show's centerpiece: a twelve-foot transparent pretzel filled with imipolex worms in a thousand different shades of blue and green; it was called "Wowo Worms."

But Fresser didn't want to take delivery on the physical item; he wanted Babs to uvvy him a copy of the software design so he could alla-make the work in situ at his house. "Too much trouble to ship it home," said Fresser. "Packing, unpacking— who needs it anymore? Give me the code and that way I can bring 'Wowo Worms' in and out of storage as needed."

The gallery owner, Kundry Asiz, was a good friend of Babs's from high school. When Babs suggested to her that they shouldn't sell the code to Fresser since money didn't matter anymore, Kundry pointed out that, yes, there was a sense in which money didn't matter anymore, but there were still several senses in which it did—first of all, it was crass human nature for people to give more attention and respect to art they had to pay for, and secondly, the rent on a space like the Asiz Gallery was something the alla couldn't finagle them out of.

So Babs agreed, and Fresser walked off with the complete code for the "Wowo Worms." And a week later, tacky little desktop copies of it were for sale in every gift shop on Fisherman's Wharf—with nary an attribution to Babs. Kundry put some heavy pressure on Fresser and got him to triple the original purchase price, but it wasn't a fully satisfying resolution.

"We gotta figure out a way to sell a design for onetime use only," said Randy. He and Babs were sitting on the ant-decorated couch in Babs's warehouse. Babs's brother Saint was there too. It was the first of May.

"Use a one-time encryption zip," said Saint. "I learned about that stuff when I was working for Meta West. You can zip your design and send the zipped version to the user with an unzipper that trashes itself after its first use. Like cheap pants. The first time you open the fly, the zipper sticks for good. You can publish the image of your work in the alla catalog, and when somebody orders it, they get a single zip of the design with its own unzipper. And of course the unzipper is tailored only to feed the information into an alla and not into any kind of a storage device."

"I get it," said Babs. "I could make an art catalog that's like a catalog used to be. There's just images of things, and you have to uvvy in some funds to take delivery on an item. And if you want another one, you have to pay again. That's a brilliant idea, Saint. I wish I'd known about that before."

"Live and learn, sis," said Saint. "Just think about the poor companies that had every one of their products put into the Metamartian alla catalog."

"Like Modern Rocks," said Randy. He liked his Spider-Man gloves and anemone boots so much that he'd looked into the fate of their manufacturer. "I found out they really did go down the tubes. The Metamartians didn't leave no holes. Whatever the aliens put in that catalog is there one hundred percent, the whole design coded up in nanotech blueprints. Those Metamartians did their homework. Now, this trick of yours, Saint, is everyone gonna know about it? It would be good to spread it around, so's artists and inventors can get some kind of reward."

"Maybe I should *sell* my trick," said Saint. "Call it the One-Zip. If I can actually figure out the details. I'm not really that much of a programmer. But you two sure went for it. Yeah, I need someone to help me productize."

"Why is everyone always talking about buying and selling

these days?" said Yoke impatiently. She'd just walked in. "You sound like a bunch of businessman numberskulls. Guys with calculator DIMs in their heads. Phil's the worst of all. Going on and on about selling his blimps. Money lags! What does anyone need xoxxin' money for anyway? And meanwhile people are killing each other for fun." Without waiting for a response, Yoke stalked across the room to study the pair of huge aquariums she'd installed. One contained a realware South Pacific reef with hard and soft corals. The biologicals were all alla-made realware: primarily coral polyps and the diatoms they fed upon. The other tank held Yoke's work-in-progress, a colony of miniaturized limpware polyps that were supposed to build an artificial reef. Yoke's polyps weren't doing so well today. When he'd gotten up this morning, Randy had noticed that Yoke's artificial reef had petered out into ugly little crumbly excrescences, not at all like the smooth, branching staghorn shapes she was shooting for.

"Xoxx it," said Yoke, staring into her tanks. "This is the only thing I'm able to try and control—and it's too hard. You have to help me tweak them some more, Randy."

"How's Phil's blimp doin'?" Randy asked Yoke.

"Oh, he's got it spread out on the roof," said Yoke, wandering over and alla-making herself a cup of coffee. "It's slowly getting better. The Phlyte Blimp. Can you hear the trademark? What is it about Phil and money all of a sudden, Randy?"

"Phil wants to make a mark on the world," said Randy. Looking into himself, Randy realized that he didn't share that ambition. He saw his role as a background guy, not a foreground guy. A consultant. Someone who helped people make connections and do things. He was happy to help Babs with her worms, Phil with his flying machines, Yoke with her reefs, and maybe Saint with his One-Zip realware alla code encryption. But he wasn't into power-driving. Hell, he was just happy to have a shot at a normal life. If only the world would let him. "For some people money's a way to keep score," he said mildly. "Practically all it's good for anymore."

"Don't forget real estate," said Babs. "Yoke and Phil need money if they ever want a place of their own. Not that I mind having you guys squatting on my wall and my roof. But you know, eventually—"

"We can leave anytime you want us to," said Yoke, getting prickly. "There's plenty of free land on the Moon. Or Mars. Or the asteroids. We'd be safer from the fighting anyway."

"I don't see you wantin' to go back into space," said Randy. "No more than I want to go in the first place. Earth's where it's at. And, look, with the allas we don't need to waste land on farms no more. That frees up a lot of cheap acreage. Or, hell, you can get an acre up on the side of some mountain any old where. With an alla you don't need power or plumbing or a place to shop. Everyone can be happy, everyone can have a nice place to live."

"So why do people keep killing each other?" wondered Babs. "Just for the rush? Thank God things are still calm in San Francisco."

"I hear things are getting really tense in Oakland," said Saint. "I'm starting to wonder if giving out the allas was such a good idea."

"If we ever get to talk to the Metamartians again, maybe we should ask them to get rid of the allas?" said Randy. "Hard to decide. Hey, did I tell you that my father's flying back down inside of Cobb? Comin' early for the wedding. He should get here today."

"I wish Darla had stayed," said Yoke, looking sad. "As soon as she talked to Whitey, she got all homesick and made Cobb fly her right up to the Moon. I think she wanted to make double sure that they didn't finish growing that new Darla clone to replace her. So, fine, now they're all together up there, but what good does that do me? I want my parents and my sister! They should be the ones coming back with Cobb, not Willy. Whitey says I should come get married on the Moon. He thinks it's getting too dangerous down here. But Phil's totally into having the wedding with his family and you guys. Xoxx it. A wedding's hard enough, so why in God's name are we doing two at once?"

"Don't look at me," said Randy. "It was you and Babs decided to make it a double. It was like you gals thought gettin' married to Phil and me was such a crazy stunt, why not push it right out to the edge. Like a viddy soap finale or somethin'."

"I know," sighed Yoke. "I can remember the mood, but I can't get myself back into it. Babs and I were so giggly that night. We'd released the allas to the public and it was going to be paradise. And now there's war everywhere. Even Phil and I had a big fight just a minute ago. Not that there's any comparison."

"Poor Yoke," said Babs. "Fight about what?"

"It's Phil's mother, Eve," said Yoke, frowning. "Maybe you already know about this, Babs. Eve got this idea that we shouldn't have the ceremonies out here in front of your warehouse like we'd been saying we'd do."

"Oh yeah," said Babs. "I know about this. I kind of agree with her."

"Well thanks a lot for letting me know," snapped Yoke, her eyes flashing. "Five minutes ago Phil tells me that Eve and Wendy reserved us a ballroom at the Fairmont Hotel. Like we're sixth-graders in a school pageant. Or no, it's worse than that. It's like we're nobles celebrating while all over the world people are suffering. Especially women. I—I really unloaded on Phil. I told him I don't want to get married at all." Yoke's chin quivered and she began crying. "This is turning into a nightmare."

Babs gave Randy a look, and he got to his feet. "Hey, Saint, let's go upstairs and look at Phil's blimp. You too, Willa Jean."

"Yaaar," said Saint. Willa Jean strutted rapidly across the floor and jumped into Randy's arms.

Phil had cantilevered a kind of staircase of mini-trampolines out from the side of Babs's warehouse. You could climb to the roof by hopping from one elastic sheet to the next. And there was a fireman's pole for coming back down. Phil and Yoke had added three more rooms to their original alley-nest; each room was level with one of the layers of the trampolines.

"Feel like one o' them fish," Randy observed to Saint as they bounced upward.

"A salmon," agreed Saint. "Heading upstream to spawn. Hey, Phil, watcha doing? We're here to spawn all over everything."

"Hi, guys," said Phil, looking up from a big flat air bag lying on the roof. "I'm working on the Phlyte Blimp. Trying to. I can't think. They're fighting in Oakland. Look over across the bay, you can see the fires."

Sure enough, across the water smoke was streaming up from the city of Oakland. Yet high above the smoke it was a pleasant spring day with fluffy white clouds against the pale blue.

"I just checked the news," said Phil. "It started as a gang thing. And now it's turned racial. Everyone getting even for getting even for getting even. How long is it we've had the allas now?"

"Two months," said Randy. "You'd think people would have it together by now." Two months ago had been when he'd realized that he loved Babs. And in another month they'd be married. If only things would calm down. If only people would remember to be kind.

"Oh, shit," said Saint. "Look at Oakland now."

Someone had just done something to make one of Oakland's office buildings collapse. Maybe they'd alla-converted part of its foundation into air. The wind shifted toward them and Randy could smell a whiff of smoke, could hear a faint crackle of gunfire.

"Make them stop," prayed Randy, and just about then a flashing bright saucer appeared in the sky over Oakland. The Metamartians to the rescue, once again. There was a distant rumble; the saucer was talking to the men fighting. And now a series of rays darted down from it; it was said that when a saucer appeared at a battle scene, it would destroy everyone's alla-made weapons.

"The allas have to go," said Randy, really believing this for the first time. "It's not going to be worth it. Especially after the aliens leave."

"Let's fly to Oakland and help," said Phil. "We can use my blimp."

"Good idea," said Randy. "And while we're at it, maybe we can get close enough to the saucer to talk to the Metamartians."

Phil used the alla to instantly fill his Phlyte Blimp up with helium. The great balloon was covered with something like impolex linguini that Phil called "Smart Hair.®" The blimp bobbed above the rooftop and a sudden breeze threatened to sweep it away. But then the plastic linguini began intensely beating, holding the unwieldy shape in place.

"It has passenger slings for us to sit on," said Phil, indicating a trio of loops that dangled from the blimp's underside.

"Have you actually tested it?" asked Saint.

"Sure," said Phil. "Well, not with three people. But if something goes wrong, we can always alla ourselves some hang-glider wings. Come on. Let's dart over to Oakland and make sure all the injured people have healer machines. We can be there in three or four minutes."

"I'm for it," said Randy. "Be nice to do something good for a change."

Once they were settled into the slings, the blimp's Smart Hair began rippling in steady waves. They slid through the air as smoothly as a pumpkin seed. Phil steered them toward the saucer, but before they got close to it, the bright disk darted away, moving too fast for the eye to follow. And then they were above the bloody streets of Oakland.

"Careful," said Saint. "Someone might shoot at us." But the saucer had temporarily disarmed everyone. The weaponless fighters were slinking away, leaving dozens of injured people on the streets and sidewalks. Phil landed the blimp, and the three boys moved among the injured, using their allas to make healer machines. Soon more rescue workers began to appear. And then some builders arrived, using allas to clear away the rubble and repair the shattered buildings.

"Looks like things are under control now," said Saint after a while.

"Let's go back," said Phil. "I have to tell Yoke I'm sorry."

"Shitfire," said Randy, checking the time. "My dad's about to come."

The ride back was a little slower, as a strong wind had started blowing from the ocean. But the blimp's Smart Hair kept them on a steady course. The boys were quiet, thinking of what they'd seen. Many people had been too far gone for the healer machines.

Back on the warehouse roof, Phil deflated his blimp and examined its skin, using his fuzzy pocketknife to tweak its little flaps. "I'm glad this worked," he said. "Those poor people."

"Your blimp is good, Phil," said Saint.

"I've been thinking," said Phil. "I don't actually need moldie-quality imipolex to make these things. Which is important, because I want to keep making them even if we get rid of the allas and imipolex is expensive again. I think regular production-quality piezoplastic would work if I used a simple enough algorithm. Your dad could help me with the code, Randy. How soon is he coming, anyway?"

"Could be any taaahm now." Randy peered up at the sky.

"Good," said Phil, patting his flattened blimp. "Okay, I'm going down to talk with Yoke." He jumped off the edge of the building and slid down the fire pole.

"After seeing Oaktown like that, I'm against the allas too," Saint told Randy. "I need to think of a career that doesn't depend on them."

"What about your water bicycles?"

"Good idea. Maybe your dad could help me with their DIM chips."

"He knows a lot," said Randy with a proud smile. "Shitfire, my father invented limpware engineering and the uvvy too. When I was growing up, I never realized I had such important relatives. I thought I was just a nobody from nowhere."

"Not anymore," said Saint, looking upward. "And, yaaar! Here he comes!"

A shiny moldie form was descending riding on the sparkling column of an ion jet. It was Cobb with someone inside him. Randy tucked Willa Jean under his arm, and he and Saint slid down off the roof to stand by the patch of gravel Cobb was heading toward. Hearing the hollering, Babs, Phil, and Yoke came out of the warehouse. Randy noticed that Phil and Yoke were smiling and holding hands again.

Cobb plopped gently to the ground and split open, disgorging a gray-haired fifty-year-old man. The man looked happy to be out in the air. He made a little bow. "Hi, everyone, I'm Willy Taze." He sized up the five of them, then stepped forward and shook Randy's hand.

"My son," said the gray-haired man, looking Randy over. "We finally meet face-to-face. Sorry it wasn't sooner. This feels good. I was a fool to put it off. I was sorry to hear about your mother, she was gone before I got a chance to talk this over with her. Quite a woman. So you're getting married, eh? Marriage is the part I never did. I'm such a geek that I only managed one single squirt inside a woman my whole entire life. And you seized that unique opportunity to get born, Randy. My very best sperm cell. Good boy!"

"Thanks," said Randy, quite overwhelmed. "So you really my pa?"

"He's my grandson and you're my great-grandson," exulted Cobb. "High time you two met! For God's sake give him a hug, Willy. You won't catch anything."

So Randy and his father hugged. It felt good. Willy beamed at him, then turned to the others, talking a mile a minute, like a man who's been alone too long. Randy knew the feeling.

"Hello, Yoke, it's great to see you again," said Willy. "That's so wonderful that you got us the allas! What a change those things are making on the Moon! So far we loonies have been too smart to get into any wars with each other. Not like the stupid mudders."

"We were just over in Oakland givin' people healer machines," put in Randy. "Things was mighty screwed up."

"Up on the Moon, everyone's been busy making sublunar parks and ponds," said Willy. "You wouldn't recognize the place anymore. And the moldies are happily stockpiling megatons of imipolex. Your parents send their best, Yoke, and believe it or not, they're getting along fine. I think almost losing Darla shocked some sense into Whitey. Joke's flying down in a few days, and Corey Rhizome is coming with her. And this must be Phil Gottner?" Willy smiled and shook Phil's hand. "Randy told me a little about you on the uvvy." Willy turned his attention to the two others. "And these other two must be Sta-Hi's kids—I think it's Babs and Saint? I mean 'Stahn,' not 'Sta-Hi.' He's still clean and sober, right? Wavy. You wouldn't want to be at a wedding with the old Sta-Hi. Isn't this something? You're such beautiful young people, all of you. Especially Randy! And Babs! Imagine having Babs for my daughter-in-law! I have to admit that I'm thrilled."

"Hi, Willy," said Saint. "I'm glad to meet you. Phil and me were hoping you'd help us with some limpware engineering."

"Don't start pickin' his brain just yet," said Randy. "Let him go inside and get some food. He's been cooped up inside Cobb for a week."

"My son!" exclaimed Willy, hugging Randy again. "You look wonderful. This is more than I deserve! Yes, I'm going inside to rest."

"I'll be there in a minute," said Randy, looking down at Cobb, who'd let himself slump to the ground. "How you feelin', Great-grandfather Cobb?"

"I'm tired," said Cobb, puddled on the ground. "And I heard some really bad news just while I was landing. I think I'll lie out here in the sun for a while. If I alla up a bottle of quantum dots, will you pour them into me?"

"Shore."

Like most moldies now, Cobb had his alla embedded inside his flesh. Without moving a muscle, he projected out a mesh and alla-made a shiny gray magnetic bottle of quantum dots. Randy held up the little bottle to the light, checking the meter.

"You want the full terawatt, Cobb?"

"You know it," said Cobb, growing a funnel up out of his chest. Randy poured the glittering dust of the quantum dots into the old man moldie. "Thanks," said Cobb. "That helps; but I've just about had it with this planet. People are so—Did my stink-eater bug catch on at least?"

"It did," said Randy. "Big-time. People and moldies are get-tin' along better all the taahm. It's just the men fighting each other that's ruining things. As for me personally—I got such a good thing goin' with Babs I can't hardly remember what I used to see in bein' a cheeseball. Leave Cobb alone, Willa Jean, run on inside." Randy pushed Willa Jean away from Cobb and to-ward the warehouse door. "Everyone's grateful to you, Cobb. But what's this about you bein' tired? We was expectin' you to run for mayor."

"No," said Cobb. "I'm ready to move further on. Politics should die. Politics used to be about dividing up scarce re-sources—and nothing's scarce anymore. With the allas here, politics is just about hatred and war. Want to know why I'm so bummed all of a sudden? Guess what I heard on my uvvy just as I touched down? People have started throwing kiloton bombs."

"Nukes?" asked Randy. "I thought—"

"Conventional explosives," said Cobb. "If you ask it to, an alla can make you a thousand ton cube of TNT. Some people just realized. Most of downtown Jerusalem's gone. And now I'm hearing"—Cobb sighed. "Baghdad too."

"We should block the allas from making weapons," said Randy.

"But what's a weapon?" said Cobb. "Gasoline is a weapon. Oxygen and hydrogen. Acid. Even a rock is a weapon if you drop it from high in the sky. I think we should tell the Meta-martians to tell Om to take away the allas."

"I saw their saucer in the sky over Oakland earlier today,"

said Randy. "And then they darted away. I bet they were going to the Mideast. Jerusalem and Baghdad got flattened?"

"Yes," said Cobb.

"What should I do?"

"Live your life, however much of it's left for you. Marry Babs."

Yoke, June 1

"Hold still," said Joke, leaning forward to touch up Yoke's eye makeup. The twin sisters had always preferred using each other to using mirrors. "There," said Joke. "Perfect." She leaned back and smiled. The two of them were in a bridal dressing room off the Fairmont Hotel's top-floor ballroom. It was almost time for the wedding. Yoke could hear music; Saint and some of his friends were brain-playing ancient flute motets on sheets of imipolex—with hints of heavy metal. "I'm glad we're doing this on Earth," said Joke. "It's so pretty down here. If only things don't keep getting worse. The heavy gravity is good for a ceremony. It makes everything seem solemn." Joke moved her arms in slow, marching motions. "Are you stoked?"

"You like Phil, don't you, Joke?"

"He's great. That blond hair and dark chin—yummy. And he looks at you like he's so in love. Emul and Berenice approve too." Thanks to some unfortunate wetware meddling, Joke had been born with two pushy robots' minds coded into the right hemisphere of her brain. It made her very knowledgeable, but her spatial perception was lousy. "They, um, did some research on him."

"Do I want to know?" asked Yoke.

"It's all good," said Joke. "Emul says Phil has a clean criminal record and he's exactly who he says he is. And Berenice says Phil's genome is not only mutation-free, but a very good fit for ours. I mean yours. So I wanted to tell you. Sorry."

"Oh, it doesn't matter," said Yoke. "I've abandoned any hope of privacy—at least for today. What a circus."

"And here comes the clown!" said Joke. A hard-looking man was peeking in the dressing room door. Their father, Whitey Mydol. He had a Mohawk strip of hair that went down the back of his head and continued on into his shirt collar. And over the shirt he was wearing a tuxedo. "I'll go check on Ma," said Joke, and moved out of the way; the tiny dressing room was only big enough for two people.

"Clown is right," said Whitey, his rough face splitting in a surprisingly pleasant smile. "I'm walking funny. How many days did it take you to get used to this gravity, Yoke?"

"Three, four weeks. Hi, Pop. How do I look?"

"You look—oh, Yoke, you look like an angel. You remind me of Darla—back when. She says our twenty-fifth anniversary is coming up this month."

"Are you being nice to her, Pop?"

"What a question!" Whitey shifted uneasily, looking too big for the tiny, white-upholstered bride's room. "Don't worry about us, Yoke, things are better. I was bad, but I'm being good again. Anyway, it's me who should be asking you things. Like are you totally sure you want to marry Phil? I can get you out of it if you want." He cracked his scarred knuckles as if thinking about a fight.

"I'm doing this," said Yoke firmly. "Are you with me or not?"

"For sure." Whitey ran his hand back and forth over his head, fluffing his Mohawk. This was the first time Yoke had ever seen him wearing a shirt and suit coat, let alone a tuxedo. "I just thought it's the kind of thing a father's supposed to ask. Phil's a good man. And we've already paid for the room." He gave a grim chuckle. "Might as well do it, then, before some dook sets off a bomb. How do we know when to march up the aisle?"

"When the music changes." And then it did.

" 'Here Comes the Bride,' " said Whitey, holding out his arm.

In the little hallway, they found Babs and Stahn, coming out of their own dressing room. While Yoke's dress was a sleek sheath of silk with a tulle veil, Babs had gone "smart art"; her dress and hair were alive with slowly moving pearl DIM beads.

The Fairmont owners had alla-remodeled the top-floor ballroom with a gorgeous parquet wood floor and white silk-covered walls winking with little diamonds. There were dozens of floor-to-ceiling windows, all flung wide-open to let in the gentle June breeze. The sweetness of it caught in Yoke's throat. If only the world could stop its downward spiral. Five more cities had been blown up in the past four weeks.

The chairs were arranged so that the ballroom's aisle was double wide; that way Yoke, Whitey, Babs, and Stahn could walk up side by side, with nobody first and nobody second. Waiting up in front by the windows were Randy and Phil, standing on either side of—Cobb Anderson.

It had developed that none of the four betrothed had a close enough church affiliation to know of a particular minister to use. So Cobb had quickly picked up a gimmie justice-of-the-peace license and offered to perform the ceremony himself. The old man moldie claimed he was tired, but he still loved to put himself at the center of things. Randy was thrilled to be getting married by his great-grandfather, and Babs didn't mind. As for Yoke and Phil, they too were glad to have Cobb supervise this religious ceremony—for had not each of the three seen the same Divine SUN?

Though it was a beautiful service, the time seemed to pass in funny spurts. Everything was crawling while they were walking up the aisle. This was the part Yoke had always visualized as a little girl thinking about weddings. Walking up the aisle in your bridal gown. It was almost as if she could feel her own eyes watching her. The man at the end of the aisle had always been vague, but now, today, he was clear. Dear Phil. Then things speeded up, and suddenly Yoke and Phil were saying "I will" and "I do." Time all but stopped for the ring part and the kiss. Phil had a brand-new ring for Yoke, which was good. Babs and Randy's vows happened in fast-forward; Yoke didn't hear a word of them. And then they were walking out in slow motion and it felt to Yoke like something she had done a hundred times before.

The waiters cleared the chairs away and set out big tables that they filled with alla-made food; Phil and Babs had made up the designs for the wedding feast. Darla was one of the first to hug Yoke, and then Whitey and Joke. And then Yoke hugged Randy and Babs.

"We're married," laughed Babs. "It's going to be so fun." But there was a shrill edge to her gaiety. Disaster was stalking them all.

Everyone was there. Yoke's bridesmaid was Joke, of course, and Babs's was her art-gallery friend Kundry Asiz. Saint was Phil's best man, and Corey Rhizome served as Randy's.

Randy and Corey had taken quite a liking to each other over the last couple of weeks. One thing they had in common was that they were both really into garage-style limpware engineering. Corey even helped Yoke to finally get her imipolex coral working. Yoke's new thing this week was growing her reefs in air instead of water; she'd started using DIM gnats for the polyps. In fact yesterday she'd grown a fabulous organic-looking headboard for her and Phil's bed. It was a struggle to keep on doing things, with the murders and battles and bombing getting worse every day. But love and art still mattered; yes, they mattered more than hate and war.

The older generation at the wedding party included Darla and Whitey, Stahn and Wendy, Randy's father Willy Taze, Phil's mother Eve, and even Phil's stepmother Willow. Phil's Uncle Rex was there too, as well as his grandmother Isolde and his great-aunt Hildegarde, who had the most astonishing face. They all thought Yoke was wonderful, and said they'd known she was perfect for Phil when they'd seen him talking to her at poor Kurt's funeral. Oh, and Randy's new aunt Della Taze had turned up from San Diego, mainly to see Willy. Della had brought her mother along, seventy-nine-year-old Ilse, a bit wobbly and sour, but Cobb Anderson's daughter nonetheless. Cobb was overwhelmed to see her.

Among the younger guests, Terri and Tre Dietz had come up from Santa Cruz with their kids Dolf and Wren, who were loving it. In honor of the happy day—and who knew how many more happy days there would be?—Randy and the Dietzes even made friends, with apologies and forgiveness all around. In fact little Wren was on the floor playing with Randy's plastic chicken Willa Jean. Aarbie Kidd hadn't been invited, but Theodore was there with a leather biker as his date. Derek and his dog Umberto had come with Kundry. There were plenty of others as well; in fact at the last minute, Yoke's friends Kandie and Cocole had even turned up from the Moon, they said they'd been wanting to visit Earth anyway, so why not now, before it was all blown up.

There were even a few moldies among the guests. Phil had asked Isis Snooks, who'd been such a help with his blimps, and Isis had brought along the flashy Thutmosis as her date. Wendy and Cobb each had a few moldie friends, and they were there too. Thanks to the stinkeater bug, mixing with moldies wasn't much of a problem anymore, so long as you had an open mind.

People were drinking champagne like there'd be no tomorrow, jabbering away like magpies, everyone jumping at every loud noise. In the last month, Dakar, Hamburg, Hong Kong, Belfast, Antwerp, and Paris had been hit by enormous bombs. Allas had repaired the buildings, but a lot of people had died. And just yesterday New York City had been bombed too. Everyone was on edge, waiting for the next thing to happen. And then it did.

"A flying saucer!" screamed Phil's mother, Eve. "Look out, Phil! Oh, what if they've come for you again!"

The saucer hanging outside the ballroom windows was a traditional metal disk with a dome in the middle. The Metamartians' ship.

"They can help us!" shouted Randy. "They can take away the allas!"

The frames and sashes of the windows quivered as if water were passing over them, and then the saucer had slid through the wall and into the ballroom. It rested there, cocked a bit toward one side, just fitting between floor and ceiling. A radial line appeared along the curve of the central dome, and then a pie-shaped sector of the curved metal slid open. Out came eight figures: the seven Metamartians from before, plus a new one, a gray little shape like a bald girl with big, almond-shaped eyes.

Yoke sniffed at the air—yes, there was the scent of old-fashioned moldies. The Metamartians hadn't yet caught the stinkeater bug.

"We are here to salute the nuptials," said Shimmer, holding up her hands and making soothing gestures. "Please remain calm, dear friends. We come in peace, seeking your aid. I am Shimmer from Metamars, and my companions are Ptah, Peg, Josef, Siss, Wubwub, Haresh. As many of you know, it is we and our god Om who have brought mankind and moldies the alla. And our gift has been mediated by these four whose marriages you celebrate today: Yoke, Phil, Randy, and Babs. We too have a blessed event to rejoice in: the birth of our sevenfold daughter Lova." The gray little Lova bent her mouth up into a U-shaped smile and bowed, making flowing gestures with her long-fingered hands.

"Skip the bullshit and take away the fucking allas!" yelled Willow. "They're ruining our world and you know it!"

"She's right," called Randy. "Tell Om to take the allas away!"

"Please, Om!" shouted Babs. "The allas are wrong for us. We aren't ready."

Lova bowed again.

"She's butt-ugly," said Yoke, all her tension rushing out into a sudden guffaw. "They're making fun of us."

"Careful," said Darla, coming up behind Yoke. "They're going to ask for something big. It's like in a fairy tale. The witches at the princess's wedding."

"You right, Darla," said Wubwub. "But what we after is no big thing: we need help gettin' outta here is all. We don't know which way to go toward two-dimensional time. And we got the notion one of you can help us. How 'bout it, Phil?"

Yoke threw her arms around Phil. "You leave him alone!"

"Wait!" said Phil, digging in his pocket. "Maybe it's this thing—" He pulled out his little black ball with the bright spots inside it. "Is this what you need, Wubwub? The fishbowl thing I got from Om? It's a star map, isn't it? Turn off the allas and use the star map to go."

"It's a map, but it ain't gonna help us none," said Wubwub, showing his crooked, yellow teeth in a long smile. "But let me see it anyhow."

"Throw it to him, Phil!" said Yoke. "Don't let him come near you!"

So Phil tossed his little ball, and Wubwub caught it. The Metamartians pressed forward to peer at it, and the beetle Josef actually crawled around upon it.

"Yes, Om already gave me one of these through my alla," said Shimmer shortly. "It's a star map, but it's of no use. It only shows your part of the cosmos. Your map shows your zone, and we have another map that shows our zone, the good part of the cosmos with two-dimensional time. But there's no master map that shows the interdimensional connection. We can't find the passage, and we can't understand Om's explanations of where it is."

There was an explosion somewhere outside, not too terribly distant. A few of the guests screamed.

"Turn off the allas right now!" cried Yoke. "Can't you see they're a disaster?"

"We can ask Om to do it," said Ptah quietly. "In fact Om can even disactualize all of the bombs and weapons that people's allas have made. Turn them back into air. All this can happen—provided that one of you will help us on our way. It's your ability to dream that we need, you see. Human dreaming is a rudimentary reaching out toward two-dimensional time. If one of you comes with us as we travel out across your galaxy, then we can watch this person repeatedly sleep and dream—and we'll be able to sniff our way out toward the fat part of time. We need a harbor pilot, in other words. A native guide. So how about it, Phil? You can bring Yoke if you like."

A sudden mesh of alla-control lines appeared around the seven Metamartians. It was Whitey, standing at Yoke's side, holding out his alla and trying to turn the aliens into air. But at the instant Whitey said "Actualize," each of the aliens hopped off to one side. Whitey accomplished nothing more than turning some air into air.

"Senseless violence," said Shimmer. "How typical. What's the matter with you men anyway? We've been trying to calm things down, but it seems to be hopeless. All we're asking today is that an Earthling accompany us as we move on. We want to take one of you who knows us a little bit. If we simply abduct some random human, they'll be too frightened to help us. And not everyone can dream in the right way. Phil's our first choice because his dreams are just right. Om's been looking through people's memories. Those mountains you always dream about, Phil—they point toward two-dimensional time."

"I can dream as well as Phil can," said Cobb, his voice loud and firm. "I dream about mountains all the time. Leave the young folks alone."

"The great old man," said Peg.

"He not human," said Siss.

"Yes he is," said Shimmer, cocking her head as if listening to an inner voice. "In fact, Om says he'll be fine. She hadn't thought to look before, but her records show that Cobb's dreams are just as useful Phil's."

"Moldies dream?" Darla whispered to Yoke. "I didn't know that."

"Of course we do," said Isis Snooks, overhearing. "What did you think we were? Machines? I'm glad Cobb is doing this. It'll get us some xoxxin' respect."

"Come aboard, Cobb," Ptah was saying. "We'll fly to the outer atmosphere and power up to just below the speed of light.

Once we get enough readings, we'll chirp into personality waves and really be on our way. We'll show you how."

"If I come, will Om turn off the allas?" asked Cobb.

"Om is ready to do that," said Shimmer. "By now she has collected a complete enough set of human memories. She'll remember your race forever. She only hopes you don't feel you've been cheated once the allas are gone. But the constant killing and the explosions—"

"I suppose we're too primitive," said Babs sadly.

"It's not just that," said Josef. "It's that one-dimensional time isn't a good place for realware. Some of your bombings weren't even deliberate. Apparently people have started setting off bombs by accident in their dreams. The more that people worry about bombs, the more bombs there will be. Your human dreaming is a risky business. Although Metamartians don't dream, we've occasionally had runaway alla misuse, our own epidemics of mass hysteria. But for us a global disaster doesn't much matter—because we have so many strands of time. No, I'm afraid that at this stage of your culture, and with your un-controlled dreaming, your single line of time is simply too frag-ile for the allas. You do well to want Om to take them away."

"Then it's a deal," said Cobb. "I'll come with you and dream the way toward two-dimensional time. And you'll ask Om to take away the allas."

The Metamartians were silent for a moment, communing with Om.

"Everyone sure they don't want no more alla?" called Wub-wub. There was another explosion outside, this time closer than before. "Om wants to know."

"No more alla!" screamed the crowd.

"Hurry up," cried Yoke. "Do it now! And have Om take away the alla-made weapons like Shimmer said she could."

"So be it," said Ptah.

Yoke felt a wriggling in the pouch at her waist. Her alla, and everyone else's, was gone. The air filled with a palpable sense of safety and ease. The people and moldies laughed and hugged each other.

"Lez go, boss," said Wubwub to Cobb. "Know what I'm sayin'?"

"Oh, Cobb," said Yoke, kissing the old man moldie.

"It's fine," said Cobb. "I've hung around Earth long enough."

"It would be easy for me to use your software to make a new one of you to live here," Willy told Cobb. "We have your software stored on an S-cube."

"Please don't do that," said Cobb. "I don't want anyone bringing me back to Earth again. I'm done here. I'll travel on with the Metamartians, but when this trip plays out, I want to finally make it into the SUN."

"He's right," said Yoke. "Cobb deserves his chance to go to Heaven."

"Good-bye everyone," said Cobb. "And bless you, my children."

He strode up into the saucer with the Metamartians. The hotel wall wavered again, and the flashing disk of the saucer vanished into the heavens.

It was a perfect day. The newlyweds' eyes were soft, their kisses wet, their hearts free, the big world real.